~The~
Dread
Penny
Society

OTHER PROPER ROMANCES
BY SARAH M. EDEN

Ashes on the Moor

<u>Hope Springs</u>
Longing for Home
Longing for Home, vol. 2: Hope Springs

<u>Savage Wells</u>
The Sheriffs of Savage Wells
Healing Hearts
Wyoming Wild

<u>The Dread Penny Society</u>
The Lady and the Highwayman
The Gentleman and the Thief
The Merchant and the Rogue
The Bachelor and the Bride
The Queen and the Knave

SARAH M. EDEN

~THE~ DREAD PENNY SOCIETY

THE COMPLETE
PENNY DREADFUL
COLLECTION

SHADOW
MOUNTAIN
PUBLISHING

Library of Congress Cataloging-in-Publication Data

Names: Eden, Sarah M., author. | Eden, Sarah M. Dread Penny Society.
Title: The Dread Penny Society: the complete penny dreadful collection / Sarah M. Eden.
Other titles: Proper romance.
Description: Salt Lake City: Shadow Mountain Publishing, [2023] | Series: Proper romance | Summary: "The complete collection of penny dreadfuls from Sarah M. Eden's Dread Penny Society series. Also includes three new stories"— Provided by publisher.
Identifiers: LCCN 2023006846 | ISBN 9781639931545 (hardback)
Subjects: BISAC: FICTION / Romance / Historical / Victorian | FICTION / Romance / Clean & Wholesome | LCGFT: Romance fiction. | Novels.
Classification: LCC PS3605. D45365 D74 2023 | DDC 813/.6—dc23/ eng/20230313
LC record available at https: //lccn.loc.gov/2023006846

Printed in China
RR Donnelley, Dongguan, China

10   9   8   7   6   5   4   3   2   1

To the nineteenth-century writers who pioneered,
perpetuated, and perfected the penny dreadful,
bringing immeasurable delight to generations of readers

ONTENTS

INTRODUCTION

by Sarah M. Eden

The nineteenth century brought unprecedentedly high literacy rates to London. For the first time, working-class individuals, and even some amongst the poorest of people, could read. Changes in paper manufacturing and printing brought down the cost of publishing broadsheets. In the wake of these changes, a group of enterprising publishers and authors took a chance on stories written *and* priced for readers who did not belong to the wealthy and privileged class.

Thus, the penny dreadful was born.

Since I learned about this facet of literary history, I have been utterly fascinated. Who were the authors who took up these tales? Where did they find their ideas? Were they celebrities in their day? Did they write for the poor and the laborers because they cared about this often-overlooked group of people, or perhaps because they were part of that overlooked group themselves?

Thus, the "The Dread Penny Society" was born.

Creating and writing about a fictional group of penny dreadful authors has been even more gratifying than I could have predicted. And to try my hand at writing penny dreadfuls fulfilled a dream I didn't even know I had.

Each story was written in the style and voice of the character who is credited as its author, with nods to the vocabulary and story structure that epitomized the literature of the time. I would often find myself rethinking and reworking a story because I realized I was telling it the way *I* would, rather than the way its "author" would. Never have I found myself so closely following the well-known writing advice of putting myself in my character's shoes. I learned a lot and grew a lot as a writer, and I had a tremendous amount of fun doing it.

The penny dreadfuls interspersed throughout the five volumes of the Dread Penny Society series were broken up, the installments spread throughout the novel in which it appeared. In this collection, each of those penny dreadfuls is presented unbroken and whole for the first time, along with three new stories written specifically for this edition.

Just like the original serial stories, some of these are adventures, others are stories of crime and justice, some have a touch of the supernatural, and some end "happily ever after." The nineteenth-century stories were varied, and so are the stories in this collection.

I hope you enjoy this taste of the literature of Victorian-era London. Happy reading!

THE LADY
AND THE
HIGHWAYMAN

by Mr. King

INSTALLMENT I

in which our admirable Heroine finds herself at
the Mercy of a dastardly Highwayman!

On a dark, windy night, hours after the sun had slipped below the horizon, its warmth little but a memory to the poor souls left to brave the thick chill left in the air by that amber orb's departure, an ancient traveling carriage, its ill-kept wheels screeching with every revolution, flew at tremendous speed down a road most people avoided toward an estate no one had lived in for decades. Inside the dilapidated vehicle, Lucinda Ledford sat with clasped hands pressed to her breaking heart.

She had long since resigned herself to this fate. All her life, she'd known that, upon her parents' deaths, she would be sent to live on this obscure family holding, far from every person or place she had ever known, alone, grieving. As she moved ever closer to her unavoidable future, the prospect weighed ever more heavily upon her.

"Oh, that Providence would choose to smile upon me!" whispered she, expecting no answer beyond the forlorn howl of the unfeeling wind. "I, who have been the recipient of nothing but Her cruel frowns!"

No matter that she was no longer a child, she was now an orphan, relegated to the loneliest corner of the kingdom, without a soul to care what became of her.

She sighed, blinking back the tears taking up residence in her eyes. How very unkind Life had chosen to be.

A voice carried on the ceaseless wind, its words indistinguishable. Hands still clasped over her breast, she listened, straining to hear this unexpected evidence that another human life existed in this abandoned corner of the world.

The carriage shook to a stop. Had they arrived so soon, so quickly? Perhaps her unasked-for new home was not so isolated as she'd feared. Oh, hope! Oh, blessed fortune!

The tension lessened in her tightly woven fingers. She lowered her clasped hands to her lap, the smallest whispers of cheer restored to her aching soul.

Outside in the darkness that same voice called again, this time discernible, clear, and sharp. "Stand and deliver!"

Those three words struck cold fear into every knowing heart. To hear them shouted on a lonely and isolated road could mean but one thing: the travelers were soon to find themselves dependent upon the questionable mercy of a ruthless highwayman.

"Oh, dear departed Father," she whispered. "How I need you here with me."

His absence—his permanent absence—was the very reason she was on this dangerous road bound for a home she knew not. Her only hope lay in the knowledge that the would-be thief of the night would discover his prey had nothing of value with which he could abscond. His nefarious efforts would be thwarted by her poverty.

She closed her eyes and forced a slow breath as she counted deliberately. The driver could surely make this highwayman aware of her state before she reached the number ten. Surely.

Her fortune ran short before she'd whispered, "Six." The handle of the carriage door turned, protesting the interruption to its rest. The coachman had never, during their two-day journey, failed to knock first before opening the door. Highwaymen possessed no such commitment to civility.

Cold, biting air rushed inside. A wide silhouette filled the empty space beyond the open door.

"You'll be stepping out, miss," a gravelly voice declared.

A shiver of apprehension slid over her from her hair to her boots. "No, I thank you." She kept her voice steady despite the tremor inside.

"I weren't askin' for your thanks. I'm requiring your cooperation."

"You will have only the former," she insisted.

To someone farther in the darkness, the man said, "We've a stubborn one this time, cap'n."

"You, Smythe, don't know how to talk to ladies." The courtliness of this new voice surprised her. Whoever the second man was, he did not seem to be the rough and uncouth villain his comrade was.

The first man stepped aside, and the shadow of a tall, lean figure assumed his place.

"M'lady," came the graceful voice once more. "I would be most obliged if you'd step from the carriage. You've my word no harm will befall you."

"Of what value is the promise of a criminal?" Fear made her bold, though her bravery was unlikely to last. If only this dastardly duo would hastily retreat before the danger of the moment overwhelmed her fragile fortitude.

An extended hand entered the carriage, lit by the dim spill of light through the opposite window. He wore no glove. No matter that he spoke with propriety, here was a reminder that he was not, in fact, a gentleman. That he currently demanded she step out into the cold night air whilst he pilfered whatever he chose from amongst her paltry belongings served as a strong indication as well.

"You'd best do as we bid, m'lady," the man behind the hand said. "Your carriage'll be ransacked with or without you in it."

Alas, she hadn't the slightest argument against that logic. Stubbornness was insupportable when it simply added to one's suffering.

"I will alight," she said, "but without your ungloved assistance."

He laughed, the sound deep and rumbling and warm. Oh, the sinister pitfalls that awaited the unwary. Such a laugh might convince the ill-prepared to think well of a man with such contemptible intentions. She was not so easily deceived.

Hand pressed to her heart and head held high, she slid to the end of the bench. She set her free hand on the doorframe and took careful step.

Despite her care, despite the fortitude with which she maintained her dignity, her ankle proved fickle. She stumbled.

An arm slipped about her, keeping her upright and unharmed. "Forgive my ungloved assistance," the gallant thief said with another of his rich laughs.

Lucinda pulled free. She turned slowly, assuming her most disapproving and regal expression. No matter that she was afraid, no matter that her ankle ached, no matter that the cold of the late autumn night sent frigid shivers over her, she would prove to this vagabond that she could be strong.

Her assailant wore a broad-brimmed hat, set so low on his head as to cover all his features except his mouth. Despite herself, her heart fluttered. His smile, not subtle in the least, produced a pair of dimples one could not help but find fascinating. She would do well to focus on his dastardly undertaking lest she be fooled by him.

"Proceed with your pilfering," she said. "Your efforts will yield you nothing beyond wasted effort and time."

He appeared not the least admonished. "That is a risk I embrace, my lady." He removed his caped outercoat.

She gasped, hand pressed once more to her heart. Did highwaymen regularly undress whilst undertaking their robberies? Surely not! With a flourish, he spun the coat around and rested it on *her* shoulders.

"What are you doing?" she demanded.

"Perhaps November is a warm month in the area of the kingdom you've called home, but in this corner, the weather is bitter."

"I do not need your coat," she said.

"Alas, my lady, I suspect what you mean is you don't want it." He turned to his shorter comrade. "Do not neglect to maintain the watch. I will search inside."

Weapon drawn, Smythe eyed the road, the cluster of nearby trees, and Lucinda herself. As the highwayman climbed into the carriage interior, Lucinda cast her eyes, now adjusted fully to the dark of night, about the area. They were not so alone as she'd believed. Several mounted men watched the encounter, though they were just far enough away that she was afforded no more details. Despite the warmth of the highwayman's unwanted coat, she shivered.

Oh, the cruelty of Fate to take away her home and parents only to send her to this dark and dangerous roadside. Was it not misery enough that she should be alone and in so unfamiliar a place? Must she also be thus accosted?

The highwayman emerged from the carriage, his face still hidden. "It ain't in there," he told his associate. "Best let the lady be on her way."

An odd turn of events to be sure. "What isn't in there?" Clearly, he sought something specific.

"Never you mind, miss." He produced another of his dimpled grins.

"You have importuned me and slowed my journey," she declared. "I will indeed mind."

He stepped nearer her. "You are new to this area, my lady. You know not the dangers that reside here."

"I have been made intimately aware of one local danger," she insisted, eyeing him with pointed accusation.

Did all highwaymen laugh as often as he? She would not have assumed them a jolly sort. Neither would she have assumed this road to be a path through treacherous waters.

"I am not the danger you should fear," he said. "On the contrary. I am all that stands between this neighborhood and a fate far worse than any of its residents comprehend."

This was not a declaration one wished to hear upon arriving in one's new home.

The highwayman took back his cloak and handed her up into the carriage. "You'd best not stop again until you are safely arrived at home."

"I had not intended to stop this time," she tossed back with greater courage than she felt.

Again, he laughed. She liked the sound, despite herself. Oh, the fickleness of a heart, finding pleasure in the warm sound of an unwanted laugh.

He slipped something into her hand, closing her fingers around it. "I found this during my 'pilfering.' Guard it, miss. It wouldn't do for you to lose it."

The door was closed. After a hard rap against the side of the carriage, the team of valiant steeds resumed their journey. Lucinda opened her fingers. A necklace lay inside, one upon which she had never before laid eyes. Had it once belonged to the distant cousin from whom she'd inherited her new home? Likely the jeweled pendant was merely paste and not an actual gem. Otherwise, the highwayman would most certainly have kept it.

She sighed, closing her hand once more. Life had too often been like this bit of worthless jewelry: the promise of something beautiful that proved nothing but an illusion. How was she to endure it?

INSTALLMENT II

in which the actions of the Dastardly Highwayman
are spoken of by All and Sundry!

The dreariness of Calden Manor, where Lucinda was to make her home now, could not possibly be overstated. The crumbling remains of long-abandoned wings of the once stately home sat in the shadow of imposing towers with parapets and arrow slits that spoke of violent days gone by. The corridors were long and winding, dark and foreboding. The staff numbered but two: a housekeeper nearly as ancient as the house itself, and the rheumatic coachman, who also served as gardener and butler. She had no neighbors near enough for spotting from the windows of the house, no promise of companionship, and little beyond the nightly moan of the wind to break the silence of her new residence.

Day after day, she watched the front drive in vain, longing with all the fervor of her tender heart for a neighbor to call. The local village must have included a church. Would not even the vicar welcome her? Had she been so abandoned by all in heaven and on earth?

"I should very much like to call upon my nearest neighbor," she told the coachman after a week of loneliness. "Do any estates lie within walking distance?"

"One mustn't walk through the forest, Miss Ledford," he answered with trembling voice. "One mustn't!"

That dastardly highwayman had undertaken his villainy on the road running adjacent to the nearby forest. Had the encounter left her coachman so rattled? Poor man. Poor, poor man!

"Have I no neighbors in the direction leading away from the fearful forest upon whom I might safely call?"

"One is not safe anywhere near the forest." The coachman shook his head as he spoke.

"Am I never, then, to have the company of a neighbor or friend? Am I forever to be alone in this place?"

The question repeated in her mind as more days passed with neither sight nor sound of anyone beyond the three unhappy inhabitants of the manor. The nights stretched long against the cacophony of the howling wind and rustling leaves of the forest.

Until finally, a fortnight following her arrival, carriage wheels could be heard. She rushed to the window of her sitting room, heart aglow with the possibility of companionship. She was not disappointed. No fewer than three coaches stopped on the drive below.

"Company!" declared she. "At long last!"

She paused long enough only to check her reflection and make certain she was presentable. A quick smoothing of her hair and a moment to straighten the paste necklace she had taken to wearing set her appearance to rights.

Excitement quickening her steps, she flew from the room to the top of the narrow front stairs in time to see a veritable crowd spill in from the cold environs beyond the front door. She had dreamed of *one* visitor; she was to have nearly a dozen!

"You are most welcome," said she, wishing her eagerness hadn't rendered her speech quite so warbly. "Please, please do come in."

A particularly beautiful lady, likely only a few years older than herself, spoke first. "Forgive our neglect of you these past two weeks. It is not safe to travel these roads alone. We have at last found a day when all of us could call at once, together."

So it was not only Lucinda's coachman who found the area too danger-ous. The housekeeper pointed the newcomers in the direction of the draw-ing room before shuffling off, apparently uninterested in or unable to see to their needs. No matter. Lucinda would make certain of their welcome.

The drawing room, empty of all adornment other than the sparse fur-nishings, proved a mismatched choice for hosting so large a group. Oh, that her first opportunity for being amongst others might have been undertaken with greater dignity. The ladies occupied the chairs and sofas. The gentle-men stood. Lucinda blushed. What an impression to make on those she hoped would be friendly companions.

Miss Higgins, as she was informed the lovely young lady was called, addressed Lucinda as soon as the group was settled. "Whisper has it you endured an encounter with our famous local highwayman."

"I fear I did." She had been afforded time enough over the lonely fort-night to reflect on that interaction. She found herself less frightened than she had been at first, and increasingly confused. "He was surprisingly kind, though unsurprisingly rude."

"Rude?" a gentleman in the group asked, his voice nearly as high as Miss Higgins's. "I've not heard him described thus."

"I was afraid," Lucinda said, "trembling, even. And he laughed. To laugh at the distress one is causing is, indeed, rude."

She received a few nods of agreement.

"Are you certain he was laughing *at* you?" an older woman in the group asked, her eyes and hair the same bright shade of gray. "Our highwayman is known for finding humor in most situations. I suspect all of us have heard that deep, echoing laugh of his."

"Keeps his face covered, though," another gentleman added. "Deucedly unfair of him, that." The man met Lucinda's gaze and, with a dip of his head, said, "Forgive my uncouth language, Miss Ledford."

"Our highwayman can be a touch unsavory in his language as well," Miss Higgins said, "but never vulgar. One suspects he might be a gentleman after all."

"Or a clever mimic," another suggested.

"Have you all encountered him, then?" How odd that none of them

THE LADY AND THE HIGHWAYMAN

spoke truly condemningly of the highwayman. Indeed, she sensed fondness in many of their recollections.

"Oh, yes," the higher-voiced man said. "Many times, in fact."

"Does he not feel he has stolen enough from all of you?" What could be left to take? Were her neighbors so very well-heeled that repeated robbery could be endured with such pleasantness and aplomb?

The older woman swatted away the thought with a gloved hand. "He never steals a thing. None of us has what he is searching for."

Reflecting on her own interaction with the highwayman, Lucinda recollected a similar declaration from him. He said he had not found amongst her humble assortment of belongings what he wished to find. Indeed, he had even returned to her the very necklace she now wore, one she hadn't realized resided in her carriage. Had he shown all his victims such consideration?

"If he found what he is looking for, would he take it, do you think?" she asked them all.

A gentleman who had not yet spoken answered. "I believe he would." His deeper voice stood at odds with the other man who'd offered thoughts on the matter. This gentleman—for everything in his manner and appearance declared him as such—possessed a pair of eyes so lightly blue as to resemble ice more than pools of deep water, yet the effect was not an unpleasant one. "And I further believe he would not feel overly guilty about simply making off with the mysterious item."

She cast her eyes over the group, searching for some indication that they, as a whole, condemned such a thing. "Do you not find his actions insupportable?"

"We are of two minds on the matter," Miss Higgins said. "Many agree with me that our highwayman, in not relieving anyone of his or her belongings, has shown that his motivations are not truly dastardly. He must be in search of something of great importance, something that, we suspect, is of utmost significance for the safety and well-being of us all. Though Sir Frederick"—she indicated the man with ice-blue eyes—"has suggested our gentleman of the road is in search of a fantastical treasure and that we ought to all be wary of him and his band of thieves."

Lucinda looked to Sir Frederick and saw confirmation in his captivating eyes, but no anger or bitterness. His well-defined jaw was not set with tension, but was at ease, and testified, somehow, of both strength and gentleness.

"You do not think as well of this highwayman as your neighbors do," she observed.

"It is possible his motivations are pure and philanthropic, but one must question his approach," Sir Frederick said. "He hides his aim and his identity, causes distress to good and innocent people. That must give us pause."

"You wish to see him punished? Or worse?" No matter that she had encountered the thief but once and had, at his hand, been made to endure very real fear for her person and safety, she found she could not be at ease with the idea of him facing imprisonment or the gallows. Heaven forfend!

"If he and his comrades are doing such gallant and admirable work, then why undertake it in such a way that can't help but call their admirableness into question?" he asked.

Miss Higgins answered. "Perhaps something about the object he seeks *requires* that he do so under the shadow of secrecy."

"Perhaps," Sir Frederick countered, "he is simply a villain."

"You are determined to think ill of him?" Miss Higgins demanded.

"Not determined," the gentleman answered. "I am simply wary. And"—his eyes moved momentarily to Lucinda—"disappointed to know he caused our lovely new neighbor distress. I wish for all the world that he had not."

The unexpected kindness touched her deeply. She pulled from the cuff of her well-worn dress a lace-edged handkerchief, holding it at the ready should this surge of emotion begin slipping from her eyes. Too many days alone. Too many nights spent listening to the unsettling wind in the fearsome forest. How she needed his gentle words. How she'd needed this visit!

Her neighbors remained far longer than most casual calls permitted. She was grateful those particular rules of propriety were lax here in this empty corner of the world.

Some two hours later, when it was time for her neighbors to depart, she thanked them again and again as they made their way to their carriages. How she wished they could remain. She said as much, only to be met with firm and insistent imploring, that, were she ever away from home, she not remain long enough that her journeys would be undertaken in the dark of night.

"Because of the highwayman?" she guessed.

"No," Sir Frederick answered, earnest and concerned. "Because what lurks in the forest is a far greater threat than he could ever be."

INSTALLMENT III

in which our Heroine is delivered a most cold
Rejection and asked a Favor quite unexpected!

Oh, the joy in Lucinda's heart each time she was included when her neighbors called on one another, making their way from one house to the next in the light of day and the safety of the group! She came to know each of them during these calls and valued their association.

Miss Higgins was kindhearted, of a sharp mind, and the dearest friend one could hope for. The man whose oddly high-pitched voice had so captured her attention when first they'd met a fortnight after her arrival in the neighborhood was Mr. Jennings, and his mother, Mrs. Jennings, was the silver-eyed older woman who'd joined them.

Also among their number during the visits was, nearly without fail, the aloof and handsome Sir Frederick. He never smiled, though he did not truly seem unfriendly nor unhappy, and he never laughed. Though he did not, in her estimation, seem to be that odd sort who lacked any sense of the humorous. He also never spoke ill of anyone beyond the highwayman, and even those criticisms weren't overly cruel nor sharp, but simply expressions of uncertainty regarding the would-be thief's character. Sir Frederick was an oddity, a mystery, and more and more, a friend.

Nearly two months after Lucinda's arrival in the area, after the passage of a lonely Christmas, Miss Higgins very kindly included her in an invitation to do a bit of shopping in the largest town of any note in the area. They departed just as soon as the morning light hit the roads, knowing that if they did not dawdle, they could achieve their goals at market and return home before nightfall. Lucinda prepared a list, one added to by her house-keeper and butler-gardener-coachman, then traveled with Miss Higgins to the various shops an hour away.

What a delight to be away from home and from the forest that she had come to eye with such suspicion! Maybe, just maybe, Fate was beginning to smile on her.

She purchased ribbons and embroidery thread. She found adornments enough for redecorating a bonnet, and salt for addressing the issue of slugs in the vegetable beds. While Miss Higgins shopped for gloves, Lucinda moved toward the stationery shop, wanting to buy parchment and ink, though to whom she would send a letter, she did not know. She simply took comfort in the warm familiarity of such things.

Her path took her past a gentleman having his shoes shined near a sparsely laden vegetable cart. She knew him on the instant, his ice-blue eyes and firm-set jaw identifying him as her handsome neighbor, Sir Frederick.

What a pleasant surprise to see him again. They had enjoyed many a conversation and had, in her estimation, developed the beginnings of a friendship between them. He would certainly be equally pleased to see her. Oh, blessed Fate, to be showing her such kindness today!

"Sir Frederick! What a pleasure to cross paths."

He met her gaze with little warmth in his own. "Miss Ledford." His greeting began and ended with that: her name, uttered with neither excitement nor any apparent desire for interaction.

Perhaps she was misunderstanding his tone. She would try again. "Have you come to town to do a spot of shopping?"

His gaze fluttered over her armful of bundles. "Have you?"

Teasing, no doubt. Amusement pulled her lips upward. "I have. My next stop is the stationers for parchment and ink. I haven't any."

Far from pursuing the line of conversation, Sir Frederick looked once more to the young boy polishing his shoes. "Mind you don't miss any spots."

"Looks a beller-croaker to me," the poor polisher said, eyeing his work. "But if you ain't satisfied, I'll scrub at it some more."

Lucinda waited, certain her friend would speak with her once more. Surely. Alas, she was to be disappointed. He never looked to her again. He acted quite as if she was not even present.

Humiliation burned in her cheeks. She refused to meet the eye of any of the passersby. Sir Frederick, who had on the many occasions in which they had been in one another's company not seemed ashamed of her presence, had issued what appeared to be a very pointed cut. Oh, that she were wrong!

"I have enjoyed our conversations these past weeks," she said, attempting one last time to draw his gaze. "Calling on new neighbors can be uncomfortable, even a touch miserable, when one is newly arrived."

"New neighbors can be miserable," he replied.

Oh. She rested her hand against her stomach, which had spun into a knot. Did he consider *her* "miserable"? It sounded as though he was saying precisely that.

"A pleasure seeing you again, Miss Ledford." The bow he offered was brief and small, and unmistakable. He kept his foot on the block used by the tiny shoeshine boy. There was not so much as a glance of farewell in her direction.

She had been dismissed, coldly and swiftly. The rejection had drawn the notice of a lady and gentleman not far removed. The lady commented behind her hand to her companion, both watching Lucinda with a humiliating degree of pity. To be made an object of ridicule when she was so very newly arrived in the area, striving to be accepted, struggling to feel any degree of hope for her future in so strange and terrifying a place was a heavy burden for her heart to bear, and proof that Fate did not, in fact, look on her with any increasing degree of fondness.

"Forgive me for disrupting your day, Sir Frederick," she said quietly before moving as far from him as her suddenly very weary and overwhelmed limbs could take her.

Cruel Fate, it seemed, took delight in her misery.

Two days passed in the silence of Calden Manor. Lucinda had ample time in which to contemplate Sir Frederick's refusal to speak with her save to indicate that her company was "miserable." What was she to do if he convinced the rest of the neighborhood to shun her as well? Could she live here year after year so utterly alone? How could it be endured?

Night had not yet fallen, though dusk threatened on the horizon. Lucinda stood at her bedchamber window, looking out over the thick forest. What was hidden within those trees that so frightened her neighbors? Their worry had etched its way into her heart, making her eye the dark expanse with great misgiving. All the neighborhood lived in terror of the forest. There had to be a reason.

She leaned against the window frame, watching the branches and treetops sway in the wind. Her lungs filled with the air of her room, air nearly as cold as that found outside owing to the lateness of her ordered delivery of coal.

She heard what she was certain was a knock at the front door. Her housekeeper took to bed every night just as Lucinda finished her evening meal, and her butler-gardener-coachman never came in the house. If she had indeed heard a knock, she would have to be the one to answer. She, alone. Undefended. With no one to turn to should the unexpected visitor have nefarious intentions.

Another knock, unmistakable this time.

"You mustn't be a simpleton," she said. "The night is not yet dark. You can most certainly answer the door."

One trembling step at a time, she descended the stairs and crossed the entryway, knocks continuing to sound at broad intervals. No matter that she assured herself she had no reason for alarm, her pulse quickened with every step she took.

She opened the door an inch, peering through the tiny crack between the door and the frame. As the identity of the new arrival became clear, her burgeoning fear gave way to confusion.

"Sir Frederick."

He dipped his head. "Miss Ledford. I am in need of a moment of your time. I have come on a matter of great importance." He motioned to a child, a girl no more than ten years old, whom she'd not noticed before, cowering behind him and watching her with concern.

No matter that he had treated her most rudely when last they met, she could not be cold to a child. She motioned the two of them inside, closing the door behind them.

"What has brought you here, Sir Frederick?" she asked.

"I have come to beg a favor."

That was unexpected. "Have you? Do you not think it presumptuous to ask a favor of someone whom you would not even speak with two days ago?"

"I would not presume to do so were the favor for myself," he said. "I ask, rather, on behalf of the child." He motioned to the small figure beside him. "Tell her why we've come, little one."

The child looked up at her with fear.

Lucinda opened her arms, and the little girl rushed into them. She leaned her slight weight against Lucinda, clinging to her.

"Please, miss," she said, her breath trembling with each word. "Please don't make me return to the forest."

"The forest?" Lucinda looked to Sir Frederick. "This child was in the forest?"

He nodded. "She needs a safe place away from the dangers she has escaped."

"And that safe place is here?" Lucinda could not account for his decision to bring the child to her.

"I am hopeful that it is, indeed." He offered a dip of his head.

This was not the apology nor the explanation she was owed, but it was a help just the same. Whatever his reasons for not speaking to her in town were, he would trust her with the welfare of this little girl.

With another nod, he stepped from the house, disappearing into the quickly approaching night. The tiny child clung to Lucinda.

"Am I to stay here?" she asked.

"Of course, dear," Lucinda said. "And I will endeavor to keep you safe from whatever you've fled from in the forest."

The girl's chin quivered. "The forest has . . . a monster!"

INSTALLMENT IV
in which our Heroine flees to the fearsome Forest and, to
her shock, encounters the mysterious Highwayman!

Lucinda's little houseguest, she discovered, was called Nanette. She, like Lucinda, had recently been made an orphan. The poor child, alone and without a home, had wandered into the forest looking for food and shelter. What she had found, according to her own vague but insistent recounting, was a horrendous, terrifying monster!

Nanette grew too distraught after only one or two questions for Lucinda to discern the exact nature of the creature she insisted resided amongst the trees. The details Lucinda had gleaned spoke of howls and moans, which might have been the wind, and flashing eyes in the darkness, which might have been moonlight reflecting off dew-wet leaves. The heavy, threatening footsteps Nanette had heard proved more difficult to explain away.

Nanette quickly found a place in Lucinda's heart. She was a dear girl, tenderhearted and eager to make Calden Manor home. Lucinda was unspeakably grateful for the child's company and felt she might be able to do some good in the girl's life.

The matter of Sir Frederick remained unresolved. That he'd cared enough about poor Nanette to rescue her from the forest spoke well of him. That he'd trusted Lucinda enough to bring the girl to Calden Manor called into question the snub he'd offered when she'd crossed his path during her ill-fated afternoon of shopping. She hadn't mentioned the encounter to Miss Higgins, who had, blessedly, not been nearby during the fateful rejection; Lucinda's heart could not bear to see pity or laughter in the eyes of her one and only friend.

Her loneliness, her confusion, and her desperate wish to see Nanette safe and happy filled her thoughts as she and the girl sat around the table in the sitting room late of an evening. Lucinda worked on an intricately detailed fire screen, while Nanette concentrated on a sampler of needlepoint.

"I do hope Sir Frederick will call on us." Nanette sighed. "He is ever so handsome and ever so kind."

Despite her thoughts, Lucinda found she wished for the same. "I too enjoy his company." In her thoughts she added, "Most of the time." He had, after all, shown himself quite capable of being hurtfully dismissive. "And I would like to thank him for bringing you here."

Nanette smiled shyly, sweetly. "He told me you would be kind to me and that I would be safe here."

"That was a kind thing for him to say." Kind as well as surprising.

"I believe he is very fond of you." Nanette's gaze returned to her needlework, though her smile remained.

"What leads you to that conclusion?" Lucinda's heart pounded in her chest as she asked the question. Did she truly wish for the answer? Was she fully prepared to hear it?

"He smiles when he talks about you," the girl said. "Nothing else makes him smile. I think he tries not to, but when he speaks of you, he can't stop."

Lucinda herself had never seen the baronet smile. Not once. Could it be true that she, the lady he had refused to even acknowledge mere days earlier, inspired that rarely seen expression in him? How utterly unexpected!

"His smile makes my heart flutter about," Nanette said. "As if I am a little nervous, but also very happy."

That was a feeling Lucinda knew well. Handsome men had that effect on many an unsuspecting woman, and Sir Frederick was decidedly handsome. She could only imagine his smile would render him even more so.

Her thoughts, jumbled yet pleasant, were interrupted as an unexpected but instantly recognizable scent reached her nose. That of smoke. She glanced in the direction of the fireplace, but, as always, it sat empty and cold. The manor was nearly devoid of coal or firewood. She had taken to keeping blankets nearby and wearing her coat during the particularly intense cold of morning.

Were this any other night, she would have assumed the housekeeper had simply lit a fire in the kitchen. But both of the manor's servants were away that evening, calling upon family and friends. Lucinda and Nanette were alone.

"Do you smell smoke, Miss Ledford?" Nanette asked, her wide eyes looking about as if expecting to see flames at any moment.

That the girl had detected the same aroma convinced Lucinda she was not imagining the worrisome smell. The oddity warranted investigation.

She rose and crossed to the window. The forest, growing dimmer by the minute due to the setting sun, showed no signs of flame. She pressed her open hand against the window, leaning so near the glass that her face almost touched the cold pane. Nothing along the side of the house appeared to be alight. Curious.

"It smells stronger." Nanette even coughed a little.

Lucinda, herself, could taste a bit of ash in the air and felt the tickle it produced in her throat. She looped one finger around the chain of her necklace, attempting to decide what was to be done. Was the fire they smelled a threat? A fire, and she alone with the girl, with no one to be of assistance!

With a calm she did not entirely feel, she faced her darling charge. "Pull on your coat, dearest. We will make a turn about the house and see if we can't solve this mystery."

They'd made but a half-circuit before the dire truth of their situation became devastatingly clear. A fire, indeed! A wing of the house glowed with the telltale amber of interior flame.

"Oh, Miss Ledford! What are we to do?"

"We must find help, Nanette. We simply must." But where? Her nearest neighbors were some distance away, and she hadn't her coachman to hitch up the horses. Neither could they simply stand idly by and watch the house devoured by fire. There was no choice but to make the journey on foot.

She took the child's hand in hers and turned swiftly toward the road— the road that led directly beside the forest. No matter that she had told Nanette time and again there was nothing to fear in those foreboding trees, no matter that she had told *herself* the same, fear tiptoed over her as they drew nearer.

"Oh, miss!" Nanette's quiet cry quivered, her tear-filled eyes watching the dim forest.

"We will do our utmost to avoid stepping within," Lucinda vowed.

From deep within the woods came a howl, the very sound she had always believed to be the wind whipping its way through the many branches.

Hearing it outside of the protective walls of her home, she no longer felt so certain.

"It is the monster, miss," Nanette urgently whispered.

No. She could not believe that. She would not. Another howl sent a shiver over her, filling her with an undeniable dread, the likes of which she had never felt before. Her steps slowed even as her pulse quickened.

Ahead, the road bent, turning directly into the forest. Had it always? She did not remember the path taking her into the woods, no matter that she'd traveled this road many times. Perhaps it was simply that her surroundings were more forbidding in the near-darkness of late dusk. Perhaps it was the influence of too many of her neighbors insisting the forest was dangerous.

"We cannot go into the forest, Miss Ledford," Nanette pleaded. "We must go back."

But looking back, Lucinda was met by the glow of the fire that was surely consuming her home. They could not return there, neither could they hope to save the manor without help.

"We must press forward, dear. We must."

Keeping the girl close to her side, she followed the curve of the road directly into the forest. Seldom had her senses been as alert as they were in that moment. Every sound, every movement pulled her attention. Her eyes could make out so little. Night was nearly upon them!

"I don't want to go into the forest," Nanette whispered.

"We must find someone to help extinguish the fire, and we need to find shelter for ourselves." Even knowing the utter truth of that, Lucinda questioned their current course. She questioned it all the more when the sound of footsteps reached her.

Footsteps. Behind them.

She tugged Nanette's hand, moving more swiftly, praying with all the fervent hope in her heart that they would reach safety and shelter soon.

The footsteps drew closer, louder, faster. Merciful heavens! She and Nanette rushed headlong into the woods, staying on the road as they plunged into darkness. This road would take them to her nearest neighbor, to help, to safety. If only they could manage!

Ahead in the darkness, spots of reflected light suddenly appeared, all in pairs, all at the height of a man. She froze, her breaths tight and painful. They were eyes, she hadn't the first doubt. Were these creatures of the forest? Or people?

Footfalls sounded heavy on the ground behind them, so near that whatever pursued them must have been nearly upon them. Creatures behind. Creatures ahead. What was she to do? What escape was there?

Nanette screamed. Lucinda pulled her close, offering what little protection she could. She held her breath, waiting for the creatures around them to attack.

"It ain't safe in the forest, miss." A man's voice. Not a creature at all.

Without exposing Nanette in the slightest, Lucinda looked up and directly at the now-familiar highwayman. Her lingering fear, coupled with her utter surprise, silenced her. She could do naught but stare.

"Are you hurt?" He spoke from under his wide-brimmed hat, just as he had all those weeks ago.

She managed to shake her head. They'd been frightened but not injured.

He seemed to look beyond her. In a carrying voice, he called, "Any sight of the beast?"

"No, cap'n," came the answer from the direction of the glowing, shimmering eyes.

"Not a single hair," another voice added.

Did all those eyes belong to the highwayman's people? She shook off the question, rising shakily to her full height once more. She'd come in search of help. Perhaps this man of questionable character would redeem himself and offer the assistance she needed.

"Please, sir," she said. "We need your help."

"I would say you do," he answered. "Being alone in these woods isn't wise."

"There's a fire at our home, and not a soul at hand to help. I fear the house is lost now, but if there's even the smallest chance—"

"Come along, men," he shouted. "To Calden Manor!"

"You know where I live?" She could not say precisely why that mattered.

Barely enough light shone to illuminate his dimpled grin. She'd forgotten how breathtaking it was. Sir Frederick's smile had set little Nanette aflutter. If Lucinda wasn't terribly careful, the highwayman's smile would have the same impact on her.

At least a half dozen men rushed past her, back in the direction of her home. The highwayman remained with her and Nanette. He, it seemed, was offering his escort and his protection.

"The men'll do what they can for your home, miss," he said.

"I thank you, and them. I would not have guessed when first I encountered you that you would be so immediately helpful."

"And why's that?"

With Nanette tucked against her side as they walked, she lowered her voice to prevent her words from carrying to the child's ears. The poor girl was frightened enough without realizing they were dependent upon the mercy of a criminal. "You were attempting to rob me, sir. Or do you not recall?"

"I assure you, I recall every detail of our time together."

Flattery. "Then you must understand why I am wary."

"If you can face the forest, you can certainly face me. I may be odd, the subject of rumor, a questionable fellow, even. But *I* am not dangerous."

"Nanette tells me there is a monster in the forest."

"There is," he said quite seriously.

"And can you be certain that monster is not you?" Though she posed the question with some humor, she asked it in earnest.

"Nanette is not the only one to have seen the horrendous beast." The highwayman gave them both a gentle but persistent nudge. "And she's one of the fortunate, to have seen it and escaped. I'd not place money on her being so fortunate again."

No matter that she remained unconvinced of the reality of a monster in the forest, she could not argue the importance of not remaining among the trees. Her home was ablaze. If it were lost, she hadn't any shelter for herself or Nanette.

"Might we send word to at least one of the neighboring estates?" Lucinda asked as she and her dear girl followed the highwayman in the direction of Calden Manor. "The more people we have, the more likely we are to extinguish the fire before the entire house is lost."

"Word's been sent to Hilltop House," the highwayman said. "One of m' men ran that way."

Hilltop House? "Sir Frederick does not have a high opinion of you or your men. Do you suppose he will heed your plea for assistance?"

"For you, Miss Ledford, I suspect he will."

She was not convinced. "Perhaps one of the other neighbors would be more reliable."

"His house is nearest," the highwayman said. "And he's reliable. He'll not neglect you."

His words proved prophetic, at least in some respect. Servants arrived to help save Lucinda's home. Sir Frederick, however, did not come. Nanette eventually stopped asking after him. It was not Lucinda's words that comforted her, though. It was the highwayman's. He said something to her, something Lucinda did not overhear, whilst the remaining flames died down. The little girl took comfort and, from that moment on, would not leave the man's side.

Odd that one who plied his trade in such unsavory pursuits could prove himself so noble. He and his men risked arrest interacting with the Hilltop House servants, yet they did not desert Lucinda in her time of need. Through it all, the highwayman kept his hat tugged low. Had he reason to conceal his face? Was he disfigured? Someone recognizable who dare not invite discovery?

Lucinda and Nanette had taken refuge in the stables, far enough from the house for safety. Blankets had been sent over from Hilltop House to guard against the bitter winter cold. They sat in the hay, wrapped in several layers. Nanette fell asleep, having worn herself to a thread, first with worries over Sir Frederick's absence, then with waxing poetic over the highwayman's kindness to her. In the silence left behind by the girl's slumber, Lucinda could hear the raised voices of those men working to extinguish the flames. The panic she'd heard earlier had dissipated. Was that a good omen, or had they simply given up?

A shadow crossed the open door of the stable. The hat was unmistakable.

"Your house ain't entirely lost, miss," he said. "But none of us thinks you'd be wise to stay until some repairs've been made. There's a touch too much ventilation just now."

She sighed, pulling Nanette closer. The girl was once again without a home. "Oh, what am I to do? I have nowhere to go."

The highwayman leaned against the doorframe, striking a casual and easy pose. For a man who seemed to have no home at all, he never appeared to be anything but *at home*, no matter where he was. What must that be like? How she wished she knew.

"Sir Frederick has sent word that the both of you are to come to Hilltop House. Rooms've been prepared for you. You're expected."

She could hardly believe it. "Sir Frederick does not particularly like me."

The highwayman slipped farther inside the stables. "I understand the one he speaks ill of is *me*. Rumor has it, he offers nothing but praise for you. Were I you, I'd accept his offer."

Nanette had said much the same thing. Yet Lucinda's mind would not clear of the painful memory of Sir Frederick's public rejection. At least *this* man treated her with kindness. Even the night he'd held up her coach, he'd been courteous.

She carefully laid Nanette down, tucking the blankets about her more cozily. She then crossed to the highwayman, holding fast to the blankets wrapped about her own shoulders.

"Thank you for all you did tonight, and for your kindness to the poor little girl."

He tugged at his wide brim. "My pleasure, Miss Ledford."

"Why is it you have chosen such an ill-advised profession? The more I come to know you, the more I see it does not suit you."

How well she remembered his laugh, no matter that she'd not heard it in some weeks. It echoed with low, rumbling familiarly. "Desperate times, my dear Miss Ledford, require desperate actions of us all."

"Are you wanting for money on which to live?" She knew the moment she asked that could not be the case. "No. When you held up my coach, you did not take anything."

"You didn't have what I was looking for," he said.

He stood so very near, the warmth of him chasing away the chill of the night.

"What was it you were looking for?"

"Hope."

INSTALLMENT V

in which our Heroine and her Young Charge take refuge
with Sir Frederick and discover a horrifying Secret!

Hilltop House was the very picture of an estate where a gentleman like Sir Frederick would live. The grounds were immaculate, yet somehow still inviting. The home itself was regal, stalwart, and elegant, yet Lucinda did not find the estate intimidating.

She and Nanette did not see the baronet upon their arrival the night of the fire. His housekeeper relayed his instructions that they should seek their beds and rest, as he was certain they were thoroughly exhausted. He also expressed his wish that they consider themselves at home at Hilltop House for as long as was necessary, insisting he was honored to have them to stay.

Lucinda was, indeed, exhausted, weary to her very bones. She was also deeply confused. The highwayman, an apparent thief and a man living outside the law, had touched her with his kindness, something she'd not been expecting. Sir Frederick, who had mere days earlier rejected her so publicly, had also offered hospitality with no apparent hesitation. How did one reconcile such contradictory behavior?

The next morning, Lucinda woke, dressed, and slipped from her borrowed bedchamber to the public rooms below. She approached the sitting room, but hesitated outside the door. Inside the room, Nanette sat with Sir Frederick on a cozy window seat, the morning sun illuminating them both.

The girl still wore a shirt of Sir Frederick's that had acted as an oversized nightdress from the previous evening.

Just as she was about to enter, she heard Nanette say her name, and Lucinda lingered, listening.

"Miss Ledford was very brave," Nanette said to Sir Frederick. "She walked straight into the forest, even though I told her about the monster. I would not be so brave."

Sir Frederick chucked her under the chin. "I suspect, my little Nanette, you are quite, quite brave."

"You go into the forest, too," Nanette said. "We are all brave, aren't we?"

"Yes, we are."

Nanette smiled up at him, her look both pleased and a bit besotted. He hadn't the highwayman's breath-snatching smile nor heart-fluttering laugh, but Sir Frederick was kind and handsome, thoughtful and good.

"Miss Ledford says that you think poorly of her." Nanette's declaration, offered with the frank innocence only a child could manage, sent waves of heat over Lucinda's face. "I tried to tell her that you smile when you talk about her, but I do not think she believed me."

"Not many people believe that I ever smile," Sir Frederick replied. "I cannot fault her for feeling that way." He made no mention of Nanette's assertion that his fondness for Lucinda had met with disbelief as well.

"Do you like her?" the girl asked.

"Of course I do," he said. "You have seen for yourself that she is good and kind."

Nanette slipped closer to him and leaned her head against his gray-striped waistcoat. "She hugs me tightly when I am afraid. I like that."

Sir Frederick set his arms around the sweet girl. "I knew she would. That is why I brought you to her. I knew you would be safe and cared for."

"Would I not have been safe and cared for here with you?"

He actually laughed, not loudly and not long, but a short, deep, rumbling laugh.

Heavens, he might have challenged the highwayman in that moment for the warmth his laughter roused within her.

"You would have been cherished here, darling," Sir Frederick said.

"Then why did you not keep me?"

Sir Frederick's embrace appeared to tighten around the girl. "Because I could not keep you as safe as I wished to. And I want you to be safe."

"I was not safe in the forest before you found me."

"I know, dear. I know."

The two sat a moment. Lucinda could not help but be touched by the scene. It reminded her quite forcibly of the way the little child had clung to the highwayman the night before. How could these two very disparate men, men who openly disliked each other, be so very similar? Heavens, but Lucinda was confused.

She stepped back into the corridor for the briefest of moments, not wishing to be caught out eavesdropping or lost in thought. With her open palm pressed to her heart, she forced back her rising emotions. Focusing her mind once more, she walked through the doorway, this time making her presence known.

"Good morning," she said.

They turned toward her. Nanette smiled broadly, sliding from the window seat to rush to her. Sir Frederick rose with his usual formal grace and offered a bow but no smile. It was little wonder everyone, Lucinda included, doubted he ever smiled.

Nanette threw her arms around Lucinda's legs. "You are awake."

"As you see." She brushed her fingers over the girl's hair, unable to hide her amusement at Nanette's haphazard appearance.

"You're wearing your necklace," Nanette said.

"And you are wearing your bedclothes." Lucinda shook her head with a smile. "Let's have you run back up to the nursery and ask the nursemaid to comb your hair and see you dressed for the day."

A nod of agreement precipitated the girl's skipping departure.

Alone with the confounding Sir Frederick, Lucinda asked the question she could no longer ignore. "Why did you refuse to converse with me when we spoke in town? You seemed reluctant to even acknowledge you knew me."

"I regretted that then. I regret it now. But, I assure you, it could not be avoided." He spoke with such earnestness that she could not doubt him.

"Why could it not be avoided?" She was being far bolder than she'd once been. Had coming to this area of the kingdom changed her so wholly? Or had she simply discovered a part of herself she'd not before known?

He approached her with a mien of humility she'd not have thought to see in him. "I cannot tell you all. There are secrets in this corner of the world that cannot be shared. In that moment when I saw you, it was imperative, for your safety as much as anything else, that you not linger long. My behavior was intended to see you on your way quickly—not to injure you."

"Was there danger?" She had certainly not sensed any on that quiet street corner.

"There is always danger, Miss Ledford."

She swallowed against the sudden lump in her throat. "Nanette has spoken of a monster in the forest, as has the highwayman."

Sir Frederick rested a gentle hand on her arm. "Our highwayman is not the only one searching for a means of ridding our forest of the threat that hides in its shadows. So long as the horrid creature remains nearby, none of us are safe. Especially the children."

Lucinda pressed her fingertips to her lips, holding back the words of worry that lingered there. "Why are the children particularly at risk?"

"Has no one told you anything of our monster?"

She shook her head.

He held out his hand to her. She accepted it, soothed by the feel of his strong hand around hers. They walked from the sitting room, down the corridor, and into the vast expanse of the portrait hall. On all sides of them, images of gentlemen who resembled Sir Frederick and ladies who also shared a few of his features filled the walls.

They stopped beneath the visage of a kind-eyed man in the fashions of a half-century past. "My grandfather," Sir Frederick said. "The monster first arrived in his time. Few saw it, and fewer still understood it." He motioned to another gentleman a bit farther down the line of frames. "My father encountered the beast more than once. He, you understand, sought it out."

"Good heavens, why?" She could not imagine going in search of a monster.

"To understand it, to separate myth from truth."

"What did he discover?"

Sir Frederick's gaze did not leave his late father's face. "That the monster was, in fact, real, and we had reason to fear it. The beast craves our fears, you see. Takes strength from our terror. Children are less likely to attempt to explain it away as mere imagination or hallucination and, thus, are more likely to be terrified at the very thought of the monster lurking in the dark."

"Does the beast hurt the children? Beyond frightening them, I mean."

"Oh, yes. We have lost a great many these past decades. Far too many." A sadness touched his words as he spoke of children he once knew, children he had not been able to save.

She held fast to his arm. "But not Nanette."

He released a pent-up breath, the sound filled with relief. "Not Nanette. I found her in time. She was fortunate, indeed. I would wager she would not be so lucky a second time."

"The highwayman you so despise said precisely that only last night."

He set his hand atop hers where it rested on his arm. "I do not despise him; I simply cannot approve of his methods. We are, however, pursuing the same goal. That makes us, no matter the oddity of it, united."

"You both seek to destroy the monster."

He nodded.

"The first time I encountered the highwayman, he searched my carriage but took nothing. He said I did not have what he was looking for. Do you know what that is? It must be connected to your cause somehow."

Sir Frederick kept her arm through his as they slowly walked the length of the hall. "Legend tells us that the beast of the forest can be stopped only by a talisman that possesses a strength greater than the fear the monster inspires. Many have conjectured what that talisman might be. We know only that it is powerful and that it will *arrive* in our area when it will be needed most."

"That is why he searches carriages when they pass through. He is looking for some sort of amulet."

"Yes." Much of the disapproval he used when speaking of the highwayman was absent from the simple declaration.

"Why do *you* not search for it?"

His eyes turned to her with tenderness in their depths. "He seeks a cure for the disease which plagues us, while I seek to rescue those already endangered by it. We each have our roles to fill."

"Then you truly do not despise him."

"As I said, I cannot approve of his methods, but I understand them."

"And you truly do not begrudge Nanette and me a place under your roof whilst ours is repaired?"

His voice dropped to something barely above a whisper. "I truly do not."

"Sir Frederick! Sir Frederick!" The housekeeper arrived in a flurry of skirts. "Terrible, it is! Terrible!"

"What has happened?" Sir Frederick asked.

"The little girl."

Lucinda's heart fell to her feet. "Nanette?"

A quick, frantic nod. "She told the nursemaid she was afraid, that she could hear the monster breathing from all the way in the forest, that it was loud and rattling inside her bones."

Sir Frederick tensed beside Lucinda.

The housekeeper continued, voice trembling. "The nursemaid turned to fetch a blanket, thinking the child was merely shaking with cold. When she turned back—" Her words cut off in a high-pitched warble.

"When she turned back—*what*?" Sir Frederick pressed, taking a single step closer to the quaking woman.

"The girl was gone. Simply vanished!"

Lucinda gasped. Nanette was gone!

"The monster," Sir Frederick breathed almost silently.

"We must get her back," Lucinda insisted. "Whatever we must do, we simply have to get her back!"

He turned to face her more fully. "We will, I swear to you. I will not stop until she is safe once more."

"What can I do to help?" Lucinda asked.

He shook his head. "It is too dangerous. You must protect yourself."

"I cannot rest knowing my dear girl is in danger."

"I will do all I can," he vowed. "And I will send for you if there is anything at all you can do."

He was gone a moment later. The determined set of his shoulders gave Lucinda a much-needed bit of hope. Yet, within moments of his departure, that hope proved insufficient.

The Lucinda who had arrived at Calden Manor weeks earlier would have waited and worried and been quite helpless. The Lucinda she was now was not content with such a thing.

Nanette was in danger. Sir Frederick, brave and noble though he was, had rushed to her rescue without the least help or support, a foolish approach indeed when one considered he had a ready and able helper already in the forest.

Lucinda rushed to her room, pulled on her thick cloak, and, though she quaked inside, marched from Hilltop House directly toward the spot in the forest where she had twice before encountered the notorious highwayman.

INSTALLMENT VI

in which our Heroine faces great Danger and uncovers
Secrets within the Forest and beyond!

Did Lucinda dare cry out? She stood at the very place on the road where she had last crossed paths with the highwayman and his band, the same road on which he had searched her carriage all those weeks ago, yet now saw not a single sign of him. She knew not where else to search, but she needed his help. Nanette needed his help.

Beneath her thick outercoat, the necklace the highwayman had found in her carriage rested heavy against her heart. Though she still did not know the jewelry's origin, she had found it gave her courage and strength. It had, before anything else, afforded her a feeling of connection to her new home and new life. She pressed her hand to it as she stood on the deserted road, surrounded on all sides by the ever-thickening fog. She would not let her courage fail her now, not when so much depended upon it.

If the highwayman and his men were not here where she had expected to find them, she would simply have to take upon herself the task of searching out Nanette.

Sir Frederick had, as far as she could recall, rescued Nanette the first time from within the shadows of the forest. Therefore, into the forest Lucinda must go. One step, one breath at a time, she moved further into the thick of the fog and the cold of the ever-shaded trees. Calling out the girl's name might draw the attention of the monster within the woods, but she had little hope of finding the poor soul if she did not give Nanette a chance to hear her voice.

"Nanette!" she called. "Answer me, if you can. Nanette!"

On and on she walked. Though her fears never fully abated, her courage rose to the occasion. She had grown strong during her time at Calden Manor. She had discovered in herself an inner fortitude.

"Nanette!"

Quick steps came toward her from the darkness, too heavy to be Nanette's. Ought she to run? Stand her ground? She hadn't a thing with which to defend herself, having assumed the highwayman and his men would see to the necessary weaponry.

Nearer and nearer the sound came, only slightly dampened by the fog and trees. Merciful heavens! Where was she to go? What was she to do? She swallowed and forced a breath. She raised her fists, ready to do all she could to fend off the inevitable attack. It was her only hope.

In a swoosh of thick, dark fabric, a man grabbed her about the waist and pulled her off the road. The movement was so quick and so sudden, she hadn't even a moment to react.

"You mustn't call out like that, Lucinda. The beast has acute hearing." Sir Frederick!

She clung to him, allowing her pulse to slow and calm. The air shuddered from her lungs. "I thought you were the monster."

"It cannot be far," he whispered. "I heard your voice quite clearly. It most certainly did as well."

"I was trying to find Nanette." Emotion broke in the words. She was so afraid for the girl, so overwhelmed herself.

"As am I."

"I had hoped to secure the aid of the highwayman," she said, "but I could not find him."

"We will simply have to make do on our own." He kept his arm around her as he led her through and around the nearby trees.

"You are not going to insist I return to Hilltop House?" She looked up at him, surprised by both the shake of his head and the disheveled nature of his appearance. He had, it seemed, already passed through an ordeal in his search. "Are you injured?"

"No, but I *am* worried." He looked out over the misty forest, mouth set in an earnest line. "I had hoped to find our sweet little Nanette by now."

Our Nanette. His choice of words touched her, even as his worry added to hers.

"Where did you find her last time? That would seem a good place to begin."

He kept his arm around her, its warmth keeping the cold at bay. "I began there, I assure you. The ruined cottage was empty, with no sign of having been occupied recently."

"Have you any other idea where to search? You know more of the beast than I do."

"There is a cave," he said. "My father believed it was the beast's lair."

She looked up at him once more. "If its lair has been known all these years, why has the monster not been hunted or expelled?"

"It is dangerous," he said, "and grows stronger when in the presence of our fear. Thus far, rooting it out has proven impossible."

Her throat thickened with worry. "And you believe Nanette is there?"

"I do not want to believe it, but I do."

Within the circle of his arms, she squared her shoulders. "Then we must go there. We must."

"Screw your courage to the sticking place. It must not fail you."

"I do not intend to allow it to falter."

His arm tightened about her. "Your courage has impressed me from the beginning. I have known from the moment I first encountered you that yours was a courageous soul. That I was not wrong on that score does my heart good, both in this moment and in all the moments leading to this one."

"I do not always *feel* brave."

"And yet you are."

And yet I am. She repeated those words in her mind as they walked on. The forest grew bone-chillingly cold. The fog, thicker the deeper they traveled, turned the midday sun dim as dusk. Just when she grew certain they could not possibly travel any farther without reaching the forest's far edge, Sir Frederick stopped.

"Have we arrived at the cave?" How she wished her voice were steadier. Sir Frederick believed her brave and bold. She wanted to be precisely that.

He motioned directly ahead of them. She took a step forward, slipping from his arms, and studied their misty surroundings. There was, indeed, a cave, its mouth wide and gaping and terrifying.

Her mind begged her to flee, to put as much distance between herself and the cavern as possible. But her heart, warmed by the touch of the necklace against her skin, insisted she remain.

"If Nanette is in there," she said, "we must go inside. We must find our dear girl."

Sir Frederick joined her. From underneath his heavy coat, he produced a small lantern, which he lit, and, together, they walked into the lair of the monster.

The air inside was dank and heavy. Long, pointed daggers of rock hung from the ceiling and jutted up from the ground. Water dripped, pooling in places. The cave ought to have been cold—no sunlight penetrated its interior—but it was not. The warm moistness of it was overwhelming, cloying.

Further into the dark deep, a growl echoed and bounced toward them. Lucinda's every hair stood at attention, her pulse quickening.

"The beast will sense my fear," she whispered to Sir Frederick.

"I do not doubt it already has. We must simply make certain it senses our bravery as well."

"What if all the courage I can summon is not enough?"

"If anyone's fortitude will be sufficient, I haven't a doubt it will be yours."

Another growl. Another rush of hot wind. They were drawing nearer. How many more steps before the beast was upon them?

Questions of the monster were quite suddenly swept aside at the sound of whimpering tears.

"Nanette?" she whispered.

Sir Frederick must have heard the cries as well. He slipped past her and, lantern held out in front of him, moved toward the sound. Around a bend in the cave, they found Nanette huddled against the wall, crying and shaking. She caught sight of them and leaped to her feet, rushing headlong into the strong arms Sir Frederick held out for her.

"We must move quickly, child," he warned her. "The beast will know we are here."

"We must go! Now!" Franticness added volume to Nanette's pleas.

Sir Frederick kept the girl close. He held high the lantern they were depending upon. He looked to Lucinda. They exchanged silent nods of equal relief and concern. They had found Nanette, but they were far from safe.

At a quick clip, they retraced their steps but did not get far before the growls and snarls grew even louder. The monster must have been very close behind them.

It senses and thrives off your fear. Be brave.

Nanette froze, eyes wide. Not a muscle in her body moved.

Lucinda looked to Sir Frederick. Worry filled his features. "The monster has seized her," he said.

"It is feeding on her fear?"

He nodded.

"Can you carry her out, even frozen as she is? Take her as far from here as possible?"

His gaze turned to something behind her, something that drained every drop of color from his face. "We are too late," he whispered.

Lucinda's lungs felt like stones in her chest. Her heart pounded against the heaviness. The weight seemed to spread, holding her arms still and her legs rooted to the spot. Moving felt increasingly impossible. Was the beast sensing her fear as well?

She yet faced Sir Frederick and could see that he, too, had grown unnaturally still, eyes frozen on the threat lurking behind her. The growling had stopped, replaced by the loud, steady breathing of something so near she could feel the heat emanating from its body.

If only the highwayman had found the legendary talisman! What hope had they of defeating the beast, or even escaping its clutches, without the protection of the missing amulet?

Against her chest, a warmth started, small and pointed at first, but spreading bit by bit. The necklace. The one the highwayman had found in her carriage! It was responding to the presence of the beast. Could it be the talisman they sought?

No. The highwayman had searched high and low for years. He would not have given it to her if he'd thought for even a moment it was a powerful amulet. Yet everywhere the warmth of it spread, her stiffness abated. It reached her neck. She could turn her head. Then her shoulders.

I am able to move. Only I am able. She and she alone could face the beast that had held so many captive for so many years, that had caused such pain and suffering. Only she.

Why had the highwayman not simply taken the amulet and faced down the beast himself rather than leaving the task to her? He'd not even told her what he'd actually given her.

Can I be so certain I am correct, that this is, in fact, the sought-after talisman? She was able to move enough that she could turn to face the beast if she chose. Whether or not the necklace she wore was the mystical charm destined to destroy the hideous beast, she had to at least try to save them all.

She set her hand on her coat, directly above the necklace. Its warmth spread farther, faster. *I must do this.*

Lucinda spun about. Mere inches away, a hideous face glared at her. A lion. A dragon. A demon. She didn't know what it was, only that it was horrifying. It growled low in its throat, steam rising from its wide, flaring nostrils, saliva dripping from its long, pointed fangs.

As when she had been stopped by the highwayman, and later, rushing to the forest to save her home, Lucinda held her chin up, shoulders back, and told herself she was braver than she felt.

"I—" Her voice shook. She began again. "I am not—"

The beast released a piercing, earth-shaking howl, the heat of its breath nearly knocking her down. She ought to have been terrified, but she felt a growing calm.

"I am not—"

Again, it interrupted her declaration with an anger-filled roar. Its enormous clawed feet scratched at the cave floor. Its broad beastly shoulders crouched, glowing eyes narrowed on her.

"I—"

It crouched lower, shifting its weight again and again from one taloned paw to the other, clearly preparing to pounce.

"—am—"

It leaped for her, hooked claws aimed for her head.

"—not afraid of you."

Light poured from her necklace, so bright it penetrated her coat, filling the cave with a red glow. The beast, in mid-flight, was tossed away from her by the force of the light.

Lucinda, herself, was thrown backward. She landed on her side, skidding along the rocky surface, glowing and hurting and confused.

Complete silence descended on the cave. No claws tearing at rock, no hot, heavy breaths. She pulled herself up on her elbows. The necklace no longer glowed. The lantern Sir Frederick had been holding was extinguished. She could hear nothing and see nothing.

"Nanette?" Her voice quavered. She was concerned for the girl, yes, but not truly afraid. No longer. The fear she had felt upon first seeing the beast was, somehow, gone. "Sir Frederick?"

"We're here." His deep, steady voice proved vastly reassuring.

"I cannot see," she said. "The beast may be—"

"You've destroyed it." Nanette spoke with surety.

Something brushed against her. She flinched back, only to realize it was Sir Frederick. He pulled her into his embrace. Her hands found Nanette there with them. She clung to them both.

"You've done it, Lucinda," Sir Frederick whispered. "I knew you would. I knew it from the very first."

"The beast really has been destroyed?"

"It has."

"And I'm no longer afraid," Nanette said.

Sir Frederick helped her to her feet. As Nanette had said, the aura of fear that had filled the place, that she had fought against while facing the monster, had dissipated.

The lantern was lit a moment later. Sir Frederick held it aloft, illuminating the cave once more. She saw no sign of the beast she had faced.

"It is gone," she said in amazement.

"When the light from your necklace reached it, the monster simply dissolved." He held out his hand.

She set her hand in his. "Then the necklace really is the amulet." She wrapped her other hand around Nanette's.

"It is," Sir Frederick said.

She eyed him as they moved swiftly but carefully from the cave. "You do not seem surprised."

"I recognized it," he said.

"Then why did you not tell me? Or take the talisman yourself? You knew where the beast was and what it was and—"

"I haven't your bravery, my dear. I could not have done what you did."

She shook her head. "If you had worn the amulet, you could have."

"The necklace was important, but it was not the crucial element. Others have attempted what you just did and failed."

They stepped from the cave into the forest. She had all but forgotten it was daytime. It had been so dark and foreboding in the cavern. She looked back at the mouth of the cave. The beast was truly gone. She, somehow, had faced it and, without knowing, defeated it.

"I have never been truly brave," she said.

Sir Frederick raised her fingers to his lips and pressed a kiss there. "Your bravery was apparent from the very first. I knew then that you were the one we'd been waiting for."

Their first meeting had been tea amongst neighbors. She'd hardly been brave then; she hadn't needed to be.

They walked through the forest, hand-in-hand-in-hand.

"The monster truly is gone?" Nanette asked as they approached Hilltop House. "It won't come back?"

"It won't come back," Sir Frederick said. "Our Miss Ledford made quite certain of that." He looked to Lucinda. "You've saved us all."

He then did something Lucinda thought never to see: he smiled. A heart-melting, soul-warming, *dimpled* smile.

INSTALLMENT VII
in which our Heroine seizes her Happiness!

Lucinda casually mentioned over tea the next afternoon that she meant to take a walk in the woods and do all she could to find the highwayman. She hinted that she meant to tell him all that had happened the day before and that the necklace he had given her was the amulet he'd been searching for. Sir Frederick had shown only minimal interest, nodding and expressing his relief that the forest was now a safe place.

She knew she was not wrong about him. His smile had given him away.

Thus, when she saw her highwayman sauntering down the forest path toward her, she could not entirely contain the excitement she felt. All that she had come to admire and enjoy about this mysterious man of daring and intrigue, and all she had come to love and cherish about Sir Frederick's generous and caring heart, were found in one remarkable gentleman.

"Miss." He tugged at his bedraggled hat. "Fine thing seeing you here."

"I looked for you in this very spot yesterday," she said, "but it seems you were occupied elsewhere."

His mouth tipped in a smile. "I was, in fact, in the forest yesterday."

She bit back a smile of her own. "I know."

Curiosity tugged at his mouth. "You do?"

"And, by the end of the day, I understood why I couldn't find you."

He tucked his hands into the pockets of his outercoat. "Did you?"

"I also discovered why Sir Frederick told me that he knew I was brave from our very first encounter, when that encounter involved no degree of courage."

The highwayman grew noticeably uneasy. "Because he misremembered?"

"No." She stepped up to him and, rising onto her toes, reached up and took hold of the brim of his hat. "Because he is you." She pulled his hat off. Sir Frederick. Her Sir Frederick. Her highwayman. "Why the ruse?"

"The amulet was found during my father's lifetime, but it did not work as it was meant to. We had the talisman, but not the one intended to wield it. Our only hope was to find someone inherently brave."

"So you held up carriages to gauge your victims' reactions?"

"I severely disliked the necessity of it. It felt cruel and was certainly not kind." All the bravado of the highwayman melted away, replaced by uncertainty and heaviness of heart. "I wished again and again I were in a position to be truthful with you about all of this. That day when we saw each other in town, I was discussing my work as a highwayman, which necessitated my dismissal of you; I could not risk you overhearing."

So many things were making sense to her at last.

He took her hand as he'd done the day before, but this time with an aura of pleading. "I will understand, my Lucinda, if you cannot forgive me for deceiving you. The secret was simply too vast and the consequences too potentially devastating."

She understood fully and deeply. "My darling Frederick." She set her arms about his neck. "My dear, brave highwayman."

In true dastardly fashion, he bent and kissed her, declaring his love and devotion through the earnestness of that very personal gesture. Lucinda clung to him, reveling in the certainty she felt within his arms, and in the promise that they could weather any storm.

Together.

The lady and the highwayman.

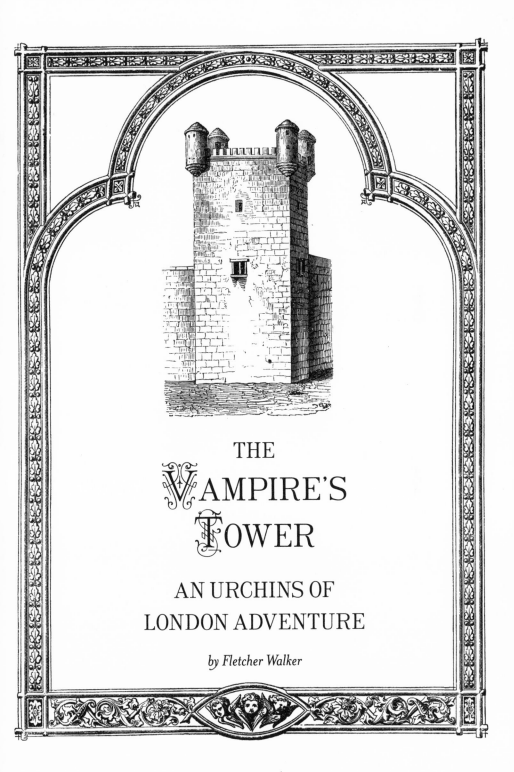

THE
VAMPIRE'S
TOWER

AN URCHINS OF
LONDON ADVENTURE

by Fletcher Walker

CHAPTER I

Morris Wood had clocked twelve years of life and had nothing but survival to show for it. He worked what reputable jobs he could scrounge, filling the gaps with pickpocketing and nipping second-rate bunts from unsuspecting costermongers and selling the bruised or misshapen apples for a few coins. He wasn't a bad sort, just a lad born under an unlucky star.

"Carry your parcels, miss?" he asked, his tattered hat in his hands, as a finely dressed woman stepped out of a milliner's shop.

She looked to her maid, walking at her side. They exchanged amused smiles.

He wasn't so easily put off. "You're like to be full knackered after a day of shopping. Allow me to lug your goods, miss."

Morris watched, hopeful. The younger misses and the oldest matrons were most likely to cross his palm with a farthing or more, sometimes even a shilling. He need only bow and scrape and try to look a bit younger than he was. Pity paid, after all. And little ones got a blimey lot of pity.

The fine lady motioned to a carriage two skips away. "I am going only so far as there."

"I'd carry your load that far, miss."

The gentry sorts had a way, when he'd worn them down, of dropping their shoulders and sighing like they had to empty their lungs all at once. Pity paid, but so did exasperation. He'd take the coins however they came.

The lady's parcels were carried to her carriage. Two sixpence were set in his hand. He pocketed them, along with the few other coins he'd managed to pull together that day. It was a meager pile, nowhere near the bunce he'd like to claim as his own. Still, it'd be enough to pay his daily due for the roof over his head that night. Another couple of morts out doing a bit of shopping, a gent here or there with a bit of silver jingling in his coat, and Morris'd have something left over after the Innkeeper took his share.

He walked down the street with his hands tucked in his pockets, whistling. The day was fine. He appreciated the weather for more than the convenience. Rainy days or windy days or otherwise miserable days tended to empty the streets. It was hard to go dipping when there were no jangling pockets wandering about. Honest work wasn't easier to claim either when the fine coves and morts kept to their houses.

Morris spotted his chum Jimmy standing by a fishmonger's cart. He gave a quick nod, pausing as he drew near. "Swiping?" he asked behind his teeth.

"Guarding." Jimmy's eyes pulled wide, looking as surprised as Morris felt. Urchins like them weren't usually trusted with *preventing* a thieving.

"You drawing bunce for it?"

Jimmy nodded. "I'm to watch all these carts and warn if someone's looking to nip off with something. The lot are paying me a shilling for the day."

"A shilling?" Morris whistled in appreciation. "I ain't never pulled down a shilling in one day for anything respectable."

"Boy," a gravelly voice called. "I don't pay you for nattering."

No more chattering. Pocketing a shilling meant Jimmy'd have loads left even after paying the Innkeeper. Morris wasn't about to rob him of that. Honest work was a rare enough thing, and they needed every penny, every shilling, every guinea they could tuck away. Jimmy and Morris meant to make something of themselves. A fellow needed money to do that. Money and a whole heap of luck.

"I'm a bit short," Morris said. "May 'ave to pick a kick or two."

"Don't get caught," Jimmy warned. "Enough of us've been swept up."

Morris knew it well enough. He kept on his way, keeping an eye out for opportunities. The Innkeeper wouldn't let him stay without the daily rent.

But nearly every night, one or more of the urchins that took refuge in the Inn didn't return from their day on the street. He'd guess, if pressed, that they'd been caught nipping off with coins or pocket watches or whatever else they could wrap their fingers around to bring back to the Inn. He didn't intend to take a ride in the Black Maria anytime soon.

He'd managed to earn a few ha'pennies here and there for odd jobs and tasks. He didn't have to go dipping the whole the rest of the day. Jimmy's shilling put Morris's earnings to shame, but they were a team. What one of 'em tucked away, they'd both be helped by.

With the relief that came from money in his pocket, Morris made his way quickly down the streets of London toward the slum where he spent each night. He'd not gone far when a sight caught him up short. The finest carriage he'd ever seen. Half at least was covered in gold. The rest, white as snow, hadn't even a speck of dirt on it, no matter that the streets were terribly dusty. On either side of the driver, who was wearing white livery with a three-point hat, two red flags flapped and flew.

"S'help me Baub, I'll have me a carriage like that one day," Morris whispered to himself, watching the awe-inspiring vehicle fly past. Someday. Someday he'd be out of the gutter. He'd be able to read, able to pay his own way without being beholden to a cracksman like the Innkeeper, and he'd have a carriage, a fine one like that'n.

He knew the way to the building that the urchins all knew as the Inn. Even with the rotting planks across gaps in the walk and the needed leaps to get safely over, he didn't have to think much to manage it any more. Easy enough.

He ducked through the misshapen hole in the side of the brick wall. No one knew when it had broken or if it'd once been a proper door, but it was their way in and out, and it was the reason the Inn was so blasted cold in the winter and blazing hot in the summer. Still, it was dry and better than sleeping on the street.

Morris stood in the usual line just inside the hole. The children always queued up when returning for the night. Some were a touch older than he was; most were younger. All were waiting their turn to make the daily payment.

Behind a tall, battered clerk's desk stood a grease-faced man, hair stringy and long. He eyed each child as he or she approached. His hand uncurled, palm up, gray fingernails extending like claws.

"Half farthing." That was what he asked of the youngest.

Little George set his nightly rent in the Innkeeper's hand and slipped past. Next, a girl closer to Morris's twelve years approached the desk.

With the same extended claw, the Innkeeper said, "Ha'penny."

"I've this watch chain," Mary told him. "Worth weeks of rent, I'd say."

He examined it, that practiced greedy eye of his not missing a thing. "Bit banged up, it is." He popped it between two of his six teeth and gave it a bite. "Gold, though." The Innkeeper nodded, dropping the treasure in the box he'd lock after everyone'd paid their due. "Three weeks for you, Mary."

She'd be in fine fettle for nearly a month. Anything she earned or swiped, she could keep. Or she could give herself as close to a holiday as any of them would ever know.

Morris's turn arrived soon enough.

"Tuppence." The Innkeeper's unwavering hand waited for payment.

He set four farthings and two ha'pennies in the Innkeeper's palm. The man counted 'em, something Morris knew wasn't necessary. The Innkeeper knew the feel of coin, knew at a glance how much he held in his claws. The coins were dropped in the locking box, and Morris was waved inside.

One more night off the street. One more night closer to the better life he and Jimmy meant to claim for themselves.

Morris grabbed a dinged and dented metal bowl from the stack in the corner and crossed to the even more dinged and dented pot hanging in the soot-blackened fireplace. He scooped out a lump of breadcrumb gruel.

Little George rose on his toes, trying to peer over the lip of the pot.

"Breadcrumb," Morris said, tipping his bowl enough to show the boy.

"Innkeeper done bobbed me." George's threadbare shoulders drooped. "Said we'd be twisting down oat gruel t'night. I like oat gruel better."

"So do I, lad." Morris dumped a heap into a bowl for George and handed it to him. "Fill up, though. It's hard to sleep with an empty belly."

He sat down on a three-legged stool, bowl on his knees, and looked out over the children, counting heads. They were two short of their usual number. One of those missing was Jimmy, but he had a longer trek back than usual. He'd be along soon, no doubt. Who else hadn't come back?

Morris caught Mary's eye. "Sally ain't back?"

Mary gave a small shake of her head, her mouth pulled low with worry. "Ain't like her to be late."

No, it wasn't.

"You don't suppose she's—" Mary didn't finish the question.

All the nearby urchins looked to him, the same nervous pull to their features. They didn't talk a lot about how many of them had simply disappeared, but everyone knew. Everyone worried.

"She'll be back soon." Morris spoke more confidently than he felt.

She didn't come back.

Even after Jimmy returned, leftover coins secreted away after paying his rent, Sally still wasn't there.

Night fell. Morning dawned. All the urchins left to make their daily silver.

And Sally didn't come back.

In the shadowy stretch of a London back alley, a sallow-faced man watched the comings and goings of the street children. Young. Energetic. Easily overlooked. A few missing here and there would hardly be noticed. Would his master be pleased at how many he was wrangling so quickly? Just what his master needed: a fresh supply . . . of blood.

CHAPTER II

"Six this week," Jimmy said as he and Morris walked through the London fog. "I ain't seen the Black Maria anywhere near these past weeks. Don't seem to be the Bobbies nipping off with urchins."

Morris didn't think so either. "But if they ain't being snatched by thief-takers, where are they all?"

"Sleeping somewhere other than the Inn?"

Morris shook his head as they turned onto Fleet Street, looking for an apple cart or ginger beer seller who'd pay 'em a few coins for guarding their goods. "We'd see the missing ones out making their coins if they were still around. No one's seen hide nor hair."

Jimmy scratched at his head, just below his hat brim. "We could look for them, but we'd not have time to earn our rent for tonight."

"I don't want to sleep on the street," Morris said. "'Specially if someone's snatching urchins." He let out a tight breath. "But we gotta look or no one will."

"We've another mystery to solve then, do we?" Jimmy grinned at the promise of a puzzle.

"Seems we do." Morris liked a riddle as much as his friend did. "Have we enough extra for the Innkeeper tonight?"

"We can use some of what we've secreted away," Jimmy said.

It'd be worth it. They might've been only twelve years old and not the oldest of the Inn's urchins, but they looked after the others.

Rather than stop at the costermonger cart and enquire after pay, they kept on.

"All the missing 'ns work this area," Jimmy said. "Whatever's snatching 'em's likely around here."

They'd solved many a mystery on the streets of London. The skeptical in Town would probably be surprised at how many of those answers were otherworldly. They'd found and defeated ghosts, encountered monsters, outsmarted villains. If history held true, they weren't searching out anything humdrum.

"John-John was the last to go missing," Morris said. "He always does his diving near Covent Garden. I'd say we'd do best to sniff around there a bit."

The market was busy, as always. Sellers shouted flattering descriptions of their wares. Most were probably lies. Ends didn't meet on the streets of London without a bit of stretching.

"I see a flower seller I know," Jimmy said. "Perhaps she's seen somethin'."

Morris nodded, looking over the crowd for anyone he thought might have something to offer. A boy with a familiar, dirt-smudged face slipped around the back of a vegetable cart, nipping a carrot before scurrying off. Morris followed quick on the boy's trail. The little one was fast, but not fast enough.

He snatched hold of the boy's arm. "Morris here, George. Only Morris."

That put an end to the fight just beginning. "Thought you was the police."

"Have the police been snatching up urchins, then?" Morris had been sure that wasn't the answer to their mystery.

George shrugged. "Someone 'as."

"Then you ain't seen nothing." A disappointment, that. "John-John works this corner of things. Jimmy and I thought maybe someone would have an idea what's happened to him."

George snapped off a bite of the carrot, talking as he chewed. "John-John told me he'd come into the cream and wouldn't need to filch here no more. I said he had the best fortune of anyone. Maybe he weren't so fortunate."

Morris could see the worry growing in the boy's eyes. "Maybe he were. Maybe ol' John-John found himself a flush post after all."

George's little brow angled sharply. "Don't sell me a dog, Morris. This ain't my first day on the streets."

He ought to've known better than try to tell a lifelong urchin to imagine the best when the worst made more sense. They learned young that it was better to be clever than rosy-eyed.

"Did he tell you anything about going anywhere or with anyone?"

George shook his head. "Only said he'd be nose-deep in the clover. He were right pleased."

Didn't sound like he'd been stolen. Maybe John-John really had just gone to a better situation.

Jimmy returned, looking as confused at Morris felt. "Becky, what sells the flowers, says John-John left to work for some swell."

Same as George said.

"Odd, though," Jimmy continued. "She said Sally, who disappeared from the Inn last week, told her the same. That she'd a chance for something better and meant to take it. Becky said neither of them seemed afraid."

Morris scratched at the back of his neck. "So maybe we ain't searching out a kidnapper but a do-gooder?"

George spoke again, still working at his carrot. "Sally wouldn't've gone off without Mary. Best mates, ain't they?"

Morris met Jimmy's eye. There was truth in George's view of things. Neither Jimmy nor Morris would trek off to a grand opportunity without the other. Sally and Mary were the same.

None of this made a lick of sense.

The three of them wandered away from the market, none speaking. Where had the missing urchins gone? Were they in danger? Had they all gone to the same place? Was none of it connected and they were just chasing steam?

George whistled low and long. "A grand bit o' wheel there, i'n'it?"

There was no need to ask what he'd seen that'd so impressed him. The same gold-accented carriage Morris had seen a week earlier rolled slowly down King Street. Fitting that it'd be on a lane named for royalty. It looked the sort of thing a monarch'd ride in.

"Could you imagine having money enough for something like that?" Morris mused aloud. "Hard to even think of when we's spending our days nipping carrots off carts and dropping coins in the claws of the Innkeeper."

"Maybe John-John got 'imself a job polishing the gold on a carriage like that." George motioned to the vehicle with his stub of a carrot. "He could eat for weeks just selling what rubbed off on the cloth."

"All the more reason to look for 'im," Jimmy said. "He might have a few cloths to spare."

George wandered off, looking for coins or whatever work he could manage before returning to the Inn. Jimmy and Morris walked on together.

"Do you really think John-John and Sally went to work somewhere?" Jimmy asked.

Morris shook his head. "Sally would've told Mary. And John-John would've crowed about it to all of us before claiming his fortune."

Jimmy stuffed his hands in his pockets. "Maybe this time, instead of going up against a ghost or a monster, we're facing down a rich man."

"Almost more scary, i'n'it?"

"Not *almost*."

Morris glanced back as they walked, eyeing the gilt carriage once more. It had stopped, and the door was open. He tugged at the sleeve of Jimmy's coat, motioning at the vehicle with his head.

A pair of bare feet, small like a child's, could be seen standing on the paving stones facing the carriage, but the open door hid the rest of the little one.

"Who's that?" Jimmy asked.

"Don't know." Morris stepped closer, studying what little he could see. "Ain't a gentry child, not barefoot like that."

Something was tossed to the ground. Green. Leafy. He recognized it in the next instant: the top of a carrot.

Jimmy sucked in a breath. "George?"

The little feet stepped up into the carriage. Morris's heart dropped to his stomach. George. Disappearing into a rich man's carriage, just like they'd worried had been happening to the urchins of the Inn.

He ran. He ran fast and hard, Jimmy close on his heels.

The carriage began rolling away, but was slowed by the press of vehicles on the busy street. Morris and Jimmy wove around hackneys and coaches, keeping track of the one they sought. If only it didn't get going too quickly.

It picked up pace. Morris made a lunge for the back, managing to snatch hold before the carriage sped out of reach. Jimmy snatched hold right beside him. Clinging for dear life, they rode the carriage further from Covent Gardens, further from the streets they knew, and, Morris feared, closer and closer to danger.

This one was smaller than the rest. The master wouldn't like that, but the children were getting wise and wary. It was becoming more and more difficult to lure them away with the promise of fortunes or food or comfort. He knew better than to frighten them; they'd raise the alarm. His master needed a full supply of fresh, young victims when the time for rejuvenating arrived. He would not disappoint his master. He didn't dare.

CHAPTER III

Just when Morris was certain he couldn't hold on to the back of the carriage a moment longer, it slowed, rolling to a stop at a tall iron gate. He and Jimmy had been in a number of odd fixes during their twelve years of life, so they knew what to do without saying a word.

They hopped off the carriage and, ducking down to stay as low and hidden as possible, followed the vehicle through the gate. They darted quick behind a hedge, waiting for the wheels to grow distant enough for them to safely move.

Morris's first glance at their surroundings shocked him; almost nothing did that anymore.

"It's a blasted castle," Jimmy said. "An honest-to-Baub castle."

They'd wandered past the gates of Buckingham and Windsor, so a castle wasn't a completely unfamiliar thing. But to have ridden the back of a carriage, one containing ragged little George, right to a castle gate? He'd not been expecting that.

"An old one, too." Jimmy's surprise hadn't silenced him. "Knights-and-armor old."

"Aye, but it ain't crumbling. Someone's living here and seeing to the ol' pile."

"Someone who convinced George to roll off with him."

They needed to find George and make certain he was safe. If the master of the castle was the one sweeping urchins off the street, they needed to know why and where they all went, and why none of them were ever heard from again.

Up ahead, the gilded carriage rolled on, not to the front portico but toward the stables. That made more sense; George weren't exactly a fine and fancy visitor. But would George be staying in the stables, or should they sneak over toward the castle and try to find him there?

"Look!" Jimmy, who was never spooked, sounded upended.

Morris followed his wide-eyed gaze to the top of a tall, narrow, stone tower. "I don't see nothing."

"It was there. A minute ago."

"What was?"

"Somethin' . . . floated by the windows up top." Jimmy hadn't looked away. "*Floated.* Swear it did."

"What kind of thing?"

Jimmy shook his head. "A person, maybe. I ain't sure."

"A person *walking* past the window?" That seemed more likely.

"Didn't look like walking."

Morris looked back again but saw nothing. There wasn't even any light up there. But Jimmy wasn't one to make things up, and he didn't get shaken easily. He'd seen something.

"We can't leave George here," Jimmy said firmly.

"But we don't know where he's being taken."

Jimmy squared his shoulders. "No. But we know where *that* is." He pointed up at the tower.

"You want to go chasing after a mysterious figure in the tower?"

"It's the threat," Jimmy said. "If George is in danger, that's where it'll be coming from."

"And if the other urchins were brought here and are in trouble, they'll be there as well."

Jimmy looked to him. "We're doing this again, then, are we? Running headlong into trouble, solving mysteries, courting danger?"

Morris allowed a cheeky smile. "It's the only thing we do better than picking pockets."

He spit into his palm. Jimmy did the same. They clasped and shook hands, then moved stealthily toward the tower.

The master was wandering the castle, still half asleep, but becoming more and more alert. Time was running short. Once he was fully awake, he would be thirsty. The consequences of not having an adequate supply for his feast would be dire.

There was little time to gather enough children.

So very little time.

CHAPTER IV

Sneaking unseen into an unfamiliar place would be far easier in the dark of night. But the sun wouldn't drop out of the sky for hours, and they needed to check on George and any others who were there, now. And they needed to find out what had slid past the tower window.

Morris waved Jimmy alongside the treacherous tower, both boys eyeing the grounds for anyone wandering about. They didn't dare get caught sneaking around, no matter if there was danger here or not. Most people took a dim view of trespassing.

Footsteps rustled nearby. Morris and Jimmy ducked down behind a thick shrubbery. They held their breath. No one ever passed.

"There's got to be a window or somethin'," Jimmy whispered, slipping farther around the tower. Morris followed, acting as lookout.

Around they went. The tower was larger than it had seemed from across the yard.

"Anyone coming?" Jimmy asked.

"No. Any windows low enough?"

"No." Jimmy abruptly stopped. "But there's a door."

That pulled Morris's attention. Jimmy wasn't looking straight ahead or even up a little. His eyes were angled down.

"A cellar?" Morris guessed. He couldn't think of anything else a door in the ground would lead to.

"Or a crypt." Jimmy really had been spooked by whatever he'd seen in the tower window to jump to that possibility.

"A crypt'd be under a church, though." Morris reached for the iron-ring handle. "I'd wager this is our way in."

Jimmy shoved out a breath. "Mind you, if this proves to be another monster, I run faster than you do."

He eyed Jimmy. "You owe me for that redcap, you know."

A bit of amusement tugged at his friend's mouth. "We escaped the murderin' goblin, didn't we?"

"*You* escaped. I fought the blasted thing." It had been one of their more terrifying adventures.

Jimmy rolled his eyes. "I came back and helped, di'n't I?"

"If there's a redcap down here," Morris said, pointing into the dimness beyond the door, "I'm closing this and locking you in with it."

Jimmy sobered quickly. "It weren't a redcap. I don't know what it was, but it weren't that."

Morris swallowed, telling himself to hold it together. They'd urchins to search out and rescue. It wasn't anything they hadn't done before.

"Are we goin' to be able to see in there?" Jimmy asked.

"I've no idea."

Turned out, they could, but only just. And being able to see when there were no windows and no lanterns and no candles wasn't reassuring.

"Where's the light coming from?" Morris whispered, carefully tiptoeing across the empty expanse, which was nothing but pillars and a stone floor, though they couldn't see the entire space all at once. The tower really was larger than it seemed.

A sound stopped them up short. A howling sort of cry.

"Wind?" Jimmy asked, voice so low it was almost silent.

"That weren't the wind wailin'."

"I didn't think so." Jimmy was an odd sort, always rallying when the danger grew. None of the worry that had shook his voice when he'd first seen the shadowy figure in the windows above remained. With firmness, he said, "Let's sniff out the stairs, see if we can't Jenny the situation."

They wove around more columns, more turns. The cellar was musty, dank, and bitterly cold. Still no lanterns or torches or candles, but somehow still plenty enough light for seeing their way. Again the cries were heard overhead. Without needing to consult, Morris and Jimmy moved faster, searching every turn for steps.

They came upon an alcove carved directly in the thick stone outer wall. Morris sucked in a sharp breath. On an iron platform at the base of the alcove sat a dusty, beaten-up, probably centuries-old coffin. The walls around it glowed, but for no reason he could see.

"Blimey," Morris muttered, a shiver sliding down his spine. "This *is* a crypt."

"Told you I ain't addle-headed."

"And I ain't so soaped that I mean to stay here, staring at a glowing coffin." Morris stepped backward, putting more distance between himself and the alcove.

"But how do we get out?" Jimmy looked around. "Never did find the stairs."

"We could back slang it." Morris poked his thumb in the direction of the door they'd used to climb into the crypt.

"Won't fudge, mate. We came to undertake a rescue. We don't walk away."

He wasn't wrong about that. They'd never once refused to help someone in danger, no matter the terror of the situation, and they wouldn't start now. "We keep looking for the way up, then. And we keep a weather eye on that dead bloke. I don't trust him one lick."

They moved quick but quiet, following the outer wall, eyeing each twist and turn around the pillars. Was it meant to be a maze, or were they simply getting turned about?

"Something ain't right about this." Morris felt certain they'd returned to a section of the crypt they'd been in before. But it all looked so alike. Same stone. Same pillars. Same odd, unearthly glow.

Before Jimmy could answer, the creak of a rusty hinge echoed throughout the crypt. A door? Or—Morris's heart leaped to his throat—the coffin?

"Cheese it," Morris said, moving swiftly away from the direction he thought he remembered the alcove being, Jimmy close on his heels.

Nothing but solid walls. Was there no way up? No way out?

"We back slang it, after all," Jimmy said. "Find another way up the tower."

"What if the door we came through is the hinges we heard?"

Jimmy didn't even slow down. "Better than the coffin."

But they didn't find the door.

They found stairs. Narrow, winding, stone steps leading up and out of the crypt. They rushed, ran.

There were no more hinges creaking.

Now, there were footsteps.

The master was awake.

CHAPTER V

Below them on the steps, heavy footfalls. Above, the crying they'd heard in the crypt, growing louder and clearer. It was children; Morris knew it was. He hadn't the foggiest how they'd get back out, but Jimmy'd been right: they never abandoned the people they'd vowed to help, no matter the danger.

Up and up, around and around. The footsteps below grew faster, louder. There wasn't much time.

The spiral stairwell led, not to a door, but to a landing. A stone floor spread far. Light spilled from a distant window, falling on a group of children huddled beneath it.

"Morris!" Little George pulled from the group and ran to him.

Jimmy grabbed hold of the boy and carried him toward the others. Morris kept beside them, searching for familiar faces. Sally was there. John-John stood guard in front of a group of smaller children who'd also made their homes at the Inn. There were others there Morris didn't know, but they had the look of urchins.

"How'd you find us?" Sally asked. "We've been here ages, and no one's found us."

"No time for tales," Jimmy said. "Someone's on our heels."

Their already pale faces turned ashen, eyes darting immediately to the stairwell.

"He's comin'," Sally whispered.

John-John pulled the tiny ones closer. "Might be he's still sleepwalkin'."

"You know who it is?" Morris turned to face the stairwell, placing himself in front of the children. A poor shield, to be sure, but it was all he had to offer.

"He's a vampire," Sally whispered. "The man who brought us here said so."

George clung tighter to Jimmy, though his fear-filled eyes were on Morris.

"The vampire's come up here before?" Morris asked.

They nodded.

"And he didn't hurt anyone?"

Heads shook.

They likely had mere moments before the monster would appear at the top of the stairs.

"Did you learn anything about him?" Jimmy asked.

John-John answered. "He stays away from the window. It's why we keep close to it."

A figure appeared at the stairs. Morris had never seen anything like it. This monster had the shape of a human, but it was bent and curled. Its head hung forward, eyes glaring at them from beneath its misshapen forehead.

The shadows made it difficult to be certain, but its skin was green. A grayed shade of green.

Behind Morris, the children cried out, panic in their voices. He looked to Jimmy. "It ain't a redcap."

"And I ain't runnin'."

The creature floated toward them. Actually floated.

Someone screamed behind them.

"Keep close to the window," Morris said. It might not be enough, but it was what they could do.

"Any weapons to speak of?" Jimmy asked John-John.

"The man that brought us here made sure we didn't have any," John-John's voice shook. "If the vampire's awake, we're done for."

"How will we know if he's awake?" Morris asked, heart racing as the monster drew closer.

"He'll eat us," Sally said.

Blimey.

The creature was close now, near enough for the icy air drafting off it to send shivers over them all.

They backed up, pressed into a tight ball of urchins, tucked under the window, brightened by the spill of light.

The vampire abruptly stopped, hovering before them, still glaring. Its lips curled backward, revealing sharp, dagger-like teeth. *He'll eat us.* Sally hadn't been telling a clanker.

Jimmy set George on the floor next to Sally. "John-John. Sally. Keep the children as near the window as you can. We'll try to bait it."

"We will?" Morris hadn't been part of the planning.

"I owe you for that redcap," Jimmy said, not looking away from the vampire. "We'll do this'n a proper, the two of us."

Morris nodded. "If we lure it away," he said to the group behind them, "you lot run for the stairs. It'll take you to the crypt, where this fellow was. Empty now. Search for the door that lets you out."

Jimmy stepped a bit to the side. Morris followed. Two bites to eat would be more tempting than one.

But the vampire didn't look away from the huddled mass of urchins.

Jimmy and Morris moved a bit farther. Then farther. They stepped clear of the group, away from the window and into the dimness beyond.

The vampire's head snapped toward them. Without warning, it flew toward them.

"Run!" Morris shouted.

He and Jimmy took off at lightning speed, moving away from the stairs. They'd led monsters on chases before. This was nothing they didn't know how to do. But this monster was fast. Their running and weaving and moving about didn't work like it should.

Its claws swiped at Jimmy, tearing at his coat. Morris whistled, pulling the creature's attention. It moved toward him. This time Jimmy whistled, and the vampire turned again. It never made a single noise. Not any noise.

A horrible realization occurred to Morris. The vampire made no noise. It floated off the ground.

Why, then, had they heard footsteps?

CHAPTER VI

"Hold!" Morris shouted at John-John and Sally.

But he was too late. A towering man stepped into the room from the stairs below, his footsteps echoing. The sound stopped the vampire's pursuit. The creature turned and looked at the newcomer.

"There's plenty enough, master," the man said. "And young. Full of vim. They'll fill you up fine. Speed you up."

Speed him? The monster was already fast.

John-John and Sally pressed the children back, away from this enormous man, while also still keeping away from the vampire.

Morris slipped over to Jimmy. "What do we do now? Two of 'em and no way out."

"The vampire wouldn't go near the window. Maybe we'd all be safer there for a time."

"But that man likely can reach us. What's to stop him from pulling us away?" Morris wasn't about to stop trying, but he didn't have the first idea how to go about the thing.

"We'd have only the one threat to contend with, though," Jimmy said. "Fighting a battle on two fronts ain't exactly a winning approach."

The vampire had done nothing but glare while they'd been by the window. He hadn't lunged or swiped at them until they'd passed into the dimness.

The dimness.

"What if it ain't the window?" Morris asked Jimmy, keeping an eye on the monster as it listened to the newly arrived man's words of reassurance. "What if he can't go in the light?"

"I've heard of that," Jimmy said. "Some creatures are done in by sunlight."

It was the only chance they had. "I'll see if I can't lure him over there. When he's near enough, shove him from behind or ram him with your shoulder—whatever you have to do. See if we can't get him to fall into the sun."

Jimmy shook his head. "He's a big'n. Don't know that I can get him down on m'own."

"Get the others to help."

"What about 'Big Bob' over there? He'll not like it."

A two-front battle weren't a good idea at all. "Just be quick. Don't give 'im time to like it or not."

Jimmy spat into his palm. Morris did the same. They shook hands, a vow of unity. They might not emerge from this alive, but they'd go into it together.

"It don't matter where you begin, master," the large man said. "You'll get around to all of them."

Jimmy motioned the urchins closer. Morris inched toward the window, keeping an eye on the children, the monster, and the towering man.

"Start with this'n." The man pointed at Morris. "Big enough to give you pep for seeing to the others."

The vampire turned to look at Morris, his glare heavy and unblinking.

This was their chance. He steeled his resolve.

The vampire floated toward him.

Morris crept backward, slipping into the very edge of the spill of light. The monster stopped mere inches in front of him.

"Out with you," Big Bob barked at him. "I'll only set him on the others."

Morris ignored him and spoke, instead, to the monster. "You thirsty, mate? I'm right here."

The vampire didn't move closer, but he didn't listen to his underling, either.

Big Bob came toward them. "I'll pull him out for you, master."

"Now!" Jimmy's shout rang out.

The thunder of a full dozen feet answered. In the instant before the urchins reached the vampire, Morris dove to the side. Caught off guard, the monster was knocked forward. He didn't fall, didn't even stumble. He simply shifted forward a single step.

But that step took him into the sunlight.

The vampire had been silent from the moment he arrived, but now the silence ended. A howl that twisted every organ in Morris's body tore through the air.

"Master!" Fear and desperation filled the word.

Morris rolled over in time to see Big Bob grasping at the disintegrating outline of the vampire.

"Out, out, out!" Jimmy'd kept his wits about him.

Sally snatched the hands of the nearest children and ran out with them. Jimmy and John-John herded the rest of the little ones out. Morris scrambled to his feet, rushing after the others. His eyes met Big Bob's. The anger there chilled him to his core.

"I'll find them again! You can't hide 'em away forever!"

Still, Morris didn't stop. He couldn't. The danger would follow them onto the streets of London, but it wasn't a danger he could stop in that moment. They'd warn the children, keep their eyes peeled. Defeating Big Bob would have to wait for another day.

For now, they were safe from that day's danger. The vampire was gone.

They had lived to solve another mystery, to have another adventure. And there always was another one. Always.

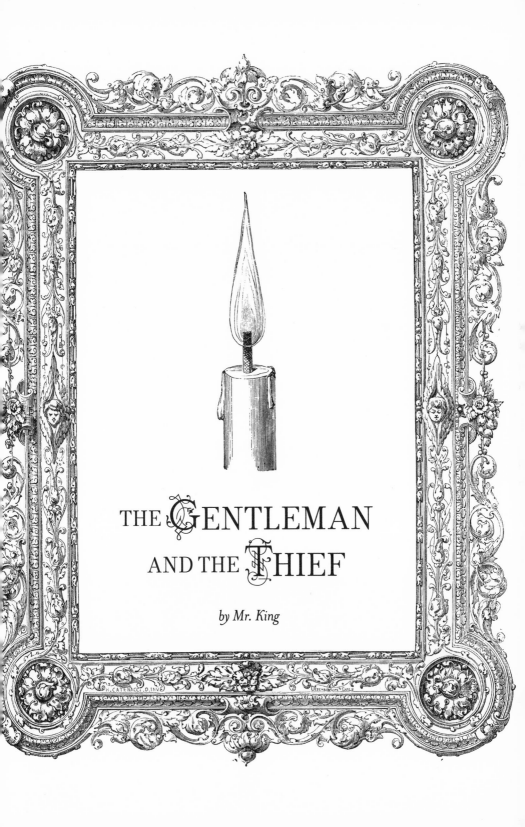

THE GENTLEMAN AND THE THIEF

by Mr. King

INSTALLMENT I

in which our Hero enlists the help of a brave and kind
Neighbor and encounters a most dire Prediction!

The grand estate of Summerworth sat nestled between a raging river
and the windswept moors. Its turrets and towers loomed large, declaring to
all who drew near that this was the home of a noble and exalted family. Yet,
within its palatial walls, a mournful sadness wrapped ice around the heart
of the only person who lived therein.

After great tragedy and heartrending loss, only Mr. Wellington Quincey
remained of those who had once made their home in the splendor of
Summerworth. His family had dwindled to only one; the Summerworth
staff had dwindled to only two.

Wellington's despondency had rendered the house an almost unbearably sad place to live. His sorrows were many. His companions were few.

For all his anguish, he was not an unkind gentleman. Those who knew
him liked him. Many a heart ached at his suffering and isolation. His family
was gone. His home was remote.

He had all but given up on finding companionship and love and a new
beginning by the time he reached his twenty-fifth year. Loneliness was his
lot in life, and he would endure it. But there was one thing he could not
sort out. How was it that an estate as far from neighbors as his, so devoid of
staff and visitors, was the victim of an unending string of thefts?

Jewelry had disappeared. Silver. Paintings. Priceless heirlooms.

His trusted servants hadn't the least idea what precisely had befallen Summerworth. The missing items could not be located. No clues had been left behind. He was utterly and completely baffled.

It was with this mystery hanging heavy on his weary mind that he mounted his trusty steed and dedicated a morning to riding a circuit of the estate. He was not at risk of being beggared by the thefts, but neither could he ignore the growing list of pilfered items. Who could possibly be taking them? What ill-intentioned thief was bringing such misery to his already painful life?

He rounded a turn in the path as it passed the cottage of the estate steward. Elmore Combs had remained in his post after the death of Wellington's grandfather some fifteen years earlier, Wellington's father ten years after that, and Wellington's older brother a mere two years ago.

Combs's daughter, Tillie, stood outside, pulling laundry off the clothesline. Wellington had known Tillie since they had been children running and skipping and laughing through the meadows and lawns and streams of Summerworth. They had been dear friends during those long-ago days. He hadn't seen as much of her the past few years as he would have liked. Life had demanded too much of him.

"Good morning, Tillie." He pulled his horse to a halt beside the house. "How are you faring this fine day?"

She folded a sheet against herself and smiled at him. "I'm well, sir."

"You needn't call me 'sir,'" he said as he dismounted. "We have been friends all our lives."

Tillie laid the sheet in her large basket. "But you're grown now, and the master of the estate. Things ain't quite what they used to be."

He pulled another sheet from the line and began folding it himself. "Are we not still friends, Tillie?"

"You're hardly here anymore. I've a closer friendship with the hedgehog who lives in back of the cottage."

Her words struck deep. Heaven forgive him, he *had* been neglectful. He'd lost his grandparents, his parents, and his brother. He seldom saw his friends from Cambridge. He had no true friends amongst Society in London, merely a list of vague acquaintances. He kept to himself, a shield against the grief of losing people he felt close to. But it meant he remained painfully lonely.

"I could come help you fold laundry," he offered. "Then we could talk as we work."

Amusement danced in her eyes. "Folding laundry ain't for the master of the estate."

"I'm doing it now." He dropped the sheet into the basket. "Besides, who will even see me working other than you and your father? This needn't be a source of teasing, unless you mean to engage in jests at my expense."

"'Course not."

He took down a serviceable-looking apron and folded it as well. "If laundry is off-limits to me, what will you permit me to do? Sweep the front stoop? Weed the kitchen garden? Are either of those acceptable for a 'master of the estate'?"

She folded a shirt, no doubt her father's. "I suspect you've spent time weeding and sweeping at your own house, it being short-staffed like it is."

"Lately, I've invested most of my time attempting to locate a virtual treasure trove of missing things."

Nothing remained on the clothesline. She took up the basket and held it against her hip. "Things've been swiped?"

"Quite a number of things," he said. "Jewelry. Silver. Paintings."

"And you've not located any of it?"

He shook his head. "I fear this mystery will prove utterly unsolvable."

He walked beside her back to the quaint and inviting cottage. The door stood open, allowing them to enter without a pause.

Her father was inside and greeted Wellington. "Welcome, Mr. Quincey. Have you come on estate business?"

"I stopped to offer a good morning to my lifelong friend but have been rightly informed by your daughter that I have not been an attentive companion to her these years."

Mr. Combs turned wide eyes on his child. "Tillie. You'd speak so critically to a gentleman of his standing? 'Ave you taken leave of your manners, girl?"

"Pray, do not scold her," Wellington insisted. "I was rightly chastised, and I mean to make amends."

"How?" Tillie never had lacked for boldness.

"We spend little time together, as you rightly observed, and I have a maddening riddle at the estate. Perhaps you might help me sort it."

She looked intrigued. If she agreed to join the hunt for the elusive thief, he would have her company again. The house would not be so empty. The joys of their childhood friendship would bring light back into his darkened world.

"Would you help?" he pressed. "I would be greatly obliged."

"I do have a knack for sorting mysteries." She carried her basket to the table. "We could solve this'n together."

"I would be deeply indebted to you." He turned to Mr. Combs. "A great many things have gone missing up at the manor house, odd bits and large pieces. I cannot for the life of me guess where they've gone or who might have taken them. You would not begrudge Tillie some time spent helping me discover what's happened to them, would you? I would not, for all the world, wish to add to your burdens here."

"We'll manage," Mr. Combs said. "Besides, I'm curious to know who— or what—has been making off with your things."

"'Or *what*'?" Wellington repeated.

Tillie nodded. "My father is quite well versed in all the old tales and creatures: pixies, fairies, changelings, redcaps."

"You suspect my thief is a mythical monster?" The moors were filled with mystery and magic, but Wellington hadn't thought such had bled onto his own estate. "Is that your theory as well, Tillie?"

"I think we'd best assume anythin' is possible."

"Mark me, children, there's more in this ol' world than can be seen or understood." Mr. Combs eyed them in turn. "Unless you proceed with a healthy dose of respect for what you can't explain, you'll forever be chasing what you can't foresee."

INSTALLMENT II
in which our Hero begins an Investigation
and accepts a most unusual Challenge!

Wellington had all but forgotten what a mischievous delight Tillie was. She arrived at Summerworth for their investigation with a jest-filled list of suspects, including everything from "a dog with a poor upbringing" to "a flock of magpies with remarkable coordination."

Her laughter had ever been a source of utter delight to him—to *all*, in fact. Had ever the heavens blessed a soul with so happy a disposition as she?

"I believe we would do well to begin where the items have gone missing," he said. "Most have disappeared from my sitting area."

"Your private rooms?" She clasped a hand to her heart. "How very scandalous!" Amusement twinkled in her eyes.

"It is a fortunate thing this house is empty," Wellington said. "You would have all the countryside whispering about me."

"Is that why you never invite me up to the house any longer?" Though her humor remained, a touch of earnestness had entered her tone.

"I ought to have come by your cottage any number of times these past years," he said. "The weight of grief can crush one's judgment."

She took his hand, as she'd so often done in their younger years. "Don't you fret it, Welly. We've a mystery to solve, you and I. That'll lift your spirits."

Was ever a man so undeservedly blessed with so forgiving a friend? They walked hand in hand up the stairs and down the corridor. She turned toward what had been his rooms when they were children.

"No, Tillie. I am in the master's rooms now."

She laughed lightly. "I forget sometimes how very much has changed since we were children."

"*You* haven't changed," he said.

She pulled away, preceding him across the threshold of the master's chambers, but tossed back over her shoulder, "You might be surprised."

Wellington had spent his share of time amongst the ladies of Society and their practiced primness. Tillie was a breath of utterly and joyfully fresh air.

"Now." She stopped in the middle of the room. "What has gone missing?"

He joined her. "A painting off that wall." He pointed. "My father's pocket watch. Two necklaces that once belonged to my mother that I have kept in my bureau as a reminder of her. A pair of pearl cuff links."

"Blimey," she muttered. "You're being pillaged."

"I know it. And this isn't the only room from which items are missing."

"Mr. and Mrs. Smith would not have taken them." Tillie had known his two remaining servants her whole life and knew well their goodness and utter trustworthiness. No, there was no question of the Smiths being anything other than loyal and good and true.

"I've not had visitors in months," he said. "And no tradesmen have come to the door. I cannot sort it. Indeed, it is a question that sits heavy upon my mind."

"How large was the painting?" Tillie asked.

"One grown person could carry it," he said, "but not without effort."

Her face twisted in an expression of contemplation. Wellington smiled from his very heart at the once-familiar sight. While she had always been of a playful disposition, no one who had known her could doubt her intelligence.

"Were any other large items taken?" she asked.

"Yes. Some that would be difficult to sneak away with."

She turned to him, excitement sparkling in her deep-brown eyes. "Any too large to remove far without a cart?"

He thought over his list. "A heavy gilded mirror disappeared from my mother's room. That could not be carried far, even by several people."

"Do you realize what this means?" She took hold of his arm, bouncing in place. "No one has come or gone. The mirror, at least, must still be in this house. Your blighter likely tucked it away somewhere to nip off with later."

What a stroke of genius! What a needed bit of luck! "If we discover where the things are hidden, we can reclaim them."

She nodded. "You'll have your treasures back and might even catch yourself a thief."

Oh, rapturous discovery! This time *he* seized *her* hand. "I know precisely where we ought to look first."

"We should do this more often, Wellington."

He laughed. How long had it been since he had well and truly laughed? Tillie had always been his sunshine on rainy days. He'd been a fool not to reach out to her during the storms of the past years.

They moved swiftly down the servants' stairs into the dim silence below.

"I thought we agreed Mr. and Mrs. Smith weren't our thieves," she said.

"They aren't. But most of the rooms on this level are shut up and never used. There is an exit on this floor of the house with no stairs to navigate."

"Ah." She nodded her understanding. "A perfect arrangement for slipping ill-gotten goods out unseen."

The belowstairs was quiet. Only the ever-blowing wind off the moors rattling the windows broke the silence. This had once been the bustling center of a lively household. Now it was little more than a cavern. Life too often demanded exacting tolls.

With an eager bounce to her step, Tillie began searching the rooms. "No pilfered goods in here, guv'nuh," she called out.

"I object to 'guv'nuh' as much as I did to 'sir,'" he said. "And, for the record, I'm no longer overly fond of 'Welly.'"

She plopped her fists on her hips and, standing outside the next room she meant to search, said, "You've become quite the pompous bore, Wellington Quincey."

"I have not."

Her head tipped to the side in a pose of theatrical disbelief. "Then prove it."

"And how would you propose I 'prove it'?"

A slow, sly grin spread over her face. "A race. I will check the rooms on this side of the corridor; you check the other side. The first one to the other end wins."

"A footrace?" He shook his head. "We are not eight years old any longer."

"Precisely what a pompous bore would say." Though she still smiled, unmistakable disappointment flickered across her face.

He could not bear to disappoint his oldest friend, not when she had just that day brought the first flicker of light back into his gloomy existence.

With an air of determination, he pulled off his jacket and hung it on the handle of the nearest door. "Prepare yourself for defeat, Tillie Combs."

"You did not best me when we were children, and you won't now."

She rushed to her first room. He did as well.

Nothing was amiss. The next room proved the same. As he stepped out into the corridor, Tillie was just slipping into her third room.

"You are falling behind," she called back.

Twice in one morning she had made him laugh. How he had needed her in his life!

He pulled open the door of the next room he was meant to check. Before he could so much as glance inside, a scream pierced the air.

Tillie!

INSTALLMENT III

in which our Hero finds himself in a most uncomfortable Situation!

Wellington rushed in the direction of Tillie's terrified scream. The room was dim but not dark to the point of blackness. Thank the heavens he could see her. He ran directly to her, putting his arms around her and tucking her behind him. His eyes scanned the room, searching for the threat.

"It was over there." Her voice shook.

"What was?" The room was empty—not even a stick of furniture.

"A flame. A bl—blue flame."

"The room was on fire?"

She clutched his arm, trembling. "No. It was floating in the air. Away from the walls. Away from the floor. No candle. No torch. Just a flame."

His gaze turned from the room to her. "Floating?"

"Don't look at me like I'm mad." She pointed near the window. "A floating flame. It was there, and then, *poof*, it blew out. But there was no one who'd been holdin' it. There was just . . . nothing."

She still held his arm, like it was a lifeline in a raging sea. Wellington didn't know what she'd seen, perhaps something outside that, when glimpsed through the high, dingy window, had seemed to be inside.

He stepped toward the window, meaning to see if he couldn't solve the mystery. She didn't release her white-knuckle grip on his arm. "You are well and truly frightened."

"You'd be as well if you'd seen what I did."

"A flame? The flicker of a candle?"

"It was too large for a candle." Her voice still shook. "It moved about all on its own. Nothin' to explain how it could possibly be there."

He unwrapped her fingers from his forearm and took her hand in his instead. He saw no singe marks on the walls, no indication that anything had been aflame. He spied nothing outside the high window that might have been mistaken for a flame. Would the mysteries never cease?

"I cannot explain it, Tillie." He looked to her. "Are you certain you didn't—"

"It weren't my imagination." Her eyes filled with growing panic.

Wellington tugged her toward the door. "Let us go back to the cottage. We can save our search efforts for another day."

She nodded, still shaken. "I think that'd be best."

Hardly another word was spoken as they crossed the estate grounds. She was pale, bless her, and very quiet, a rarity for Tillie Combs.

Her father took note of her condition immediately. "What's happened?"

Tillie dropped onto a spindle-back chair, apparently not able or ready to answer. Wellington did so instead.

"During our search for the missing things, she saw something she cannot explain."

"What?" Mr. Combs looked from one of them to the other.

"A blue flame," Wellington said. "It floated with no explanation."

"A blue flame?" He repeated the description in a tone of awe, his wide eyes falling fully on his daughter. "Moved about, did it?"

Tillie took a shaking breath. "It was unnerving, Papa. Cold and . . ." She shook her head. "I didn't like it."

Mr. Combs rubbed at his unshaven chin as he paced away. "Odd, bein' where we are. Odd, indeed."

"You know what it was?" Wellington asked. What a boon it would be if he could, indeed, explain it.

"I've a notion." Mr. Combs motioned him out of the house. "I'll give it some thought, sir. If m' Tillie saw what I think she saw, you've a bigger mystery on your hands than you realize."

He was offered no further explanation than that. In a moment's time, Wellington was outside the cottage, alone, confused, and already longing for the return of Tillie's smiles and spirit-lifting company.

Two days after the blue-flame encounter, Mrs. Smith rushed into Wellington's library, a mixture of excitement and panic on her face. "You've visitors, sir!"

"Visitors?" He very seldom had anyone call on him at Summerworth. It was an isolated estate, and his period of mourning for his parents had necessitated the estate be quiet and lifeless. Even with that period past, nothing much had changed.

"Two carriages, sir," she said. "And the young people spilling out look fine indeed."

He rose from his desk and crossed to the window. Two carriages sat in the drive, but both appeared to be empty.

"The visitors are in the drawing room, Mr. Quincey," Mrs. Smith said.

The house was so out of practice with visitors, Mrs. Smith had managed the thing in quite the wrong order. "I will be there directly," he said.

She nodded and rushed from the room.

Visitors. He didn't know whether to feel pleased or concerned. What if his as-yet-unidentified thief had made off with the tea set or the chairs in the drawing room? What if these new arrivals were hoping for a place to stop their journey for the night and they, too, found themselves victims of this thief?

Wellington made himself presentable and joined his guests in the drawing room. One mystery solved itself immediately. Two of the gentlemen— Alsop and Henson—were known to him, they having been acquaintances at school. Perhaps not truly close friends, but near enough to make a call, even an unexpected one, completely acceptable.

Bows and curtsies preceded formal introductions. His one-time chums had brought with them a Mr. Fairbanks, his sister, Miss Fairbanks, and Miss Porter, an acquaintance of the Fairbanks family. Their manner of speaking and dress marked them all as residing firmly in the upper class. There would be no footraces among this lot.

"You've not been to London in ages, Quincey," Alsop said.

"I have been in mourning," he reminded them.

"Not for the last six months."

The truth of that could not be argued. "The estate has occupied much of my time of late. Leaving it unattended has not been an option."

Henson was walking the length of the drawing room. "The place seems nearly abandoned. Has some tragedy befallen the area?"

"Many of the servants left after my parents' passing." That was all the more detail he meant to furnish them with on that score. "As for tragedies, would a string of thefts suffice?"

The ladies pressed shocked hands to their hearts—not the theatrical jest Tillie had employed, but a gesture made in earnest. The gentlemen looked to him with alarm.

"Thefts?" Mr. Fairbanks clicked his tongue and shook his head. "What is this world coming to?"

"I believe I will catch out the culprit soon enough," Wellington said. "But at the moment I am baffled."

Mrs. Smith appeared quite suddenly in the doorway, a frantic expression on her aging face. "Another visitor, sir. Miss Combs."

Tillie slipped inside with her usual adventurous spirit firmly in place.

"I've a notion to search again if you're—" Her gaze fell on the others. "Oh. You've callers."

Wellington waved her closer. "Miss Combs, this is Miss Fairbanks and Miss Porter. Mr. Alsop, Mr. Henson, and Mr. Fairbanks."

They offered half-hearted bows and curtsies. Tillie's effort was a touch less refined than was generally seen in more exalted circles, but there was no malice in it, no disrespect. She was a good soul.

"How do you two know one another?" Miss Fairbanks asked.

"Miss Combs"—it felt odd referring to Tillie so formally; they'd been friends so long, he struggled to think of her as anything but his one-time playmate—"grew up on the estate. Her father is the Summerworth steward."

"Ah." More than one of the visitors made the exact same noise of dawning understanding.

"Do you still live on the estate?" Miss Fairbanks asked Tillie. "Few people do, as I understand it."

"The butler and housekeeper and m'father and I are the only ones left," Tillie said. "We see to it the grand ol' place keeps standing."

"Mr. Quincey is fortunate to have all of you," Miss Porter's words were kind, but something in her tone was not.

Tillie seemed to notice it as well. Her brow drew down, and she watched the gathering with more wariness than before.

Alsop returned his attention to Wellington. "We're bound for a house party at George Berkley's estate. You remember him from Cambridge. He said he'd be most pleased to have you there."

An invitation to a house party. This was the first he'd had since leaving behind his mourning period. When first he'd finished school and entered Society, he would have jumped at the opportunity, but now he found himself hesitant.

"Do come, Mr. Quincy," Miss Fairbanks said. "It promises to be a very enjoyable week in the country."

"While I am grateful for the invitation, I do need to sort out the matter of these thefts. Else, I might return home to find the house entirely empty."

Tillie still hadn't moved from her spot. Her eyes darted from one person to the next, her concern and confusion clearly growing. What had her so frozen? Tillie was not usually one to be rendered so withdrawn.

Mrs. Smith arrived with a heavily laden tray. She set it on a nearby table, then tossed him a look of apology. "I'll be back with the actual tea, sir. I'm a bit at loose ends, being out of practice and such."

Before he could reassure her, Tillie spoke. "I'll help you."

"Oh, bless you, Tillie."

The two women slipped out, but Tillie looked back, meeting his eye before dropping her gaze and hurrying from the room. Where had her unflagging spirit gone?

"Does Miss Combs often make herself so at home here?" Henson asked. "Seems a bit forward for a servant."

"She's not a servant," Wellington insisted. "She's the daughter of the estate steward."

"A minor difference," Miss Fairbanks said. "She is most decidedly bold."

"She is helping me search for the thief."

"Helping you *find* the thief?" Alsop shook his head. "Has it occurred to you, my friend, that she might *be* the thief?"

"Tillie?" He guffawed. "She would not steal so much as a dandelion from a meadow much less items belonging to another person."

Alsop shrugged. Henson gave Wellington a look of pity.

"I do hope we are wrong, Mr. Quincey," Miss Fairbanks said, "but you would be well-advised to keep a close eye on her."

"I will take your advice into consideration," he said through tight teeth.

"I see we have offended you." Miss Fairbanks fluttered over to him, all solicitousness. "That was not our intention. Do come to the house party with us. Allow us to show you we hold no ill will."

"Again, I thank you." He addressed them all. "But I will have to decline. Estate matters require my attention."

Conversation grew more general, ranging from topics of Society to the weather. The visitors were not unpleasant, neither had they been outright rude, yet Wellington felt dissatisfied with their company. He missed Tillie. He had missed her the past two days. Heavens, he had missed her the past two years. If only she hadn't run off to the kitchens. If only this group hadn't sent her fleeing there. If only, if only, if only!

Tea was brought up, but by Mrs. Smith alone. Tillie, it seemed, did not mean to make another appearance.

The callers prepared to depart, insisting they needed to be on their way if they were to reach their stop for the night, the last before arriving at their final destination. Farewells were exchanged as were hopes that they would meet again, perhaps in Town.

"Do think on what we said," Alsop offered, one step from the front portico. "You may be chasing a thief who knows where you are looking. When one hands an arsonist matches, one is playing with fire."

Wellington motioned him on. "I will bear that in mind."

A moment later, they were gone, yet Wellington did not rest easy. He hadn't even a moment in which to do so before Tillie spoke from behind him.

"They think I am your thief, don't they?"

He spun about. There she stood, looking somehow both hurt and defiant. "They don't know you."

"But *you* do, and you gave some thought to their warning."

"Tillie—"

She pushed past him. "You didn't believe me 'bout that flame, and you don't full believe me that I'm not thieving from you." She pointed a finger at him. "We're friends, Wellington Quincy. Perhaps it's time you treated me like we were."

INSTALLMENT IV

in which our Hero makes a most gentlemanly
Apology and a shocking Discovery!

The house was far too quiet. For two days, not a sound had been heard. Mrs. Smith, Wellington suspected, was upset with him. Mr. Smith, who was seldom seen as it was, made not a single appearance. The most glaring absence of all, though, was Tillie's.

Wellington had gone by her house repeatedly, but she hadn't answered his knock, neither had she come by the manor house. How was he to apologize, to convince her that he did not, in fact, believe her capable of anything so underhanded as thievery if she would not allow him a moment in which to do so? His visitors had cast that aspersion, yes, but he had not. He would not. He could not.

Oh, was ever a man so vexed with the impossible task of apologizing to a woman?

Some three days after he'd last had a conversation with anyone inside the walls of his house, Wellington walked the corridors with his hands tucked in his pockets. His shoulders drooped under the burden of his loneliness. Even the elusive thief had abandoned him. Not a single item had gone missing in the past few days.

"I haven't a single soul with whom to share my change of fortune." It was his own fault, truly. He ought to have immediately risen to Tillie's defense. He ought to have said more to discount the hints of accusation his visitors had lobbed in her direction. The weight of regret only added to the stooped nature of his posture.

On and on he walked, making one lonely circuit after another. Minutes passed. His mind did not clear. If only Tillie would return and be his friend once more.

Into the cavernous quiet came the sound of footfalls, not rushed or threatening, but at ease and at home. Wellington kept perfectly still, listening and pondering. The steps drew closer. He stood his ground, unwilling to cede more of his peace of mind than the thief had already taken from him.

But it was no thief who appeared from around a bend in the corridor; it was Tillie.

So surprised was he that Wellington could not even manage a greeting. Fortunately for him, she did not appear to need one.

"Things are being stolen from our cottage," she said without preamble.

"Unless you think I am thieving my own things, I'd say your mystery thief has changed locations."

"I don't think you are stealing from yourself."

She folded her arms across her chest and tipped her head to the side. "Only from *you*."

"I don't think you're stealing from anyone," he insisted. "Those visitors said that; I didn't."

"You didn't disagree with 'em," she said. "You said you would think on it. That ain't a vote of confidence, is it?"

"I was trying to get them to leave faster," he said. "Arguing the point would have prolonged their visit."

She lost a bit of bluster. "I know I ain't fine and proper like they are."

"And I far prefer your company to theirs." He reached out to take her hand, but she stepped back. The rejection was warranted, yet still it stung. He took a breath and regained his footing. The business at hand would be his best step forward. "What has been taken from your home?"

"A few coins," she said. "My little amber cross that I wear on the chain your mother gave me. A spade."

"A spade?" That was a decidedly odd thing for a thief to make off with.

She shrugged. "That one didn't make sense to us either."

"You helped me search my house for clues," he said. "Might I be permitted to offer the same assistance?"

"I'd not object." She jerked her head toward the front of the house. "Shall we?"

He walked at her side all the way to the front drive, then along the path that would take them to her cottage. A fair stretch of moorland separated their two homes. They would have time and plenty for either talking and repairing things between them or sinking ever further into the awkward silence between them.

"I am sorry for what happened with my guests," he said.

She shook her head. "I forget sometimes how much things have changed over the past years. You're a distinguished gentleman; I'm still the steward's daughter."

"You are my favorite steward's daughter."

"My father is your favorite steward?" A hint of her usual mischief returned to her tone.

Wellington bumped her lightly with his shoulder. "I believe you know perfectly well what I meant."

She smiled fleetingly. "We have always been good friends, have we not?"

"The very best."

She looked up at him. "Then why is it you didn't believe me about the blue flame? You didn't ridicule me for it, but I could tell you thought I had cobwebs in m' attic."

"I thought no such thing," he said with a laugh. "I don't doubt what you saw. It was simply unexpected, and I hadn't an explanation for it."

Tillie stopped in her tracks, eyes trained up ahead. She pointed a slightly shaky finger. "Perhaps that will shed a bit of light on the matter."

Up ahead, floating above the ground, moving back and forth, not diminishing, not growing, was a light. Not any light. A blue one.

A blue flame.

Tillie's shoulders set. "After it!"

And she ran.

INSTALLMENT V

in which our intrepid Couple give chase and
discover more than Expected!

Tillie was going to land herself in deep trouble chasing after a mystery on the moors. Many a soul had grown hopelessly lost in the vast nothingness of the wild hills.

Wellington called her name, but the wind carried it away. He ran after her, reaching her just as she reached the blue flame. But it had disappeared without a trace. No one stood where the flame had been, carrying a candle or torch or lantern.

"You saw it this time, di'n't you?" She looked up at him.

"I did." He stared at the spot where the flame had vanished.

She nodded again and again. "And you can see for yourself there ain't nothing it could've been a reflection of or anything we might've simply mis-seen."

"We didn't mis-see. But what *did* we see?" He turned his head, slowly, searching.

Tillie looked around as well. "There." She pointed into the distance. "It's there."

And so it was. A blue flame, just far enough to be barely visible. If he wasn't mistaken, it was moving.

"We'll catch it this time, Tillie." He snatched up her hand and ran with her out onto the moors.

On and on they went. Whenever they drew closer, the flame disappeared, only to reappear elsewhere a moment later. The mystic blue flame led them on a chase over hills, down rounded valleys. Over and over and over. Still, it eluded them.

Exhaustion was setting in, mingled with a heavy dose of frustration. What if their quarry proved uncatchable? How could they endure endless years of pilfering and thievery?

They stood breathless on the gaping moors, waiting for their prey to reappear. How long had they been chasing it? How far afield would it lead them?

"Why hasn't it come back?" Tillie whispered, spinning about, eyeing the landscape. "It's been gone longer this time."

The flame was nowhere to be seen. But something could be heard.

"What was that?" He turned in the direction of the sound.

"It sounded like a child cryin'."

"Out here?" Merciful heavens, a child lost on the moors was in danger indeed. "Hulloo?" he called out. "Where are you, child?"

A whimper answered, one hardly loud enough to be heard. But hear it, they did. Tillie, her hand still in his, pulled him around more bends and over a hill as they followed the heartrending cries.

"We have to find the poor child, Wellington."

"We will," he vowed.

And they did. A tiny, shivering boy, likely no more than six or seven years old, cowered behind a large rock, eyes wide with fear.

Tillie approached first. She could be mischievous and adventurous. Her temper could flare hot, or she could be tender as a newborn lamb. In that moment, she was soft and quiet and still.

She knelt beside the boy and gently, slowly, set her hand on his arm. "Are you lost, dearie?"

"I were running away." Tears clogged the child's voice.

Wellington knelt next to Tillie. "Why were you running?"

"I'd've been in a heap o' trouble."

Tillie sat beside the child. "You'll be in a mountain of it if you're out here when it grows dark. Come with us, dearie. We'll see to it you have food in your belly and a warm fire."

"I'll be in trouble."

"You won't be, I swear to it." Tillie looked to Wellington. "Will he?"

"Not a bit of trouble," Wellington said. "We'll take good care of you."

The boy shook his head. "You'll be angry at me."

"Why would we be angry with you?" Wellington could not ignore the real worry in the child's expression.

The boy took a shaky breath. "Because I stole it."

Wellington met Tillie's eye. Could this little slip of a child be their elusive thief?

"It's not him," Tillie whispered, apparently understanding his unspoken question.

"He's just said he stole something."

She shook her head firmly. "It's not him."

The little boy whimpered. His safety needed to come first.

"Come along," Wellington said. "We'll see to it you're fed and warm, then we'll settle whatever needs settling."

He agreed, but clearly wasn't at all convinced he was safe. Tillie took the boy's hand and smiled reassuringly. The child walked alongside them but didn't speak. Wellington kept a weather eye out, watching for the elusive blue flame, but it made no return appearance. He suspected Tillie was keeping close watch as well.

They arrived at the Combses' cottage just as the sky was turning pink with the first blush of the coming sunset.

Mr. Combs was home and eyed them with curiosity. "You've found a child."

"On the moors," Tillie said, leading their new addition to the low-burning fire. "We were chasing the same phantom I saw at Summerworth."

"You were?" Mr. Combs looked to Wellington. "Did you see it as well?"

"I did. We attempted to catch it, but it proved too fast and agile."

"Of course it did." Mr. Combs actually snorted with disdain, though there was no unkindness in the sound. "No one can catch a bluecap."

A bluecap? Wellington had heard of redcaps, murderous little goblins, but he was not familiar with this variety of spirit. "I don't know what that is."

"A little creature that appears as a blue flame, wandering about on its own, popping from place to place."

Precisely what they'd seen.

"Is it known to steal things?" Wellington asked.

Mr. Combs shook his head. "Not generally, but it expects to be paid. If no one is paying it, the sprite might be . . . collecting payment on its own."

"What would I be paying this creature for?" Wellington could not make sense of it at all.

"The bluecap is found in mines," Mr. Combs said. "The miners pay it for warning them about cave-ins."

"My house is not a mine, and there is no danger of a cave-in."

"It may be doing something else," Tillie said. "Something it thinks it ought to be paid to do."

Could this truly be the cause of his difficulties? A little creature that ought not to be anywhere near his house?

He motioned subtly to the little boy, huddled under a blanket near the fire. "The little one confessed to stealing."

Tillie shook her head. "It isn't him. He couldn't have moved the mirror or the painting."

"But the other things, maybe?" Heavens, did he have more than one thief?

"I didn't steal anything from you, sir." The little boy's voice was filled with misery.

"Then what *did* you steal?" Wellington asked.

The child took a quavering breath. "The blue flame."

INSTALLMENT VI

in which our Hero has a startling Revelation!

The little boy, whose name they had discovered was Pip, had made his declaration about stealing the blue flame, then had cried so ceaselessly he'd not managed another word. Not knowing exactly what harm the bluecap might bring, Wellington had thought it best that Pip, Mr. Combs, and Tillie all remove to the manor house. Of all things, he wished for them to be safe.

In return, he found greater joy in his house now than he'd known in years. He and Tillie, sometimes accompanied by Pip, made another search of the house, looking for the items the bluecap had nipped off with. Mr. Combs was of the opinion that the creature was inclined to stash his "payments" rather than spirit them off, but where that pile of treasures might be, they didn't know.

Pip was cheerful enough on their searches so long as neither of them brought up the topic of the bluecap. The reminder of the sprite he claimed to have stolen would turn him once more into a trembling heap. It made getting information from the child difficult, and they had no other help in finding the creature or the things it had taken.

Four days after they'd rescued the boy from the moors, Wellington walked alongside Tillie through the back corridors of the house, having come no closer to rooting out their mischievous visitor. Pip had fallen asleep, so they'd left him in his room and undertaken this search without him.

"I wish we could do somethin' for the little imp," Tillie said. "He's terrified of the creature he stole, and I suspect he's drowning in a sea of guilt as well."

"If only we could sort out how he caught it in the first place, we could rid ourselves of it."

"And of him?" she asked quietly, cautiously.

"He must be *from* somewhere," Wellington said. "And his family must be worried."

Tillie shook her head. "I don't think he has one."

Wellington motioned her out through the door of the music room; they hadn't found any missing items hidden there. "Why do you suspect that?"

' She shrugged as she passed. "Because that's what Pip said when Papa asked him."

Tillie was a delight. He never laughed as much as he did when he was with her.

"Your father took the less-interesting approach." Wellington caught up to her. "Did he also happen to ask Pip where he came here from?"

"Ipsley, on the other side of Ipsley Moor," she said. "Slipped out of the workhouse, he did."

The workhouse. Mercy. "We can't send him back there."

Without warning, Tillie threw her arms around him. "Oh, Wellington! I had so hoped you would say that. I can't bear thinking of him in so miserable a place."

Something odd happened to Wellington Quincey in that moment. Something entirely unexpected. His heart, which had always been whole and entirely in his possession, gave itself over to his lifelong friend. Her arms around him felt like the warm embrace of home. He set his arms around her as well and held her, feeling his heart undertake its change of ownership.

"Papa and I can keep Pip at our cottage if need be," she said. "But he'd be happy as a cat in the cream here. He'd have long corridors to run through, and an entire nursery to make his own." She looked up at him. "Oh, Wellington! Say he can stay. Please."

"Of course, he can. This house has been far too empty for far too long."

In the instant after that declaration, the house suddenly filled with voices.

Tillie's head turned toward the noise, but she didn't drop her arms from around him. "Who's doing all that bellowing?"

He locked his hands behind her back. "I couldn't say. I never have visitors."

"You did a week ago," she said.

"I suppose I did."

Tillie leaned her head against his chest. "Could they be back?"

"I think they might be. They had said the house party they were attending would last a week."

She slipped back. "You should go greet 'em."

"You should come as well," he said. "Then they can meet you."

"They already have. They didn't like what they saw." Quick as anything, she hurried down the corridor without looking back.

Sometimes it seemed she was forever running from him! His heart ached for her to remain at his side.

He entered the drawing room and discovered his group of acquaintances there, dripping wet. The weather had turned whilst he and Tillie had been searching the house.

"Forgive the intrusion," Alsop said. "This deluge made the roads impassable. We find ourselves in need of your hospitality."

"Of course." Wellington would never turn anyone away in such circumstances. "We are short-staffed, so I cannot guarantee you the most comfortable of stays."

"If you can guarantee us a roof and a warm fire," Henson said, "we will be more than satisfied."

Mrs. Smith saw them all to the guest wing. Mr. Smith made certain each room had a fire burning. Wellington went in search of Tillie but did not find her. Pip was still sleeping in the nursery. His home was the busiest it had been in ages, yet he felt lonely again.

He went through the motions of being a proper host. The guests were checked on by Mrs. Smith and provided with a tray in their rooms so they could rest and warm themselves. He consulted with his housekeeper and butler about the trickiness of looking after five unexpected visitors with only the two of them on staff.

"Tillie will help," Mrs. Smith said. "She's a good 'un, she is."

"She is a guest here as well."

"Not the same, though, is it?" Mrs. Smith sighed. "She's your dear friend, yes, but the daughter of your steward. She's not one of your fine and elegant friends. They know it. And so does she."

"I could go the rest of my life without seeing any of today's arrivals again, and I would not be the worse for it," Wellington said. "But these past days, having Tillie's company so often, I know I could not say the same about her."

"She's not your equal," Mrs. Smith reminded him.

"No. She is a better person than I."

Mrs. Smith handed her husband the stacked linens he would be delivering to the guest rooms. "You and I know her worth, but Society wouldn't agree with us."

"We aren't in London. Those things don't matter much in the wilds of Yorkshire."

Mr. Smith watched Wellington with narrowed gaze. "You've lost your heart to the girl, haven't you?"

"She's been my friend all my life," he said. "But she's more than that to me now. She's everything."

"Not everyone'll see things the way you do," Mrs. Smith warned. "She'd not be welcomed with open arms in Town or at Society dos."

"I've never put a great deal of store by such things." A smile blossomed on his solemn face. "I would rather spend the rest of my life running around the moors with her than bowing and scraping my way through all the ballrooms in London."

"Then might I offer you a word of advice?" Mr. Smith asked.

Wellington nodded. He hadn't a father any longer to help point him in the right direction. He welcomed whatever wisdom was offered him.

"Make certain *she* knows that."

Wellington awoke to the sound of shouting. He'd slept later than expected, having been up longer than he'd wished. Preparations for breakfast for so many additional people in the house had required all their efforts. Tillie had undertaken hers from a distance, volunteering for every chore that would take her away from the visitors at the manor house.

He hadn't the opportunity to tell her of his feelings, and it seemed there would not be peace enough this morning for doing so any time soon.

All his guests were in an uproar, standing outside Miss Fairbanks's assigned bedchamber. The lady, herself, was flailing her arms, her words frantic. Tillie appeared on the scene a moment later, watching the group with the same expression of confusion he must have been wearing.

Miss Porter suddenly pointed an accusing finger at Tillie. "She took it. I know she did!"

Though Tillie paled, she didn't flinch. "I have a name, and you clearly have an accusation. See if you can't spit out both."

Wellington bit back a laugh. His light o' love was no shrinking violet. Still, fisticuffs erupting in the corridor hardly seemed advisable. "Miss Porter, what has been taken? Whatever it might be, I doubt Miss Combs was involved in its disappearance."

"We tried to warn you," Alsop said. "You're being robbed left and right, and you refuse to see the likely reason."

"I know the reason," he said firmly. "And Miss Combs is not part of it."

"You do not—" Alsop managed no more words as Wellington interrupted him.

"I have offered you my hospitality. I should hope you won't repay that by insulting my most honored guest, nor by casting aspersions on my judgment."

That brought the chaos to a swift end. Wellington took advantage of the silence.

"Miss Fairbanks, what has gone missing?"

"My diamond-and-pearl brooch. I set it on the bureau last evening when I retired to bed. It was not there when I awoke." She held up a hand to forestall any commentary. "I searched the room. It is gone."

Wellington looked to Tillie. "The little monster is at it again."

"So it would seem." Tillie frowned. "It was bad enough when we was the only ones being robbed. We can't let it go any longer now."

She was completely correct. This group, however, was not likely to give her the benefit of their good opinion.

Wellington set his shoulders and assumed his most authoritative air. "We know the identity of our thief. Thus far, though, the culprit has managed to evade capture. Miss Combs and I will redouble our efforts to corner the criminal and reclaim all that has been taken."

That seemed to appease them a little. Very little.

"Now, if you will all take your time breaking your fast and enjoying one another's company, Miss Combs and I will recruit help from someone hereabout who can be trusted." He eyed them all individually. "I hope there will be no more unfounded accusations."

A few looked at least a little embarrassed to have been so unfeeling. The rest accepted the chastisement without showing the least remorse. So long as they stopped causing Tillie distress, he would let that be enough.

He offered her his arm. "Shall we, Miss Combs?"

"Yes, please." As they walked arm in arm down the corridor, she whispered. "What precisely do you mean to do?"

"Exactly what I said: catch a thief."

INSTALLMENT VII

in which our brave Hero and intrepid Heroine
face Danger and Mystery on the Moors!

Pip sat on Tillie's lap, wrapped in her protective arms while they reassured him he wouldn't be required to face down the sprite he'd stolen from its home.

"We simply need to know *how* you captured it," Wellington said. "It cannot continue roaming about, causing mischief. Its antics are causing people a great deal of distress."

Pip nodded. "It steals things."

"I'd wager it don't know it oughtn't take those things," Tillie said. "The little creature is away from the only place it knows, trying to make sense of somewhere so strange."

The boy looked up at her. "Do you think it's scared?"

"Might be. It's a frightening thing being surrounded by people you"— her eyes met Wellington's—"know you don't belong with. That's likely why it's hiding."

He fully understood the layer beneath her words. She too had been hiding, ever since his Society acquaintances arrived. Just as Mr. and Mrs. Smith had observed, she "knew" she didn't belong among them. Oh, how his heart ached for her!

"If only our little thief realized we wouldn't harm it for all the world," Wellington said. "That we only want what is best for it."

"But having it here is causing so much trouble." She didn't look away, didn't drop her gaze. "What is 'best' is for it to return home."

"Is that why it's scared?" Pip asked. "It wants to go home?"

The thought of that idea applying to Tillie sat heavy on Wellington's heart. "Is it scared, dear?" he asked her.

She held the little boy closer. In a voice quiet and less confident than he'd ever heard it, she said, "Terrified."

Wellington sat near enough to reach out and gently brush his fingers along her cheek. "There is nothing to be afraid of."

Pip broke into what would otherwise have been a very tender moment. "But it's so far from home. All the way across the moors."

Tillie looked at the little boy. "You know where its home is?"

He nodded. "A mine, over near Ipsley."

A mine. Just as Mr. Combs had said.

"Do you suppose," Wellington said, "if we could catch it and return it to the Ipsley mine, it might remain there and stop causing mischief here?"

"If I had a home," Pip said, "I'd always want to be there."

Tillie held him closer. "You can have your home with me, Pip."

What would it take for her to offer him a home "with *us*"? How could Wellington show Tillie that such a future was not only possible but perfect?

"You'll not make me go back to the workhouse?" Pip looked from one of them to the other, worry and hope warring in his expression.

"No, Pip. We'd not want you so far away as Ipsley," Tillie said.

The boy sighed and leaned against her. He looked less burdened. "It likes things that are shiny. That's how I got it to come out of the mine—with shiny things. And I had a shiny box that it went into. And I closed the lid so it couldn't get out, and then I ran with it. But it wasn't happy in the shiny box. It bumped around inside. I ran and ran, but then I dropped the box and the lid came off and the blue flame came out and darted into your house." He looked to Wellington. "I should've told you, but I was afraid."

"How long were you out on the moors by yourself?" The creature had, after all, been undertaking its thefts for weeks.

"I hid in the stables." Pip curled into an ever-smaller ball on Tillie's lap. "The blue flame was angry. I didn't want it to find me."

"We'll lure it away," Tillie promised. "And we'll get it back home. Nothing will happen to you, dearie."

Pip climbed down. He assumed the determined stance of one attempting to be brave. "You'll need shiny things. And a box."

Tillie nodded solemnly. "We'll fetch 'em." She stood and took Wellington's hand in hers. "Let's catch us a tiny blue monster." Tillie waved Pip along. "You can stay here with my papa."

"He likes me," Pip declared.

"We all do," Wellington said.

Tillie squeezed his hand and smiled up at him. A man could quickly grow accustomed to such a look from such a woman. Pip skipped off down the corridor, his joyfulness restored.

"What do your guests think of Pip?" Tillie asked. "They couldn't have missed that he's an urchin."

"I don't know that they've interacted with him yet."

Her gaze returned to the corridor, though he suspected she wasn't really looking at anything in particular. "Are you afraid they'll disapprove of him as well? Or accuse him of being the thief?"

"They might," he admitted. "Civility requires that I give them shelter from the rain, but there is no requirement that I allow them to be insulting."

"Pip and I are beneath them," she said. "Their behavior is expected."

"But it won't be endured. Should they cause you further pain, my dear, I will toss them out on their ears, rain or no rain."

Her expression softened. "Not many gentlemen would make that choice."

"They would if they knew *you*."

She swung their linked hands between them as they walked. "I think you've grown fond of me these past weeks."

"I've always been fond of you," he said.

"Fond enough to undertake ridiculous and likely dangerous adventures?"

He let his amusement show. "Increasingly so."

Tillie tugged him onward. "Let's go fetch some shiny things."

They'd been out on the moors for an hour without any sign of the elusive blue flame. Tillie was wearing every piece of shining, sparkling jewelry at Summerworth. Wellington kept near her with a wood-lined silver humidor at the ready. It was the shiniest box they could find.

And, yet, they'd had no success. To compound the difficulties, the skies above were turning leaden. Heaven help them if they were caught out in such a place under such circumstances!

"Perhaps we should come back another day," Wellington said. "I'd not want you to catch cold."

"Pip will not rest easy until the bluecap is home. And your guests aren't likely to leave until we recover the missing brooch."

He squared his shoulders. "That is all the motivation I need."

Tillie snorted, something a well-bred lady would never do, but which he enjoyed immensely. She was sunshine and fresh air.

She held up two fists full of dangling bracelets and chains of precious metal, bouncing them about so they sparkled. "Mr. Thief," she said in a singsong voice. "Come steal these fine things from us."

"That hasn't worked yet, it won't—"

A blue flame appeared, no more than fifty yards ahead of them. Wellington pulled in a tight breath.

Tillie shook the jewels.

The flame darted forward then disappeared.

"No, come back," Tillie whispered. She kept the jewels up high.

Wellington adjusted the silver box he held so the dim, cloud-infused sunlight glinted off it a little brighter as added incentive.

The blue flame reappeared, but for only a moment.

"We mean you no harm," Tillie called out. "Truly we don't."

"We want to take you back home," Wellington added.

Suddenly, the bluecap was visible again, closer this time. And it remained.

"We know you come from the mine by Ipsley," Tillie said. "We can take you back there."

Wellington opened the box. The flame disappeared.

"Perhaps it ain't fond of traveling in a box," Tillie said.

"I can't say I blame it." He tucked the silver humidor into the leather sack he'd borrowed from Mr. Combs. "Maybe we can convince the little sprite to follow us over the moors."

Tillie flourished the enticements again. "Mr. Bluecap! We want to take you home."

Nothing.

She looked at him. "Perhaps if we start walking in the direction of Ipsley, it'll follow?"

Wellington shrugged. "It's worth trying."

"I'd imagine it'll take an hour of walking," she warned. "And we've been out here an hour already."

He took the dangling jewels from her nearest hand, then slipped his fingers around hers. "I'm game for a long walk if you are."

They walked hand in hand, waving the sparkling lures about. The occasional backward glance revealed the blue flame following. But in the moment after they looked, it always disappeared.

"It is following us," Tillie whispered.

"I know."

On and on they walked. The sky overhead grew heavier and darker. The wind blew fiercer with each passing moment. The moors were no place to be in a storm. They were too far from Summerworth to turn back and too far from Ipsley to be at ease. A bone-chilling gust nearly knocked Tillie over.

"Perhaps we should've made this trek in the pony cart," she said.

"The flame would have spooked the pony. This could only be accomplished on foot."

After nearly an hour of winding through the moors, Ipsley came into view. The mine would be nearby. But where, exactly?

Tillie looked around, uncertainty in her face. She, apparently, didn't know either. "We cannot come this close only to fail. Where is it, Wellington?"

"The mine or the bluecap?"

"Either one," she said. The wind pulled at her hair and dress, yet she stood stalwart and fixed. How could anyone not see and admire the strength of this remarkable woman? She spun and motioned with her handful of jewelry. "There's the flame."

Wellington rushed alongside her toward their flickering quarry.

"Please," she called out. "We'll help you find your home."

"Truly." Wellington added his voice to hers. "Your mine is nearby; we know it is."

The blue flame flew further afield. They rushed after. They could not lose it. Not now. Not when they were so close to returning it to its home and ridding Summerfield of Alsop, Henson, and their lot!

The bluecap suddenly stopped. It hovered in place, flickering but not truly moving. In the instant before they reached it, the flame dropped straight down and vanished, not into thin air. Into a *hole*.

Wellington grabbed Tillie's arm and pulled her to a stop, her toes mere inches from the edge of a mine shaft. He drew her back to safety. The hole beneath their feet glowed an otherworldly blue.

"I believe our mysterious visitor is home at last," Wellington said.

Tillie leaned the tiniest bit forward and called down into the mine. "Could you return the things you stashed away? We've a shrew back at Summerworth who won't leave us in peace without her brooch."

The light grew brighter. Tillie stepped back. Wellington put his arm around her, unsure what was happening or what threat might arise next. The last weeks had taught him to expect what he could not possibly foresee.

A full dozen blue flames shot up out of the shaft and swirled around the two of them, whipping up even more wind than the storm brewing overhead. Tillie turned, burying her face against Wellington's chest. He set both his arms firmly and protectively about her as they were enveloped by the flames.

No heat emanated. Indeed, the flames were cold, like a draft from the dark corners of a . . . a mine. Stronger and stronger it blew, the pull of it twisting and turning. The vortex tugged at Tillie, threatening to yank her out of his arms.

"Wellington!"

He tightened his grip. "Kneel down." The wind carried his voice away. Had she even heard him? "If we're lower, it'll be harder to topple us."

The whirlwind pulled her further, stretching his fingers painfully.

"The wind is too strong." Tillie's voice pleaded with him.

With every ounce of strength he had, Wellington pulled her against him as he lowered himself—and her with him—to the muddy ground below, kneeling in the midst of the onslaught.

They hunched there as the blue whirlwind continued. They'd returned the wandering bluecap. Did its "family" think they'd kidnapped it in the first place?

Tillie was still sliding away. Her slight frame was no match against the pull of azure wind. She would be torn from him, perhaps tossed into the mine shaft. He wrapped the open sides of his jacket around her, then crouched over her, trying to shield her and weigh her down.

"We brought it home," he called out into the cold, blue cyclone. "We mean no harm. Let us go. Please."

With a flash of white, the flames disappeared. Only the gusts of humid moorland wind remained, and the first raindrops of the breaking storm.

Wellington kept still, waiting, watching for the bluecaps to return. Nothing emerged from the mine shaft. No light. No sound. No movement.

Tillie peeked out from her protective cocoon. "Are they gone?"

"I believe so."

She sat up straight, trembling and muddy. "I thought they'd blow me right off my feet and into the shaft."

"So did I." He kissed her temple. "You weren't hurt were you, my dear?"

"No lasting damage."

They scrambled to their feet, muddied but otherwise well.

"We make a fine team, Tillie Combs."

She smiled up at him, rain pelting her face. It was coming down harder now. They likely had time enough to reach Ipsley before the sky fully broke open, but only if they moved quickly.

"We'd best hurry," he said.

He kept her hand in his, and they moved swiftly toward the town. It wasn't until they were nearly there that Tillie stopped abruptly.

"Our sparklies."

He looked at her, unsure what she meant.

"All the jewels we were holding, to lure the bluecap onto the moors." She held up her empty hands. "They're gone."

He hadn't even noticed. His handful was missing as well. "Did we drop them?"

She shook her head. "I was clutching them tightly as I could manage."

He had been as well.

Tillie looked back in the direction of the mine. "They took it. They took the treasures." Her shoulders drooped. Rain dripped from her sodden hair. "I suppose this means Miss Fairbanks won't be getting her brooch back."

"Likely not." The wind blew rain up his sleeves and down his collar. They'd be soaked in another minute or two. "She'll rail and bluster, but I'll settle with her. Then she'll be on her way. They all will be."

"Is that a promise?"

"A solemn vow." He took her hand once more, the rain coming down in buckets. "But for now, my dear, it's time to run for cover."

INSTALLMENT VIII

in which our brave Couple finds their Happiness!

Having procured a cart and pony at the coaching inn in Ipsley after waiting out the storm in a private dining room, Wellington made the drive back to Summerworth with an exhausted but joyful Tillie at his side.

"I am a bit disappointed." Her amused smile contradicted her declaration.

"What has disappointed you?"

"Our thief proved to be none of the things on m'original list." She shook her head and clicked her tongue.

He laughed. "You were hoping for ill-mannered dogs and well-coordinated magpies?"

"Oh, mercy, that would have been a lark to sort out."

He grinned at her. "I believe we had quite a lark regardless."

She sighed and leaned her head against his shoulder. "Chasing mythical creatures out onto the moors. What greater lark could there be?"

He pondered that for the length of a breath. "Mere weeks ago, I would not have thought racing over the moor was a worthy pursuit. I fear I was every bit the pompous bore you accused me of being."

"I really did call you that, didn't I?"

"You did, indeed." He led the cart around a bend in the path. "And you were utterly correct. I've spent too many years alone. The only company I'd kept with any degree of regularity was that of . . . well, people not unlike Mr. Alsop and Miss Fairbanks and their ilk. I'd lost sight of the Wellington I was when we were children."

"I loved *that* Wellington," she said. "He was my dearest friend."

"What do you think of *this* Wellington?"

She wrapped her arm around his. "I think he's wonderful."

"And I think *this* Tillie is rather remarkable as well."

They reached the front portico of Summerworth. His unwelcome guests would still be inside, likely moaning and groaning over Miss Fairbanks's missing jewelry. Wellington would do his best to settle the matter, offering to replace what was stolen and subtly pushing them out the door.

Mrs. Smith met them in the front entryway, her expression frantic. "What a scene!" She fanned herself with a dishrag. "You'd not believe what's happening."

Oh, mercy. Wellington met Tillie's eye. She clearly expected as much theatrics as he was anticipating.

"We'd best go face it," he said.

"And if they lob accusations at me again?"

Wellington set his shoulders. "Then I will toss them out with none of the civility I've been silently rehearsing."

She lifted an eyebrow and popped a fist on one hip. "I'm not afraid of a horde of creatures. We've faced down a number of them today already."

He took her hand in his, the lightness in his heart entirely at odds with the discomfort of the coming confrontation. On the first-floor landing, Pip found them. He bounced and jumped, grabbing for their hands.

"Come see. Come see."

"Come see what?" Tillie asked.

"All of it!" Pip dragged them up another flight of stairs and through the door to Wellington's rooms. "See. All of it!"

There, piled as high as Pip's knees, was a small mountain of jewelry, shiny metal boxes, silver brushes, and even the missing mirror and paint-ing. Heavens, the Combses' spade was there as well, as was a hand plow and a milking bucket. The items Wellington and Tillie had taken out onto the moors, the ones that had disappeared from their hands during the blue whirlwind, were there also.

"All of it," Tillie said.

"One of these will be Miss Fairbanks's brooch." Wellington began dig-ging for it.

Tillie dropped to her knees and joined the search. Mr. Combs, upon entering and hearing of their task, joined in the effort. As did Pip. And Mr. and Mrs. Smith.

Within the hour, Miss Fairbanks was in possession of her brooch, the rained-in houseguests were on their way, and Summerworth was peaceful and joyful again.

"They won't be the last visitors to disapprove of my being here," Tillie warned as the traveling coach disappeared from view.

"I will remove anyone and anything that makes you less than happy, my Tillie. And soon enough, visitors, whether human or not, will learn that you matter to me more than they do."

"And Pip?" Tillie asked.

"He will learn that he matters to us too."

"*Us.*" She sighed. "I do like the sound of that."

"Then you are going to *love* this."

He kissed his beloved Tillie, holding her close as the wind whipped over the moors, cold and wild and tinted blue.

HIGGLEBOTTOM'S
SCHOOL FOR THE DEAD

A GHOST OF A CHANCE

by Lafayette Jones

CHAPTER I

Ace Bowen had been a student at Higglebottom's School for the Dead for a few months and was quickly becoming the school's most legendary pupil. He was learning the art of being a ghost faster than anyone before him, and he did it with flair.

He walked the corridors of Higglebottom's with an otherworldly strut. Ghosts *could* walk, no matter that the living seemed to think all they did was float. Floating, in fact, was more difficult.

The other students always waved to him as he passed. The staff shook their ghostly heads in amusement. He was the life of the school, so to speak. He, along with his friends, Bathwater and Snout, was also the source of most of its mischief.

"Pouring ink into the laundry cauldron so the haunting shrouds all turned light-blue. Tightening all the floorboards so none squeaked during the Third Form's 'Ghost Walking' exams." Professor Rattlebag had been listing the boys' pranks. He wasn't likely to finish before the end of the dinner hour. "Teaching the school parrot to mimic the sound of rattling chains so Professor Dankworth could not be heard during her 'Disguise Ghost Conversations with Sundry Sounds' lesson."

Oh, the parrot could mimic more sounds than just chains. Bathwater sputtered, trying to hold back a laugh. Ace lounged in a chair that wasn't there—a skill most students didn't master until at least Third Form.

"I think it best you three go directly to your dormitory," Rattlebag said. "There will be no dinner for you."

Skipping dinner wasn't much of a punishment as ghosts did not actually need to eat, but learning to pretend as if they did proved helpful when wanting to go unnoticed amongst hungry Perishables.

The boys rose and made their way toward the office door. Ace aimed his path toward the wall.

"Not through the wall, Mr. Bowen," Rattlebag said, sounding far too tired for a ghost who'd not needed sleep in nearly a millennium. "You haven't mastered the skill yet. Nurse Snodsbury was quite put out the last time she had to reassemble you."

Willing to save Snodsbury a bit of bother, Ace passed through the open door with his ghostly feet a few inches off the floor, another skill a First Form was not meant to have mastered.

No, Higglebottom's had never seen a student quite like him.

"Rattlebag has no sense of humor," Snout said as they walked toward their dormitory. "Those gags were brilliant."

Bathwater shrugged. "Maybe things stop being funny after you've been dead nine hundred years."

"Rattlebag certainly stopped being funny," Ace said.

They all laughed, not the least worried about punishments or expulsion. The teachers liked them, despite the havoc they wreaked.

"Two weeks until the Spirit Trials," Snout said. "Do you mean to ask Cropper to join our team?"

Ace was considering it. They needed a crack team for that term's trials.

For eight hundred years, school terms at Higglebottom's School for the Dead had ended with the Spirit Trials, a series of tests in which the students demonstrated all they had learned about being a proper ghost. A high enough score allowed the winning team to advance to the next Form early.

Ace was bored to death, as it were, of First Form studies. "Cropper's whip smart. But he's not a lot of fun."

Bathwater attempted to sit in an absent chair but mismanaged the thing, spilling onto and partway through the floor. "I guess I'm not so whip smart, myself," he said, pulling himself up with some effort. He managed to not leave any bits of himself behind.

Snout eyed Ace with curiosity. "Would you rather have a diverting teammate or a helpful one?"

"The three of us could do well enough to at least pass the Spirit Trials," Ace said. "Might as well have a lark doing it."

"Even if it means not skipping to Form Two?" Bathwater asked.

If ghosts had actual hearts, Ace's would've dropped a bit at that question. He wanted to be challenged at Higglebottom's. But he'd not had much time for larks and absurdity in life. He meant to enjoy a hardy helping of both in the afterlife.

"If we don't qualify to skip ahead early, we can make the most of our final term in Form One."

"Rattlebag might advance us anyway," Snout said. "Anything to get us out of his classes."

"All the more reason to make certain the Spirit Trials are a highlight."

"Are you aiming for more mischief?" Bathwater sounded worried. Though he enjoyed their mischief and joined in eagerly, he did worry a bit over it.

"You bet your afterlife, I am."

Somewhere in the room something thudded, a common sound in a school full of ghosts learning to be proper haunters. But nothing had fallen or shifted or lay in a heap.

"What was that?" Bathwater asked.

"I don't know, but I mean to find out." Ace floated—a bit of showing off helped build a touch of confidence—to the noisy side of the room.

Nothing seemed amiss.

Then the bed skirt rustled. The wind wasn't blowing outside the ancient school. No one in the room was practicing making a draft.

Ace knelt on the floor, careful not to slip through, and peered under the bed, directly into the eyes of a boy. But not just any boy.

A *living* one.

CHAPTER II

"Blimey!" Snout declared over Ace's shoulder. "It's a Perishable."

"What's it doing here?" Bathwater asked.

Ace shrugged. "Beats me. I've never heard of a *living* person being at Higglebottom's." He eyed the terrified face under the bed. "What are you doing here?"

"I was caught in a storm," the boy said. "I came inside to get out of the rain."

"It hasn't rained since yesterday."

The boy rested his chin on his upturned fist. "I know."

"You've just been hiding?"

The boy's eyes darted around. "This place is full of *ghosts*."

Ace rested his ghostly chin on his ghostly fist, his position mirroring that of the boy's. "I know."

"Are you going to eat me?" the boy asked.

"Ghosts don't eat."

"Lock me up somewhere?"

Bathwater dropped onto the ground beside him, stopping his movement at the moment his spectral form would've stopped if he had a body. "Why didn't you just leave after the storm ended?"

The boy took a deep breath, something else ghosts didn't *have* to do but practiced as a way of either blending in or causing distress, whichever was needed. "I've nowhere to go."

"You don't have a family?" Bathwater asked.

The boy shook his head.

"A school of your own?" Snout asked.

Another headshake.

"A name?" Ace dropped in dryly.

"Frank," he said.

"Ace, Bathwater, Snout, and *Frank*?" Ace would have rolled his eyes if he'd learned the trick of it yet. Ghost bodies didn't work quite the same way Perishable bodies did. "You'll need a better name."

"Does that mean we're keeping him?" Snout asked.

"Where else is he going to go?" Ace motioned the boy out from under the bed. "No point hiding anymore."

"We should probably tell someone," Bathwater said. "We're only First Forms. We don't know what to do about something this big."

That was a temptation no ghost with ambition could pass up. Ace grinned. "Then let's be the only First Forms in the history of Higglebottom's to manage a *prank* this big."

Bathwater hesitated for a fraction of a moment, then both he and Snout turned to him eagerly. They were the best partners in crime a fellow could ask for.

Ace spoke to their newest arrival. "Would you like to stay at Higglebottom's, Frank?" *Frank.* He really needed a better name.

Frank nodded.

"That's our challenge, lads. We're going to pass off this Perishable as a ghost."

"To the professors, even?"

Ace nodded. "It wouldn't be much of a prank if we didn't pull the wool over *anyone's* eyes."

Bathwater circled Frank, eyeing him. "No one'll believe he's dead. He doesn't look it."

"Because I'm *not*," Frank tossed back.

"We can teach you to play the part," Ace said. "Learning how to be a ghost is what we're all here for anyway."

"You don't know how?" Frank asked.

"It ain't something you die knowing," Ace said.

"He has to have a uniform," Snout said. "Everyone'll know he's not a student if he's wearing that."

The boy wore high-collared shirtsleeves and buckled-at-the-knee trousers. Though both were crusted in mud, they weren't tattered and billowing like the Higglebottom's uniforms. He looked like a muddy Perishable, not a ghost.

"He's closest to your size, Snout. Fetch him an extra of yours."

But when Frank tried to put on the frayed shirt and trousers, they just floated through his arms and legs. It seemed Perishables couldn't wear ghost clothes.

"Well, there's that plan busted." Bathwater sounded as disappointed as Ace felt.

Ace, however, was not one to give up easily. "The Hauntings Department has an entire storeroom of things that aren't made of phantom fabric. We could make him a uniform."

Snout nodded enthusiastically. "We could."

"How are you at walking quiet so you don't make a sound?" Ace asked Frank.

"Never tried it." The boy made a go of it.

His first few attempts were dismal. He'd make a rotten ghost as loud as he was. The element of surprise was key to any proper haunting. Stomping around would give him away straight off. But as he slowed down, he got quieter. After a lot of attempts and a lot of advice, Frank could move with an impressive degree of stealth.

When he spoke, he didn't sound much like a ghost, but Ace couldn't pin down what it was about his voice that gave him away. That bit of training would have to wait until he pieced the puzzle together. "Don't talk to anyone but us. That'll sort that difficulty."

"But we do have to worry about his face," Snout said.

"A fine thing to say," Frank said, "considering I know why they call you 'Snout.'"

Even Snout laughed at that. This Perishable was going to fit in nicely.

"I think he means your face isn't pale enough," Bathwater said. "We could tell you weren't a ghost right from the start, and we hadn't seen your clothes or heard you walking or anything."

Frank turned to Ace. "You're heading this expedition. What do *you* suggest?"

While Ace pondered the trouble of Frank's complexion, the silence was broken by a sound never heard at Higglebottom's School for the Dead: a stomach growling.

Frank's already too-colorful face turned redder. "I'm a little hungry."

"We have food here," Ace said. "We don't have to eat it, but there's plenty around."

"I'd die for just a bite or two."

Ace chuckled. "Seems to me you'd die *without* a bite or two." He turned to Snout. "Could you sneak a bit of food up for Pudding, here?"

"Pudding?" Bathwater asked. "Is that his name now?"

"He's aching for food. Seems to me, naming him *for* food would be fitting." He held Frank's gaze. "What do you think?"

The Perishable shrugged. "I don't mind."

"'Pudding' it is."

Snout slipped from the room.

"I know why I'm called what I am, and where Snout's name came from." Pudding looked at Bathwater. "Why do they call you 'Bathwater'?"

Ace was the one who'd given him the name, so he was the one who answered. "Because he objected to being called 'Baby.'"

"So you threw out the 'Baby,'" Pudding said, "with the 'Bathwater.'"

"A brilliant solution if you ask me." Ace had figured out another "brilliant solution" for their current difficulty. "While Snout's fetching you food, let's see if we can't find a classroom with a good amount of chalk dust. We'll have you pale as death in no time."

"And then?" Pudding asked.

"As soon as we've got a uniform for you, we'll test your disguise with a stroll around the school."

Pudding looked intrigued but wary. "And if the disguise doesn't work?"

"Then Bathwater, Snout, and I won't be the only ones of the four of us who're dead."

CHAPTER III

The more time Ace spent with Pudding, the more he liked him. He had gumption. He was funny. And, Ace suspected, he would always be up for a prank or two.

It was a deuced shame the boy wasn't dead.

"Is that enough chalk?" Bathwater eyed Pudding's pale face.

"Can't be," Pudding said. "I can still breathe."

"Are you accusing us of trying to kill you?" Snout laughed.

"It'd make this transformation easier."

Ah, yes, Pudding was funny.

Snout had sewn a uniform for Pudding, a feat that had amazed all of them—including *Snout*. He hadn't been a tailor's apprentice or anything like that during his Perishable years.

"Do you think we're ready?" Bathwater asked. "If he's caught out, we're all in the wringer."

The risk was most of the fun. "We're ready," Ace declared.

Pudding stepped lightly as they made for the dormitory door. He'd been practicing and could move almost as silently as the others. If only Ace could figure a way to make it seem as if, now and then, Pudding unintentionally slipped through the ground like First Forms so often did.

They took the stairs down to the ground level and sauntered out into the open-air commons. The school didn't hold classes one day each week, giving the students some leisure time. This was one of those days, so the commons was busy.

Students took note of Ace as he passed; they always did. He was always about with friends, so that didn't cause much of a stir. One of the four of them held his breath each time someone looked too closely. The scrutiny, though, always ended with the other student moving along.

"We're managing it," Snout said.

"The 'we' feels questionable." Pudding kept his voice low, apparently remembering that he didn't sound quite like he ought.

"You could always saunter about on your own," Ace said.

"We could always saunter to wherever the food is," Pudding tossed back.

Ace shook his head, managing not to accidentally spin it all the way around. "You Perishables and your obsession with food."

Pudding shrugged. "It's more an obsession with staying . . . perishable."

"Hush, lads," Snout growled. "Rattlebag's coming this way."

They formed something of a clump, chatting like nothing was odd about them. Pudding tucked himself a little behind Bathwater. It'd be best if he weren't too easy to see.

"Professor Rattlebag," Ace greeted. "I hope you're proud of us; we haven't made any mischief lately."

"Proud?" Rattlebag hitched a pearly eyebrow. "I think the better word is suspicious."

"Of *us*?" Ace used his most innocent voice. "We've been perfect angels."

"I doubt that." Rattlebag glanced over the others before returning his gaze to Ace. "Remember, I have my eyes on you."

He floated away. The professors had been practicing ghostliness for centuries and could manage all the tricks with hardly any effort. Someday Ace would as well.

The other three were grinning broadly when Ace looked in their direction.

"We snuck Pudding past Rattlebag," Ace said. He'd have given them a one-ghost round of applause if he'd learned yet how to make actual noise that way. That was a Second Form skill. "We're well on our way to becoming legends, my friends."

"Including me?" Pudding asked.

"The only Perishable to 'attend' Higglebottom's? That's legendary in anyone's book."

From across the lawn, Cropper approached. He wasn't a regular in their group, but he wasn't an enemy either. Further, he was clever. Would he see through Pudding's disguise?

"Who's the newdead?" Cropper asked, nodding toward Pudding.

"Not entirely newdead," Ace said. "But still fresh. We're taking him under our shroud, so to speak."

Cropper watched Pudding a moment longer. "How far under your shroud?"

"What do you mean?" Bathwater asked.

"Whispers around Higglebottom's is that you need a fourth for your Spirit Trials team."

A Perishable on their Spirit Trials team? That would be the prank of the millennium. But it also might cost them the opportunity to skip ahead to Second Form. Another term in First Form would be a dead bore. Literally.

"That explains the addition," Cropper said, nodding like he'd just answered a puzzling question. "We'd all wondered why the Gang of Three now had four. He's your new teammate."

Snout and Bathwater looked to Ace, keeping their expressions unreadable to anyone who didn't know them as well as Ace did. If they said Pudding *wasn't* their new teammate, those wondering about him would wonder more. They'd be caught out for sure and certain.

"We're being charitable," Ace told Cropper. "Showing up newdead so close to the Spirit Trials is a recipe for failure. We're going to save this new arrival from that fate."

"That'll cost you the top prize," Cropper warned.

He knew it. He knew everyone else knew it. But knowing something was impossible had never stopped Ace before.

"Oh, we'll take the top prize. And we'll be the first team to manage it with a newdead."

Cropper shrugged. "I wish you luck, then."

"We won't need it."

Cropper walked away, only slipping a foot through the ground twice—not too rubbish for a First Form.

"Pudding's going to be on our team?" Snout asked.

"He'll have to be, or this whole thing'll fall apart." Ace eyed them all, including their chalk-covered new friend. "It'll be the most ambitious prank we've pulled yet. And we only need one thing to make it work."

"What's that?" Pudding asked.

"A whole heap of luck."

CHAPTER IV

Pudding sat on Snout's bed with a high-stacked plate of Bakewell tarts on his lap. He'd already eaten the bowl of boiled potatoes and chipped beef Bathwater had brought up from the dining hall.

"None of you want any?" Pudding held up one of the round pastries. "Best I ever had."

"If eating was one of the Spirit Trial challenges, we would have this competition wrapped up and tucked in our pockets." Snout watched Pudding with amazement. "How does he do it?"

"He's a Perishable," Ace said. "Some things come naturally to them."

Pudding set aside his tray of tarts and leaned against the headboard. "Can't believe you told everyone I'm going to be on your team for some sort of ghost challenge. What do I know about being a ghost?"

"Nothing really." Snout leaned his shoulder against the bedpost but didn't quite do the thing properly. Half of him slipped through.

"You look like you've been impaled." Pudding cringed. "That would make a person run like a fox in hunting season."

"Good to know." Snout righted himself. "Fourth Forms have 'Terrify a Perishable to the Point of Hysteria or Loss of Consciousness' in their Spirit Trials. I'll have to remember the impaling."

"Do we have to scare peop—I mean, Perishables?" Pudding asked.

Ace shook his head. "First Forms are limited to dogs and cats."

"We have to scare dogs?"

"That test is called 'Artful Dodging,'" Bathwater said. "We have to sneak past a dog and a cat without either of them noticing us." Bathwater had struggled with that one. Even talking about it now he sounded nervous. "Animals see a lot more than Perishables do. And cats are malicious about it."

"Both of them would spot me straight off." Pudding's mouth twisted to one side.

Ace tried subtly mirroring Pudding's expression, but he couldn't quite get it. He'd learned to float through walls with only the occasional mishap, but he couldn't work his own face.

"There's also 'Churchyard Chase,'" Bathwater continued. "The student chases a stand-in for a Perishable all around a churchyard, with the aim of getting them to stop at a particular headstone."

Pudding slipped his hands behind his head. "I'm a fast runner."

"Won't work," Ace said. "If you fall, you'll scrape yourself up. Blood would be a dead giveaway."

"A not-dead giveaway, more like." Pudding had a way of making them laugh even when they were weighing heavy matters.

"If not Artful Dodging or Churchyard Chasing," Bathwater went on, "then maybe 'Is That the Wind, or Is This Place Haunted?'"

Pudding's eyes pulled wide. "That's the name of the test? That whole mouthful?"

"Rattlebag said it used to be called 'Ghostly Sounds, Beginner Level.'"

"Ghostly Sounds," Pudding repeated. "Like moaning and wailing and saying things like 'Who dares disturb my eternal slumber?'" He pulled the last word out long and singsongy, throwing his hands up like he was towering over something.

They all burst out laughing.

"Pathetic!" Ace said between chuckles.

Pudding pretended to be offended; no one seeing his exaggerated pout and pulled brows would believe he was in earnest. "If that was so bad, you try it."

Ace rose up from the bed—floating for effect—and hovered slowly closer to his new friend. He pitched his voice low and rumbling, dropping the volume and speaking almost painfully slowly. "Who dares disturb my eternal slumber?"

For just a moment, Pudding truly looked scared. But the fear dissolved on the instant. "That was brilliant! I could feel your voice shaking inside of me. Can you teach me to do that?"

"I don't know," Ace said, returning to his bed. Sitting on a bed without falling through was one of the first lessons at Higglebottom's.

"We don't have time for being wrong about what he can do," Snout said. "Pudding has to take one of the four tests. Which one do we give him?"

Ace gave it a moment's thought. "Snout, you're best at Artful Dodging. Bathwater, your strength is Churchyard Chase. I should probably take Is That the Wind, or Is This Place Haunted?"

"What does that leave me?" Pudding asked, another Bakewell tart disappearing into his mouth.

"Shroud Wearing," Ace said.

"And what does a fellow have to do in 'Shroud Wearing'?"

In unison, all three of them said, "Wear a shroud."

Pudding laughed. "No jesting. What's the challenge?"

"We're telling you the truth," Ace said. "The test is wearing a shroud."

"A fellow puts on a shroud and says, 'There you have it'?"

"Keeping something on that isn't made of phantom fabric is a difficult thing," Bathwater said. "My head still slips through at least half the time. Sometimes, I raise my arms to look bigger and more threatening, and the shroud doesn't come with me. Humiliating."

"Oh, blast it all, we're thick." Ace let himself drop through the bed and onto the floor beneath. This time, he didn't leave any pieces of himself behind. He slid out from under the bed, addressing them all. "Shroud wearing. Perishables don't need practice not floating through their clothes. We can toss a shroud on Pudding, here, and he could walk out, make the circuit, and come back the reigning king of First Form shroud wearers without having to learn a blasted thing."

Bathwater and Pudding whooped, both clearly seeing the genius in his suggestion.

Snout still looked skeptical. "A First Form shouldn't be perfect at it, though. That'd make the professors start thinking too hard about who this unfamiliar student is."

Ace nodded. It was a valid point. "So we figure out how to make it look like he's slipping into the ground a little. They'll assume he's concentrating so hard on staying inside the shroud that he's neglecting his feet a bit."

"And he'd be entirely covered up," Bathwater said.

Ace looked at each of his friends in turn. "What do you say?"

"It's brilliant!" Pudding declared. "And if it means staying here, out of the rain, with food to eat, I'll pretend to float through all the ground you want me to."

Ace was getting excited. They were going to sneak a Perishable into the Spirit Trials, and they were going to get away with it.

Ace, Snout, Bathwater, and Pudding were about to become Higglebottom legends!

CHAPTER V

The day of the Spirit Trials arrived cold and cloudy, but the school was in bright spirits. Spirit Trials were the highlight of the entire term.

Ace and his crew entered the cricket pitch with a great deal of swagger—Ace in front, Pudding directly behind him, with Bathwater and Snout on either side. The other First Form teams were assuming their places, but none with quite so much confidence.

Pudding pointed to the seats where the staff sat. "Which one of them is Higglebottom?"

Ace shrugged. "Couldn't say."

"You don't know?"

"No one knows. Might not be any of them. He runs the school, but no one sees him or knows who he is."

Pudding gave him a look thick with doubt. "The teachers and staff must know."

Ace shrugged. "If they do, none of them will say so." The identity of Higglebottom was one of the afterlife's great mysteries.

"And that doesn't bother anyone?" Pudding was clearly having trouble accepting this.

"It is what it is," Ace said, repeating a phrase he'd heard more times than he could count during his own time as a Perishable. "School runs smoothly. The big decisions go over well. No use restringing a fiddle that plays in tune."

Pudding eyed the gathered staff through most of the welcome speech given by Professor Rattlebag as well as the instructions from Professor Dankworth. Ace was grateful Pudding's event would be last or else he might have been too distracted to even take part.

Artful Dodging was first. Ace slapped Snout on the back, managing to send his hand all the way through him.

He grimaced, knowing all too well how unnerving that sensation was. "Apologies."

But his teammate was too focused to take note of it. His gaze never left the animals gathered in the middle of the pitch. He watched the students who made the run before him, seeing what they did and how the animals reacted.

"You'll be brilliant," Pudding said quietly. "Even if I don't cheer out loud for you."

They'd all decided it'd be best if Pudding kept mum. His voice didn't echo or rattle enough. The others would notice if he spoke too often.

Snout's turn arrived. He closed his translucent eyelids, pressed his ethereal hands together. Slowly, the light drained from him. He could still be seen—total disappearance wasn't taught until Fourth Form—but he was much easier to miss.

With silent, careful step, he cautiously moved behind the redtick hound sitting at the ready. At one point, its ears perked, but it didn't turn around, didn't take notice.

"That's one success," Ace whispered to the rest of the team, watching from the edge of the field.

Snout took the same approach with the gray-and-white striped tabby. Again, a tiny twitch of an ear, the littlest bit of awareness, but no real notice. He was going to hand the team a full-marks finish.

At the last minute, the cat spun about and hissed, back arched and fur on end. Snout returned to his usual near-opacity, shoulders drooping. He'd been blasted close.

The cat who had snatched victory away swished its tail and sent Snout a sassy look. It had known what it was doing, making him think he'd bested it. Bathwater'd had the right of it when he said cats were malicious.

The score card was displayed. They were penalized only two points for the cat catching Snout, no doubt owing to his having crossed almost the entire distance.

Ace leaned toward Pudding. "Bathwater's bang up with Churchyard Chase. He'll fetch us full points easily."

And he did. The Perishable stand-in, a mop wearing a woman's dress and being flitted about by one of the professors to look almost like a living person, rushed about the churchyard, darting in one direction until Bathwater showed up and scared it back. In half the time of the other competitors, Bathwater had herded the mock-Perishable to the headstone of

Kipper Kettlesworth, the destination he'd been given moments before the chase began.

Their team received full marks, placing them in a tie with Cropper's team.

"Next up," Rattlebag called out once the Churchyard Chase was completed, "'Is That the Wind, or Is This Place Haunted?' Teams, select your competitor."

"That'd be me." Ace tossed the others a cocky smile—he'd perfected that ghostly facial expression early on in his days at Higglebottom's.

The others heckled him, jesting that he would be the lowest-scoring First Form in history, but no one was actually worried. Ghostly sounds came easily to Ace.

His turn arrived. He met Rattlebag at the center of the pitch and waited for his instructions.

"Wind at a distance," Rattlebag requested.

Ace made precisely that sound. In another year or two, he would learn how to make his voice actually emerge at a distance, but the appropriate volume was all the Trials required of First Forms.

"Wind inside the house."

That one was trickier, since Perishables would know there was a jig afoot if they heard wind right beside them but felt nothing. Beginning haunters weren't meant to reveal that ghosts were nearby, simply lay the groundwork for the more advanced ghosts to build on. Still, Ace was not the least challenged by the request.

"Otherworldly gurgling," Rattlebag said.

Ace did so.

"Muttered gibberish that sounds vaguely like someone speaking a language other than the one the Perishable speaks."

That one was Ace's favorite. "Tippione traw groppier mantar." He kept the sound in the back of his throat and spoke without opening his lips. Sound could still emerge from a ghost's closed mouth, just more garbled and confusing. "Lessier noddle cooppinter."

Even Rattlebag looked impressed. He motioned Ace back to his team.

When the score was posted, it was the very top mark, a perfect score.

"That puts us in first place," Bathwater said. "As long as Pudding wears his shroud well, we have victory in the bag."

"And our ticket to Second Form," Ace said. "We'll be riding high."

Some twenty minutes later, after all the other teams had chosen and sent out their competitors, Pudding put the tattered shroud over his unghostly head and made the walk across the pitch.

They'd practiced for hours, trying to make him look like an expert without looking like too much of one. He was doing a fine job . . . for a Perishable, at least. Ace couldn't help thinking again what a shame it was Pudding wasn't actually dead.

Pudding changed up his pace a couple of times, sometimes slowing as if needing to regain his confidence. And he'd gained a real knack for bending at the knee, below the shroud so no one could see, and tipping to one side. It was the perfect picture of someone sinking a foot through the ground. He would recover, take a moment to collect himself, then walk forward again.

"A convincing performance," Bathwater said, his tone one of relief.

"I plan to call for an encore," Snout said.

"I plan to go straight to whichever Second Form dormitory catches my fancy and claim my bed." Ace wasn't delaying that move one moment longer than he had to.

Pudding was almost to the edge of the pitch when the heavy-laden skies burst open, and rain poured down like a waterfall. Rain wasn't generally of much concern among ghosts, but it did make the non-afterlife items they interacted with heavier and trickier to move.

At the end of the field, Pudding stood beneath an increasingly weighted shroud. It clung and grabbed at his form beneath it. So much for the subtlety of First Form hauntings. Still, subtle or not, Pudding had been by far the best in his test. They had their victory!

Cropper rushed across the pitch toward him. Rattlebag was drawing closer as well.

"C'mon, lads," Ace said. "Something's afoot."

They arrived in time to hear Cropper say, "A rain-soaked shroud is too heavy for a First Form to hold up. No First Form—not even Ace—could do this."

Gads, if the fellow wasn't right about that. They'd worried about Pudding giving away the game by being too good at his challenge. They hadn't counted on the rain making that glaringly obvious.

"He ain't an upper Form," Ace said. "My word of honor."

Cropper and Rattlebag looked at him, clearly attempting to find the gap in his words. More testers and onlookers had drawn nearer.

"He's not an upper Form," Rattlebag repeated. "But he doesn't seem to be a First Form, either. What, then, is he?"

Rattlebag reached for the edge of the shroud. Ace watched, worried. They would soon know if Pudding's chalk disguise was good enough to fool a professor at close range.

The shroud yanked off him and floated to the ground. Ace groaned at the sight before him. Rain had sent the chalk running down Pudding's face in translucent gray rivulets, revealing ample amounts of his Perishable complexion.

A collective gasp swirled around the crowd. Whispers began immediately.

Rattlebag's eyes took on a threatening glow. "All four of you. Higglebottom's office. Now."

CHAPTER VI

Ace had pulled a lot of pranks and caused a lot of mischief in his time at Higglebottom's, but he'd never once been sent to the headmaster's office. He didn't know anyone who had been.

"We're in for it now," Bathwater said, as they made the trek up the cobweb-covered corridor that so few students ever saw.

"At least they can kill only one of us." Snout's bit of humor lightened all of them.

Even Pudding smiled. Then he looked to Ace. "We're in deep trouble, though, aren't we?"

"We're headed to Higglebottom's office. 'Trouble' doesn't begin to sum it up."

"I'm sorry," he said to all of them. "This is my fault. I shouldn't have stayed."

Ace shook his head. "Where else were you going to go?"

They'd established straight off that Pudding didn't have a home or a family waiting for him anywhere. Sneaking him around, sorting out a way for him to stay had been a lark, yes, but they'd also come to like him. Not one of them would want him tossed out to live under a rock or something.

Rattlebag, who'd been walking ahead of them, motioned toward a heavy wooden door. It opened. Moving things without touching them was something else Ace looked forward to learning.

They followed Rattlebag to the center of an empty room. Entirely empty. No furniture, no rug on the floor, no paintings on the wall. If there'd been chains and wrist cuffs on the wall, it would have looked exactly like a dungeon.

"Do we just wait here, or . . . ?" Ace let the sentence dangle.

"Hush," Rattlebag said. Then, in a suddenly booming voice, he called out, "Higglebottom, I've brought our troublesome students for your verdict."

Verdict. That didn't sound good.

A gust picked up in the room, swirling the dust around.

Under his breath, Pudding said, "Is that the wind, or is this place haunted?"

Ace and the others laughed for a moment before Rattlebag's glare silenced them.

The dust formed a whirlwind in front of them. Rattlebag, oddly enough, addressed it.

"These are the students and the Perishable they've been passing off as dead."

The swirl of dust broke apart and formed, in its place, words hovering in the air. *How did the Perishable get here?*

"I was lost in the rain," Pudding said. "I saw the school and slipped in to dry off."

How long have you been here?

"Just over a week, uh . . . sir."

Why did none of you report him here?

There was no voice to go with the questions, but it wasn't difficult to imagine the hard and angry voice behind them.

"He didn't have anywhere to go," Bathwater said. "And he was hungry. Perishables are fragile."

The question didn't change or disappear. Had Higglebottom—Ace was assuming this was the mysterious headmaster—not received the answer he wanted?

"And it was a challenge," Ace admitted out loud. "If we could hide a Perishable without being caught, that'd be something worth talking about for centuries."

You did get caught.

"I know, blast it," Ace muttered.

What do you suggest we do now?

The question was likely meant for Rattlebag, but Pudding answered.

"Let me stay?" He flashed an awkward but amusing smile.

"Let all of us stay?" Bathwater added.

The question didn't rewrite itself. Higglebottom hadn't heard what he wanted. Again.

Ace took a step closer and, likely for the first time since arriving at the school, took a stand on something other than the joys of mischief. "Pudding is a deuced good ghost, even if he's a bit too alive for our tastes. We have food here, which he needs. We've a roof. Beds. Enough non-phantom fabric to make sure the boy ain't walking about in the altogether. He could learn what we learn, but he could also teach us about Perishables, things we might not know otherwise. If he stayed, it'd be good for all of us."

Still the question remained. The boys looked at each other, unsure what else they could say.

Into the silence, Rattlebag spoke. "These boys hoodwinked all the students for a week. If not for the rain, they might have managed it even longer. Disguising a Perishable as a convincing ghost requires knowing what makes a ghost. And teaching a living boy enough to participate in the Spirit Trials is not a small feat."

Shocked silence gripped all of them. Rattlebag had defended them.

Professor Rattlebag and the Perishable will remain. The others will wait in the corridor.

Ace didn't like the idea of Pudding in here without a defender. "But we—"

Rattlebag's hardened expression warned him not to press the matter. So he, Bathwater, and Snout slipped out, waiting just on the other side of the door. If they'd had breath to hold, they'd have held it.

"What do you think Higglebottom will do to Pudding?" Bathwater paced, every third or fourth step slipping through the floor.

"What can a dirt whirlwind do?" Ace said with a shrug. His usual jovial tone fell flat. He wasn't sure what came next. None of their pranks had ever felt this . . . dangerous.

"If Pudding gets tossed out, I'm going too," Snout declared.

"So am I," Bathwater said.

Ace looked at both of them, feeling the strength that comes in numbers. "So am I. We're a group of four now. There's no going back on that."

In the next moment, the wooden door opened. Rattlebag floated out. His face gave no clues. Pudding was directly behind him.

All of them watched their friend, eager for anything he could tell them. He, too, was unreadable.

Ace couldn't wait another moment. He turned to Rattlebag. "Is Pudding being tossed out?"

"He is being kept on as a special consultant. An expert in Perishables, as it were." Rattlebag eyed the rest of them in turn. "The three of you will complete your First Form on the usual schedule, no matter that you took top prize in the Spirit Trials."

It was both disappointing and an utter relief.

"But we get to stay at school?" Snout said.

Rattlebag nodded. "Now, off with you. The Spirit Trials are still on-going, despite the, shall we say, legendary disruption this morning." A hint of amusement tugged at the professor's lips. He was stern and often frightening, but Ace would wager Professor Rattlebag liked the mischief Ace and his friends undertook.

Bathwater, Snout, and Pudding offered their thanks and ran off, no doubt headed for the rugby pitch.

Ace stayed behind a moment. "Why did you stand up for us, professor? You had a chance to be rid of us."

"Never in my hundreds of years of teaching have I had a student even the least capable of hiding a Perishable in plain sight. You have potential. I'd hate to see that wasted."

"You like us," Ace said. "Admit it."

Rattlebag's expression hardened once more. "Do not press your luck."

Ace snapped a salute and sauntered down the same path his friends had taken. There were four of them now. Four friends with years of mischief ahead of them and a professor who, despite his gruffness, would take their part.

The afterlife was looking good, indeed.

THE MERCHANT
AND THE ROGUE

by Mr. King

INSTALLMENT I

in which our lonely Heroine is forced to endure the company of a Person with a most Roguish reputation!

In the village of Chippingwich was a confectionary shop where sweets of unparalleled deliciousness were sold by a woman who had not long been a resident. Tallulah O'Doyle's arrival in the picturesque hillside hamlet had gone mostly unnoticed until she opened her shop and became quite quickly a favorite of many villagers. She created and sold peppermints and taffies, anise candies and sweets with soft cream centers. She included cakes and biscuits in her offerings and showed herself quite adept at all that she made. Indeed, she had no equal in the matter of confectionary delights.

Alas, her life was not nearly so honeyed as the sweets she sold! Tallulah was quite alone in the world, without parents or siblings, without the dear friends she'd known when she was young, without the beloved granny who had raised her on tales of the Fae and warnings of creatures lurking some-where between myth and reality. Tallulah now lived far from her childhood home in Ireland, far from the familiar paths and fields she'd daily traversed. To England she'd come to build a new life, and, for all her show of bravery and determination, she was lonely and terribly uncertain.

"Lemon drops, please, Miss Tallulah." Seven-year-old Belinda Morris clinked a ha'penny onto the shop counter, the top of her head barely visible.

"Not peppermints?" That was Belinda's usual choice of sweets.

"Marty likes lemon drops."

Tallulah leaned forward across the counter, the better to see the dear child. "And he has convinced you to try them?"

She shook her head. "He don't have a ha'penny. I'm sharin' with him." Her eyes darted toward the shop window.

Little Marty, near in age to Belinda, stood on the other side of the glass, watching with a look of earnest worry. She knew his family was not particularly flush; the sweets he purchased now and then came dear to him. That this girl, whose situation was not much better, would buy *his* favorite in order to brighten his day . . . Dear, kind Belinda!

"Perhaps I could give you three lemon drops and three small peppermint sweets," Tallulah said. "Then you would both have your favorite."

"How many candies is that?" Belinda asked.

"Count them on your fingers, dear."

Belinda did, her lips moving silently. "Six! But I usually only get four with a ha'penny."

Tallulah simply smiled. She pulled three of each candy from the glass display jars on the nearby shelf and wrapped them in a small bit of paper. "You are a good-hearted girl, Belinda," she said, handing the prized sweets over the counter. "And a very good friend, indeed."

"Oh, thank you, Miss Tallulah!" She skipped from the shop. Her exchange with Marty was visible through the windows, an innocent bit of kindness. A mere moment later, Marty rushed into the shop and behind the counter.

He threw his arms around Tallulah's waist. "Thank you, Miss Tallulah."

"Make certain you thank Belinda. 'Twas her ha'penny."

"I will, Miss Tallulah. I promise!"

He rushed out and rejoined his friend. Tallulah smiled at the sight and, after they'd slipped from view, at the memory. She'd once had dear friends like that as well. She was gaining acquaintances in Chippingwich, but she was often lonely. And far too often alone.

As she wiped down the counter, she allowed her thoughts to whirl in the winds of time, carrying her back to Ireland and the life she'd lived there. It had always been home to her. Could this tiny village feel that way? Could she find home again? How heavy was her heart with so difficult a question resting upon it!

The shop door opened once more, and the local squire stepped inside. Tallulah did not know him well. He spent far more time at the pub than the confectionary shop, a not unusual preference amongst the men of the village. Mr. Carman was a man of great influence and importance in the village.

Tallulah greeted him in a tone of deference. "Welcome, Mr. Carman. How may I help you?"

With a flick of his red cape, the squire placed himself at the counter but somehow seemed to fill the entirety of the shop. He wore a hat in the same shade of crimson. Tallulah had never seen him without either accessory. It made him quite easy to identify. As did the almost putrid smell of him. Tallulah struggled against the urge to hold her nose when he was nearby. Yet, no one else seemed the least bothered.

"I am hosting a fine family who are passing through the area, and I am in need of a very elegant cake."

"Of course." Tallulah jotted down his requirements for flavor, size, and style, and the time and date he would need it.

While they discussed the particulars, the door opened yet again. For a moment, she was entirely distracted from her purpose. The man who had just entered was known to her by reputation, and that reputation was not an entirely angelic one.

Royston Prescott was known for two things. First, he was the local haberdasher and quite good at what he did. Second, he had a reputation for being a rogue. Not a true scoundrel or someone a person ought to be afraid of. Rather, he was playful and mischievous. He made trouble, but in a way that people liked him all the more. Liked him, but perhaps did not entirely trust him. He was known to flirt with any and every female he came across. He was known to joke when he ought to have been serious, to take lightly those things which ought to be taken quite seriously.

Tallulah was not afraid of him. She doubted anyone truly was. But he was a rogue and a flirt. Men of that sort were best taken with an enormous grain of salt.

"I will be with you in a moment," she said.

He smiled a very personable smile and accepted his lot.

To the squire, she said, "Have you any other requirements for—"

A sound echoed off the walls—a gurgling noise that sent shivers down her spine.

Neither the squire nor Mr. Prescott seemed to have heard it. Odd.

She gathered her wits and tried once more. "Have you any other requirements for your cake?"

"Let me see your list, and I will make certain it is correct." He reached for the paper.

For just a moment, Tallulah thought she glimpsed, not a hand, but a claw. She looked again and saw nothing out of the ordinary. Her gaze shifted to his face, but the shadows of his hat hid most of it. An uncomfortable sensation tiptoed over her, but she dismissed it. Her mind, no doubt, was playing tricks on her.

"All is in order," the squire said. "How fortunate the village is to have you. Do you mean to make your home here permanently?"

"I do hope so," she said.

The squire, despite having posed the question, did not seem entirely pleased with the answer. Odd, that. He *had* said the village was fortunate to have her.

He stepped back from the counter and past Mr. Prescott. The two exchanged looks that were not easily discernible. Tallulah couldn't tell if the two men were on friendly terms or if 'twas animosity she sensed between them. The squire's crimson cape fluttered behind him as he left the shop.

Mr. Prescott stepped up to the counter. Even his swagger held a heavy hint of self-admiration.

Fortunately, Tallulah was rather immune to such things. She too could flirt and make lighthearted conversation. And she was known to toss about an expert bit of banter. But she was unlikely to fall under the spell of a scoundrel.

"You seem to have secured the patronage of our most significant local personage," Mr. Prescott said.

"And it appears I'm soon to have the patronage of our town's most *flirtatious* local personage."

He tipped her a crooked smile, one complete with a twinkle of the eye and a raise of an eyebrow. "My reputation precedes me."

"And what reputation might that be?"

The man chuckled lightly, far from offended. "You cannot deny that I have a reputation."

"I don't intend to deny any such thing. I simply wondered if *you* are aware of what is said of you."

He leaned an elbow against the counter, watching her with a gaze that was at once curious and assessing. "Let me see if I can sum it up. I am a man of exceptional taste. I run a successful business. I am quick with a word of praise, predisposed toward finding beauty in everything around me. I enjoy banter and flirting, but all the women in the village are warned not to take me too seriously."

It was, in all honesty, a good summary of what she'd heard.

"You've left something off," she said.

He tipped his head to one side, clearly attempting to sort out what he might have left out.

Tallulah went about her business, wiping the counters and removing finger smudges from the glass displays about the shop, not offering him the least clue.

"You have baffled me, Miss O'Doyle," he said. "What aspect of my rumored character have I omitted?"

"You neglected to mention the weakness you have for sweets, and"—she motioned to the colorful display on the wall behind her—"your intention to buy a great many confections while you're here."

That brought the smile to his face once more. Oh, he had an intriguing smile indeed! His reputation was widely spoken of, as was his ability to cut quite a fine dash. The fact that he was handsome and personable was mentioned at every opportunity. Yet, even with all of these warnings, Tallulah found herself ill-prepared for the impact of his roguish smile and knee-weakening good looks.

She would do well to be on her guard with this one.

INSTALLMENT II
in which an Unkind Deed causes sorrow in Innocent and Roguish hearts alike!

Royston Prescott could not understand why he was so very bothered that the local confectionery merchant didn't seem to care much for him. He'd heard talk of Miss Tallulah O'Doyle and had been intrigued over the weeks since her arrival. At long last, his curiosity had gotten the better of him, and he had slipped in to discover for himself if what he'd heard of it was true.

The children in the village adored her, proclaiming her the kindest lady of their acquaintance. Many throughout the area applauded her generosity. A few expressed some concerns that her tender heart would make it more difficult to turn a profit, but overall, she was declared an excellent addition to the shops at the market cross.

He had seen her about town, always from a distance. She was lovely, animated, and seemed a decidedly happy sort of person. He also saw in her something he recognized: loneliness. There was a certain melancholy resting deep in her eyes that spoke of someone who felt out of place, longed for someone to recognize what she struggled with.

She had taken up his banter readily and had thrown back as many quips as he had tossed at her. She was funny and clever, and he appreciated that. But it had become quickly obvious that she saw him as everyone else did—as he made certain everyone else did—dismissing him as little more than a hopeless scoundrel bent on shallow and meaningless interactions.

It shouldn't have bothered him, but it did.

He stepped inside her shop two days after his initial visit and found the place quite busy. She, of course, had children inside staring longingly at the jars of colorful candies and displays of petits fours. This was a place of dreams for young, poor children. How easily she could have made it torturous for them, but she didn't. When a child produced a ha'penny or, if they were particularly blessed, a pence, she helped them select the very best assortment of candies.

"You're very kind to our little ones," Mrs. Morris said. "We've never before had a confectionary shop in town. Your corner of Chippingwich has become a place of dreams."

"*My* dreams as much as anyone else's," Miss O'Doyle said. "I like the baking and making, and the children are a delight to have about. And the town is proving right friendly, which I'm needing being so far from m' home."

"Perhaps this'll become a home to you." Mrs. Morris echoed the words of the squire from two days earlier, but *she* sounded sincere.

"Miss Tallulah." Georgie Kent, one of many children in Chippingwich seen pouring in and out of the shop, held a ha'penny up to her. "Anise candy, please, Miss Tallulah."

She accepted the coin. "You are in luck, Georgie. Anise candy is reduced in price today. You'll get an extra piece."

Georgie bounced in place, his eyes pulling nearly as wide as his grin. He left, as so many did, utterly delighted with their local confectioner.

"Mr. Prescott," Miss O'Doyle greeted, his turn having arrived. "What may I do for you?"

"I have heard quite a lot of praise for your petits fours." He offered what he knew was a very winning smile. "I simply must judge for myself."

"You realize, of course, I will charge *you* the full price."

He pretended to be affronted. "Am I not endearing enough to be granted the Adorable Village Youngster price?"

She made quite a show of regretting the necessary answer. "Even were you endearing, you would be disqualified on account of your advanced age."

Oh, she was a delight!

"Do you not offer generous pricing to the exceptionally aged?"

"The shock might send you into your somewhat early grave."

He tipped her a flirtatious glance. "I'd be willing to take the risk."

She quoted him the usual price, but with a laugh in her eyes he felt certain was answered in his. He purchased two petits fours and sat at one of the two dainty tables in the establishment set there for the use of the customers. He would enjoy watching her interact with the villagers as he ate the tiny cakes. There was something very calming and pleasant about Miss Tallulah O'Doyle. Even one such as him could appreciate that.

Before any of the little ones or their parents could request their preferred sweet or baked good, Squire Carman slid inside, making his way directly to the counter. He was not one to wait his turn. Neither was he one for any variety in his clothing. Always the red hat and cape. At times, like this day, he wore a crimson waistcoat as well.

"I've come for the cake I commissioned," he said.

"Of course."

Miss O'Doyle turned to the curtained cooling cabinet in the corner and pulled from a low shelf a queen cake, dusted liberally with confectioners' sugar and decorated with candied fruit. Sugar came dear. This offering, elegant and no doubt delicious, would not be inexpensive. Of all the people in Chippingwich, only Clancy Carman could afford such an indulgence.

The cake was set on the counter before him. The other customers looked on in awe. It was a beautiful creation, one sure to inspire envy in the hearts of everyone not permitted to partake. The squire's lofty guests would be duly impressed.

Was Miss O'Doyle? Or did she see the squire for what he truly was?

"This is not what I asked for." Mr. Carman eyed the baked marvel in much the way one would a decaying corpse.

"It *is* what you asked for," Miss O'Doyle replied, calm yet firm.

Mr. Carman raised his chin to an authoritatively arrogant angle. "I remember my requirements precisely."

She opened the drawer directly beside her and pulled out a slip of paper. "And *I* wrote down your requirements." She held the paper so he could see the writing thereon. "Which of these demands does the cake fail to meet?"

The shop had gone quite still and as near to silent as two children and four adults could be. The squire was not known to be a generous man, and many people whispered a warning about his temper. Miss O'Doyle might not have known that.

"If your list"—he sneered out the word—"matches what you have just placed on this counter, then you wrote down my requirements incorrectly."

"I did not."

"Are you calling me a liar?"

The snap in his tone silenced Miss O'Doyle. She watched him, brows drawn, expression both confused and concerned.

"The cake is a disappointment," Mr. Carman said, an infuriating veneer of satisfaction touching every inch of his face, "but I haven't time to obtain a replacement. I'll pay you half."

"Half?" Miss O'Doyle's eyes opened so wide one would not have been surprised if they simply fell from her head. "I paid more than that just for the ingredients."

Carman was unmoved. "You are fortunate I am willing to pay you *at all*."

Miss O'Doyle's eyes darted about the room, clearly searching for someone who could help her make sense of this turn of events. Royston left his petits fours on the table and moved with feigned disinterest to the counter, stopping behind it, beside her, and addressed the baffled woman in a low voice.

"He has done this before. I doubt we've a merchant in the entire market cross that hasn't had him balk at some purchase or another."

She kept her voice to a whisper like his. "He's claimed disappointment at your haberdashery? I find that difficult to believe; you do have a reputation."

A corner of his mouth tugged in an unfeigned show of amused pleasure. "Let us simply say he has saved a great deal of money in my shop."

"And no one ever fights him on it?" she asked.

"He is powerful. It has generally seemed best not to rock the boat."

"Until the boat capsizes," she said.

"What are you two whispering about?" Squire Carman demanded.

Royston looked over his shoulder at the weaselly man. "I was telling Miss O'Doyle that I am enjoying the tiny cakes I just bought from her."

The squire's gaze narrowed on him, and a chill washed through the room. Mr. Carman had that effect. The people of Chippingwich could not say precisely why, but he made everyone uncomfortable in eerie and disconcerting ways.

"Does he ever grow violent?" Tallulah asked in an even quieter whisper than they'd been employing.

"No one doubts him capable of it," Royston said.

She released a small, heavy breath. "I suppose some payment for the cake is better than none. And it would afford me time to decide what I mean to do moving forward."

He nodded, not necessarily to give approval of that particular course of action over any other but as a means of acknowledging that she had chosen a path.

Miss O'Doyle looked once more to the squire; Royston got out of the way.

"Have you come to your senses?" Mr. Carman asked.

"I have come to the realization that I am neglecting my other customers by prolonging this transaction." Miss O'Doyle held her hand out for the meager coins she had been offered.

The squire dropped the coins not in her upturned palm but on the counter before taking up his ill-gotten cake and leaving with a smug air.

The other villagers present in the shop stood frozen on the spot. Carman held enough sway to inspire wariness, and he was enough of a fiend to inspire fear. He was not missed when he left a place and gained few friends by arriving.

How would their relatively newly arrived confectioner respond to the man who'd been making life miserable in Chippingwich for years? Would she rant and rage? Weep and crumble? Loudly decry the unfairness of it all? They were reasonable reactions, each and every one.

She did none of those, however. She simply looked out over the gathered customers, her dignity firmly in place, and said, "Next, please."

INSTALLMENT III

in which our Heroine makes a most shocking
Discovery about the Town in which she lives!

The squire's refusal to pay for his cake put Tallulah's ledgers in tremendous jeopardy. Two nights in a row she spent hours searching for a means of recovering from the financial blow he'd dealt her. If she was quite careful, she could manage it, but she could not endure another swindling from the man. And yet, Mr. Royston Prescott had indicated this was a common practice for the local squire.

Under normal circumstances, she would not have selected a known tease as a primary source of information on such serious matters, but Mr. Prescott had shown her a degree of support that had surprised her. He'd not told her what to do, neither had he defended the squire. He was the closest thing to an ally she had.

She closed up her shop a little early, two days after the incident with the cake, and made her way down the road to the haberdashery shop where she knew she would find him.

She stepped inside and found the establishment empty, though she knew he did excellent business. But Fate was smiling on her. She'd found him at a time when he was not overly busy.

He looked up as she entered. A flirtatious smile spread across his face. "Miss O'Doyle. Have you come to purchase a waistcoat?"

"Wouldn't I be quite the sight? Walking up and down the market cross while dressed in men's clothing?"

The twinkle in his eye told her the possibility did not, in fact, horrify him. Why this brought her pleasure, she couldn't say. Most any other man would have offered words, however hollow, of horror at the idea, accompanied by lofty praises of her femininity. He simply looked more roguish.

Her first impressions of him were proving accurate: he was a rogue, but not the threatening or dangerous variety. In fact, she found herself sorely tempted to smile along with him.

"I've come to ask you a question," she said.

"As I'm not currently inundated with customers, this would be an excellent time to ask any and every question you might have."

"You say that as if you hope my question will be something overbold."

He shrugged elegantly and walked with careful and graceful strides to where she stood. He leaned a hand on the table, tipping his posture ever so slightly askew, granting him a casual connectedness to her that might've been a touch too familiar for an ordinary man. It seemed almost subdued for a rascal.

"What is your question, Miss Tallulah O'Doyle?" He even said her name in a way that was a touch scandalous. And, heaven help her, she liked it.

Forcing herself to focus on the business at hand, she asked, "Why is it that the squire has been permitted to mistreat so many for so long? Why has no one tried to stop him?"

His eyes narrowed, and his head tilted. "Why do you assume no one has ever tried?"

How *had* she come to that conclusion? "At my shop when the squire declared he meant to cheat me, not a single person looked surprised or outraged. And you said he'd done this before. I suppose I assumed it'd been ongoing long enough that it would've been stopped by now if enough effort had been made."

Royston shrugged. His posture and expression remained quite casual for one discussing a tortured town. "Your assessment, then, is that Chippingwich hasn't tried hard enough."

"Or that even the best efforts haven't managed the thing."

"Well sorted," he said.

She folded her arms, not in a show of defiance but in a match to his playful posture. "I believe you will find I'm terribly clever."

"Are you?"

She took the slightest step closer to him, lowering her voice a bit. "Clever enough to know that you're not telling me everything."

The smile he offered was playful. Was he ever anything other than devil-may-care? He'd shown her concern in her shop while the squire was there, but that had been fleeting and not without a heavy hint of impishness.

He motioned her toward the table not too far distant. It was where he, no doubt, took orders from his customers and offered his customers' companions a place to rest while they waited.

She took the seat he offered her. He sat beside her, sitting with as much swagger as he employed when on his feet. "What would you like to know? Your every wish is my cherished command." Had her hand been within reach, he likely would have kissed it. The man never stopped flirting. Tallulah hoped he'd be serious long enough to explain a few things about Chippingwich.

"Am I the only one who finds the squire's company . . . rattling?" She wasn't explaining her feelings very well. "He makes me feel as though I'm about to crawl out of m' skin."

"I don't know a soul who doesn't find his presence uncomfortable," Royston said.

"And not merely on account of his odor?"

That brought confusion to the man's expression. "Does he smell strange to you?"

"Doesn't he to *you*?"

Royston didn't answer, but narrowed his gaze further, as if trying to make sense of her confusion. She didn't dare ask if he heard noises when the squire was about. Tallulah did quite regularly. Mostly, it was a gurgling sound, but sometimes, though, she heard a distant, echoing laughter that sent chills down her spine.

"Someone has obviously tried to stop the squire, but hasn't succeeded," she said. "What was tried? And who did the trying?"

"I've been here two years now, and there's only been one attempt I know of to thwart Mr. Carman," he said. "His reign of terror was a well-known and well-established thing by the time I arrived."

"And who was the person who stood up to him?"

"The man who owned the shop that you now claim as your own."

A weight settled on her heart. Her shop had become available, she knew, not because the previous owner had grown too old for running it, nor because he had moved to a larger or different location. It had been available because it had been empty.

"Was his opposition to the squire the reason he lost his shop?"

"Not exactly."

Not exactly. "What happened to him?"

Mr. Prescott released a breath before he answered. "No one knows."

"He disappeared?"

A slow nod answered her quavering question.

Cheating the local merchants was not, then, the true threat they all faced. 'Twas little wonder Squire Carman held such power over them all.

"I'd not realized how difficult the situation was."

"I did tell you that day in your shop that he's believed to be violent."

She rubbed at her forehead. "I didn't take your warning entirely seriously." She felt her cheeks flush at that admission. She did try not to judge people too quickly, yet she'd done precisely that with him. He seemed to be a rather shallow, swaggering blatherskite, so she'd assumed everything he said was somewhat empty.

The shop door opened, pulling both their eyes in that direction. Kirby Padmore, the proprietor of the local pub, shuffled inside, his expression as weary as ever yet still maintaining kindness and welcome. He was the reason his pub was so popular a destination.

Mr. Prescott rose and crossed to the new arrival, strutting as always. "How may I help you, Kirby?"

"I'm in need of new shirtsleeves," he said. "I've ruined my last."

Mr. Prescott crossed to the ceiling-tall shelves along the back wall, shelves that held a tremendous amount of fabric, but he did not pull out a bolt. Instead, he reached behind one particularly wobbly pile and removed an already sewn shirt.

Kirby accepted it.

"What did he toss at you this time?" Royston asked.

"Guinness."

Mr. Prescott looked to Tallulah. "I hope that doesn't pain you too much, hearing of this senseless waste of a drink your country holds in such esteem."

"I might be pained, were I not so confused."

Kirby sighed. "The squire's temper can run a touch hot. When he's put out with me, he has a tendency to douse me with whatever happens to be in his glass."

'Twasn't difficult to imagine that scenario. "Does he grow 'put out' with you on account of you asking him to pay his bar tab?"

"That's generally the trigger."

A plague, indeed. "You must miss the years before he was the squire."

"I've never known a time when he was not," Kirby said.

The man was noticeably older than Mr. Carman. Kirby, like Mr. Prescott, must have come from elsewhere.

"How long have you been in Chippingwich?" she asked.

Kirby paid Mr. Prescott for the shirt that had been waiting for him, no doubt a long-standing arrangement between the men. "I've lived here all my life." With that, he slipped from the shop.

All his life?

Kirby was seventy if he was a day. Mr. Carman didn't look a day over forty, yet he'd been squire throughout Kirby's memory.

How was that possible?

INSTALLMENT IV

in which the Threat to the village reveals itself in Terrifying ways!

Tallulah watched for the squire as the days passed. She hadn't the least doubt he would return, and she needed to decide how she meant to respond. Knowing he was, by all estimations, at least eighty years old despite appearing to be only half that, she knew there was something otherworldly about him. That explained the putrid air that hung about him, and the unnerving noises that seemed to follow him about.

Her gran had told her stories of the Fae, of monsters and fairies and mysterious beings. If the squire belonged to *that* world, then he was dangerous in a way no one comprehended. And yet, refusing to stand up to him simply allowed him to hurt the village all the more. He would continue his reign of terror if he was left unchecked.

"You must know what it is you're facing," Gran had said. "To unknowingly cross paths with the Fae is a danger greater than any human can imagine."

But what was he? She wasn't at all certain, and saints knew she needed to be.

Belinda and Marty stepped inside, their eyes immediately on the colorful displays of candies.

She adored the children of Chippingwich. "What's it to be today, loves?"

"We want to try anise candies," Belinda announced. "Georgie likes them."

"He does, indeed." She set a ha'penny's worth of anise candies on a slip of paper and folded it up, trading the sweets for their coin.

"Do you have any new candies, Miss Tallulah?" Marty seldom spoke, and when he did so, he was very quiet.

Tallulah kept her own voice gentle and calm when answering. "I have chocolate-covered almonds. They come very dear, though, so we'll have to save those for a very special treat."

Marty nodded, eagerly eyeing the folded paper in his friend's hand. The two little ones would most likely have the anise candy eaten long before reaching either of their homes.

A flurry of red announced the squire's arrival. He slid into the shop with all the arrogance of someone who knows he will not be challenged or denied what he wishes for. Tallulah didn't know what he had come to demand this time, but it was clear he believed he had won already.

The children inched quickly away from the counter, watching the squire's approach with a deep-seated wariness. They were, no doubt, all too familiar with the sort of person he was. Tallulah kept her posture straight and her demeanor sure.

The squire likely did not know she had pieced together that he belonged to the world of the Fae. She hid her discomfort with his smell; she ignored the distant laughter.

"What can I do for you, sir?" she asked in a tone that was as neutral as she could make it.

"I have decided to give you the opportunity to redeem yourself," he said.

He meant to humble and humiliate her before making his demands, did he? Well, she didn't mean to allow him.

"Whatever do you mean by that?" she asked.

"I was referring to the cake," he said.

"I do recall the cake, but I do not understand the reference you're making." She understood completely, but giving him the impression that it was of so little consequence that she had already forgotten might take a bit of the wind out of his sails.

"The cake you produced was a failure," he said. "I am certain you remember that muddle."

She pursed her lips in a confused frown. "I do not recall a failed cake."

He eyed her more closely. The man, no doubt, wasn't certain what to make of her. Good. If he were upended, he might not be quite so sure of himself. Lack of confidence might render him less dangerous. Perhaps he'd even offer a clue as to who or *what* he truly was.

"I'm here to place another order," he said. "I have decided to be generous since you are new in the village, and it is the job of a squire to see to the good of his people, even if it means risking another disaster."

"I don't understand," she said, still feigning innocence.

His narrowed gaze grew bewildered and increasingly annoyed. She would do well to tread lightly.

"That ridiculous haberdasher said that your petits fours were well done. I should like to place an order for enough of those to impress visitors who are coming to Chippingwich. I will be hosting them in two days' time, and I should warn you they are not easily impressed."

"I'm afraid that will not be possible," she said.

For a moment, he said nothing. Then, in a bit of irony she struggled not to smile at, he repeated the same words that, coming from her, had so frustrated him a moment earlier. "I don't understand."

"You've declared my cake was a failure. I'd not see you disappointed again."

"I have told you I am generously willing to allow you another opportunity."

She shook her head. "I have learned my lesson, Squire Carman. I am simply not talented enough to provide someone of your eminence with confectioneries for your exalted guests. You had best ride to the nearest village with its own confectionery shop."

The entire shop fell silent. She wasn't certain the children were even breathing.

"You would rather not make money?" he asked through a tight jaw.

"On the contrary." The last time, he had paid her only a portion of what he'd promised for the cake. It would not surprise her in the least if he decided that the petits fours ought to be complementary. He would find some reason to argue that they were not worth paying for. She refused to be swindled again.

"As I said, there will be no confectioneries for you to pay for. You will simply have to go elsewhere."

"You are refusing?" The squire asked the question in so tense a tone that she felt some of her courage flee. But no. Someone had to stand up to him.

"It appears I *am* refusing." The declaration emerged firmer and surer than she had anticipated. She was proud of the steadiness of her voice. The children, however, did not seem to feel quite so much confidence. They bolted for the door and out onto the street.

"No one in this village has the audacity to oppose me," the squire said.

Something in the air changed. Literally. It was colder, heavier. Her very breath sounded different. Her voice likely would as well, but she refused to stay silent.

"I've not improved as a baker in the last few days. Nothing I make is likely to meet with your approval, so it makes no sense for me to bake you anything else. It's for your own good, and for the good of the impression you hope to make on your distinguished guests, that you obtain what you wish for from a shop that you trust."

"I am not the one who ought to be concerned with what is in my best interest."

Tallulah set her hands on the counter, feeling the shift in the balance of things. She had the oddest sensation of not being entirely stable on the ground.

"Now," the squire said in a tone that could never be mistaken for patience, "do you intend to take the order I have come to place?"

The fear she felt growing inside insisted she bow to his demands. He was frightening, and powerful. If she didn't stand up to him, she doubted anyone ever would.

She swallowed. Breathed. And pushed on. "You will have to place your order elsewhere."

The displeasure in his eyes grew quickly to fury. The very ground beneath them began to shake. Items on shelves shifted and moved, jumping dangerously about. A glass bowl of candies fell to the floor and shattered.

Confections flew from shelves and boxes, landing in ruined heaps on the floor.

All the while, the squire watched her, unblinking. The hatred in his eyes gave them an unholy glow. One she was nearly certain was literal. Literal and heated and radiating red.

The glass in the window wobbled, an unnerving rolling motion she knew glass was not meant to make.

The squire's expression twisted with hatred. And with it, his face changed. It seemed to pull, elongate, grow misshapen.

Faster and faster the window shook and waved. More and more grotesque grew the squire's face.

Then—a cracking sound.

Tallulah dove to the ground, her head tucked in and her arms covering herself as much as she could manage. In the very next instant, a blast of air shook the space and the window gave, showering her and the shop with shards of wood and glass.

"You, Tallulah O'Doyle, have made a very grave error."

From her position ducked behind the counter, she heard the sound of the squire's exiting footfalls, crunching on the bits of glass and candies and debris strewn about the floor.

She remained there, curled in a ball, shaken more than she cared to admit. He had done this. He had done it while standing in place, and without causing himself the least harm. Though she was uninjured, she suspected he could have hurt her if he'd wished to. It was a warning, an easier consequence than what he would likely inflict the next time.

All was quiet in the shop. She could hear nothing beyond the sound of her breathing and the wind whistling in through the broken window. She was grateful the children had already left the shop. How many others in town would know soon enough what had happened? Her determination to help them by standing firm might simply have made them more afraid, put them in more danger.

"Tallulah?" Someone was calling her name. The sound of glass crunching beneath heavy footsteps told her the speaker was in the shop. "Tallulah, are you hurt?"

Royston Prescott. She recognized his voice now. And she felt better.

Slowly, carefully, she stood once more. Glass and bits of cake and biscuits and candies rolled off her as she straightened.

"All the market cross saw your window shatter," he said. "And even before the squire stepped out, we knew what had happened."

"You knew he had this power?" She tried not to let her fear show, but she was not at all certain she'd succeeded.

He nodded. "None of us knows where his abilities come from, but we have all had our own experience with them. He is a dangerous man."

"He is *not* a man. I know enough of the Fae to know he is some variety of monster."

Royston brushed bits of debris from her shoulders with his gloved hands. "Whatever he is, he's dangerous."

"All the more reason none of us can face him alone."

He looked her in the eyes. "This has not scared you off? Hasn't convinced you to stop trying?"

"If the children had still been in here when he did this, they might have been hurt or worse. I cannot shrug and walk away simply because I'm afraid. It's time this village escaped the grip of whatever the squire truly is."

A smile spread across Royston's handsome face. "Kirby said he was certain you wouldn't flinch. I'm happy he was right. Chippingwich has been waiting a long time for someone like you."

INSTALLMENT V

in which terrifying Secrets are revealed about
the grave Danger facing the Village!

Bob Kent stood in the doorway, looking over the destruction. "She stood firm?"

Royston nodded.

"Is it time to try again?" Bob asked.

"I believe it might be." He looked to Tallulah. "Are you injured?"

"No, but I'll likely be a bit bruised." She watched them both, clearly confused and curious.

"We'll see to this." Bob motioned to the mess. "Best consult with ol' Kirby. This may be our best chance."

"Kirby Padmore?" Tallulah asked Royston.

"He knows more of this than any of us, and you need to understand it better as well."

Royston offered her his hand, unsure if she would accept, but there was not even a moment of hesitation on her part. She set her hand in his and walked with him through the broken glass and scattered confections and splintered wood—all that remained of her once-impressive shop.

Just outside, a crowd had gathered, looking at the blown-in window and debris with a heaviness that spoke of familiarity. Whether Tallulah realized it or not, this had happened before.

He walked with her, their fingers entwined. She was quiet, not surprising considering the harrowing experience she'd passed through.

"Are you certain you are not injured? There was a fearful amount of glass strewn about."

She nodded. "I was not hurt, but I am worried all the same."

He met her heavy gaze. "This village harbors a terrible secret, Tallulah. Kirby can explain it all far better than I can."

They stepped into the pub. Royston glanced around, wanting to make certain the squire was not present, but only Kirby was there. Someone must have whispered to the proprietor the details of all that had happened at the sweets shop because he didn't appear the least surprised at their arrival.

"Revealed himself, did he?" Kirby asked.

"Aye," Royston answered, "though how much, I'm not certain."

Kirby motioned them to a small table tucked up near the low-burning fire. Royston saw Tallulah seated, then sat himself.

"I'd already sorted out that Mr. Carman is some sort of creature." Tallulah jumped straight into the matter at hand. "When you said a few days ago that he'd been squire here for as long as you could remember, I knew there had to be something otherworldly about him. And, blessed saints, the smell of him." She grimaced. "He can toss noises around, make a body hear things that aren't there. All that confirmed my suspicions. But after what he did in my shop today . . ." She wrapped her arms around herself as a shudder shook her frame. "He is something other than a man," she whispered. "I'll not be convinced otherwise."

"Because of the damage he did?" Royston pressed. It was crucial they know precisely what the squire had revealed of himself to her.

"Yes, but more than that." Her gaze darted from Kirby to Royston and back. "His eyes glowed. I realize that sounds ridiculous, but they did. They glowed red."

Royston looked to Kirby. "She saw his eyes glow."

"So did you," Kirby reminded him.

"We tried then," Royston said. "We must try again now."

"Begging your pardon," Tallulah said with a bit of dryness in her voice, "but I'd like to be part of this conversation, especially considering it's meant to be about me."

He couldn't help a laugh no matter the heaviness of their topic. "A thousand apologies, my dear." Royston then dipped his head to Kirby. "If you'd be so good as to explain to our fair companion."

"Even in a time such as this, you flirt," she said to Royston with a smile.

"Is that a complaint?"

Her eyes twinkled as she shook her head. "Not in the least."

Oh, he did like her. Royston set his hand atop hers, and she threaded their fingers together once more. As her fingers bent around his, small scratches pulled, tiny bubbles of blood emerging from some. He hoped she had no further injuries.

Calm as could be, Tallulah turned to Kirby. "Tell me what we are facing."

"My father first told me when I was very young about the creature. He has lived in these parts for an age, though we do not believe he originated here. Many a tale has been told of cruel tricks and dastardly doings perpetrated by him. He fools people into doing embarrassing or dangerous things. He destroys crops, buildings, belongings. As near as I've been able to tell, he began his reign as our local squire on a lark and discovered he liked it—liked the ability to do mischief and to cause terror."

"And does he play such dastardly tricks on his exalted visitors as well?" Tallulah asked.

Royston breathed a small sigh of relief. That Tallulah had not dismissed the otherworldly explanation out of hand was a good sign.

"We aren't certain what becomes of his visitors. It is whispered about that he can change people into other forms, at least temporarily. There is some worry that he might . . . eat people."

"Then why order baked confections to impress them if he means only to do them harm and—" The question halted and understanding dawned in her expression. "In order to inflict his mischief upon *me*."

Kirby nodded. "And he doesn't take well to being irritated or ruffled. His tricks are to be endured without complaint else his ire be earned."

"The citizens hereabout, I've discovered," Royston said, "do not see his glowing red eyes, even when he is using his ability to blow open doors or break windows or such things. Only you and I have ever seen that."

"And we both come from somewhere other than this village," Tallulah said.

"That, we believe, is a clue to his origins," Kirby said. "He has remained here so long because he can do so in disguise. Only the arrival of outsiders threatens to reveal his true shape and form."

"It was not merely his eyes that changed," Tallulah said. "In his most angry moment, I felt certain his nose and face elongated, pulling out almost into a triangular snout, almost like a—"

"A rat?" Royston finished the thought in unison with her.

Her wide eyes turned on him, and she nodded.

"When angry, he also has a tail," Royston said. "It is hidden beneath his cloak and, I suspect, cannot be seen by any of the villagers."

"Rat features," she repeated in a contemplative whisper. "Does he ever *not* wear his red cap and cloak?"

"Never," Kirby said.

"He has rat-like features, plays dastardly tricks, smells of something rotten, produces unnerving noises, and, I suspect, no one has ever seen him eat."

Royston looked to Kirby, unsure of the answer.

"He's thrown back many a pint in here," Kirby said, "but never have I seen him eat so much as a crust of bread."

Tallulah tapped her free hand on the table. "He's a *fear dearg*, I'd bet m' life on it."

"A far darrig?" Royston repeated the words phonetically, not being at all certain what they meant.

"'Tis a lone Fae, a solitary creature, and not one at all inclined toward friendliness. These monsters are known to play horrid, often cruel, tricks on humans. They look like humans except for their rat-like fur, face, and tail. And they always wear red: sometimes limiting themselves to a cloak and cap, sometimes wearing red from top to tail, as it were. In Irish, *fear dearg* translates to the Crimson Man, named so on account of the color they always wear."

"Any idea why it is that we, who are from here, cannot see the squire in his true monstrous form?" Kirby asked.

"The Fae are connected to their homes in strong and often mystifying ways," Tallulah said. "It could be that tucking himself in this foreign-to-him corner of the world protects him, hides him."

"Could be, could be." Kirby leaned back in his chair, stroking his chin as he pondered. "Royston could see him because he is not from here. And you could as well because your origins lie away from this village."

"Not only away from Chippingwich," Royston said, "but your origins reach back to the country of the *fear dearg*. I'd wager you can see him better than any of us. And perhaps that is why you can smell things we can't and hear things we don't. He cannot hide as entirely from you."

"Have you any idea why he doesn't eat?" Kirby asked.

"The *fear dearg* do eat," Tallulah said.

"Do I dare ask *what*?" Royston had a suspicion it wasn't anything pleasant.

"They eat carrion, carcasses."

"Human?" Kirby asked, his voice small and cracked.

She nodded. "And animal."

A heavy silence filled with uncertainty and worry settled over the all-but-empty pub.

"As far as we have been able to discover," Kirby said, "he cannot be killed. Many have tried, and all have failed."

"He can be," she said, "but only with the right weapon."

"And what weapon would that be?" Kirby sighed, his voice weighed down by years of defeats and frustrations. "We've tried everything we know."

"They can be defeated only with a blade of iron," she said. "Iron is dangerous to most Fae," she said. "'Tis the reason we hang iron horseshoes above a door; not for general luck but to protect ourselves from the Fae."

"Have you tried iron?" Royston asked Kirby.

"I can't say that we have. It isn't a common metal for weapons any longer."

"Can one be obtained?" Tallulah asked.

"I will see to it, but we must be careful about the arranging of it. Should our efforts be discovered . . ."

"I have a shipment of cloth arriving in a few days," Royston said. "We can secret the weapon in that. My disguise will go far to preventing the squire from growing suspicious."

"Your disguise?" Tallulah asked.

"We did not know how to defeat him. And, had he known how well I can see his true form, he'd have killed me, I'm certain."

"What disguise did you assume?" she pressed.

"That of an unreliable, selfish, flirtatious—"

"Rogue," she finished in a tone of realization. "You make yourself seem too frivolous to appear to the squire to be a threat."

"Facing him would require selflessness, and he is certain I have none." A sudden, horrifying thought occurred to him. "Did you let on that you could see what he truly looked like?"

"Not intentionally," she said. "I spent most of that encounter attempting to hide from flying glass."

"You and I alone can see him for what he truly is, though only entirely when he is at his most dangerous. It is for us, then, to face him and free this village of his reign of cruelty and terror. But that is a task fraught with danger. I do not for a moment believe anyone in Chippingwich would hold you to that knowing you did not arrive here with this end in mind."

"Courage that exists only when one has a choice is not courage at all. True bravery lies in facing those dangers one did not expect and is not required to face simply because it is the right thing to do."

"Then we'll face him?"

She nodded. "Together."

INSTALLMENT VI

in which Time runs short and our Heroine is
faced with unfathomable Danger!

The damage to the confectionery shop was significant enough that Tallulah had not the time to resume her candy making or baking despite the passage of three days. The villagers had been remarkably kind and generous. They had begun cleaning while she'd been in the pub learning the horrible truth of their situation. They'd continued their efforts for hours afterward and into the next day. Given time, she'd have the means to replace the glass in the front window. For now, the town had kindly supplied her with enough greased paper to fill the gaping hole left by the squire.

A *fear dearg* of all things. And in England rather than Ireland. The Fae could, of course, travel, but didn't usually go so far afield. Had she encountered in her homeland what she had in Chippingwich, she would have recognized the signs, would have known much sooner what they were facing. Then again, were she in Ireland, *everyone* would have realized what they were facing, and she wouldn't be struggling with the enormity of defeating the monster on her own.

"There are many reasons the Fae avoid the mortal realm, iron being chief among them." She could hear her gran's words in her mind. "Iron bends the Fae. It twists them about, interferes with their magic. The most dangerous among them can only be felled by weapons of iron."

Heaven help them all if Kirby and Royston were unable to obtain an iron axe or sword. *Fear dearg* grew bolder with every bit of mischief and torment. They came to enjoy the misery they caused, yet quickly found it insufficient. They grew worse and worse with time, and this *fear dearg* had been at his current mischief for nearly a century. That the village suspected their monster-turned-squire had killed the last shop owner to push back against him didn't surprise her, but it did worry her. The squire would soon grow quite bold in that respect as well. Chippingwich would move from being tormented to being decimated.

The door, splintered but still functioning, opened. Her heart hammered on the instant but settled when Royston stepped inside.

He sauntered toward her, the same dandified gait he'd employed when first they'd met. It was a disguise; she could see that so clearly now.

"What news have you?" she asked once he'd reached her.

"My shipment of fabrics arrived today," he said. "*Only* the fabrics."

She rubbed at the back of her neck. "Without the remainder of that shipment, we are in dire straits." They simply had to have an iron weapon.

"I do believe Kirby secured what we were looking for. It simply has not reached us yet."

She sighed. "Let us hope we receive that shipment in time."

"And with no indication of what's inside," he added.

Saints, that'd be a disaster. "We cannot risk raising a certain . . . person's suspicions."

He tugged at his lace-edged cuffs. "Tosh. I meant only that it's far more enjoyable to open a packet when one has no idea what might be inside."

How was it she hadn't seen through these antics sooner? He had managed to fool the *fear dearg* but had also pulled the wool over her eyes. "If you have no idea what is inside the packet we are anticipating, then I have concerns about your intelligence."

He chuckled. "Let us hope the squire harbors those same doubts."

"About both of us," she said.

Royston took her hand and raised it to his lips, pressing a warm kiss to the backs of her fingers. "I do not believe I have ever met your equal, Tallulah O'Doyle. You are brave and kind and, yes, intelligent."

"And you, Royston Prescott, are showing yourself to have excellent taste."

Again, he lightly laughed. With obvious reluctance, he slipped his hand from hers and stepped toward the door. "I will watch for our delivery. In the meantime, take care."

"I will say the same to you."

He dipped his head in a flourishing bow. A moment later, he was gone, and she was, once more, alone. Before the squire's destructive visit, her shop had seldom been empty. The villagers, bless them, had continued to come by, to look in on her, to offer what help they could. She loved the people of Chippingwich, and she was determined to free them from the grip of the dangerous monster in their midst, one they could not fully see for what it was.

"What a shame all your customers have fled." A whoosh of red and a waft of putridity accompanied the sardonic observation.

"Mr. Carman," she said, keeping her tone as calm and disinterested as ever. It wouldn't do to tip her hand before they were ready to truly do battle with the monster. "I have not yet begun replacing the candies and sweets and baked goods that were lost when the window broke. I do not know how soon I will do so."

"I only came to offer a friendly greeting." He turned his head toward her as he spoke, a shaft of light spilling across his face. It appeared as a double, both the human visage the villagers saw and the rat-like face of the *fear dearg* beneath. Each face faded in and out, repeatedly replaced by the other. His disguise was breaking down.

"You've offered your greeting," she said. "Now, I need to get back to the matter of repairing m' shop."

Squire Carman made a slow, dramatic turn, eyeing the room with a mock expression of concern. "A shame what happened."

As he turned, his cape rustled, and a rat's tail became momentarily visible. Why was it she was seeing so much more of the monster beneath the disguise? What had changed?

Perhaps knowing what he was made it more difficult to be fooled.

Or, perhaps, just as his mask had first cracked in her presence when he'd grown angry with her, the disguise fell to bits the more upset the *fear dearg* was. And if she was seeing him so clearly, then he was not as calm as he appeared.

"It would be a true shame if more damage occurred here," Mr. Carman said.

"Yes, it would." She held her ground, watching him warily and closely. Heavens, that tail of his wasn't hidden in the least. How odd that only she and Royston could see it.

"And yet, it seems unavoidable." The squire turned back slowly. His eyes glowed as they had before. His human face had grown nearly transparent. His disguise was all but gone.

"What makes it unavoidable?" she asked.

"The way you look at me." The *fear dearg* inched closer, his demonic gaze unblinking and hurling actual physical heat at her. "You hide it well, *bean*." That he called her by the Irish word for *woman* worried her. He understood that his origins in her homeland had offered her insights none of the others had. "You know what I am."

"Irish children are taught young the dangers of the Fae."

"And, yet, you've stumbled right into that danger."

Newly repaired shelves began to rattle. The paper in the window ripped. All the while, the *fear dearg* didn't look away from her, didn't take another step.

"I've a good arrangement here," the monster said. "I'll not let you destroy it."

"I've good friends and neighbors here," she said in return. "I'll not let you destroy them."

"I've not eaten any of them." His mouth turned up in a sinister smile, revealing sharp, jagged teeth. "Yet. But I'm running out of 'distinguished visitors.'"

Once a *fear dearg* discovered a liking for some bit of cruelty, he never lost his taste for it.

If only the iron weapon had arrived! What was she to do?

"Now"—the Crimson Man took a single step closer—"how to rid myself of both you and that ridiculous haberdasher at once."

"What has that rogue to do with anything?"

"He knows what I am, just as I know what he is." The *fear dearg* flipped back one side of his cape. "I suspect I'll have to invite him to cook dinner."

Invite him to cook dinner. She knew what that meant. Every Irish child knew what that meant. Any human invited to cook dinner for a Crimson Man found themselves roasting a fellow human over a spit. And if Royston were invited to cook, she'd no doubt *she* would be the unfortunate main course.

The new position of the squire's cape revealed something Tallulah had not seen him carrying before: a burlap bag. She ought to have known he had one. All *fear dearg* carried them. Always. And always for the same purpose: kidnapping and hauling off their human victims. If she was seeing it now, then she was moments away from being stuffed inside.

"I've delayed this bit of mischief for a long time." Mischief. Not a strong enough word for what she knew would come next when that burlap sack appeared.

There was a means of preventing it, though. She had been told there was. But what was the method? It didn't stop *fear dearg* entirely, but it prevented being kidnapped. Heavens, what was it?

"You played me a dirty trick sending off the little ones." His hand inched back toward his bag. "I *do* know that children are delicious."

It was something she was meant to say. Her gran had told her. 'Twas a particular phrase.

He came closer, reaching for the bag.

What was it? *What was it?*

His free hand reached for her. Once he caught hold, there would be no escape.

Across the years, the voice of her gran whispered to her. Tallulah spoke her words as they entered her thoughts. *"Na dean fochmoid fàin."*

He froze, his expression turning putrid with anger. "That will save you from the confines of my burlap bag, but you may very well wish you were there."

The chairs at the table flew at her. She dove out of the way, only to have something else deal her a blow. She could hear the heavy, scurrying footsteps of the Crimson Man. He couldn't abduct her, but that didn't mean he couldn't kill her.

She groped around until she found something heavy that could fit in her hand—a shattered chair leg. Tallulah rolled enough to lean on her opposite hip and swing the leg with all her might at the *fear dearg*. He nearly toppled but managed to remain on his rat-like feet.

The stumble was enough to grant her time to scramble to her feet, the chair leg—now cracked—still in her hand.

He spun about with a jerk, eyes glowing so brightly the entire shop was lit in red. "I am tiring of these games."

"Perhaps we ought to stop playing."

He shook his head, no longer bearing even a shadow of human shape. "My games end only one way."

"With me on a spit?"

A grotesque grin grew on his rat face. "I *will* enjoy that. I'll have to continue playing after you are gone."

Once *fear dearg* had a taste for something . . .

Royston stepped into the shop. "I propose, rather, *we* continue playing after *you* are gone."

"You will be easier to defeat," the Crimson Man declared. "You haven't the fire of this one."

"Perhaps not, but I do have this." He raised a mighty axe.

The monster was unconcerned. "'Though blade of stone or axe of steel, the Crimson Man you'll never kill.'"

Royston's face filled with pity. "How very misinformed you are."

With a chuckle that sent ripples of dread through every inch of Tallulah, the *fear dearg* threw his rodent head backward in amusement.

"I need him within swinging distance," Royston mouthed.

She circled back, holding her pitiful chair leg with as much confidence as she could muster. The monster eyed her doubtfully, amusedly. She swung the leg with no intention of actually hitting him.

"How very pathetic," their enemy said. "And how very futile."

"I am protected from your bag," she said. "I must protect him."

Realization filled those glowing red eyes. Tallulah swung more frantically, more wildly. With annoyance, he stepped farther from her, but not near enough to Royston.

The supposed rogue held the axe firmly in both hands, eyeing his target with a firmness of purpose that belied his assumed character.

"He is not safe from my bag." The *fear dearg* cackled and turned. "Abandon your pathetic axe. It will avail you nothing."

"I like it," Royston said, securing his grip. "It is unlike any weapon I've yet yielded."

Claws on his burlap bag, the Crimson Man began to close the gap between him and Royston. "And you and your unique weapon can both turn over a fire."

"I wouldn't recommend it," Royston said. "Iron can be difficult to digest."

The *fear dearg* stopped, frozen to the spot.

Tallulah took a giant step forward and swung the splintered leg hard against his back, sending him reeling forward. Royston did not miss his opportunity.

A swing of the axe.

An otherworldly cry.

The shaking of the very ground.

Then all was still, and dark, and quiet.

INSTALLMENT VII

in which Fear becomes Hope and Worry turns to Jubilation!

The creature had disappeared. Vanished. Royston had swung his iron axe, and he knew he had hit his mark. But the moment the cries of agony from the otherworldly monster pierced the air, the beast dissolved into millions of granules of glowing red light before dissipating entirely. Nothing remained. There was no blood, no body, no remnants of a creature that had, for nearly one hundred years, ruled viciously in this area.

In but a moment, he turned to Tallulah. Where was she? Had she emerged unscathed? With the boldness and bravery that would have inspired the poets of old, she had attacked the monster without the needed weaponry, making certain the squire did not fully realize what Royston was preparing to do. They had worked together, taking on a desperate task. But she, far more than he, had been willing to embrace true danger.

"Tallulah?" The shop was not entirely dark, but there was a heaviness in the air that made everything confused and difficult to navigate. He suspected it was the aftereffects of the death of the monster. The feeling would, no doubt, dissipate soon enough. In the meantime, he needed to know she was well and hale.

"Royston?" She spoke from so nearby he was shocked that he couldn't actually see her. He reached out a hand. His fingers brushed what he was certain were her fingers. "There you are."

"Is he gone?" she asked, slipping her fingers through his.

"He's gone, evaporated into tiny particles of glowing red."

"Do you see his bag?" she asked.

"I cannot see a thing."

"Search about for it. The bag contains magic of its own and must be burned."

He dropped down, feeling about on the floor, searching in the darkness. The space was growing less befuddling, but he still felt upended.

"Wait, I found it," she said. "Let's go outside. The lingering magic will make this task impossible in here."

He fumbled, tripped a bit, but made his way outside. She stepped out of the building just as he did, her arms burdened with an enormous burlap bag easily big enough for a person to fit inside.

All around the market cross, villagers spilled from buildings, eyes wide with worry and questions. Kirby stepped from the pub, his bushy white brows pulled with concern.

Royston turned to face them all and, in a ringing voice, declared, "The monster has been defeated. We are free!"

Shouts of jubilation rang out around them, the perfect juxtaposition to the horrible shrieks of an evil monster who had met his demise moments earlier.

"There remains yet one more thing to be done," Tallulah said. "We must destroy this bag, burn it to ashes." She dropped the bag on the ground in front of her. It made an enormous lump of rough fabric. "It is the last lingering remnants of his magic. It must not be permitted to remain."

The villagers needed no encouragement. Torches were lit in the various fires of the establishments all about, from the pub to the mercantile, from the milliner to the butcher. Royston himself slipped into the haberdashery and to the small fire at the back of the shop, and lit a torch of his own.

One by one, those who had been tortured and held hostage by the creature who would have used this bag to steal away every one of them if given a chance, lit it on fire. Again and again, they touched torches to the fabric and added to the growing flame that was consuming it.

The fire spat out flames of purest, deepest red. No smoke emerged. No sparks flew. There was nothing about this fire that was natural. But it was undeniably cleansing.

Royston stood beside Tallulah as the villagers sang and cheered and danced. Their joy changed the glow of the flame from crimson red to a soft pink. Rather than being attacked by the dark magic of the one-time squire, they were being lit by the soft glow of his final demise.

"They are free," Tallulah said. "They are safe."

"Chippingwich has waited a long time for you, Tallulah O'Doyle. Only with your knowledge and bravery were we at last able to defeat him."

"Your role in this was not insignificant," Tallulah said. "I believe the key was not me, but *us*."

"Us." He liked the sound of that. "We did show ourselves to be a remarkably good team."

She slipped her arm through his and rested her head against him. "Yes, we did."

"It may take time for your shop to open again," he said. "If we were to combine efforts, you could resume your business while waiting on the repairs."

She met his eye, clearly curious. "What are you proposing?"

"That we open the first Haberdashery and Confectionery Shop. We will begin a new trend, I'm certain of it. And being the fine team that we are, we will make an inarguable success of it."

A hint of a smile played over her features. "Is that the only thing you are proposing?"

He leaned in and, adopting the roguish tone he had long ago perfected, he said, "That is not remotely the only thing."

"I should very much like to hear your schemes." She didn't seem to harbor any lingering doubts about his character. She'd seen past the rogue he'd pretended to be to the person lurking beneath. And she seemed to like who she saw.

"Well, let me tell you the first and the last item on my list." He raised her hand to his lips and kissed her fingers. "The first part of my proposal is that you join me at the pub for dinner, and I will hold your hand and look lovingly into your eyes the way a man does when courting a woman."

"I like the beginning of this list," she said.

"Then you're going to love where the list ends." He slipped his arm free of hers and wrapped it instead around her waist.

"And where does it end?" she asked.

He rested his forehead against hers. "It doesn't. There's no end. This, Tallulah O'Doyle, is meant to last forever."

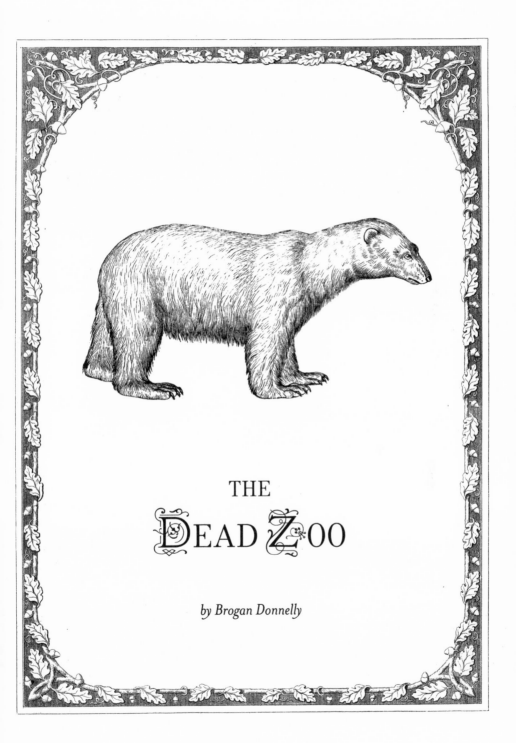

THE

DEAD ZOO

by Brogan Donnelly

DAY ONE

In the heart of Dublin City, between the River Liffey and the Grand Canal, surrounded by Merrion Square, Trinity College, and St. Stephen's Green, sits the imposing and stately Leister House where meets the Royal Dublin Society. And housed in the newest wing of this residence-turned-Society premises is a museum of a most unusual nature. Its contents are not unknown elsewhere; its function is not strange for a museum. It is made unusual by the oddity of its name, a moniker both amusing and dark.

This place of learning and study and preservation is a museum of natural history, filled with the remains of animals large and small, bird and insect, mammal and fish. Skeletons sit alongside wax models that occupy displays alongside taxidermy of a most realistic nature. Whales and eagles, rodents and trout, a Tasmanian tiger and a polar bear. The species are too numerous to name here, but the museum is far from empty. And its contents have earned it, amongst the locals, the name "The Dead Zoo."

Early on a spring morning, Amos Cavey, a man who had earned in his thirty-five years a reputation for intelligence by virtue of having mentioned it so very often, stepped inside the zoo of no-longer-living creatures, having been sent for by William Sheenan, keeper of the exhibit of mammals.

William had asked this tower of intellect to call upon him at the zoo, not out of admiration but desperation. Amos never ceased to brag of his intellectual acumen, and William was in need of someone who could solve a very great and pressing mystery.

Amos walked with unflagging confidence up the Plymouth stone stairs to the first floor where the mammals were housed. He was not unfamiliar with the museum and its displays. Indeed, he had once proclaimed it "quite adequate, having potential to be impressive indeed." He had made this observation with a great deal of reluctance as it might very well be seen as a declaration of approval of the Royal Dublin Society, which he did not at all intend it to be.

Alighting on the first floor, he stepped into the grand hall where the preserved species were displayed, some on shelves, some behind glass, some posed on pedestals. The ornate ceiling rose three stories above the stone floor. Two upper stories of balconies overlooked the space beneath. Tall columns supported those surrounding galleries, giving the room a classical look, one designed to complement a place of learning.

He held back his inward expression of frustration at having to step over and around a mop employed by a janitor. The man offered no acknowledgment of their near collision, but simply continued his efforts, so intent on his work that one would assume he was expunging the worst of muck and grime rather than polishing the floor of a museum that was kept quite clean.

"Do not mind Jonty," William said as he approached. "He is so very dedicated to his work. We owe the beauty of this building to his unflagging efforts."

Jonty grunted but didn't speak, neither did he look up from his mopping. As William had declared, he was quite good at what he did, and no oddity of character would see him dismissed from his position. Do we not endure things in people when we value something else enough?

"Your note," said Amos with his usual air of superior intelligence, "indicated you are faced with some puzzle you find *unsolvable*." He spoke the last word with an unmistakable tone of doubt.

"Indeed, I am." William's tone held far too much worry for anyone to mistake his sincerity.

"I fancy a challenge," Amos said. "Tell me of your mystery, and I will find your answer."

The reader may find this declaration a touch too arrogant, but Amos did have a most impressive intellect. He was not wrong to rate his abilities so highly, though his tendency to regularly regale people with acclamations of his intelligence made him a difficult person with whom to spend any length of time. Were William not truly in need of Amos's particular assistance, the self-assured intellectual would not have been offered so sincere a welcome.

"How familiar are you with our collection?" the harried keeper asked as he motioned for Amos to walk with him amongst the displays.

"I have visited a couple of times." Amos looked over the nearest animals with an eye to evaluating them. "I found the musk ox mother and calf intriguing. The particularly large trout, however, I take leave to declare might actually be a salmon."

William let the criticism pass, not wishing to dwell on anything other than the matter at hand. They passed the dodo skeleton, a particular favorite of his, though why it was displayed amongst the mammals, he could not say.

"I am, however," Amos said, "quite intrigued by the polar bear."

As William was partial to the Arctic predator, he found himself better pleased with his current company than he had been. "That bear was brought back by Captain Leopold McClintock after his Arctic search for the lost Franklin expedition. The bear's fatal wound has been left in the fur, giving us a perfect picture of how the creature looked in its final moments."

They'd reached the taxidermied animal they were discussing. Amos eyed it with curiosity. Something about it was different from what he remembered. He prided himself on his eye for detail and would not be satisfied until he knew what had changed since he last saw the animal.

"We have recently added this Arctic ringed seal." William motioned to the large pinniped, displayed in all its taxidermied glory in a wood-framed glass box. "Our collection of ice-bound animals is growing."

Amos took pointed notice of the seal before studying the bear once more. Two glances at each were all he needed to sort out the change in the massive polar bear. Its positioning had been changed from the last time he saw it. The museum had turned the bear's head to be looking not at the lions, as it had on Amos's previous visit, but at the seal.

Clever, he thought to himself, as the seal was a polar bear's natural prey. He hadn't realized the taxidermied animals could be repositioned.

The Dead Zoo possessed an unavoidable degree of eeriness, being so full of creatures that had met their demise. Row after row of skeletons, of long-dead and, at times, not-long-dead animals frozen in poses meant to mimic life but never fully capturing it. How chilling was the effect of a dangerous, deadly animal, focused unblinkingly on the very animal that constituted nearly the entirety of its diet, but both animals nothing more than skin and fur stretched over expertly formed frames.

The janitor trudged past, pulling his mop and bucket with him, grumbling something neither William nor Amos attempted to overhear. As soon as he was out of sight, William addressed the matter at hand.

"I've asked you here because pieces of our collection have gone missing. I dismissed the first few disappearances as items being misplaced or pulled off their shelves for repair or cleaning, but they have never returned."

"You wish me to solve for you a string of petty thefts?" No man in possession of as much pride in his cleverness as Amos could help but feel disappointed at the request.

"These are no ordinary thefts." William guided him past kangaroos, posed in mid-jump, and an armadillo preserved in full armor. All around were skeletons and glass-eyed forms. Tall displays cast odd shadows. Rows of displays broke up the large space into small, sometimes confining sections.

Amos glanced backward as they walked, fighting the oddest sensation that someone was there, watching or wishing for his attention. But he saw no one. Only row upon row of animals. Bears. Lions. A magpie.

From the long-ago years of his childhood came the familiar refrain of the well-known nursery rhyme about magpies.

One for sorrow.

Two for joy . . .

He'd long ago outgrown superstitions, but that lone bird sent a shiver over him, one he clamped down with effort.

The two men paused at a display of rodents, many of a variety unseen in Ireland. William indicated three separate empty places. "These are newly missing, but they were held in place by strong metal bands and thick bolts. Freeing them from their confines is not a simple task. These specimens couldn't simply be picked up and slipped in one's pocket. This required time and effort, yet we've seen nothing."

That bit of additional information did offer some degree of intrigue to the mystery.

"And what does the museum director have to say about these thefts?" Amos asked.

William glanced in the direction of the director's private office. "I would rather not tell Mr. Carte about this, not if we can discover the thief's identity and recover the stolen items."

While Mr. Alexander Carte was not a vindictive man, there was no doubt he would be none-too-happy to hear that the museum, whose collection was not yet what he wished it to be, was being diminished by thievery. The director's displeasure might very well cost William Sheenan his position.

"Are these the only specimens to have been stolen?"

"No," William said, "only the most recent. We have lost mammal skulls, taxidermied rodents, even a couple of small felines."

"And how long has this been happening?"

William's expression grew ever wearier. "For a week now. Something has disappeared every day. That is all I know for certain. The items disappear, though I know not when or how. I've seen nothing, can explain nothing. I am at a loss."

Amos took a slow look around the enormous display room. Row after row of specimens spread out over three floors, the ground-level floor not yet completed. The museum was quite popular, owing in no small degree to Carte's exhaustive efforts to raise funds, expand the collection, and build interest.

Discovering who amongst the many visitors could possibly be pilfering items would be a challenge, indeed. A challenge worthy of a finely honed mind.

Amos tugged at his right cuff, then his left. He smoothed the front of his sack coat, then straightened his neckcloth.

"I will return in the morning," he said, "when the museum is open once more to visitors. I will observe, study, sort, and, I have no doubt, solve these mysterious thefts."

William offered his gratitude along with expressions of confidence in Amos's ability to do just as he had promised. One would be quite justified in wondering if he offered the praise as a matter of sincerity or in the hope of convincing himself that the disaster awaiting him, should his superior discover the thefts, could yet be avoided.

"Until tomorrow." Amos dipped his head quite regally.

"Tomorrow," William repeated.

He watched as the would-be detective left, a spring in his step and an unmistakable confidence in his stride. He watched with heavy expression, tight pulled lips, and tension radiating from him. The situation was a dire one, more so than Amos Cavey yet realized.

DAY TWO

Amos did not begin his investigative efforts until the day after being asked. He'd told William Sheenan that would be the case but hadn't confessed that there was no reason for the delay. Truth be told, Amos simply wanted to seem quite in demand. A reputation was only as impactful as one made it, after all.

With an air of casual authority, he stepped into the expanse of the collection of death. From a scientific perspective, it was the very height of anthropologic intrigue. To one who possessed even a modicum of superstition, it was the very height of horror. Amos Cavey never permitted any mental anxiety he experienced to hold greater influence over his decisions or behavior than the more logical part of his mind did.

The museum was not empty, but neither was it bustling yet. This was the perfect opportunity for gathering clues. Amos had armed himself with a small notebook and a lead pencil sharpened to perfection. With both firmly in hand, he began a slow, pointed circuit of the first floor where the mammals were displayed, along with a few oddities from other corners of the animal kingdom. He chose to overlook how utterly sloppy a bit of work that was. He had been asked to solve a series of thefts, not teach the keepers the proper classification of species.

All seemed well around the largest displays. Nothing appeared amiss with the rhinoceros or American bison. He walked slowly around the open-air display of a walrus. All was well. A bit of dust hung about the zebra.

The wooden frame of the glass case surrounding the seals was a bit beaten up. The museum really ought to place their older cases in lesser visited corners of the room, not on full display such as this.

Mr. Carte had gone to such lengths to build the reputation of the Dead Zoo. Carelessness would only undermine it. Then again, so would knowledge of the thefts Amos had agreed to try to solve. He ought not be surprised to find other flaws beneath the veneer.

His investigation took him up the stairs to the second-story balconies where the museum housed its display of birds and fish. Amos spotted a gap in the display of birds and made directly for it. Not seeing a placard indicating the specimen had been removed for repair or cleaning or such, he studied the spot more carefully.

As with the case that had once housed the now-missing rodents, this case containing the display of birds boasted a bit of injury, precisely what one would expect after someone had quickly and inexpertly used a tool of some sort to loosen the bindings. The scratches he saw were not scattered in every direction, as one would expect from the natural wear and tear of years of visitors, but concentrated, repetitive. Someone had removed this bird without the precision one would expect from the keepers of this odd zoo who valued their animal population.

A disconcertingly familiar sensation—that of being watched—tiptoed over him just as it had the day before. It set his neck hairs standing on end. He swallowed, but not without a little difficulty. There were far too many eyes in the museum, not all of them human, not all of them seeing, for some sensation of being observed not to be felt. He told himself it was merely a trick of the mind.

But his eyes fell upon a murder of magpies—made still by death—watching him. Seven. Seven magpies.

One for sorrow.
Two for joy.
Three for a girl.
Four for a boy.

He could not stop the rhyme from echoing in his thoughts.

Five for silver.
Six for gold.
Seven for a secret, never to be told.
Seven for a secret.

Amos pushed down the feeling of foreboding. He would not allow himself to be ridiculous.

William arrived at his side not a moment later, no doubt the real reason for Amos's premonition. He *had* been observed by the man who had asked him to be there. With his logical nature firmly in charge once more, Amos felt himself far more on solid ground.

"You should know that this bird has also been pilfered," Amos said. "The display shows the same subtle damage, the same pattern of gouging."

Though the keeper was, understandably, a bit embarrassed to not have realized the issue extended beyond the mammals exhibit, he did not grow offended. "I ought to have realized the thefts would not be limited to only my section of the zoo. Please tell me if you find any other specimens you believe we have lost to this unknown criminal."

"He will not be unknown for long," Amos said. "I can assure you of that."

William dipped his head. "There *is* a reason I asked for your participation in this."

It must be remembered that the Dead Zoo was run by none other than the Royal Dublin Society, the members of which were not precisely dunces. To not ask one of their membership to oversee a matter such as this was a good indication that either the mystery was indeed an exceptionally difficult one to solve or William Sheenan was particularly keen to keep the matter a secret. It is for the astute reader to ascertain which was, in fact, the case.

Amos continued his searching circuit of the museum, first on the second story, then making his way to the galleries on the third. He found in his perusal a number of missing items. Some showed not the least indication of having been tampered with. Others, however, were scarred with the same careless marks as the other hapless dead creatures. All totaled, he found nine specimens had been taken.

Seating himself upon an obliging bench at the far end of the mammal exhibit, Amos acquainted himself with all his notes, searching for the connection he knew he would find there. Visitors glided in and out, each awed by the displays and most filled with amazement at the collection. Few paid him the least heed. He did not mind.

Nine missing.

One feline.

Four rodents.

One fish.

Two birds.

One bicolored lobster.

All were small enough for an enterprising individual to tuck under a jacket or shawl. These thefts, he grew more and more certain, were not the work of a particularly gifted thief. Perhaps the items were taken by youths challenging one another to undertake what they saw as a lark. Perhaps it was a person with a propensity toward thievery for reasons even they could not explain; he had read that some people could not help the inclination. Perhaps someone wished to undermine the museum.

He rose from his place of pondering and meandered amongst the visitors, listening in with a degree of subtlety he felt quite proud of. None, he felt certain, would realize he was investigating them.

The mother and child peering at the whale skeleton were quickly eliminated. To undertake something like this in the presence of a child would be difficult indeed.

He hovered just beyond a group of young students from Rathmines as they spoke at length of how very bored they all were.

"We'd not be seen if we slipped off and moved a few things about," one lad said. "Could pose the animals for a rugby match or some lark like that."

His friend shook his head. "They're likely all bolted in. And the museum man said once the animals are put on display, they don't get moved about."

The boys, then, were certain the specimens couldn't be stolen or moved from their spots. They'd not think that if they were the ones making off with them.

Amos realized, of course, that the perpetrator might very well not be present that particular day and at that particular hour. But the museum was open only three days per week. For so much to have gone missing in so short a time, he reasoned, the person must have been coming in every open day to make off with something new.

On he wandered. As has been established already, he was not one to admit to any insufficiencies in his intelligence. And he certainly wasn't likely to admit defeat after a single morning.

His footsteps took him past the polar bear once more. It was really a magnificent animal. Something in its eyes was more realistic than the other creatures strewn about. The glassy expressions one saw in all directions made clear how very dead the Dead Zoo really was. But this bear somehow gave a person pause. Perhaps it was simply the decision to have him perpetually watching the animal that might once have been his dinner. Even the least scientifically inclined visitor could understand hunger at a glance.

Amos wandered on, listening in on every conversation. Back up the stairs. Past the fish. Back to the birds. He ignored as he went the eyes that were deceptively upon him. He knew better than to believe the trick this place played on the senses.

Two gentlemen stood near the ostrich skeleton, having a lively conversation. A quick assessment of their attire told Amos they were relatively well-to-do. Their manner of speaking confirmed that evaluation.

"A remarkable specimen," the taller of the two said to the other.

"Indeed," was the response. "And the mounted birds are quite exquisite, as well."

"Have you observed the penguins?" The taller gentleman indicated the birds in question by pointing at them with his cane. "I find myself quite envious. Something of that caliber ought to be in *my* collection."

"Indeed."

"There is, you understand, but one thing to be done." The man's mustache twitched. His silver brows arched haughtily.

"Indeed."

"I must have a penguin of my own. I will not rest until I do. I have certainly managed to add to my collection of late." The man's tone was both self-satisfied and suspicious. "It would be a small matter to do so again."

And with that, the miscreant sealed his fate.

"Sir, if you will be good enough to follow me." Amos assumed his most demanding, unwavering tone.

"I beg your pardon." The man eyed him disapprovingly.

"The keeper of the mammal exhibit requires a word with you."

"Does he?"

Amos motioned him toward the stairs, counting on the man's good manners to prevent a scene. He often depended upon people doing what he thought they ought. He was both cynical and trusting by nature, and he was not always a good judge of when to employ which. In this instance, he chose correctly.

William was easy to find. He seldom left his precious mammals, and there he was found.

"Mr. Sheenan, I have solved your mystery." Amos held himself in a proud and defiant posture. "Your collection is the envy of many, some to the point of abandoning their good breeding to obtain what you have that they wish to possess."

William looked from Amos to the tall gentleman and back once more. His confusion was lost on the self-assured detective, who was quite proud of having so easily solved a question that had baffled others. Had he paid greater attention, he would have noticed that William and the gentleman did not seem at all surprised to see one another. Neither had they asked for an introduction.

Confident in his conclusions, Amos pressed forward. "This man wishes for one of your penguins to be part of his collection. He spoke of it in quite strong terms, almost foregone terms. I contend that—"

"Pray pardon the interruption, Lord Baymount," William hastily said to the man at Amos's side. "I hope you will continue to peruse the collections here at your leisure."

"Lord or not," Amos resumed, undeterred. Oh, the follies one reaps when unwilling to give ear to others. "He spoke of his collection—"

"With pride, I hope," William quickly interrupted. He knew the path Amos meant to trod and intended to save him from it. "Do go look them over."

He breached protocol so much as to nudge his lordship away, desperate as he was to avoid the humiliation Amos had very nearly caused.

"You did not allow me to finish." The intellectual was all wounded dignity.

"And for that you are quite welcome." William pointed to the back of the retreating lord. "He has contributed a great many specimens to our museum. His 'collection' of items are on display *here*. That he saw the penguins and wished one were part of *his* collection was not a threat of thievery but a determination to add something of equal intrigue and significance to those items he has already donated."

Few times in his adult life had Amos experienced the odd sensation of being embarrassed. It was a feeling he had as much experience with as being wrong. That he'd experienced both at once would astonish anyone who knew him.

His pride whipped up a frenzy of determination. He refused to be defeated by so simple a task. And he further refused to be humiliated again. The mystery would be solved, and it would be solved by him. His worth would be proved to William Sheehan, to the haughty Lord Baymount, to himself.

And, if it were the last thing he did, he would find a way to shake the unnerving weight of an unseen gaze that followed him all around the Dead Zoo.

DAY THREE

Amos had hardly slept. Such was the burden of one whose self-declared claim to fame was unparalleled intelligence but who had endured a monumental lapse in judgment. Burdened with questions of identity, Amos arrived at the Dead Zoo worse for wear yet unwilling to abandon the challenge he'd been issued.

The museum was not open every day. On this morning, no visitors would be admitted. Members of the Royal Dublin Society, however, had ready access.

If Amos were not so certain of his eventual success, he might have been ashamed to have not realized sooner the significance of thefts occurring while the museum was closed. Lord Baymount's misleading conversation had planted in Amos's mind a trail of thought he'd followed during the long sleepless hours of night.

For a collector of taxidermied, mounted, or skeletal animals, the Dead Zoo presented a treasure trove of possibilities. Someone without the preferred scruples might see in its displays a shortcut to the collection he desired. And who could wish for such a thing more than members of the society whose interest in such things had led to the Natural History Museum in the first place?

Still, he did not mean to storm into the mammal exhibit with accusations falling from his lips. He would build a case, gather proof. He would not be made the fool again.

William Sheenan was not the first to greet our unlucky detective upon his arrival. Amos's path crossed Jonty's first. The gruff man was not mopping as he had been that first day. Indeed, Amos had not seen him mopping since. On this day, he was dusting displays.

He grumbled as Amos passed, his words indiscernible but his tone unmistakable. He did not care for Amos, did not like him being there. The feeling was growing more mutual with every encounter.

William, however, was pleased at Amos's arrival. Though he'd not cared for the near run insult of the day before and had needed to patch things up with Lord Baymount, the situation at the museum required greater and quicker effort than previously.

"Our colobus monkey is missing," William told him.

"The long-haired, black and white one, yes?" Amos asked, unable to hide the hint of pleasure in his expression. Another missing specimen offered opportunity for more clues. Though he was reluctant to admit as much, he needed more information than he had if he was to avoid another embarrassing misstep.

He followed William to the display. Amos checked the now-empty display and found it just as the others had been: a bit scratched, a bit scuffed. Whoever had undertaken the theft had done so with more care than before, but only a very little more.

He froze. That same feeling—a horrid, unnerving feeling—of being watched seized him. Even more than his failure of the day before, *this* flaw in his reasoning caused him great distress. He was not easily overset. He was not intellectually weak. Amos Cavey would not give way to illogical whimseys.

He told himself he would ignore any magpies he should see. Surely there were no more displays than the two he'd already seen.

He was wrong. The nearest shelves contained more. Ten this time.

Eight for a wish.

Nine for a kiss.

Ten for a bird you must not miss.

It is all rubbish. Nonsense. This place oversets the mind, is all. I will overcome it.

With himself firmly in hand once more, Amos stepped back from the vandalized display and set himself to a study of his surroundings. He had, of course, made a thorough inspection the day before, but that had yielded nothing but near-disaster. Today, however, would be different.

The comings and goings were fewer and focused. His primary group of suspects were present and no one else.

He could not err today. He would not!

Two members of the society entered the room, both looking quite pleased with themselves. Amos had interacted with them before and had found them unbearably arrogant. He was not opposed to confidence of character, mind you—he possessed quite a lot of it himself, after all—but he did not approve when he saw it in those who had not fully earned it. Some members of the Royal Dublin Society had offered inarguable proof of their intelligence. Others, like Mr. McClellan and Mr. Kearney, hadn't.

They crossed paths in front of the hippopotamus, something Amos made look unintentional. "Gentlemen," he said with a dip of his head.

"You do realize the museum is closed to visitors," Mr. McClellan said. "Only members of the society have access to the collection today."

"Unless one who has chosen not to join the society has been particularly invited by the keeper of the mammals." Amos watched them for any signs of worry.

They did seem to find that odd, but not in a way that seemed to alarm them. Curiosity appeared to be the crowning response.

"Why has William asked you to be here?" Mr. Kearney asked.

Amos allowed a pitying look. "Alas, if you do not already know, then you were likely not meant to."

Far from felled by this subtle insult, Mr. McClellan and Mr. Kearney simply exchanged looks heavy with amusement and walked away. Oh, yes. The members of this haughty and insufferable society were prime suspects. Prime, indeed!

Amos meant to trail them as unobtrusively as possible. They would not suspect his efforts. If luck were with him, they would unintentionally provide him with incriminating evidence.

His pursuit brought him past Jonty, who watched him with obvious disapproval, though what he'd done to earn the man's dislike, he didn't know. Still, he could not be bothered with such things at the moment. His intellect was at work, and he would not allow himself to be distracted.

His quarry must have sensed him following them. Now and then, they stopped and glanced backward. If he were, in that moment, within view, he busied himself with studying whichever specimen was nearest at hand. If luck favored him and he were not visible, he simply tucked himself more firmly out of sight and waited.

It was during one of these moments of hiding that the sensation of being watched washed over him once more. Every time he felt the weight of eyes upon him, the feeling grew heavier and more difficult to explain away.

This time, his gaze sought out the janitor. But Jonty was nowhere to be seen. That, of course, did not preclude him being tucked away just as Amos was. The man had made clear his disdain and disapproval. It was, no doubt, his glares which Amos felt crawling up his neck.

Around the corner, Mr. McClellan, fully ignoring the card instructing otherwise, touched the skin of the moose on display. Such disregard for proper behavior. Oh, yes, these were his miscreants.

He stepped closer. Then came the sensation of someone stepping closer to *him*. He looked behind him. No one.

What was the matter with him? He never allowed his imagination to flourish, let alone run rampant.

Amos focused all his attention on the two suspicious men. They were very intent on the displays, but not in a way that spoke of true appreciation but rather amusement. They were in the Dead Zoo for entertainment, and what could be more entertaining than thievery to those inclined toward such things?

William was fast approaching. Now was Amos's opportunity. He would denounce the men, insist William check their coats and pockets for something they meant to slip off with, and leave a hero. The Royal Dublin Society would ask him *again* to join. He would refuse *again*. But he would likely be invited to lecture and present and otherwise make even more of a name for himself. His prowess would see him praised not merely in Dublin, but in London as well.

He opened his mouth to begin what he anticipated would be a very impressive denunciation, but William spoke before he could.

"We've something else missing," he said in a low voice. "I saw it was not in its display this morning but assumed it had been taken out by order of Mr. Carte. I have only just learned it was not."

Something of panic lay in William's words. That hadn't been present before when he'd spoken of missing items. This, then, was different.

"What is it?"

With a shaking breath, William said, "Our hartebeest is missing."

"Hartebeest?"

Amos quickly thought back to his previous wanderings in the Dead Zoo. He could picture the animal in his mind's eye. An antelope, two- to three-hundred pounds in life. No doubt, lighter in taxidermied preservation, but still quite large. Too large for carrying off undetected. Not without assistance, and assistance beyond a single partner. One would have to have access to a cart of some kind. And it could not be done in sight of others.

A sense of foreboding settled over him. He'd nearly lobbed another accusation that would have proved humiliating. He'd nearly made an absolute quiz of himself once again.

How had he been so wrong twice? *Twice?*

What was happening to him? What dark spell was this place of death casting over him?

DAY FOUR

William watched from the first-story windows of the museum the next morning as Amos paced the grounds below. The man had arrived nearly three-quarters of an hour earlier but had not come inside. The calm air with which he had taken on the task of solving the mystery William had presented to him was growing thin. His once-tidy appearance had given way to a haphazard one. A frantic detective was, he supposed, better than no detective at all.

Unaware he was being observed, Amos made yet another circuit of the wide expanse of lawn situated outside the Dead Zoo. How was a simple matter of thievery baffling him so entirely? He couldn't wrap his powerful brain around it. It wasn't even a sophisticated scheme. Displays were hastily opened. Specimens were made off with while no attempt was made to cover up the effort.

This was hardly a complicated matter, and he was not a simpleton. On and on he paced. The tension in his shoulders grew by the moment. He'd not slept more than a few moments here and there. Though he'd not passed anyone upon his entrance to the grounds, he felt certain the Royal Dublin Society members stood about somewhere, laughing at him. Mocking him.

"That's why I feel eyes on me," he muttered to himself, pushing his mess of hair away from his face. "That's why I feel followed."

He eyed the museum. He remained on the grounds, not out of fear of going in but as a means of watching delivery persons coming and going. Who else could arrive regularly with a cart and haul items in and out without arousing suspicion?

That was who he was looking for. It had to be. He could not be wrong again. He was Amos Cavey, an intellectual and a logician. He would not be felled by so simple a mystery.

Yet half the day passed without a single workman coming onto the grounds. Nothing entered or exited the museum beyond a few members of the society. Even William Sheenan didn't make an appearance outside of the building.

The two men's eyes met in midafternoon, Amos standing in the grass, William standing inside at a window. Long minutes passed with them simply watching each other. Neither knew what the other was thinking but would, no doubt, be surprised if he knew.

William was holding out hope that the man he'd selected to undertake this difficult task did not mean to abandon it.

Amos's frustration was turning to anger. He, who prided himself on his logic, on his unflappable intellect, stormed toward the building, his movements angular and stilted.

Mere steps from the door, he froze. More magpies—living this time— sat perched in a line on the branch of a tree. Twelve. All watching him.

Eleven is worse.

Twelve for a dastardly curse.

For the length of a breath, his heart froze. *Twelve. Twelve.*

No, he would not be undone by this. He would not give way to childish superstitions.

He pushed onward and through the museum doors. Amos stormed into the large display hall so forcefully that he nearly tripped over Jonty's push broom.

"Watchya," Jonty grumbled.

Amos might normally have pointed out the preposterousness of telling someone who had nearly tripped over a broom stretched across a doorway that he was the one needing to show greater care, rather than the one who had put the broom in the doorway in the first place. But he had larger fish to fry, as the saying went.

"What day are your deliveries?" he demanded the moment he reached William at the very window where he'd spotted him from the grounds below.

"We do not have a specific day." William turned to him as he spoke. He was a patient man, as calm as Amos prided himself on being, but even his endurance was wearing thin. His frustration did not stem from thinking the mystery was taking overly long to solve—only four days had passed, after all, since he had recruited Amos Cavey—but rather the fact that he was finding himself the aim of Amos's angry darts.

"How often have deliveries been made over the past fortnight?" Amos demanded more than asked. "How many were made by the same people? By people *employed* by the same people? Did they deliver with carts? Or wagons?" His questions came rapidly, almost without breath between. His wide eyes darted about.

"Are you unwell, Mr. Cavey?"

"Am I not permitted to be anxious in the solving of these thefts? Would you rather I shrug and leave you to face Mr. Carte's wrath?" Had he been less overwhelmed, perhaps Amos would have recognized the unwarranted intensity in his questioning. He could not recall the last time he had failed in an intellectual endeavor. He hadn't the least ability to endure it.

"A mere four days have passed since I first told you of our situation," William countered. "That we do not yet have the answers is not a failure."

"I do not fail," Amos said. "Not ever."

The man seemed horribly on edge. William judged it best to give the man room to breathe and calm himself. In a tone he hoped was soothing without being patronizing, he answered the earlier questions. "We had one delivery of note. It was a replacement pane of glass for a display case. That was brought almost exactly a fortnight ago, before these disappearances began. The courier did bring it on a wagon, but he and his wagon have not returned since."

"Was anything taken from the case that needed the glass replaced?" Amos asked.

"No. Not a thing." William had truly begun to worry about the man. He appeared quite rattled. "Perhaps you ought to return home for the remainder of the day. Rest a spell."

"I am not unwell." He took a breath, his jaw still taut. "The thefts are not occurring during the day. They must be the work of someone here at night."

"No one is here at night," William countered.

Amos pointed a finger in his direction. "No one *you know of*."

"You suspect someone is sneaking in?"

"I am nearly certain of it." Amos paced a few steps away before returning to where William yet stood. "I will stay here after closing tonight and watch. By morning, your mystery will be solved."

"You sound very confident."

Amos raised up to his full height. "By morning, you will have your answer."

Not quite as sure of himself as he wanted to appear, Amos returned to his own home long enough to have a bite to eat and a cup of tea. His appearance, he knew, had grown haggard. In his eagerness to resume his investigation that morning, he had not stopped to shave, nor had he invested any effort into his appearance save running a comb quickly through his hair and remembering to change out of his nightclothes. He did not bother addressing the state of himself before returning to the Dead Zoo.

Mr. Carte was leaving the museum as Amos approached. The director was not meant to know about their situation, so Amos slipped behind some tall shrubs, shielding himself from discovery. Once the path was clear and he was no longer likely to be caught, Amos stealthily moved to the doors of the Dead Zoo.

William awaited him there. "Mr. Carte is beginning to ask questions.

Please take care not to disturb any displays or leave behind any indication you have been here overnight. I would struggle to explain that without digging quite a pit for myself."

"I am not entirely inept." Amos's defensiveness came as naturally now as his arrogance once had.

With a barely withheld sigh, William motioned him to the door, which he held open. "Best of luck, Mr. Cavey."

"I do not need luck. I will use my mind."

"Such as it is," William muttered not quite loud enough to be overheard.

As soon as Amos was inside, William pulled the door closed and locked it.

Night had not entirely fallen. Dim light spilled through the windows, illuminating the rows of displays and glass cabinets. The galleries, though, were in complete shadow.

Amos lit the lantern he'd brought in anticipation of this difficulty. He climbed the stairs to the lower gallery and placed himself in a corner he had specifically chosen for its view of the museum. The vantage point wasn't perfect, but he could see enough to spot someone making off with an animal or a skeleton. And he could see the doors.

He would catch the no-good thief. He would!

For more than an hour, he stood rooted to the spot, studying every shadow, every still form. His eyes darted about, quick to examine any movement, though his mind told him there was none. He was the one doing the watching, and yet he couldn't shake the all-too-familiar sensation of the situation being reversed.

The museum was empty. He was the only living thing inside, and yet he didn't feel alone. The Dead Zoo had an unnerving effect on the senses. Surrounded by death, by animals captured in lifelike poses but with empty glass eyes, even the strongest of minds would struggle—did struggle.

His eyes might have been playing him for a fool, but he trusted his ears still. And his ears heard something below.

The lantern cast quivering light as he made his way down the stairs to the mammal exhibit. The sound was clearer now.

Scraping. Scratching.

Someone, he felt certain, was attempting to jimmy open a display or loosen fastenings as had been done before. He was about to find his culprit.

The sound echoed off the walls and three-story high ceiling, bouncing off glass and huddling around taxidermied animals. The muffled confusion, nevertheless, grew more distinct as he grew nearer to it. Past the warthogs, past the goats. He'd studied the Dead Zoo enough to know what lay around each corner, which species was housed where. He passed beneath the suspended skeleton of the giant whale and approached the seals.

Suddenly, the sound stopped, and silence fell heavy around him. He held the lantern aloft as he circled the seal display. The light scratches he'd seen in the wood frame were not the only signs of wear he spotted now. Deep gouges marred the surface. New gouges. A powder of wood bits made a light coating on the floor below.

Someone meant to make off with a seal. How in heaven's name did the miscreant intend to do that? Such a thing would require multiple people and a large wagon with a strong team. Seals were enormous, their only natural predator being the massive polar bear.

Amos glanced over his shoulder at the creature in question. But it was gone.

The polar bear was gone.

How had someone made off with such a large item without making noise, without being seen? It was impossible. Utterly impossible!

He studied the stand on which the bear was—or *ought to have been*—displayed. There was absolutely no sign of tampering. None at all. There was not even the tiniest speck of dust. It was almost as if the polar bear had simply walked away.

His mind insisted that was impossible even as his eyes darted frantically around.

Something heavy and soft, by the sound of it, landed upon the floor somewhere out of sight. The same sound again. Then again.

It sounded not unlike the pad of a dog's feet on the floor. A rolling paw, soft enough to muffle the noise but made loud by the weight it bore.

Paws. Against the floor.

An empty polar bear display.

An inelegant attempt to gain access to a seal, the polar bear's natural diet.

Amos shook his head, insisting the theory forming in his mind was too ridiculous to be true. There had to be another explanation. There simply had to be.

Heavier and quicker came the sounds of paws on stone.

Amos's heart rate rose. He backed up, watching and holding his breath.

He could hear breathing—heavy, deep-throated breathing.

The wide expanse of the museum, its columns and high ceiling, turned even the tiniest sound into a cacophony, and nothing about these sounds were tiny. Fast, heavy paws and threatening growls came at him from every direction.

He did all he could think to do. He ran. Every turn he made, the sounds followed him. He swore he could feel hot breath on his neck, though he did not turn back long enough to look. He ran. Ran. Ran.

The door to the museum was locked. It would not give at his frantic pulling. He pounded and shouted, his own voice bouncing off the walls and attacking him anew. Perhaps another door? A window?

He raced back into the enormous room. Where were the windows? Why could he not find them? He knew there were windows. He'd seen William standing at one, looking at him. There were windows. There were! But where?

He could find nothing. His mind refused to identify anything. The shapes around him shifted and contorted, monstrous collections of limbs and heads. They moved. He swore they did. They turned and watched him as he ran past, and he never felt their eyes leave him.

He was running in circles, passing the same skeletons, the same animals, over and over again. But they were positioned differently, facing him no matter where he was. And all the while the fall of heavy paws continued.

Out of the corner of his eye, he saw a flash of white. He dove behind the glass-sided display of deer.

A roar split the darkness. The display shook. Glass shattered.

Amos tried to scramble to his feet, but he couldn't rise.

Closer came the sound of paws on the stone floor. Closer. Louder. Slower.

Deep, growling breaths.

A shadow fell across him. A shadow despite the darkness.

And then a face.

DAY FIVE

Sebastian Hines considered himself quite a paragon of gentlemanly achievement. That the keeper of the mammals at the Museum of Natural History had, in an official capacity, asked for him to call was yet another feather in his cap. He stepped inside what the uncouth locals referred to as the Dead Zoo, feeling quite pleased with himself.

The museum was not open to visitors that day, which made his presence there all the more flattering. Yes, he was sharing space with two delivery men, but he did not permit that to dampen his spirits. The men carefully set down a pane of glass beside a display case in need of mending.

Nearby, a grizzled janitor bent over a mop, applying himself with pointed and focused effort to cleaning something off the stone floor. It was not exalted company, but *they* were there as tradespeople. *He* was there as a sought-after guest.

"Do not mind Jonty," William Sheenan said as the new arrival approached. "He is so very dedicated to his work."

"No bother." Sebastian pressed a lace-edged handkerchief to his nose, managing to hide his look of displeasure. "I am curious as to why you've sent for me."

"I have encountered a mystery here at the Museum of Natural History that I cannot solve."

Sebastian was taken for a tour, past a display of a missing rodent, past a disgruntled Jonty working hard to clean something from the floor, past a display case in need of new glass. Past a taxidermied polar bear looking unblinkingly at a seal.

It had all happened before.

It would happen again.

Dear Reader, should you visit Dublin, should you jaunt past Merrion Square, should you wander into the Museum of Natural History, take care.

Not everything at the Dead Zoo . . . is dead.

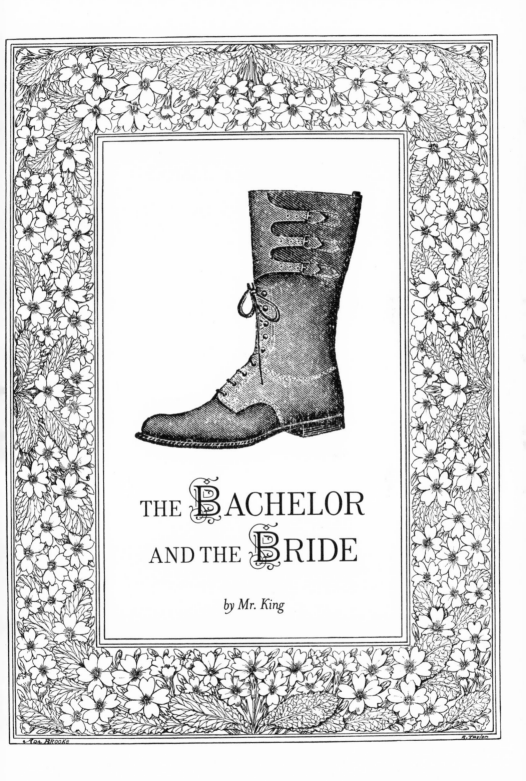

THE BACHELOR AND THE BRIDE

by Mr. King

INSTALLMENT I

in which our Hero inquires of a Wise Woman and
receives Instructions of a most unexpected nature!

Centuries ago, in a quiet corner of the border country, a young man
of medicine by the name of Duncan worked tirelessly on behalf of those
who placed their well-being in his hands. Not having the expertise nor the
implements of our doctors today, the pull he felt to protect the people in his
care often sat heavy on his heart and mind. He dedicated himself to healing
and comforting, but, as was far too often the case in years gone by—and,
alas, in our time as well—he found himself as familiar with the churchyard
as he was with his own cottage.

As had happened far too often before, he found himself tired, discouraged, and heartbroken after a harrowing few weeks of looking after
impossible-to-cure patients, an illness having ravaged his area of the kingdom. One patient remained in his care, her recovery entirely in question.

The young girl was now an orphan, Duncan having been unable to cure
her parents of the very ailment that still threatened his patient. He had tried
but failed in his attempts to cure the ill-fated family, and he had little hope
of saving the child's life. Duncan was not one to simply declare defeat when
faced with considerable obstacles, but he *was* the sort who was willing to
admit when he had exhausted his own knowledge.

And thus it was that Duncan Endicott, man of medicine, donned his
best linen shirt and doublet, though both were several years out of fashion,

and smoothed his Van Dyke beard and moustache, before placing his capotain hat on his head. Satisfied he would make a favorable impression, Duncan undertook the rambling walk through the nearby forest to the cottage of an aged woman known to all in the area as Granny Winter, or *Geamhradh Seanmhair* as she was called in the ancient tongue of Scotland.

It was widely believed—and Granny Winter had never disabused anyone of the assumption—that she was, in fact, the legendary Wise Woman, the *Cailleach*, the figure from ancient tales who had come into existence shortly after the dawn of mankind, making her younger than the salmon but older than the eagle. The *Cailleach* was the bearer of great wisdom, the holder of great secrets, the creator of the hills and valleys, the queen of autumn and winter, the bringer of storms, the overseer of life on earth. She was revered, and a bit feared. Whether or not Granny Winter was the Wise Woman of old, she *was* an old and wise woman.

Her cottage was not hidden, neither was it difficult to reach, but few people drew near it. Whispers and hushed conversations about the mysteries of this aging woman revealed that arriving at her doorstep was not a quest undertaken by the faint of heart.

Duncan Endicott had never been the least fainthearted.

He knocked at the rough-hewn door of the thatched-roof cottage, a sprig of wildflowers in his hand, hoping the offering would convey to Granny Winter that he had not come with ill intentions.

His knock was answered by a young woman who had lived with Granny Winter for a handful of years. No one knew her origins nor how she had come to make her home there. Duncan had not been born in the area and had even less idea of her origins than anyone else did. It was widely acknowledged that Miss Sorcha Báirbre and Granny Winter were not actually kin, and yet, they looked upon each other quite as if they were.

Sorcha was near about Duncan's age. He had taken notice of her the first time he'd seen her after moving to this corner of the kingdom only two years earlier. He'd been struck by the sparkle in her deep-brown eyes and by the eagerness with which she undertook anything and everything. And he had hardly been immune to her soft and quiet beauty. Mystery surrounded her, yet she was clearly liked and embraced by the townspeople.

Seeing her at Granny Winter's door lifted his spirits and fortified his courage.

"*Geamhradh Seanmhair*," Sorcha called back into the cottage, "the doctor is here."

From within came the craggy voice of the old woman. "Call him in, lass. He has come on an important matter."

It was moments like this, when the wise woman seemed to know things she ought not know, that solidified the belief that she was more fairy than human.

"She has been expecting you," Sorcha told him in her soft and reassuring way. She even smiled, which Duncan found particularly pleasing.

He removed his hat and stepped inside, allowing his eyes a moment to adjust to the dim interior. He approached the chair near the fire where Granny Winter sat watching him through her stringy silver hair. He presented his handful of flowers to her. For a moment, she didn't move. Was she displeased? Was his offering not acceptable enough to find favor with her?

At last, she spoke, but not to him. "Lass, take the offering and hang it to dry."

Acute relief passed through the young doctor. He had come to ask a favor; being deemed welcome was of utmost importance.

Sorcha accepted the flowers on the old woman's behalf. Voice lowered, she said to him, "Do not lose heart. She'd not have let you in if she didn't intend to hear you."

"Thank you," he said. "I'd not wish to make a nuisance of myself."

Again, she smiled.

Again, the sight buoyed him.

"Sit yourself down," the old woman said, motioning toward a three-legged stool. "Tell us what it is you have arrived to ask."

He moved to sit, his long legs bent at awkward angles as he lowered himself down. He faced her, his posture penitent and his expression humble.

"We have endured a string of illnesses of late, Granny Winter," he said. "I have done all I can, but my knowledge is limited, and my cures are insufficient. I have in my care a young girl, Donella. Her parents succumbed to the same illness their brave daughter fights fiercely all day and all night, clinging to life with ferocity. My heart aches to think her fire might extinguish despite my great efforts to save her."

Granny Winter nodded slowly. She spun in her hand an old and battered hammer. Beside her was a small stack of firewood. The cottage smelled of herbs and earth. There was something in the scene that was at once inviting and disquieting.

"What is it you wish for me to do for the lass?" Granny Winter asked.

"I have come to ask if you, in your wisdom, know of something that might help her, something I might do for her. I know I am presumptuous in asking you to give of your knowledge and time. Were I asking merely for myself, I would not do so. But I wish for the girl to live. I wish to see her restored to health."

"You have asked well," Granny Winter said. "That you inquire not to elevate yourself but for the sake of another speaks well of you."

"Will you help me save the girl?" Hope bubbled as it had not in weeks.

"Alas, I have not the answer you seek."

His heart fell to his feet. He knew not where to seek knowledge if she did not have it.

"Pick your face up, lad. I do not mean there are no answers, only that they will not come from my lips. The answers to your questions must be sought at Loch Dreva."

On the other side of the cottage, Sorcha took in a quick, audible breath, something very near to a gasp. Loch Dreva was unknown to Duncan, but he hadn't a doubt Sorcha knew it well and not through pleasant recollections.

But if that was where he would find the answers he needed, then that was where he would go.

"I'm willing to make any journey, however long, however treacherous," he said. "But I do not know where Loch Dreva lies, nor do I know how to reach it."

Granny raised one bent and bony hand and waved Sorcha to her side. "Sorcha knows this land well. She lived her earlier years as a vagabond, traveling often and traveling far. She knows the mountains and valleys, the streams and meadows."

"Will you give me instructions on how to find this loch?" he asked the lovely young woman.

"It cannot be found by being told," Sorcha said. "One must be shown. But, be warned, Loch Dreva is a place frequented by fairies and monsters alike. Certain death awaits the ill-prepared traveler."

"I confess," he said, "I am quite ill-prepared for fairies or monsters or anything of their ilk."

"Sorcha knows the tales and warnings well," Granny Winter said. "I have seen to that."

"I do not know how much time I have before Donella will slip beyond saving." Duncan worried mightily for the young girl. "I will learn as quickly as I can and do whatever I must to discover the location of this loch and gain the knowledge I need."

Granny Winter shook her head slowly, her silver hair wafting about her. A chill breeze rustled everything inside the cottage, though the door remained snuggly shut. "You must begin your journey now. Sorcha will lead you to Loch Dreva, and, as you journey, she will teach you how to escape the traps that await you."

Sorcha offered a humble agreement. To Duncan's relief, she didn't seem upset at the prospect of making the trek, though she'd not chosen it.

"But you mustn't set out without this." From beside her chair, Granny Winter produced a sack made of rough-hewn fabric, lumpy and awkwardly pieced together. "Everything you most need for your journey ahead lies within."

She held out the sack to *him*, not to Sorcha, which was surprising. She entrusted to him, whom she hardly knew, something he suspected was of value to her.

"I will guard it well," he promised.

Granny Winter shook her silver head. "Do not *guard* it well. *Use* it well."

"How long do you expect this journey will require?" Sorcha asked her. "It is nearly *Bealltainn*."

Bealltainn was a holiday of some significance in this corner of the world. It fell upon the first day of May, less than a week hence.

"Your wanderings can be concluded by then," Granny Winter said. "See that they are. I will look after the young girl, tend her until your return. But should you not take my place at her bedside by the going down of the sun on the first day of May, all will be for naught."

And thus began a journey into the world of fairies and monsters, walking a path riddled with danger in pursuit of answers to questions the two wanderers had not yet thought to ask.

INSTALLMENT II

in which our Hero learns much from our Heroine
of Things both odd and dangerous!

Sorcha and Duncan had long since left their village behind. The bag Granny Winter had provided them hung over Duncan's shoulder. Sorcha was not one to be left out of the difficult work of any undertaking and, therefore, carried another bag filled with food for their journey.

The two were not entirely unacquainted with each other, which made their arrangement more comfortable than it might have been otherwise. They'd spoken often at village gatherings when their paths crossed. Sorcha had burned her arm a few months earlier, and Duncan had tended to it. If she had to put a name to their connection, she would likely have attempted to think of a word somewhere between *acquaintances* and *friends*. What she would not have admitted, though, was that she deeply liked him.

He was a good man. Everyone who knew him felt that. But he was the respected and loved bachelor doctor in the area, and she was the odd, spinster woman who'd simply arrived one day and now lived deep in the woods in a cottage. The woman who was surrounded by whispers, who had passed the majority of her life without a home, without roots, and was now without family.

"How long will it take to reach Loch Dreva?" Duncan asked.

"We are likely to arrive on its shores this afternoon. The distance is not significant."

"And one truly cannot find the lake unless one already knows where it is?"

She nodded. "Everyone who knows its location has been brought there by someone who had previously been brought there by someone who had themselves been brought there by someone . . ." She motioned with her hand to indicate this was a pattern that repeated endlessly.

"Who, do you suppose, was the first to impart this knowledge?" He did not ask with mocking tones or dismissal but with genuine curiosity.

"No doubt a creature from the realm of fairies and monsters brought someone from the human realm there, and that person, in turn, brought someone else."

"And who was it that showed you?" he asked.

She did not always grow emotional when speaking of her family, but she found herself reluctant to answer on account of the lump forming in her throat. "My father."

Duncan must have sensed the emotion bubbling inside her. His expression filled with the same empathy and concern she had seen every time she'd watched him treat an injury or illness. "One never entirely recovers from the loss of one's parents." He spoke as one who knew.

She nodded, unable to add words to the sentiment. How sorrowful was her heart! How heavy were her reminiscences!

He managed to slip his sack from his back to his chest as they walked. He opened the bag, searching its contents. "I wonder what Granny Winter has provided us for this errand."

Sorcha had long since come to value the endless wisdom of the woman who had taken her in, but she was no closer to comprehending the enormity of it.

"I see a pair of soft leather shoes and a small stone butter crock. Odd items to be sure." He pulled from the bag a taxidermied vole. "This was certainly not expected." He set it back in the bag.

"Is that all?" she asked.

He shook his head. "There also appears to be a pair of spurs and a bottle of some sort."

Sorcha hadn't the first idea why Granny Winter had chosen those particular items, but Granny Winter seldom explained herself.

"There does not seem to be a single item in here that might aid in our defense," Duncan said.

"Seldom can the creatures that inhabit the realm of fairies and monsters be defeated by the clash of arms. Most are overcome through cleverness and an understanding of the laws that govern them."

Duncan peered inside his bag once more. "I cannot imagine a stuffed vole proving useful in a battle of wits."

"Somehow, it will," she said. "Granny Winter is as clever as the fairies. I would wager that even the strangest things in that bag will prove absolutely vital."

"Even the vole?" Duncan asked with a raise of his eyebrows and a tip of his mouth.

She smiled in return; she couldn't help herself. She was often reserved, struggling to show lightness even in pleasant moments. He brought that out in her, miracle worker that he was.

As they continued on their journey, the land around them grew more untamed, more untouched. The trees grew taller. The thistles grew thicker. On and on they walked. Closer and closer they came to the first of many dangers such a journey must hold. Oh, courage! Oh, selflessness!

"Where did you live before you came to our village?" Sorcha asked as they walked along the edge of a crystalline river.

"I lived in a village in the north of England, not terribly far from the border country."

"Do you miss it?" she asked.

"A little. My family is no longer there, and they were the strongest tie I had to it."

Had her family a proper home, a place that was theirs permanently, that is where she would have felt a pull as well. As it was, she felt them everywhere and nowhere all at once.

"My family traveled a great deal," she said. "We spent most of our time in places like this." She motioned to the surrounding vista. "There were times when I would wonder if we were the only humans to have ever seen what we saw or heard what we heard. I grew up more acquainted with fairies than with children, more with monsters than with people."

"Were you scared?" he asked.

"Sometimes. My family taught me of their ways and kept me safe. Until the end, at least."

He glanced at her but didn't press. She suspected that he, good man that he was, meant to save her from the misery of recounting such a difficult moment in her life. But she was made of stronger stuff.

"I was fourteen years old. My family, in our travels, found ourselves at a crossroads. Those are dangerous places, you must realize. For while *we* might see only the meeting of two roads, crossroads are where the human world and the fairy world often meet as well. And not every creature that emerges into *our* sphere does so with good intentions."

"Was that the case on that day?"

She nodded. "We were intending to pass the night in a small, nearby cottage and regain our strength. We had only just come to the crossroads when an enormous dog appeared. It had the look of a wolf but the size of a calf. When the light hit it in precisely the right way, we could see something even more extraordinary about this canine. It glowed an otherworldly green.

"My father shouted to all of us to run, that we must reach the cottage as quickly as possible. We immediately obeyed and ran as hard as we could toward the shelter in the distance. One piercing, terrifying howl called after us. The sound filled me with terror like I had never felt before. I ran faster, more desperately. My family did the same.

"Another howl pierced the evening air. I didn't know this creature well, but the sound of its horrifying cries told me in ways words could not that it was to be feared and for good reason. The terror I felt nearly stopped me in my tracks, nearly froze me to the spot. I sensed that one more howl would literally stop my heart.

"The time was approaching when it must, with surety, howl once more. I reached the cottage, threw open the door, and tumbled inside. In the very next instant, that third howl sounded. I huddled in the corner with my back against a wall, shaking, terrified for my very life."

"And your family?" he asked gently.

"I emerged the next morning after the light shining through the windows of the cottage revealed that I was in the home alone. I searched for my family but found nothing of them beyond my father's hat. For days, I wandered those roads, hoping to find my family but terrified I would only find that dog again. I kept at my search, going to places we had been before, all the while losing hope. It was nearly a year later when Granny Winter found me and took me in."

"You searched for a year?"

She nodded. "And I would be searching for them still if not for her. I told her all that had happened. She told me the creature we had encountered was the *cù-sìth*. It is, as I had suspected, from the realm of monsters. It hunts with howls. Humans who hear its terrifying cry but don't reach shelter under a protective roof by the time the third howl sounds . . . they die."

He took gentle hold of her hand and squeezed. It was a friendly and kind gesture. "I am so sorry for your loss."

"Granny Winter has spent these past years teaching me of the dangerous difficulties my father hadn't time to explain to me. I suspect there is little of the fairies and monsters I do not now know. I have taken refuge in her cottage for a long time, afraid to return to the paths I once knew."

"Did this quest force you to do so before you were ready?" he asked.

She pondered his question. "I was ready, but I needed a reason to take that leap again."

"Well, I thank you for being willing. I could not bear the idea of losing Donella without having exhausted every resource I have. And I could not accomplish this journey on my own. Beyond not knowing the location of the loch, I know very little of what we might encounter while we are out here. My knowledge of fairies and creatures is limited to a vague understanding of will-o'-the-wisp and an even less-specific knowledge of hobgoblins."

"And I know very little of doctoring," Sorcha said.

"It's a fine thing for people to offer each other their expertise, is it not?"

His hand still held hers. He swung their arms between them. It was, perhaps, a childish gesture, but it lightened her heart and eased her mind.

"So, tell me," he requested, "have you any idea what we might encounter at Loch Dreva?"

Quick as that, her heart grew heavy.

"I know precisely what we will find. Though I understand why Granny Winter is sending you there, I was terrified to hear her speak the destination."

Her declaration did not appear to surprise him. "Is there a horrible monster at Loch Dreva?"

"Not in the sense you are likely thinking. This particular creature has the appearance of a cantankerous old woman. She looks more human than monster."

"But she is not human?"

Sorcha shook her head. "She is the *Bean-Nighe*, the Washing Woman. She is often found at lakes and rivers, washing clothes."

"What is terrifying about washing clothes?"

"Her laundry is the death shrouds of people who are soon to die. And anyone who comes upon her is doomed to wear the shroud she is washing. Death will soon claim him or her."

"Granny Winter sent us to this bringer of death for answers?"

"The *Bean-Nighe's* expertise is the realm of death. She knows the answers to many things about life, healing, death, fate. She will know how to cure Donella."

"How do I speak to her without seeing her?"

"There is a way," she said. "But it is difficult and dangerous."

"All the more reason for you to explain it to me. I need to be as prepared as possible to undertake whatever task is required of me."

His courage warmed her and impressed her. "The first thing to remember is that once you see her, you must not look away. If you do, the shroud will be yours. Further, if she sees you, the shroud will be yours. You must come up behind her, never looking away, making no noise that might give you away. You must snatch her up off the ground before she knows you are there.

"Once you've done this, you will have power to prevent her from declaring you the next to die. While you have her, she will ask you what you require of her to secure her release. Tell her you require that she answer three questions of your posing."

He nodded. "So if I manage to lift her off the ground without looking away from her, and without being seen by her, and, in response to her asking what my demands are for releasing her, I say she is to answer three questions of my posing, then I may ask her how I can cure Donella?"

Sorcha nodded once more. "She must answer all three of your questions, and you must be very careful how you ask them. The *Bean-Nighe* is very clever. She answers questions in unexpected ways, tricking her capturers into asking questions which will not give them the answers they seek."

He did not seem discouraged but also did not seem to be taking the task lightly.

"There is more," Sorcha said. "While you do have power over her and she *must* answer your questions, the laws of such interactions require you to answer three of her questions in return."

"This is quite an ask," he said, looking wary but just as determined as ever.

"Do you feel equal to it?" she asked. "For if you don't, I will undertake this in your place, though I will not necessarily know what to ask, especially if she proves as clever as legend says she is."

"Could we not help each other navigate her tricky questions?"

Sorcha shook her head. "Only one of us can approach her, else the other, having been seen by her, will die."

He took a deep breath. "Then it is something I must do alone."

"There is no other way."

"How am I to approach quietly? Even as we have been talking, I've been able to hear my own footsteps. I will not have the cover of conversation to hide the sound."

Immediately, the answer popped into her thoughts. "The soft leather shoes in Granny's sack."

The moment she said it, he seemed to understand the epiphany she'd had. It was precisely what was needed. His feet would be protected from the rocks and thorns and thistles, but his footfalls would be rendered much lighter and much quieter.

They talked over the difficulties and worked out a few strategies. They spoke of their worries and their hopes as they continued their journey toward Loch Dreva. Soon enough, Sorcha recognized the hill around which a path led to the loch where the *Bean-Nighe* could be found undertaking her gruesome washing.

Sorcha stopped. She could pass by the hill without making the turn and remain hidden from the Washing Woman, but Duncan needed to continue directly toward his fate.

"This is where we part, is it?" He looked to her for confirmation.

"If you follow this hill, you will see Loch Dreva—and the back of the Washing Woman."

He took a deep breath. "Do you mean to wait here for me?"

"I fully anticipate you returning, successful and ready to save your dear little patient. I will wait here for you to complete your mission."

"I suspect you have more faith in me than is actually warranted."

"So prove to me that it is warranted."

He raised her hand to his lips and pressed a kind and gentle kiss there. "I will return shortly."

With that, he slipped slowly out of sight.

In her mind, she could hear the howl of the *cù-sìth*, could feel the fear of sitting alone in the silence of the dark cottage, waiting for loved ones who would never return.

INSTALLMENT III

in which our Hero encounters the *Bean-Nighe*!

Duncan paused as the trail he was on began to turn. Before he knew it, he would be facing Loch Dreva and the feared Washing Woman. Now was the time to switch his sturdy boots for the soft shoes Granny Winter had provided for him. How much quieter they would be!

The shoes fit him perfectly, which would have been surprising had they come from anyone other than Granny Winter. There was a reason she was so widely assumed to be the *Cailleach*.

He slung his sack on his back and once more began walking carefully and slowly toward his destination, amazed at how quiet his steps had become. However, as he began to hear the sounds of water, his heart pounded so loudly he wasn't certain the soft-soled shoes would help at all.

Once I see her, I must not look away. Mustn't make any noise. Mustn't let her see me. Must snatch her up off the ground. Must require her to answer three questions.

He silently repeated the list as he walked, hoping that by making the instructions quite clear in his mind, he would be able to adhere to them without difficulty. He would have but one chance.

His heart ached as he thought of Sorcha waiting for him on the other side of the hill. She had waited alone for her family all those years ago, not realizing they had been unable to escape the monster as she had. He didn't want her to suffer like that again. And he most certainly didn't want to die.

His footsteps, silent under the influence of his borrowed shoes, took him closer and closer to the sound of water. After a time, the swishing sound of water being agitated joined the cacophony. That, he would wager, was the *Bean-Nighe* washing her terrifying shrouds.

Duncan searched the area, determined to know where she was so he wouldn't accidentally give himself away. Closer and closer he drew. Nearer and nearer he came. A slight rise in the path afforded him a view of the entire loch—its pristine, luminous waters, the mountains on every side. And what appeared to be a haggard old woman hunched over on the shore, her back to him, washing.

The *Bean-Nighe*.

He stepped closer and closer. How he wished he could look down to make certain of his steps and avoid disturbing any rocks underneath his foot. But looking away meant certain death, so he kept his eyes on her.

She was muttering to herself, though not in any language he

understood. Her voice was just loud enough to mask what little noise his footsteps made. He drew closer, keeping extremely quiet.

Don't let her see you.

So long as he didn't distract her from her gruesome task, she wouldn't look in his direction.

Careful.

Quiet.

He was closer than ever, close enough to hear the clink of rocks hitting each other, no doubt being used to scrub shrouds.

Lift her off the ground, or the shroud will be mine.

He was so close. One more step. He held his arms out. He could not afford even the tiniest mistake. He swung his arms together and wrapped them around the twisted figure, lifting her immediately from the ground.

The *Bean-Nighe's* piercing scream was harrowing and unnerving. She was so light that she felt almost like nothing in his arms. It was a trick, no doubt, meant to convince people they'd not actually taken hold of her so they would release her without their demands being met and their survival secured.

She squirmed and screamed at him, in what language he knew not.

"I'll not release you until you meet my demands," he said firmly and authoritatively.

Her voice crackly and grating, she said, "And what are your demands?"

He recalled perfectly what Sorcha had told him of this part of the inter-action. "You must answer three of my questions, and then I will release you, and you will allow me to leave unharmed."

"Someone has taught you our ways."

Unsure if conversation was permitted, he simply repeated himself. "You must answer three of my questions, and then I will release you, and you will allow me to leave unharmed."

"Very well," she said. "You must answer three of mine in return."

He knew that would be required of him. "Very well."

The Washing Woman ceased her wriggling and wailing.

"My first question is this: How do I cure Donella's illness?" he asked.

"And my first question is this: How do you define 'cure'?"

He held his peace a moment, remembering what Sorcha had told him of the woman's cleverness. The way he defined the word, he didn't doubt, would change the answer he received. "I define it as treating an ailment or injury or other such difficulty in such a way that the person being treated makes a full recovery."

"Then my answer to your first question—How do you cure the girl's illness?—is this: through great difficulty."

She had, indeed, answered the question, but she'd not done so in any helpful way. He had to think of a different manner of posing his question so that she could not escape answering it. "My second question is this: What are the *precise* means, methodology, and anything else necessary to the accomplishing of it, that will cure Donella?"

"You learn quickly." The *Bean-Nighe* sounded none too pleased. "My second question for you is this: How much are you willing to risk for this cure?"

Not wanting to give her reason to make his efforts more dangerous than they had to be, he was careful in his reply. "My answer to you," he said, "is to observe our current situation and allow that to serve as your answer."

She growled in her throat. "Then my answer to you is this: You must travel to the churchyard in Carrifran and gather water from the mouth of the gargoyle. If the girl drinks it, she will be cured according to your definition."

He was not familiar with that town. How many days would be required to reach it? How many days to return home? How he wished he were granted limitless questions so he could learn all he needed to know. Instead, he asked what seemed the best question for obtaining the most pertinent information. "My final question is this: What is the most important thing for me to know if I am to make this journey and return home safely?"

"My final question is this: How do you define 'safely'?"

Again, she meant to trick him into limiting what she was required to do for him. "I define it thus: to be made and remain whole in body, mind, and spirit."

"And *my* answer is this: the most important thing to know is that no one emerges whole from a harrowing journey when that journey is undertaken entirely alone."

It was not at all the helpful bit of advice he'd hoped for. It was, however, true to her nature. Still, he had asked his allotted three questions and had answered hers. He felt certain that, were he to not honor their agreement, the consequences would be dire.

"Having obliged me in my requirements, and I in yours, I will release you, and you will permit me to go on my way."

"As agreed," she said.

His heart pounded, but he trusted Sorcha's knowledge of these things. He lowered his arms so the *Bean-Nighe's* feet touched the ground once more. He released his hold on her and stepped back. She picked up the shroud she had dropped when he'd grabbed her, and she returned to her washing, muttering to herself and not looking at him.

He hadn't thought to ask Sorcha if he was required to keep looking at the *Bean-Nighe* as he made his way back. It seemed best to do so rather than risk being wrong.

He walked carefully backward away from the loch, over the rise, and out of sight of the Washing Woman. Only when he was certain she could no longer see him, and already knowing he could not see her, did he truly breathe again.

Water from the mouth of the gargoyle in the churchyard at Carrifran.

Duncan did not know where that journey would take them, but he suspected the danger was far from over.

INSTALLMENT IV

in which an unexpected Danger places our Hero
and Heroine in a most dire Situation!

Sorcha felt as though hours had passed, though it had likely not been more than thirty minutes. She told herself to breathe, to remain calm, to not grow overly worried. But her mind returned rapidly and repeatedly to a similar wait undertaken in a dark cottage on a fear-filled night.

She tried to tell herself she had given Duncan ample warning about the dangers he faced, that his knowledge of it would protect him. But her father and mother had understood the threat of the *cù-sìth*. Her father, after all, had shouted for them to run for the cottage; it was the cottage, and the cottage *alone*, where they would have been safe. They had known what they faced; they simply hadn't had time to escape.

She alternated between pacing the road and sitting on a large rock nearby. She kept herself out of view of the path, not entirely certain how far one had to travel before seeing the *Bean-Nighe*. But, heavens, how she was tempted to look for Duncan!

Hers was more than merely the concern one human being ought to have for another. She liked Duncan. She knew him to be a good and kind-hearted person. He was clever and caring. Handsome. Generous. How strange that he had never been married. Few in their village remained bachelors, but he had, despite his caring and generous heart.

She rose from her rock once more and began pacing. Duncan was undertaking the task, would be successful, and would return. Of course he would.

She hoped.

She turned back toward the rock on which she'd been sitting, but she didn't take a single step.

There, standing where she'd been, was Duncan. He had arrived silently. Granny's shoes were very effective. She hoped they had proven just as effective in his very dangerous task.

She remained rooted to the spot, watching him, unable to even speak.

"She was there," he said. "I never looked away. She didn't see me."

Sorcha began breathing a little more easily.

"I snatched her up off the ground, asked my required three questions, and answered hers. Then she let me go."

Sorcha pressed a hand to her pounding heart. "Then you're safe? The shroud will not be yours?" Her voice emerged a bit breathless. She'd been so very afraid for him!

"It will not. And, further, she told me how to heal Donella."

Most of the tension in Sorcha's body eased. She crossed to him. "What do we need to do?"

"We have to fetch water from the mouth of the gargoyle in the church-yard at Carrifran. If Donella drinks it, she will be healed."

"Then our journey is not yet complete." She hadn't anticipated that. They hadn't a great deal of time before they must return.

"I don't know where Carrifran is," he said.

"I do," Sorcha said. "It lies at least a day's walk from here."

"If we begin now, we should reach Carrifran tomorrow," he said, clearly thinking out loud. "That still leaves us three days before *Bealltainn*."

"Yes, but I have my suspicions that the Washing Woman is not the last creature we will encounter. You see, they are not solitary. They are not un-connected. That you had one interaction with a member of their race, and emerged triumphant, means others will be watching for you, determined to best you as the *Bean-Nighe* was unable to do."

"And what of your encounter with the *cù-sìth*? You emerged triumphant in that encounter," he said.

"The very reason Granny Winter has taught me so much of the ways of fairies and monsters. She is hopeful that the passage of so many years without significant interactions means they aren't particularly upset at my escape. Likely because they were successful in causing me so much pain."

"Are all creatures from that realm so vindictive and bloodthirsty?"

Sorcha shook her head. "Some are rather benevolent. Some are neither good nor bad. But those that mean harm are more than capable of inflicting it."

"If you don't wish to continue," he said, "I will understand. You need only give me directions, and I will make the remainder of the journey on my own."

"I am not afraid."

"Neither am I," he said.

She'd long suspected he was quite brave. It was a wonderful thing to realize she was right.

"We had best begin," she said. "We have a long journey ahead."

They paused long enough for him to switch from the soft shoes to his sturdier boots. Granny's shoes were placed in the bag, and the bag slung over his shoulder. Sorcha pulled from her bag an apple for each of them, which they ate as they walked.

"What do you know of this town we are heading toward?" he asked.

"Not very much. I know where it is, but I've not been there myself. Granny Winter showed me a map a few weeks ago, talking about the various places and some of their history. She pointed out that town on the map, but she didn't tell me anything about it."

His face pulled in an expression of pondering. "I have my suspicions she knew you were going to be making this journey. Why else would she have a bag ready with things that were needed, and why else would she mention this town to you?"

Sorcha smiled to herself. Granny *had* likely known, or at least had had an inkling. There seemed very little that woman didn't know or couldn't predict. How she hoped Granny Winter had foreseen the possibility of success on this journey, even if success wasn't entirely promised.

They had been walking for nearly an hour, speaking of inconsequential things, sharing stories from their lives and their likes and dislikes, recounting things that had happened in their village and the people they knew there. It was one of the most pleasant conversations she'd ever had. The villagers were not unkind to her, neither did they ignore her existence. But they kept her at a distance, likely because she lived with Granny Winter, who was treated with respect but also with uncertainty.

The path Sorcha and Duncan walked took them into a meadow. Grass fluttered in the breeze. Wildflowers were abundant. No matter that the countryside held difficult memories for her, she still found it the most beautiful and inviting of places. Duncan hunched down a few steps into the meadow and plucked from the ground a beautiful purple flower. Not all men would notice such things, but she wasn't surprised he did. He had a gentle heart and a kind soul. She was surprised, however, when he offered the flower to her.

She accepted it. "No one has ever given me a flower." She spun it between her finger and her thumb, mesmerized by the whirl of purple hues.

"Not ever?" The revelation clearly surprised him.

"I know giving flowers to ladies is something men often do. I suppose I'm simply not the sort of lady they think of doing that for."

"I don't see why that would be." He stroked his pointed beard and mustache, his expression one of deep pondering. "You're clever and kind. You're the very best of company. Beautiful and pleasant. You have a kind heart, and you care about people."

She felt herself blushing all the deeper. She was never paid such compliments. Granny Winter was not unkind to her, but hers was not a disposition which leant itself to saying flowery things. Sorcha breathed in the floral scent, then tucked the stem behind her ear.

They continued walking through the meadow. She couldn't imagine being more content with anyone than she was with him in that moment. They'd very nearly reached the other side, where the meadow gave way to a small copse of trees, and their path continued on. A niggling doubt tugged at her mind. They were going in the right direction, weren't they?

He was trusting her to get him to Carrifran. Was she certain they were indeed on the right path? She paused, still in the meadow, still within sight of the path through the trees. She turned and looked in the direction they'd come. Why was it she felt the need to go back? She couldn't ignore the very real pull she felt.

"What is it?" Duncan asked.

"I find myself wondering if we're proceeding in the correct direction. Something in my mind is telling me we should be going back."

"Back in the direction of Loch Dreva?" He clearly did not agree with her assessment.

"Perhaps not that far," she said. "We may have missed a break in the road or a turn we ought to have taken."

"I didn't see any," he said.

That he was doubtful of her settled frustratingly on her mind. Did he not feel this same insistence that they were going the wrong way?

She studied the meadow, hoping to discover some clue as to what was pulling at her. She spied a flash of blue light at a distance, dancing on the tips of the blades of wild grass. The light called to her. Beckoned to her.

"We need to go that way." Without hesitating or looking back at him, she rushed toward the spark, but it extinguished the moment she reached it.

Frantic, her eyes swept the area, searching.

The blue light appeared again, a bit farther ahead, back the way they'd come.

She chased it only to have it extinguish and reappear farther away. It moved faster, though she did too. The pull was undeniable, unmistakable. She couldn't have stopped chasing it if she tried.

Back it went, back along the trail. On and on she followed, not to the path they'd been on but into a nearby wood. There was no path, just flickering blue lights, tiny blue flames popping up everywhere, guiding her in the direction she knew she had to go.

Duncan caught up to her, running alongside her, digging in his bag. He pulled out the crock of butter and tossed it toward the blue flame. It stopped. Hovered.

She stopped.

Duncan set his arms around her, his embrace firm but gentle. "I know this creature," he said. "You mustn't follow it, Sorcha."

"I need to. It's taking me where I must follow."

"It's the will-o'-the-wisp. It is leading you astray, and it will lead you to your death if you allow it. You have to resist the urge to follow."

Something in his words penetrated the fog clouding her mind. The will-o'-the-wisp. It called to those who wandered, those who felt pulled toward something new and something different. It twisted around the mind, convincing people to run ever deeper into dangerous paths, away from the path they were meant to trod. It tugged at her wanderer's heart, tucked itself into her vagabond's mind, and pulled her almost beyond resisting.

She closed her eyes tightly and leaned against Duncan. She wrapped her arms around his middle and held fast to him, knowing her life depended on it. The mystical flame would eventually extinguish itself, searching for another unwary wanderer. She simply needed to resist its call until it did.

"I can still hear it," she whispered, afraid.

He stood steadfast, a lighthouse in a storm, holding her to him and whispering words of reassurance and promises to remain with her for as long as she needed him to.

"The flame has flickered out," he said after a time.

But its pull continued twisting around her mind. She held fast to Duncan, depending on him to keep her from following the lights again.

"There is a hollowed-out old tree nearby, one large enough for us to tuck ourselves inside," he said. "We'll be warm and safe there."

He kept hold of her as they walked, held her hand as she set herself in the protective embrace of the tree, then sat beside her.

"We know now why Granny Winters included a crock of butter in her bag," Duncan said. "The will-o'-the-wisp is known to steal milk from cows to make into butter. Offering butter provided a needed distraction."

"I shudder to think what would have happened if you'd not helped me." Sorcha leaned against him.

He set his arms around her once more. "We make a fine team, Sorcha." There was comfort in that. Comfort and hope.

INSTALLMENT V

in which the Promise of a New Day turns to Fear!

Dawn broke, sending rays of soft morning light into the protective hollow of the tree where Duncan and Sorcha had sought refuge. The will-o'-the-wisp had not returned. Its call no longer seemed to pull at Sorcha, but Duncan could tell she was shaken by the experience. He was a little shaken himself.

Seeing her run, seeing her leave without so much as glancing back at him, had struck something more than fear into him. His heart had actually cracked, broken a little. Even before realizing what she was chasing, he'd been weighed down by the realization that she was leaving him behind.

How had he come to care so deeply for someone he'd only just met? How was it his heart had grown so partial to her so quickly?

Waking up to the promise of the new day, the clear sky of a bright spring morning, with Sorcha sleeping soundly in his arms and Granny's miracle bag on the ground beside them, he felt strangely at peace. Just as Sorcha had said the day before, he was certain they would yet encounter more creatures before their journey ended. He didn't know what could possibly remain, what dangers awaited, but he wasn't afraid. And he wasn't alone.

"No one emerges whole from a harrowing journey when that journey is undertaken entirely alone." Was this what the *Bean-Nighe* meant? Was her answer not merely an avoidance of his question but also a useful piece of advice?

A moment passed, and Sorcha woke as well. Sleep remained heavy on her eyelids. Her movements were slow with lingering slumber.

"How are you feeling today?" he asked.

She smiled up at him. "Ever the doctor, aren't you?"

He laughed a little at that. "I suppose. I *am* asking as more than a man of medicine, though."

Color touched her cheeks. She blushed so beautifully, just as she had when he'd offered her the flower in the meadow yesterday. It was a joy to see her do so again.

"I am well," she said. "A little embarrassed to have been so quickly taken in by the will-o'-the-wisp. I do know better."

He took her hand in his. "The pull of that creature goes beyond logic and knowledge. You've nothing to be embarrassed about."

"I suppose I hadn't realized how much of a wanderer's heart I still have."

He pressed a light kiss to her hand. "Which is also nothing to be embarrassed about."

She sighed, the sound one of relief. "Thank you."

"We likely have a long day of walking ahead of us," he said. "I'm hopeful you still have some food in your bag."

She took it up and opened it. "I do."

"That is a relief," he said, turning his tone to one of absolute teasing. "I feared for a moment we were going to have to eat the vole."

She laughed, the sound of it settling like music on his ears. Had there ever been another person who brought him such easy and soul-warming delight?

He opened up his bag, intending to make a show of reaching inside for the vole. But he stopped, staring in confusion.

"What's the matter?" she asked.

"The soft slippers are gone."

"Did you leave them somewhere?" she asked.

He shook his head.

"Then they have disappeared?"

"So it would seem. I suppose there must be some sort of enchantment on them."

She shrugged. "I don't think Granny Winters would play us such a trick if we still needed the shoes."

"Then," he said, "perhaps they disappear when they are no longer needed."

Sorcha handed him a bit of bread and a slice of hard cheese. "What is left in your bag?"

"The spurs, the vole, and the stoppered vessel."

Her brows pulled together in thought as they ate their humble breakfast. Duncan hadn't any idea what the items could possibly be used for. But one thing felt quite certain: they would be useful, *essential* even. And he meant to guard the bag closely.

Their morning meal completed and the sun fully above the horizon, they began their journey, walking as they had the day before, crossing miles, over hills, around rivers, through meadows.

Whenever they walked across the broad, open areas where flowers and wild grass grew, she took hold of his hand. He knew she was worrying that the will-o'-the-wisp would return and she would be unable to resist the siren call to wander. That she took comfort and strength in his touch was a fine thing indeed. After the third such meadow, she kept her hand in his, walking along quite as if it was the most natural thing in all the world. Truth be told, it felt natural.

The day was waxing long, though not entirely over. Sorcha said she felt certain they were going in the right direction, but the trek was taking longer than expected. Though she didn't say as much, he suspected she felt a bit guilty for having added to the length of their journey by running after the will-o'-the-wisp. But Granny had sent them with precisely the object needed to break that spell, which meant she had anticipated the need. And if their task was doomed to fail from the beginning, she would not have sent them. Duncan took great reassurance in that.

It didn't mean the outcome was guaranteed. But it meant there was a chance.

The road they were on grew more defined and easier to see. Trees grew on either side, and mountains loomed in the distance, but the path was clear.

Until it unexpectedly broke in two.

Sorcha kept back, clinging tightly to his hand and eyeing the area. "Crossroads are dangerous things," she said.

She had warned him about that before.

"Do you know which way we are meant to go?"

She shook her head. "Not entirely." She continued eyeing the area, but she didn't seem ready to run or abandon their mission. Hers was not an aura of fear but of vigilance.

"There must be some clue," he suggested. "Surely something will tell us which road to take."

She nodded and peeked down one road, then took a few steps, but not many, in that direction. He did the same down the other.

Just at the edge of the road, tucked among the trees, was a horse. It was calm and docile, dipping its head to take a mouthful of grass before looking around quite as if it hadn't a care in all the world. This was clearly not a wild horse, one inclined to bolt and jump at the slightest thing. It likely belonged to someone. And it likely could be ridden.

Ridden.

Granny Winter had placed spurs in his bag. She would not have done so if they weren't meant to be used. Being quite careful to not spook the horse, he removed the spurs from the bag and pulled them onto his boots, strapping them in place.

"I see a large outcropping of rock down the other road," Sorcha said, still at a distance. "I remember that was on the map of the road to Carrifran."

"How far from Carrifran?" He kept his eye on the horse as the sound of Sorcha's footsteps grew louder.

"A half-day's journey, likely." She was at his side. "Where did the horse come from, do you suppose?"

"I'm not certain."

"Granny did include spurs," she said. "That cannot be mere coincidence." Clever as she was, Sorcha had pieced together that bit of the puzzle almost instantly.

"I can only assume we are meant to ride it. A horse would get us to our destination more quickly."

She still looked uncertain. "Finding the horse at a crossroads does not feel like a *safe* discovery. The animal may very well be something other than it seems."

"Is there a creature belonging to that realm who appears in the form of a horse?"

She nodded. "Several."

"Are they all dangerous?"

She shook her head. "But at least one of them is: the kelpie. It is quite dangerous, in fact."

They approached the horse with caution. There must have been a body of water nearby; water dripped from its mane. Perhaps the animal was docile because it was tired. Perhaps it had been trapped for a time in a downpour. Except, it hadn't rained that day.

"What do you suppose we ought to do?" Sorcha eyed the horse with misgiving.

"Granny would not have given us the spurs if she didn't mean for us to use them."

Sorcha shook her head. "It's possible she included them on the chance that we did decide to ride the horse, even though doing so would be a mistake."

It might very well prove to be one. But could they truly risk returning too late to save Donella? Their time was running worryingly short.

"I think we should ride it in the direction that we need to go," he said. "It will speed our journey and increase the chances we can return home by *Bealltainn*."

Sorcha agreed, though she seemed reluctant.

He climbed onto the horse's back, and Sorcha, using a fallen tree as a step, sat behind him, the rough fabric of her dress bunched up around her. Riding a horse very nearly atop its hind legs would not be terribly comfortable for her. He hoped, for her sake, this proved a gentle ride. She wrapped her arms around his middle. He took hold of the damp hair of the horse's mane, the only thing available to him. Not merely wet, the mane contained bits of seaweed.

Duncan pulled out a piece and, keeping hold of the mane with his other hand, held the seaweed up for Sorcha to see. "I've never known a horse to collect this in its mane."

"Seaweed!" she gasped. "It's the kelpie."

The kelpie. She'd said that was the most dangerous of the monsters appearing in the form of a horse.

Something about the feel of the creature beneath him began to change. It softened and grew more enveloping, almost as if he were sinking into it.

"Tell me what to do," he said.

"It will become sticky, making escape impossible. It will ride with us directly back to whatever loch it lives in and drown us in the depths."

The kelpie bolted.

Duncan needn't have held on to the mane; the kelpie had become so adhesive he couldn't have come loose if he'd tried. "What of the spurs? Why would Granny give us spurs?"

"The spurs are made of iron; they must be. Iron alone can control it."

Her grip on him tightened. She was holding so fast he could hardly breathe.

He dug his spurs into the flanks of the beast, which was twisting and shifting in shape. The harder he dug, the more solid it became beneath him despite feeling less and less like a horse. Using his legs and the spurs on his feet, he pushed and turned and nudged the creature in the direction they were meant to go. It bucked and jumped and made every attempt to loosen the grip of the iron spurs. Duncan held on for dear life, and not merely his. Sorcha's life depended on it as well.

From behind him, she called out directions, telling him which way to turn the kelpie, which way to direct it.

On and on they went, dodging trees, jumping over rocks and obstacles, moving faster than any horse ever could. Duncan's legs burned with the effort to keep control of the beast even as it made every attempt to dislodge him. The muscles in his legs were turning to gruel. He didn't know how much longer he could maintain control of the dangerous monster.

At last, the creature came to a jarring stop. Rearing up on its back legs, it slung them to the ground, then darted off on the instant.

Stunned, the air knocked entirely from him, Duncan lay on his back, hurting in every muscle of his body, his mind refusing to accept the reality that they might be safe. He could summon only enough strength to turn his head and look for Sorcha.

She lay on the ground nearby, looking up at the moonlit sky. Her breath clouded above her in the chill of night.

Night. How was it that so much time had passed? Could they truly have been riding for hours?

Using what little strength remained in him, he pulled himself over to where she lay. He set an arm around her.

"Are you injured?" he asked.

"Exhausted. But whole."

He rested his head against hers, letting himself simply breathe. He closed his eyes, rested his body and mind, and silently prepared himself for whatever further dangers awaited them on this most perilous of journeys.

INSTALLMENT VI

in which our brave Duo's destination proves quite unexpected!

Aching and sore after the terrifying ride they'd had on the back of the kelpie, Duncan and Sorcha pulled themselves up off the ground. Night had, indeed, fallen. They were at the end of their second day of traveling, and they had only two days to make the journey back home. There was no time for setbacks.

They kept their hands clasped as they walked along the road toward Carrifran. Only the moon in the clear evening sky lit the scene. No lights emanated from inside any home or building. No fires appeared to be burning in any hearths. The town was completely and utterly quiet.

Their steps took them down a street to the remains of a market cross. All was still. The buildings were in disrepair.

"Carrifran appears to be abandoned," Duncan said, unsure what that meant for their current endeavor.

In the distance, he could see the spire of the church. The road they were on would take them directly there. Sorcha kept near his side, but her steps were slow. He didn't know if she was weary from the journey or wary about what they might encounter next. He himself felt a great deal of both.

They arrived at the outer gate of the churchyard. It too appeared abandoned.

There was no way to tell how long it had been since anyone had lived in this town or worshiped in this chapel, but the eerie emptiness of it filled him with misgivings. And, yet, he could clearly see on the corner of the dilapidated chapel a stone rainspout carved to look like a gargoyle. This was their destination. This was where they needed to be.

"I do not imagine it will be as easy as it appears," Sorcha said. "More needs to be done, I'm certain. Something else must be waiting for us here."

He wished he didn't agree with her assessment. After all they had encountered, this seemingly clear path proved terribly unsettling.

Holding tight to Sorcha's hand, he took a single step forward. She did as well. The moment their feet touched the churchyard soil, a flash of lightning cracked the cloudless sky.

Without warning, without sound, without pause, a woman appeared before them. A ghost.

She hovered in the air, her feet not touching the ground, her green dress wafting as if in a breeze. She was impossible to miss, and yet her form was not entirely solid. Duncan could still see the church behind her, through her, obscured by her.

She stared at them, watching them with a look that clearly foretold danger. But she said not a word.

"What is your assessment?" he asked Sorcha.

"If I had to guess, I would say she's a Lady Grim."

"I had heard churchyard grims were animals—usually dogs."

Sorcha nodded. "Traditionally, the first living thing buried in a church-yard is an animal whose spirit guards the resting places of all who follow. But if that is not done, then the duty to protect the spot lies with whomever was buried there most recently. That person's spirit remains until someone else is buried, who then takes up the role, which is later inherited by the next to be laid to rest."

To the still silent and still watchful Lady Grim, he said, "We mean no harm. We have come only to fetch water from the mouth of the gargoyle. We need it to cure a very ill young girl in our village."

The Lady Grim said nothing. She watched him, but her expression changed from anger to something very nearly pleading.

"Is there something you need from us?" Sorcha asked.

The Lady Grim motioned with her ghostly hand toward a nearby grave. Duncan hunched down low enough to face the stone. He wiped the dirt from its face, making the inscription clear. The grave belonged to a woman buried more than one hundred years earlier on what, according to the inscriptions, was to have been her wedding day. She had been merely twenty-five years of age.

From his position, he looked up at the ghostly guardian. "Is this you?" he asked gently.

She nodded.

"No one has been buried here since?" Sorcha asked.

The Lady Grim shook her head.

Duncan stood once more, looking at the dilapidated church and thinking about the crumbling village they'd walked through. She was the last person to have been buried here. And no one lived here any longer. No one else would ever be buried in this churchyard. She was trapped as the guardian of this place, held here for more than a century, unable to obtain her eternal rest.

"She is a prisoner here," Sorcha said, following his thoughts. "There must be a way to free her."

"I've never freed a grim," he said. "Is it even possible?"

Sorcha shook her head. "Grims aren't freed; they are exchanged."

They stood in silence for a time. Surely neither of them was meant to die and be buried here for this journey to be completed. Granny Winter would never have subjected Sorcha to such a fate.

He looked to the Lady Grim, who watched him with a sad, silent countenance. How desperately she must have wanted to leave, but it was not in her power to do so. He felt called to be a doctor, a healer. He did all he could for those amongst the living, but he had no ability to heal the dead.

"I am sorry," he said to her. "I don't know how to right this wrong."

She still didn't speak, didn't move.

Duncan tried to take a step toward the church. He was immediately flung back by an unseen hand. He landed on the ground, painfully but not injuriously.

Sorcha helped him to his feet. "It seems the only way to reach the church is to release her."

"Exchanging a life is out of the question," Duncan said.

"Whoever began this churchyard did not spare her this fate. There is no means of freeing her other than finding someone to take her place."

"I will not sacrifice either of our lives for this." He could not. He *would* not. "The past two days have been life-altering despite the danger. I could never again imagine my life without you in it. I refuse to believe Granny Winter would send us on a journey that would bring us together only to tear us apart again."

She set her hand lightly on his arm. "I cannot imagine my life without you either."

There had to be another way to free the grim and save Donella. This could not be the end of their perilous journey.

"If only a true grim had been buried first," Sorcha said. "Animal spirits do not require an exchange."

Animal. "Does that hold true only if the animal is the *first* to be buried?"

She shook her head, her expression turning to one of deep consideration. "An animal could take over the duties of a grim even now."

And they had an animal. He pulled Granny's bag off his back and opened it. All that remained was the stuffed vole and the bottle. The small animal had seemed such an odd thing, but it now made perfect sense.

"Are there any rules about grims that say the thing buried must be newly dead?" he asked.

"I do not know." She met his gaze, hope shining in her eyes. "It *is* possible the vole can serve this purpose."

"It is worth trying," he said. "It is worth seeing if Granny Winter knew of our plight in such detail."

He turned his attention to the Lady Grim. "We are going to try to free you," he said. "If we succeed, will you allow us passage to the gargoyle?"

She dipped her head in agreement. This was their chance, then.

In a bit of dirt under a nearby tree, Duncan began to dig. He'd no implements, only his fingers. He clawed at the soft dirt. Sorcha soon joined him. They didn't dig a large hole, nor a deep one. Simply enough to bury the animal sent with him.

As they dug, the wind picked up and swirled the tree branches. The smell of rain filled the air. He glanced at the Lady Grim as he continued his effort. Her hair and dress whipped with greater vigor, greater motion. She, he did not doubt, was creating this storm, but whether out of excitement or nervousness, he couldn't say.

At last, the hole was of sufficient size. He placed the vole in it, and he and Sorcha pushed the dirt back in to cover its resting place. They packed it down, making certain the remains were hidden, held fast, and safe. Sorcha placed a rock at the grave site, allowing it to act as a headstone.

They both stood and stepped back, looking from the tiny, makeshift grave to the Lady Grim. Was it enough? Would it work?

Lightning once more cracked, sending flashes of light across the sky. It disappeared quickly and with it the guardian of the graveyard. She'd come without a word, left without a warning. In the next instant, the sky opened, and rain began to fall.

Duncan and Sorcha rushed across the churchyard, crossing as quickly as they could over the rough, unkempt land, directly to the corner of the church where the gargoyle stood sentinel.

All that remained in Duncan's bag was the bottle. He pulled it out, realizing what its purpose was. In it, they would collect the water that would save Donella's life. He pulled off the stopper and held the vessel directly beneath the grotesque stone face. As rain filled the gutters of the church, water began to pour over the teeth and snarled lips of the carving. It splashed off Duncan's hands, off the sides of the vessel, soaking him and Sorcha but also filling the vessel.

Once the water reached the very brim, he plunged the stopper in place once more, then returned it to his bag and pulled the bag onto his back. He hoped it would be enough to heal young Donella.

He and Sorcha huddled beneath the archway of what had once likely held the church doors. It offered minimal protection from the elements, but it was enough. He wrapped his arms around her, holding her to him as the rain fell.

"We've managed it," he said. "We've managed it together."

"We still need to return home safely," Sorcha said. "I shudder to think what awaits us on that journey. And we've only two days remaining. I'm not certain it can be done."

From behind them, in the ruined remains of the church, he heard voices. They both turned, keeping hold of one another.

The church was filled with ghostly apparitions, people dressed in clothing of eras gone by, reaching back centuries. At the front of the chapel, in the chancel near the altar, was the Lady Grim, though now she wore a crown of ghostly flowers and held a matching bouquet. A man clothed in the garb of the same era as she was gazed lovingly at her face.

Hers was the appearance of a bride, and the man was, no doubt, the one she would have married had she lived.

The ghostly bride gave her faded bouquet to a woman standing near her. She set her hands in her groom's. A ghost in priestly raiment stood before them.

"Their wedding," Sorcha whispered. "How long they must have waited for this day!"

Duncan pulled her closer. "It's a sight that could melt the heart of even a resolute bachelor like myself."

From within his arms, she asked, "Are you resolutely a bachelor or a bachelor who happens to be a resolute sort of person?"

"Bachelorhood has, of late, lost its appeal."

At the front of the church, the ceremony reached its joyous conclusion. The husband and wife embraced to the silent cheers of generations of their families. The sight, indeed, touched the heart.

With her groom's arm tenderly around her, the Lady Grim smiled at Duncan and Sorcha, then motioned back in the direction of the churchyard.

They looked that way. A bright doorway of light appeared. It emanated warmth and a sense of safety. Duncan could not express exactly why he felt secure in doing so, but he knew they needed to step through this bright passageway.

"I suspect that is a doorway home," Sorcha said. "They are offering us a safe return."

She felt as he did. That was reassurance enough.

Hand in hand, they moved from beneath the stone arch to the doorway of light and stepped through.

INSTALLMENT VII
in which our Hero and Heroine discover the Grandest Adventure of all!

Passing through the doorway of light set Duncan and Sorcha directly in front of his humble cottage in their home village. The return journey, one that would have, no doubt, been filled with terrifying creatures, was avoided entirely. They'd returned with ample time, several days remaining before *Bealltainn*. Duncan still held the vessel of water in his hand, Granny's now-empty bag on his back. And he still had Sorcha at his side. She kept hold of his hand, giving no indication she had any intention of letting go.

They rushed inside the cottage without having to discuss it. There, sitting beside the cot where Donella had lain ill and suffering for nearly a fortnight, was Granny Winter. She rocked slowly back and forth, watching them enter without the least bit of surprise.

"We've returned," Sorcha said.

"I knew you must have been close." Granny Winter motioned to the floor directly beside her. There, piled neatly, was everything that had disappeared from the sack she had given Duncan. All the items must have returned to her as they'd vanished.

To Sorcha, he said, "Help the little one sit up. I'm going to give her the water."

Sorcha rushed to do so, no hesitation, no uncertainty. She gently assisted the poor girl, weak with illness, to a seated position, holding her and speaking soothingly.

Duncan sat on the edge of her bed. "Sip this," he said. "It will make you whole."

She gave a weak nod of understanding. Slowly, one drop at a time, she began to drink the contents of the small vessel. Her strength returned quickly. Sips turned into full swallows. Sorcha no longer needed to hold Donella upright. The last remaining mouthful of water, Donella took on her own, having strength enough to do so. She handed the vessel back to Duncan, smiling brightly for the first time in weeks.

Duncan looked to Granny Winter. She nodded. And she rose. She held a hand out to the little girl. "We've come to an agreement, Donella and I. This little one has lost her family, and I have room in my cottage. She means to come stay with me."

"Just as I did when I was orphaned," Sorcha said.

"You are welcome to remain as long as you wish," Granny Winter said. "But I suspect you are ready to begin anew."

Sorcha nodded. "For so long, I have feared what the world held. But I have faced it again and have discovered I am equal to it."

Granny Winter dipped her head. She turned to Duncan. "Sorcha has a wanderer's heart. It will pull her away, seeking adventures and journeys. You must decide what pull *you* feel."

He hardly needed to think about it. His life would be unimaginable without her. A mere few days on the road, facing dangers they'd never expected and finding in each other the welcome rest and steadfast connection they both needed, had taught him to trust her more than he had anyone else. To cherish her. To love her.

"I may not have spent much time journeying, but I've no objection to wandering the lochs and hills and valleys, especially if I can do so with her."

Sorcha reached her hands out. He took them both and pulled her into his embrace.

To Granny Winter, he said, "I believe you have your answer."

"But heed my warning," Granny said. "You have caught the attention of the fairies and monsters. You will not be free of them now. They will search you out."

"Then we will face that difficulty head-on," Sorcha said. "And we will help people along the way."

"Perhaps you would consider making us a gift of your magical bag," Duncan said. "Just as you promised, all we needed was found inside."

Granny Winter smiled, deep wrinkles crinkling in an expression of amusement. "All that you needed was inside *of you*. Courage, determination, cleverness. Together, you have all you need."

Duncan turned his gaze back to Sorcha. "Together, we have all we need."

And they did, indeed. As they walked the paths of life, they found in each other everything they had ever dreamed of.

ᛒODIES

OF

ᛚIGHT

BEING A FICTIONALIZATION
OF REPORTED
AND CORROBORATED
MYSTERIOUS PHENOMENA

by Dr. Barnabus Milligan

CHAPTER ONE

In recent years, in the area of London near Belsize Park, a young physician by the name of Sefton Palmer established himself as a reliable man of medicine and an individual of inquisitive disposition. Dr. Palmer was trusted by his patients, well-thought-of by his colleagues, and, it seemed, destined for extraordinary things.

Though his practice tied him to his particular corner of the metropolis, he was not opposed to travel and, thus, one day found himself in the countryside of Ireland, visiting with others of his profession. A detailed discussion of various medical discoveries with one colleague in particular had lasted longer than either had anticipated, setting him behind his intended time to make the journey over the then-frozen bogland toward the home of another colleague who waited in anticipation of his arrival.

Dr. Palmer and his trusted horse began the journey on a late-January evening long after the going down of the sun.

Reader, please bear in mind that bogs freeze in winter—they are nearly as much water as soil—and such bogs are easily disturbed by the pounding of horses' hooves, even when the beast is kept to a sedate pace. Failure to remember these well-established truths will render the following narrative perplexing in the extreme.

Dr. Palmer undertook his traversal of the boggy countryside with an eye to efficiency, not wishing to arrive at the home of his fellow physician at too late an hour. Thus, he set his horse to a quick clip, not as mindful as he ought to be of the dangers of a dark country lane with which one is not familiar.

The oddest of sounds reached his ears. He slowed his horse, to which the animal did not seem to object. In the dark stillness, he listened. Pops. And snaps. After a moment, he realized what he was hearing: the ice in the bogs was cracking. While he intended to remain on the road, it was easy to grow lost on a dark night, something he ought to have considered sooner. And growing lost in the bogland came with a risk of being plunged into a boghole or finding himself unknowingly riding into a lake and drowning.

As if to add to his sudden realization of the precarious nature of his situation, a thick fog began rolling over the land. The already dim landscape grew dark as ink. The cracking of ice grew louder and more frequent. He grew increasingly frustrated. And increasingly concerned.

"Slow and careful." He offered the instructions as much to himself as to his horse.

What little calm he'd managed to acquire disappeared as a sudden explosion of reddish-white light shot toward the sky. Followed by another. And another. Immense cones of fire appeared all around him. Their size and magnitude varied greatly. Some were six feet in diameter at the base, others five times that size. Their heights differed every bit as much—some no more than the height of a man, others reaching thirty feet into the air.

Two dozen, perhaps more, appeared and disappeared at unpredictable intervals and at vastly different distances. Some must have been at least a mile away. Even as he carefully led his horse onward, the cones of flame continued to appear and extinguish.

The effect was dazzling, shocking, and yet these columns of fire made little impact on the darkness, the light they produced being disproportional to their size. Neither did these pillars of fire add warmth to the frigid night. Dr. Palmer eyed them all with growing confusion and increasing interest. Though the blazes flickered without warning all over the landscape, each individual column stayed in place while it was visible, never wavering from its position.

What were they? What had caused them?

Rain began to fall, and with it, the columns of fire disappeared into the mysterious night.

The icy bogs continued to crack. But no more towers of fire appeared.

In three-quarters of an hour more, he found himself at the home of his colleague. Despite the shocking oddity of all he had seen, Dr. Palmer no longer felt upended nor worried. His was, after all, a mind more predisposed to curiosity than to concern.

"Palmer," he was greeted, "I had nearly given you up."

"I left after my time." He set his hat on a hook near the door and pulled off his dripping wet coat. "The journey itself took longer than anticipated due to a most extraordinary experience."

He was forthwith shown to a bedchamber where he could change from his damp clothing. Though the hour was terribly late, his interest in all he'd seen proved greater than his exhaustion. While his fellow physician most certainly longed to seek his own bed, Dr. Sefton Palmer thought not of that possibility. A mystery weighed on his mind, and his mind never permitted itself to be ignored.

"Have you ever, whilst traversing the bogs, experienced anything odd?" Palmer asked his colleague.

"Odd in what way?"

Palmer proceeded to describe what he'd seen in as much detail as he could. Only after expending tremendous energy on the endeavor did he realize that his account might not be believed, that his colleague might deem him confused or even mad.

"Strange things are spoken of on the bogs," the other doctor acknowledged. "Though I cannot say I've heard tell of precisely what you describe, I would not dismiss the encounter out of hand. 'There are more things in heaven and earth, than are dreamt of in your philosophy.'" Ending his reply with a nod to the Bard was quite common for Palmer's colleague. He himself, though, was not so poetic.

"I know what I saw, but I do not know how or from whence it came," Dr. Palmer said. "Neither do I know in what other forms it might occur. But, mark my words, good sir. I will solve the mystery of these sudden bursts of light even if I am required to dedicate the remainder of my life to doing so."

Such declarations should not be made lightly, for they have a most disconcerting tendency to come true in surprising and far too often destructive ways.

CHAPTER TWO

The question of lights appearing without warning or explanation took root in Dr. Palmer's mind in the months that followed his shocking experience on the bogs in Ireland. He had formulated more theories than he had produced on that night, but he still had no definitive answers.

What he'd seen had not been a reflection. Though the lights had looked like fire, they were nothing of the sort. He had not eliminated the possibility of phosphorescence as was rumored to occur in marine life. He was also determined to learn more of any oddities peculiar to organic matter. He had heard of a very odd sort of lightning he meant to investigate. He had every intention of raising the question at the next meeting of the Royal Society.

Late of an afternoon, whilst his mind spun on the question of the reddish-white cones of fire-like light, Dr. Palmer was summoned to the bedside of one of his patients, a woman of heartbreakingly young years whose health was severely impacted by pulmonary consumption. Though he hoped to be proven wrong, he suspected she was approaching the end of her short earthly sojourn.

The door at Lavinia Abbott's home was answered by her ever-faithful maid, Jane. Dr. Palmer was shown to Miss Lavinia's bedchamber, where she had spent the entirety of the past three months unable to leave her bed, her condition deteriorating.

"I fear I'm not long for this world, Dr. Palmer."

He crossed to her bedside and sat on the edge. Death was part of doctoring every bit as much as life was. That did not, however, render the experience less heartbreaking.

"What has convinced you of your imminent departure?" he asked her.

"I was earlier today seized with a horrible suffocation. How I resumed breathing, I do not know. I fear the next time I will not be so fortunate."

Palmer evaluated her condition as she spoke and continued doing so in the silence that followed. Her pallor was significant. Her breathing was shallow and belabored. Her body had grown thin and frail.

"Are you in pain?" he asked, entirely willing to provide for her powders or tisanes to assure her comfort.

"Pains of mind," Miss Lavinia said. "I fear I shall suffer another suffocation and you will be far away. I'll not have you near to aid me."

He took her hand in his, careful of her paper-thin skin. "If you wish," he said, "I will remain here throughout the day and into the night to keep close watch on you."

She smiled weakly at him. "You are a good man and a good doctor."

"I try very hard to be." He did, indeed. The matter of unexplained lights had distracted him of late, but he was determined to focus his attention on his ailing patient.

He settled himself in the room, keeping watch over Miss Lavinia.

Jane brought her broth and made certain the bedside pitcher was well supplied with water. She cast sad eyes upon the woman she'd looked after for a half decade, clearly agreeing with Miss Lavinia's assessment of her own mortality.

Truth be told, Palmer agreed as well.

The remainder of the evening passed without incident. Miss Lavinia drifted into a light sleep not long after the sun dipped beneath the horizon. The lamp in the room was lit, casting a soft glow.

Dr. Palmer sat upon the edge of the bed once more as a cot was placed upon the floor. He meant to pass the night there, recognizing that the woman was fading. He'd only just checked the rhythm of her pulse and watched the rise and fall of her chest when the lamplight flashed bright and sudden upon her face, illuminating it in odd and unexpected ways.

"Jane, please move the lantern. Its light upon her face will wake her, and she needs as much rest as her body will allow."

From behind him, the maid replied, "The lantern ain't casting any light on her face, Doctor."

Palmer focused his powers of observation once more upon the countenance of his patient. Unmistakable light darted over her features. It flashed and danced, producing enough light to illuminate her head but cast no light upon the room in general.

He stood once more, taking a step back and observing the unexpected sight from more of a distance. He was not mistaken in what he saw. A silvery light, not unlike that seen when moonlight is reflected on water, danced upon her face. The curtains in the window were drawn, eliminating that possible source. The light rendered her skin so white one might believe it to have been covered in paint. Indeed, the skin took on a look of having been glazed. All the while, the mysterious light continued to dart about.

The learned and curious doctor spoke not a word, even as his heart pounded in anticipation and wonderment. There was no heat emanating from the light, nor did it shine beyond the precise location where it emerged.

Though the color was different, it put him immediately and fully in mind of the columns of fire-like light he had seen on the bogs months earlier. This time, though, the inexplicable phenomenon had made itself known on the face of a human being.

"This ain't the first time I've seen this happen, Dr. Palmer," Jane said.

"When have you seen it before?" he inquired.

"This morning," came the reply. "Miss Lavinia's face lit in just this way. I found it quite dazzling, I did."

"And did you tell anyone else what you'd seen?"

"Blimey, no. None of the other staff'd believe me, and Miss Lavinia would likely say I were being superstitious. Fine folk are always assuming that about us lowly folk. But I won't never forget what I seen."

Palmer checked the position of the lantern once more, confirming to himself that it was, indeed, not in such a place as to be the source of the lights which continued to appear on Miss Lavinia's face. For an hour, the phenomenon continued before disappearing as suddenly as it had begun.

He stayed at Miss Lavinia Abbott's side for the remaining days of her life. The lights returned twice more, though he could determine neither cause nor source nor pattern for their rising and extinguishing. The evening before her passing, the lights returned for a final time, fainter than on the previous occasions and lasting a shorter interval.

Palmer had theorized the lights he'd seen on the bog were the result of the freezing and thawing of organic material. As Miss Lavinia lived out her remaining days, her condition deteriorated. Perhaps it was her deterioration that had caused the mysterious light to appear. Perhaps it was deterioration in the bogs that had done the same.

He would have answers. He vowed that he would. For, as much as the bog lights had sat upon his mind, this experience added weight tenfold.

People could glow. And he would not rest until he knew why.

CHAPTER THREE

The paper Dr. Palmer submitted to the College of Physicians on the luminescence he had observed was met mostly with silence. Though he was frustrated, he was not surprised. He'd filled the submission with details and theories but no data, no scientifically sound information. His next paper, he vowed, would be overrun with both.

It was in pursuit of this that he returned to Ireland, returned to the peat bogs where he'd first observed the cones of fire. He sat in the dark and the cold, watching and waiting for a return of that most extraordinary sight.

It did not return.

He did, however, experience something not entirely unrelated. The peat of those bogs, when cut, emitted an unmistakable, albeit brief, glow. It occurred when the peat was disturbed, and the light disappeared almost on the instant. Could this, he wondered, be related to what he'd seen more than nine months earlier? Could there be a connection?

Determined to know more and return to London with answers, he made an examination of the peat himself. He cut a bit, causing the momentary glow to continue. As it disappeared, he immediately sliced off a bit more, and the glow returned.

He guarded the slice of peat fiercely as he returned to the cottage he had let for a few weeks in pursuit of the answers he required. No one else was present; he could not permit the distraction. Palmer laid out his medical tools, quite as if he was about to undertake an examination of a patient or a dissection in a lab. He set his large cutting of peat on the table amidst his instruments. He lit a lamp and brought it near. Palmer set magnifying spectacles on his nose and bent over the peat block.

A bit of careful cutting and breaking revealed the presence of tiny white worms no more than half an inch in length. Palmer poked at them and nudged them and, in whatever way he could, caused the animals a bit of irritation, hoping to discover that they were the source of the soft glow he'd seen in the bog peat.

It did not seem to be enough.

Palmer refused to believe he was wrong yet again. The College of Physicians had dismissed his discoveries and hypotheses because he could not provide any evidence. He would have it this time. He swore he would. He would not rest without answers. *Could* not.

What else could irritate or cause excitation in the worms without causing them any harm? He looked around his cottage, searching for something, anything. His eyes fell upon a bottle of strong spirits. He could not place the worms in the alcohol as that might drown the creatures. The vapors, though, might prove sufficient.

He took careful hold of one worm with his smallest pair of tissue forceps. He filled a small, shallow dish with the alcohol, then held the worm over it, near enough for the vapors to envelop the creature. Mere moments later, it began to glow.

At last! At last he had succeeded in forcing a naturally occurring glow to appear!

The phosphorescence was a brilliant, beautiful, clear green that illuminated the entirety of the worm's body. But it lasted a mere instant.

He subjected several of the worms to the same treatment and achieved the same result. With enough of these tiny creatures in peat, agitation of that peat would cause dozens upon dozens to produce the green light at once, creating the twinkling glow he'd seen.

It did not, though, explain the columns of fiery light he'd seen at the beginning of the year.

It did not explain the lights that had illuminated Miss Lavinia's face.

And it did not explain the further phenomena of light he observed as the weeks and months continued to pass. For he'd committed himself to searching them out. Dedicated himself to the pursuit.

Palmer had attended the bedside of a woman dying of a pulmonary consumption not unlike that which had claimed Miss Lavinia Abbott. He had not tended to many patients since Miss Lavinia's passing. One could not pursue elusive answers and doctor at the same time. At least not often.

As he had in Miss Lavinia's home, he observed in this new location a moon-like light dancing upon the woman's face, with something of the look of lightning, something of the look of the glowing peat, but not precisely like either one.

He was not alone in observing the phosphorescent illumination of this particular patient's features. The unfortunate soul was attended also by her sisters and mother. The word of women was not generally considered by the medical establishment to be authoritative, but their corroboration of his observations might still have proven useful despite that prejudicial opinion—if only their recounting of the experience had matched his.

The light they had observed, the women insisted, had not been *upon* her face but hovering *above* it in the air she breathed out. It danced in diagonal glimmers, shimmering about near the head of the bed.

He did not think he had misjudged what he'd observed. He was too meticulous an observer. That this mystery held such weight in his mind made him even more aware of the details.

A fellow doctor in Ireland wrote to tell him of a similar experience occurring in a neighboring village. A man suffering with pulmonary tuberculosis was known to emit a glow as well. It was said, in fact, that these periods of body-produced light appeared nightly. It was described by the local people as a luminous fog or a sparkle of phosphorescence, but Palmer's colleague could not confirm this. He further indicated that all he had heard pointed toward the odd light existing, as the sisters previously mentioned had insisted, in the air rather than upon the person of the patient.

That, while intriguing, was not the phenomenon Palmer was chasing. It was not the mystery he grew more and more determined to solve. He would not—*could* not—rest until he did! It was no longer a matter of mere curiosity but of necessity.

Back in his own home once more, Palmer became all but consumed by the pursuit of answers. He attempted to coax a glow from every living thing he could get his hands on. None cooperated.

The question rested heavily on his thoughts as he went about his days and even as he attempted to sleep. He thought upon it as he ate his meals and as he dressed for the day and undressed for the night.

Early one morning as he brushed through his hair, now a bit overgrown and less well-kept than it had once been, a spark of light emitted, jumping about between the strands of hair. He'd seen such a thing happen before but had paid it little heed. Until now.

The same thing happened on occasion when pulling a nightshirt on or off. A bit of a crackling feeling would emerge. The spark would follow, only to disappear as quickly as it had appeared. Could not the various lights he'd seen on bogs and on faces be related to this?

And thus he spent weeks rubbing together various materials, pulling out strands of his own hair, applying various substances, attempting to determine what, precisely, could force the spark of light to return. Linen rubbed against skin sometimes worked. No matter the amount of hair he pulled, only that left upon his head ever showed any success, and that only rarely.

He might have continued his experiments indefinitely if not for the whisperings of two strangers he passed on the street as he returned from seeing a patient, something he did with less frequency. The two men were discussing the widely held belief amongst those of the lowest classes that human bodies could produce light . . . after death.

CHAPTER FOUR

When Dr. Sefton Palmer arrived at the college where he had, a mere dozen years earlier, undertaken his medical education, he did so with an unmistakably frantic air. He would prove the existence of the lights he'd seen. He would discover their source, their cause, their nature.

He would, if it required pursuing the answers for the rest of his life.

Had his attention not been so entirely upon his pursuit, he might have noticed the odd looks he was receiving. He might have been concerned that people received him so quizzically. He was no more aware of these reactions than he was of his own haggard and unkempt appearance.

His steps took him to the office of the professor he'd most respected during his time at the college. Dr. Sherman would help him find the answers.

"Palmer." The good professor looked entirely taken aback at seeing his former student upon the threshold of his office. "I had not expected you."

"What do you know of the presence of lights in the human body?" Palmer had no time for pointless niceties.

"I know that you submitted a paper on the subject not many months ago." Dr. Sherman did not seem pleased.

"I had hoped for help in solving these mysteries, but I have received nothing but silence or ridicule." Palmer held his hat in his hands, crushing the brim in his frustration. "You said, when I was a pupil of yours, 'The moment a doctor believes his learning to be complete, he ceases to be a good doctor.' It seems to me there are a great many poor doctors who have dismissed out of hand what I have actually seen. I pray you will prove an advocate of your own advice."

That seemed to soften the man. He waved Palmer farther inside his office. "The phenomena you described in your paper is not one that is recorded or known amongst your fellow men of medicine. It was met with skepticism, which is not unhealthy nor unheard of."

"Skepticism and dismissal are not the same thing." Palmer only just managed to keep himself from growling out the response.

"Not everyone has entirely dismissed it."

Palmer looked to Dr. Sherman once more. "Who is not dismissing it?" He wanted names. Locations. He needed others to pursue this with him.

"There have been a few whispers," Dr. Sherman said. "Some have seen twinkling lights on bogs or at sea. And the ability of some insects to glow is well known."

"I am not speaking of such things." He took to pacing, something he did with some regularity of late. "There is a connection to human beings. I know there is, and I've heard that some in the dissection room have seen corpses glow."

"When did you last sleep, Palmer?" Dr. Sherman asked. "You look exhausted."

"I don't need you to be my doctor. I need to know if you've heard of these postmortem glows."

"I have not," he said.

Dr. Palmer shook his head, speeding up his pacing. "But that does not mean that it has not happened, that it is not true."

Sherman stepped in the way of Palmer's pacing, necessitating he stop. "Take my advice, young man. Return to your flat. Rest. Alleviate this worry from your mind."

"It is not a 'worry.' It is a scientific mystery. I cannot merely abandon this pursuit."

"I fear if you continue, it will drive you mad," Dr. Sherman said.

"If I do not find the answers I need, it most certainly will."

Dr. Sherman watched him for a long moment, brows drawn in concern, as if Palmer was unaware of the dire nature of his own condition. Palmer did not flinch under the pointed gaze. He knew Sherman was mistaken; pursuing these answers was *not* an ill-conceived quest. It had become his life's mission.

A sigh emitted from the older doctor. "Blackstone still oversees the dissection room. Perhaps he will have some familiarity with the manifestation you speak of."

Realizing his one-time idol did not intend to offer much else in the way of help, Palmer left without a backward glance. The struggle for knowledge abides no sentimental loyalties.

He knew perfectly well how to find the dissecting room. He might have been struggling to find answers to difficult questions, but he was not struggling with his memory. Blackstone's office, located directly beside the room where the cadavers were kept, was empty, its usual living occupant apparently occupied elsewhere.

Irritated with the ceaseless obstacles he encountered, Palmer made his way into the dissecting room without waiting for its overseer to grant permission. The room was dark. No candles or lanterns were lit. The windows were covered in thick draperies. The odor of the room was not one any medical student ever forgot nor truly grew accustomed to. Palmer refused to be felled by olfactory discomfort.

He closed the door behind him, extinguishing every bit of light in the room, though there'd been precious little to begin with. Though he could see nothing, he knew what lay before him—a half-dozen tables with cadavers laid atop them, awaiting examination. Another encounter in this room that students struggled to not find disconcerting.

Palmer inched his way along the wall on which the door hung and placed himself in the corner, and waited. Waited for lights to appear. Waited for the rumors he'd heard to prove themselves true.

"Light up," he whispered in short bursts of breath. "Light up."

The room remained dark. Minutes ticked by. Perhaps hours. Still, he remained in his corner, watching, whispering, waiting.

And then . . . the lights came.

The subjects upon the tables became quite unexpectedly lit by a remarkably luminous appearance, emanating, as it would seem, from the cadavers themselves. They were lit to such a degree that their forms and shapes and various parts were as clear to see as if every lantern in the school had been lit and brought into the dissecting room, as if the heavy curtains had been pulled back and sunlight allowed to stream inside.

Palmer made mental notes of all he saw, memorizing the details, taking in every possible aspect. The whispers he'd heard were showing themselves to be true.

He would be vindicated. He would be listened to at last.

He stepped out of the dissecting room, searching out someone to act as witness to the phenomenon. Dr. Sherman and Dr. Blackstone were emerging from the latter's office. Neither seemed overly surprised to see him, but they also did not look overly pleased.

"It is happening just as I said it would," Palmer announced. "They are glowing in precisely the way I've seen others. You doubted, but it is happening. It is happening now."

With looks of doubt, they followed him through the dissecting room doors once more. Soon enough, their disbelief would be turned to apology.

Again, the smell of the room rushed over Palmer. Again, he dismissed it. He pushed the door closed, plunging the room into the darkness necessary to see the glow.

But the glow was gone.

Utterly gone.

"It was happening," he growled out. "It was."

He could not see his colleagues, but he knew they would be considering him with equal parts pity and annoyance. He knew because that had become the near-constant response he received to his declarations.

"I am not lying, and I am not mad," he insisted. "I saw what I saw."

"Perhaps, Palmer, you should take a bit of time away," Dr. Sherman said. "Find a quiet corner of the country and rest your mind."

"I have not gone mad. And, somehow, I will prove it."

With that proclamation, he stormed out. He knew now that bodies could glow after death, and he knew of one other means of observing the recently deceased.

He needed to find a Resurrection Man.

CHAPTER FIVE

Weeks had passed since Dr. Sefton Palmer had seen patients, attended bedsides, or interacted with any of the society he once had kept. Nothing was given place in his life but the question of lights. Nothing.

He stood in a graveyard at the very outskirts of London on a January night, one year to the day when he had first seen the columns of fire over a bog in Ireland. One year with more questions than answers. One year of replacing his doctoring with this pursuit. One year that had brought him to this place of death in the company of one who made his living disturbing the peace of the dearly departed.

Palmer had thrown his lot in with a resurrectionist.

They, a man who had once dedicated himself to healing people and a man who stole bodies from graves, stood in the dark, looking over the rolling mounds of dirt and the near-toppling headstones.

"You've seen corpse-lights?" Palmer asked his companion, not for the first time.

"All of us what ply our trade in these yards 'ave seen 'em." The man spoke in gravelly tones, with no indication he found the occurrence the least intriguing. "I've a mate who comes from Wales. He calls 'em *canhwyllan cyrph*. Another bloke what plies the trade quotes some Scottish poet, writing about dead knights and their graves glowing bright in the dark."

It was a poor summary of Sir Walter Scott's *Minstrelsy of the Scottish Border*, but Scott was hardly the only writer to recount such a thing. Irish poet Thomas Moore spoke of them as well. Many accounts existed of such things. And if Palmer's theory that these lights were the result of decomposition were true, the sight of them in graveyards made perfect sense.

Then, where were they?

Palmer paced among the graves, making note of those headstones still standing, careful of those toppled over. The grass grew high and wild. Perhaps that was hiding the lights he'd come to see. Perhaps conditions weren't right. But he didn't know what the "right" conditions were.

"Have you seen corpse-lights in *this* churchyard?" Palmer asked the resurrection man.

"Oi."

"And was it on a night like tonight? Clear skies. Cold. The previous night was quite wet."

"Oi."

That, Palmer had decided, was part of the equation he was attempting to discover. The air needed to be cold. The ground and therefore the body needed to be wet, though it need be not raining at the time when the lights were expected. That the pattern still held true was a promising thing.

He would find his answers tonight. He was determined to.

"Have you ever seen these lights when the ground was not wet?"

"This 'ere's London." The man spoke sardonically, a tone he'd struck from the moment Palmer had first approached him about this undertaking. "When is the dirt at our feet ever not wet?"

It was a fair enough question. "Have you seen these lights anywhere other than graveyards?"

"Oi. And I've heard tell of them appearing in odd spots. There were a man drowned at Ettrick. Couldn't find his body at first, but then the corpselight gave him away. Found him straight off."

Bodies even glowed in the water. This was not a trick of his imagination. Palmer was right. He would be believed, and he would not rest until he was. If he had to hire the assistance of dozens of resurrection men and house breakers and criminals of every ilk, he would do so. No more would he be ignored and dismissed and pitied.

He paced the churchyard, eyes constantly surveying the expanse of it, the crumbled remains of the nearby church, the tall, flowing grass, the quiet of this all-but-abandoned corner of the world. The glow would come. It must.

"Can you not encourage the corpse-lights?" Palmer pressed. "Agitate the soil or some such thing."

"They don't come because you demand it." The resurrectionist picked at his fingernails with the point of a sinister blade. "It needs the right timing and a new body."

"So resurrect one," Palmer shot back. "It's why we're here, isn't it?"

"I'm here for a body, yes. The freshest ones fetch the best price."

The freshest ones also, it seemed, produced the most light. "Where is the body you've come to harvest?"

He could see no newly turned-over dirt, no grave newly dug and filled. Indeed, not a thing in this churchyard appeared to have changed in decades, perhaps centuries. Had he been duped? How dare the man!

Palmer bristled. "I cannot see these lights if you've not brought me to a place where you mean to ply your trade."

"I mean to ply it, never you fear." Moonlight played upon the man's ghastly features. "I'm not one for wasting m'time."

"Neither am I. So point me to this body you've come for."

With a look of pity not unlike the one Palmer had seen in the dissecting room but this time filled with a stomach-turning dose of amusement, the resurrectionist smiled at him. "The freshest ones fetch the best price."

It was long after whispered in the College of Physicians that a young doctor by the name of Palmer had driven himself mad in pursuit of an unanswerable question. He had abandoned his patients, his home, and his faculties. In the end, he had disappeared. That was offered as a warning to his fellow men of medicine not to allow the inexplicable to become inescapable.

Dear reader, remember: Though this tale be cautionary, at its heart are two truths. The first, that lights have indeed been known to appear in all the places where our Dr. Palmer pursued and encountered them. The second, and far more important is this: Some questions are best left unanswered.

THE

QUEEN

AND THE

KNAVE

by Mr. King

INSTALLMENT I

in which a brave Queen plans a Celebration
but instead faces a grave Danger!

Long ago and far away, the proud and prosperous kingdom of Amesby
lost its beloved king. With broken hearts, they passed their period of na-
tional mourning, with no one so sorrowful as his only child. The kingdom
was now under her rule: the very young, very grief-stricken Queen Eleanor.
Though she had been raised to one day ascend to her father's throne, she
did not feel herself at all prepared to do so at merely twenty years of age.

Fate, in its oft-cruel sense of timing, set before her the task of hosting
the once-a-decade Unification Ceremony, in which the country's ruling barons gathered at the royal palace to declare their loyalty to the kingdom and
confidence in its monarch, who in turn pledged to hear the counsel of the
barons and listen to the needs of the people.

Eleanor had been queen but a month! A month in which she had
grown *less* sure of herself, not more. A month in which she had made more
missteps than she felt herself able to ever forget or overcome.

Failure to complete the Unification Ceremony would send her kingdom
into chaos and warfare.

Thus, summons were sent to all corners of the kingdom by way of the
fastest messengers available. All the barons in the land—and there were a
great many—were required to make their way to the royal palace. There
would be a week of gatherings, contests of skill and strength, the ceremony
itself, and, at the end, a grand ball.

All was predetermined. All was required.

In the afternoon of the day of the barons' arrivals, which the queen was required to *not* be present for—a tradition held over from the days when the monarch was often at odds with the barons—Her Majesty took to walking about her private garden, the only part of the palace, beyond her personal quarters, where no one was permitted to be but herself.

Oh, Father! she silently bemoaned. *I am not equal to this. I am not the leader or diplomat you were.*

Should the worst happen and the Unification Ceremony not be completed properly, her father's kingdom would fracture. Should that fracture widen and deepen, peace would be lost, and countless people would suffer. Horrifyingly many would die.

It was too much for her inexperienced shoulders to bear. But what choice did she have?

Her feet took her past the sentry box where a guardsman stood, keeping the monarch's private garden private. She knew this sentry. His father had also been a guardsman—the Captain of the Guard, in fact—and Eleanor had come to know Reynard Atteberry when they were both children. They had played together. They'd once even been friends, a rare thing for a princess. She was too often kept separated and isolated, and that meant she was often lonely.

"Good morning, Reynard," she said as she reached his post. "Thank you for watching over the garden."

"My pleasure, Your Majesty." He spoke without taking his eyes off the path beyond the gate he guarded, watching for anyone approaching. He had a duty to fulfill, after all. Duty always came before friendship, even before happiness at times.

Duty.

Always.

Eleanor continued onward, beginning a second circuit of her only place of solace. If she could find a bit of peace, she might feel less disheartened.

She'd only just stepped beyond the shadow of the sentry box when a new shadow fell across her path.

Amesby was home to a great many barons with a history of warring with one another and a peace brokered between them every ten years. But the kingdom was also home to those who possessed magic but not the right temperament for utilizing it without causing pain and suffering.

Dezmerina was one such sorceress.

Eleanor had seen her but twice before: shortly before her mother's death and shortly after.

The sorceress now stood on Eleanor's path, watching her with the hard and unyielding expression Eleanor had seen in her nightmares.

"They are all arriving today," Dezmerina said, her inflection flat but still sinister, calm but still threatening.

"You are not amongst those required to be here this week." Eleanor attempted to sound like *Queen* Eleanor, but somehow managed to sound like a tiny child.

"I require myself to be here," Dezmerina said. "I am owed this moment."

"And what moment is that?" Eleanor tipped her chin, trying to hide her worry.

"Amesby has ignored me long enough, has withheld from me what I am entitled to. Your father refused to cede to me what was mine."

"And what is that?"

Dezmerina took a step closer to her. Eleanor stepped backward.

A smile slowly pulled at the sorceress's lips. "A throne. Mark my words, it will be mine."

The air around them began to stir, though not a single blade of grass moved. Dezmerina raised her arms at her side. Her eyes turned dark and sinister. Her voice pitched low, she intoned,

> "Whene'er the sun lights Amesby skies,
> Her queen will see through pine marten's eyes.
> While battles rage and chaos reigns,
> Her life will ebb whilst mine remains."

The swirl of air wrapped itself ever tighter around Queen Eleanor, squeezing and pressing her from all sides, and her body shrunk with it. She tried to call out, pleading for help from anyone who might be near enough to hear, but the transformation stole her voice.

Dezmerina cackled an evil laugh, pleased with herself and pleased with the pain her curse would cause the daughter of the man who had made himself her enemy. Throwing her arms downward, she disappeared in a crash of thunder.

Sentries were forbidden from leaving their post. The sentry box was to always be directly beside them, the gate to the garden ever behind them. Reynard Atteberry was not one for breaking rules nor doing things he oughtn't. He was honest, dependable, as steadfast as stone.

He'd seen and heard all that had happened, having been overlooked by Dezmerina, no doubt on account of his lowly birth and place of comparative unimportance. What, after all, mattered a single guardsman to one whose entire focus was on destroying a monarchy?

Reynard abandoned his post that day, violated every rule he'd been taught about being a sentry and a guard. He rushed toward the small creature, its dark fur glistening in the sunlight.

Her queen will see through pine marten's eyes.

And that was precisely what the ice-hearted, villainous sorceress had transformed Queen Eleanor into. No larger than a cat, but with the proportions of a weasel and the distinctive cream-colored fur "bib" about its throat. There was no mistaking that Queen Eleanor, only a month on the throne, had been transformed into a pine marten.

How the curse could be undone, Reynard knew not.

But he knew this: he had sworn to safeguard his queen, and he would do so at all costs.

INSTALLMENT II

in which our valiant Sentry faces a Perilous Decision!

If Reynard had harbored any doubts about the true identity of the pine marten in the queen's garden, the fact that it willingly allowed him to pick it up and carry it back to the sentry box and then sat watching him with pleading and hopeful eyes would have managed to convince him. Pine martens, as a rule, were neither tame nor cooperative. This one acted more like a sweet-tempered kitten than a wild animal.

"I confess, Your Majesty, I haven't the first idea what is to be done now." How odd it was addressing an animal as "Your Majesty," but, no matter appearances, he knew who she was. "Were I to tell anyone that you are Queen Eleanor, they not only would not believe me but I would lose my post, you would likely be tossed into the forest, and Dezmerina's declared desire for revenge would be fully and horribly realized."

Few people would have kept such a level head in the face of so strange a situation. But Reynard was no ordinary sentinel. His father had been Captain of the Guard and had raised him to be both adaptable and brave, both open-minded and focused. And, though their stations in life were very different, Reynard and Queen Eleanor had known each other from childhood and had even, when still little children, played together quite as if they were equals. They occasionally now even had very brief but friendly conversations.

He felt as if he knew her, as much as any commoner could ever know his queen. He liked the person she was. He cared what happened to her. And all that, no doubt, helped him keep his composure. Survival in a crisis seemed somehow more possible when the outcome impacted more than oneself.

Inside the sentry box was a single stool for sitting on, though the only time it might have ever been used would be when two sentries were present but only one standing at duty. Reynard had never known that to happen. He'd often inwardly scoffed at such a permanent solution to a nonexistent problem, especially when the box could hardly spare the space. He was grateful for it now.

Her Majesty sat on the stool, watching him as he spoke, making their conversation less odd—as much as was possible when a conversation was being held between a person and a pine marten.

"If I don't stand at my post, the Captain of the Guard will be summoned. I'd do best not to draw his attention until I've thought of a believable explanation."

The pine marten queen tipped her head, giving him a quizzical look.

"I am not usually one for inventing stories in order to avoid the truth," he assured her. "You must admit, this is a very unique circumstance."

She dipped her head, a movement very close to a nod.

"I will stand at my post and do my utmost to look as though nothing is at all amiss, but I will also spend that time trying to sort out what ought to be done next."

Queen Eleanor curled into a ball of deep brown fur and rested her head on her tail. No matter that her features were now that of a weasel-like animal, her expression was easy to interpret. She was sorrowful, worried, but not defeated. Reynard felt certain she, too, was pondering how to thwart Dezmerina's determination to destroy the newly crowned queen.

Reynard had not the first idea how to accomplish that. He'd once known someone who could have helped. A woman who'd had magic, but who'd not used it to cause hurt or harm. She'd healed and helped and benefited everyone she could. She'd been one of the most remarkable people Reynard had ever known.

But his mother was gone now, and with her all the knowledge she'd had.

His father had passed away two years earlier, meaning Reynard answered to a Captain of the Guard who was far less likely to believe him should he present to him such an odd tale as he had to tell.

What was to be done?

So few people in the kingdom had magic. Dezmerina had spent many years hunting those who did and killing any who refused to lend their gifts to her cause. Some were forced into doing her bidding under threat against their families. Those who were most able to assist in their queen's current distress would, most certainly, be too afraid to make their abilities known.

Were he even able to find someone with magical ability, how was he to leave the palace grounds with a pine marten without drawing undue attention? Should anyone ask why he left the sentry box at the end of his shift and took with him a wild animal, he'd have great difficulty explaining it, never mind justifying having kept the creature in the sentry box.

While Reynard was trying, without success, to determine his next step,

Queen Eleanor was pondering many things herself. Her form had changed to that of a woodland creature, but she was still herself, still had her own thoughts and feelings and memories. She still had her intelligence and determination to be the best queen she could be. But how could she possibly be any sort of queen at all if she remained a pine marten?

Whilst she was required to be absent during the arrival of the kingdom's barons—a fortunate bit of timing, considering her current state—she was absolutely required to offer a welcoming speech the night of the Barons' Feast. The Unification Ceremony would not occur for two more days, but failing to give the opening speech would put the feast in such jeopardy that the ceremony itself might as well be canceled.

Her father would have known what to do; she was utterly certain of it. But she hadn't his wisdom to call upon. If not for Reynard, she would have been utterly alone, struggling to feel even a modicum of hope. Though they'd not interacted nearly as much in their grown-up years as they had while still children, she trusted him as much now as she ever had. He was a good man, kind and brave, with just enough of a rogue's love for adventure to give her added confidence that he wouldn't simply abandon her in order to fulfill his duty to stand where he was and ignore all else.

Eleanor could not recall ever having heard a pine marten make noise. They must have had the ability, but she could not predict what she would hear when testing her voice. Would the sound be quiet and weak? Would there be no sound at all? Truth be told, when she spoke as her human self, she often felt weak. She couldn't deny other people thought the same.

But she needed Reynard's help. She needed him to stay with her. And she wanted to help find a solution to her problem. Being able to speak to him would facilitate that.

She hesitantly attempted to speak. What emerged was a shrill, almost catlike sound. She tried again, concentrating. The sound changed ever so slightly, but it did change. With effort, she might find her voice. She might manage to talk or to at least communicate.

Reynard stepped close once more, speaking to her whilst still facing forward, looking, to anyone glancing in his direction, as if he were doing nothing but keeping watch.

"Two palace guards are coming toward us. They will be here either to take up their position on watch or to bring a message to the sentry on duty. They will spot you the moment they arrive." He looked back at her without turning more than the smallest bit. "If you will go to the back of your garden where the weeping birch grows and hide yourself well, I will meet you there as soon as I am able."

The pine marten queen nodded, grateful she could do so.

"I will not abandon you, Your Majesty," Reynard promised.

She slipped from the sentry box and moved with the swift grace of the creature she had become, moving easily between the iron slats of the gate and into the garden, aiming for the tree Reynard had specified.

With Queen Eleanor safe from the notice of the approaching guards yet still in danger of being spotted by a gardener or gamekeeper, Reynard, feeling nervous but determined, watched his colleagues arrive.

"Her Majesty's lady's maid reports the queen has not yet returned from her walk in the garden. Have you seen the queen?"

Reynard nodded. "She did walk in the gardens earlier. The last I saw Her Majesty, she was walking in the direction of the back wall. It is likely she returned to the palace by way of the entrance there."

"Was anything amiss?"

If only Reynard knew if these two would believe him were he to tell them the truth. All the kingdom knew of magic, and all the kingdom knew of Dezmerina's violent and destructive use of it. But, somehow, their fear of her had translated into a certain stubborn refusal to believe that the harm she had caused had truly been caused by her.

The horrid sorceress had such full hold on the kingdom that she either forced cooperation or frightened into denial.

"Queen Eleanor appeared to be deep in thought," Reynard said. "I very much had the impression she did not want to be interrupted." Somehow he'd managed to offer an answer that wasn't entirely false.

The taller of the two guards, Chester, motioned with his head toward the other. "George will stand sentry in your place. I am to search the garden. The Captain has asked that you make a search of the surrounding forest in case the queen decided to wander further afield."

At last, a spot of luck.

The changing of guards was quickly accomplished. George stood at full attention. Chester slipped into the garden. And Reynard made his way as quickly as he could without drawing their notice into the adjoining forest, following the curve of the garden wall to the place where the weeping birch stood.

He spotted the pine marten queen quickly. She climbed agilely down from a high branch to one that grew out over the wall. From there, she leapt to him, and he caught her, wincing at the piercing of her claws on his arm.

Holding her protectively and watching for signs of other searchers, wanderers, or Dezmerina herself, he rushed further into the woods. It would be dark soon; they daren't go far. But neither dare they remain within sight.

Reynard knew of a small cottage in the woods. It had belonged to his mother, and it was the place she had retreated to when Dezmerina had begun her efforts to gather or destroy those with magic. It was protected through charms and enchantments. They could be safe there. But what they would do after that, he did not know.

The sun was setting, the light disappearing quickly. The small animal in his arms grew heavier, more awkward to hold. He stopped his forward rush and set her down. As he did, the last rays of light disappeared.

And, in a twist and swirl of impossible movement, the pine marten transformed once more into Queen Eleanor.

INSTALLMENT III

in which Clues are discerned and Hope is not lost entirely!

For a moment, neither Reynard nor Eleanor could speak a word nor take another step. What had undone the spell? What had caused the queen to resume her true form? Was it a trick? A trap?

Both must have had the same thought in the same moment as they both said in near perfect unison that they would do best to seek a place of hiding whilst they sorted what had occurred.

This was, of course, the very reason Reynard had suggested they flee into the forest. "There is a cottage," he told her, "not far distant from here that had once belonged to my mother. I believe we will be safe there."

"Will not Dezmerina find me there?" Eleanor did not seem afraid, simply cautious.

"It is protected," he said. "In fact, it is protected specifically against Dezmerina and her aims."

Eleanor was no stranger to the history of her kingdom, allowing her to understand instantly what Reynard was saying. "The one who lives there has magic."

"*Had* magic. She is no longer among us. I am thankful, though, that she was not, in the end, destroyed by the evil sorceress. Avoiding that fate is the very reason she enchanted this cottage."

Wishing not to remain in the open much longer, they rushed in the direction of the protected cottage. They quickly lit candles, illuminating the interior and its dust-covered furnishings and supplies. A trunk of blankets allowed them to guard against the cold without needing to light a fire that might draw undue attention. The cottage protected them from Dezmerina but it would not, necessarily, prevent the palace guard or any of the barons from discovering them there.

"I cannot imagine Dezmerina's curse would be so quickly and easily dispersed," Eleanor said. "Yet, I am in my own form now. What could possibly account for it? And how long will it last?"

"I wish I knew those answers." Reynard was, indeed, frustrated not to know.

"I am meant to address the barons at the opening feast tonight." Eleanor's brow pulled in thought. "That will occur an hour after dark, which is not long from now. If I could be certain I would remain myself for any length of time, I would rush back to the palace. This week is vital to the continued peace in the kingdom. I dare not risk destroying what generations have worked to achieve."

"The wording of the curse is crucial," Reynard said. "It cannot behave in ways that are contrary to what was spoken. The difficulty comes in interpreting what is actually said as the wording is always, by design, confusing."

"You seem to know a great deal about such things." Eleanor did not sound horrified at his knowledge of magic.

"Like many in Amesby, there are some in my family who have magic—who *had* magic. I was taught that curses follow a pattern," Reynard said. "The first line indicates the circumstances under which the curse manifests, the second is how. The third line predicts the impact of the curse, while the fourth lays out the requirements for ending it."

Eleanor's mind returned to the curse once more, thinking through the wording, through the details.

> *Whene'er the sun lights Amesby skies,*
> *Her queen will see through pine marten's eyes.*
> *While battles rage and chaos reigns,*
> *Her life will ebb whilst mine remains.*

"The second line is why I transformed into a pine marten," Eleanor said, thinking aloud. "And the situation has already led to chaos. The guards and household are searching for me. I can only imagine the panic is growing as the time for the welcome speech approaches." She felt more than a small amount of that panic herself. Her first significant duty as the new monarch, and she would fail at it. "The *how* and the *impact* have, thus far, proven quite accurate."

"The first line contains the rules of the curse." Reynard thought on it as well. "'Whene'er the sun lights Amesby skies.' The sun is not lighting the sky just now. I had thought it simply meant so long as there existed a sun, which would mean forever, but that might not be the case at all."

"I am only to take the form of a pine marten during the daylight," Eleanor sorted out loud. "And it is currently not daylight."

Reynard met her eye. "And will not be again until morning."

Eleanor pulled the wool blanket more closely around her. "I could return to the palace and make the welcome speech. I'm not meant to remain at the feast, so no one will remark upon my departure. And tomorrow is the Baron's Consultation Day, when the monarch is not to be present. So long as I escape the palace before dawn, my transformation will not be seen by anyone. There would not be panic created by my current circumstances, but neither would I neglect any crucial parts of this excruciatingly crucial week."

"I can help you return to the palace," Reynard said. "And I can help you escape in the morning."

"Will not your absence be noted by the Captain of the Guard?" She knew the guardsmen were held to strict schedules, and desertion was not tolerated.

"Once we have discovered how to lift this curse, my absence will be easy to explain. Until then, the future of the kingdom depends upon our successful navigation of the difficult road Dezmerina has laid before you. The barons must be appeased. The kingdom must retain confidence in you as monarch. And the transformations the sorceress has subjected you to must be stopped."

His firmness of purpose and unwavering dedication helped to bolster Eleanor's. She was not a person of weak principles, neither was she in any sense a coward. The enormity of all that had happened was, however, a weighty and difficult burden.

"Let us return to the palace forthwith," Eleanor said, sounding more like a queen than she had in some time. "I will deliver my welcome speech, then retire to my chamber, insisting I wish to give the barons full opportunity to enjoy their feast and prepare for their work on the morrow."

"Do you wish to escape the palace tonight or shortly before sunrise tomorrow?" Reynard could not assist in her escape if he did not know when she would be undertaking it.

"Tonight, I believe. If I wait overly long, I might find myself mistaking the time of sunrise, and my maids will find a pine marten in my chambers. Heaven only knows what they would instruct the gamekeeper to do with me."

While all the kingdom knew of Dezmerina's power and nefariousness, few would believe the wild creature found in the queen's bedchamber was the queen herself. And were they faced with proof, far too many people, especially amongst the kingdom's barons, would either panic at such a fate befalling their monarch or seize upon the sudden vulnerability of the kingdom to claim power of their own.

Their only hope was to keep Eleanor's current state a secret until the means of ending the curse was discovered. A problem with a known solution, however difficult, was less terrifying than one which could not be made right.

Reynard pulled a small leather box from a high shelf. He removed from its interior a carved stone hanging from a length of leather. "This amulet will offer some protection as we journey back to the palace. Its magic is not impenetrable, and we will not be as safe as we are within these walls, but it will offer us some defense."

They each took hold of one end of the leather strap, the arrangement offering them both claim on the amulet's powers.

"Where shall I meet you after you complete your speech?" Reynard asked.

"There is a small sitting room adjacent to my bedchamber. Inside is but one chair. It faces a window with a heavy curtain, the hem of which pools on the floor. Tuck yourself behind that curtain where it sits against the wall so you will neither be seen inside the room or through the glass of the window. I will meet you there."

Reynard nodded, committing her instructions to memory.

They rushed through the forest, both holding fast to the amulet, both grateful for the other's bravery and cleverness, both unsure of how they might thwart Dezmerina.

Once inside the castle, having entered through a door well-hidden but known to Eleanor, they were greeted with a dilemma. Eleanor needed to make her way to the great hall to deliver her address, while Reynard needed to hide himself in the small sitting room to wait for her. They could not both hold the amulet if they did not remain together.

"I will be surrounded by the barons and the household," Eleanor said. "Dezmerina's efforts are dependent, in part, on the power of uncertainty. I do not believe she will harm me whilst I am among a crowd. You, however, do not have that protection."

"Your life is more essential," he said.

She shook her head. "I feel firmly in my heart that we are both necessary to undo what the sorceress has done. I will have the protection of witnesses. You must have the protection of the amulet."

Before he could offer another objection, they both heard the approach of footsteps.

"Go," she said. "Down this passage to the winding stone steps at the end. Three revolutions, through the door, down that corridor. The third door is the one you want. Go. Quickly."

And on that declaration, Eleanor let go of the amulet and hurried in the opposite direction. How she hoped in her heart he reached his destination without incident, without harm! She had harbored such worry over her duties this week, over the speech she was about to make, yet it now seemed so insignificant compared to the obstacles in front of her.

She reached the exterior doors of the great hall just as the Master of the Royal Wardrobe arrived, flanked by dressers and servants who all looked remarkably nervous. That their concern visibly ebbed when they saw her gave Eleanor a surge of both relief and pride. She knew, logically, that their relief likely came from having feared she would not fulfill this duty rather than simple pleasure at seeing their queen, but she embraced the feeling just the same.

Gold-threaded gloves were placed on her hands. Her shoes, stained by grass and mud, were replaced with ones of silk and ribbon. A mantle of deep purple velvet and lined with ermine was fastened around her, draping at her sides and covering all but the front hem of her dress.

The royal coiffeuse quickly brushed and pinned her hair, undoing the damage of so difficult a day in an instant. The lighter of the queen's crowns was placed on her head, the one she wore when seeing to official duties while not seated upon the throne.

Queen Eleanor turned to face the doors through which she was to enter the great hall. She took a calming breath, then nodded to indicate her readiness.

Two footmen opened the large, heavy oaken doors. The din of voices inside dropped immediately to a curious hush. Chair legs scraped the ground, and the rustle of fabric indicated the barons had risen, which was required of them when their monarch entered a room.

In her brief time as queen, Eleanor had practiced this moment as well as the others she would undertake that week. She knew where to stand and what to say. She'd feared she would quake her way through the ceremonies, but to her great surprise and relief, when she stepped into the hall, she felt her legs firm beneath her, felt her pulse maintain its quiet rhythm.

She climbed atop the dais and faced the gathering.

"Barons all, you are welcomed most warmly to the royal palace to begin our week of unification." The speech was the same every time it was given, and Eleanor had long ago memorized it. "The Kingdom of Amesby is proud and dignified. There is abundance in the land and goodness in her people. You, dignified barons, are come to make ironclad once more the peace that has for generations seen us prosper and progress. In the spirit of that unity, I offer you this feast."

At that final declaration, known to all who heard it, the rearward doors flew open and servants carrying salvers of food and ale stepped inside the hall to deliver the monarch's offering to the newly arrived nobility.

"Huzzah!" the barons shouted, as was required of them. "Huzzah! Huzzah!"

As the third shout was made, Eleanor retraced the path she had taken mere moments earlier and returned to the corridor beyond the great hall. The barons were left to enjoy their feast, casually discussing over the meal what would be formally discussed among them the next day.

The week of unification had begun.

But after the Baron's Consultation Day, Eleanor would no longer have an excuse to be absent during daylight hours. If a means of ending Dezmerina's curse was not found quickly, the Unification Ceremony would not be completed, and the chaos and battles the curse predicted would become reality.

She and Reynard had but one day.

And one day could not possibly be enough.

INSTALLMENT IV
in which Heartache proves itself a most painful Affliction!

Reynard kept perfectly still and perfectly quiet while waiting behind the heavy curtains in the queen's personal sitting room. To be found there would mean imprisonment, charges of trespass and treason, likely death. Though he knew Queen Eleanor would come to his defense and spare him such a fate, she could not do so during daylight hours. And if he were caught in so compromising a place and the queen was found to be missing again, the conclusions jumped to would be devastating indeed.

All had remained calm and peaceful in the residence wing of the palace, a sign, he hoped, that the welcome speech had gone as planned without disaster or misstep. He hoped that was true not merely for the sake of the kingdom but because he knew the ceremonies surrounding this week weighed on Eleanor's mind—on *the queen's* mind.

He'd found himself making that mistake of late: thinking of the queen in friendly and personal terms. They had once, when children, been friends, even using each other's given names quite freely. He'd fallen too easily back into that once-permitted indulgence, though to his relief not aloud.

Quick, quiet footsteps brushed over the carpeting of the room and, in a swift bit of movement, the curtain fluttered then fell back into place with this new arrival positioned with him behind it. He'd not lit any candles in the room nor were those in the corridor bright enough to illuminate his sudden companion. The person was near enough for Reynard to feel the warmth of them. He didn't speak, not knowing if he'd been spotted or if he was, quite by accident, sharing the space with someone who hadn't yet realized he was there.

"My speech went as it ought." The queen spoke softly, her breath tickling his face. She must have been standing very close indeed.

"I am pleased to hear that." He spoke in a whisper. "Were you chastised for your earlier disappearance?"

"There was not time. I did, though, receive a few quizzical looks." Her hand brushed his arm then settled against his chest.

There was something unexpectedly reassuring in that simple touch, one that ought to have made him take a few steps back in order to regain an appropriate distance from his monarch. But, instead, he found himself setting his hand atop hers, holding it gently above his heart.

"There are enough from the household staff still in this wing of the palace that we dare not make good our escape yet," she said softly.

"Will they not be searching for you?"

She shook her head, though he did not see the movement. "I informed my lady's maid that I was retiring early and asked that the curtains around my bed be drawn. I further insisted I not be bothered all night and that I would most likely stroll my garden in the morning for a constitutional. That should prevent my absence from being discovered tonight and offer an explanation for my disappearance in the morning."

"How late are the staff likely to be active in this area of the palace?" Reynard asked.

In a movement she gave no thought to but found entirely natural, Eleanor leaned against him. She spoke even more softly. "Another quarter hour, most likely."

Hesitantly, Reynard set his other arm about her, keeping her tucked close.

Both participants in the clandestine embrace insisted to themselves that the arrangement was entirely a matter of safety, an effort to remain undiscovered. Both firmly ignored the insistence of their hearts that holding each other was proving both deeply enjoyable and utterly peaceful. And both knew better than to speak a word of those feelings to the other.

The quarter hour passed as if on the back of a tortoise. They stood so near that they could hear each other breathe, that the cold of the stone wall warmed behind them, that neither, for the first time in far too long, felt alone.

But neither did either of them look at each other, though the room was too dark for them to have realized as much. And as neither spoke, their thoughts were also unknown to each other.

How heartbreaking are moments of connection when those experiencing them are not free to express what they are feeling!

The residence wing outside the queen's sitting room grew silent, most of the candles had been extinguished, and the intrepid pair were able to slip from the palace, doing so with as few words as could be managed.

They held fast to the amulet as they rushed into the forest and directly to the cottage waiting for them there and the enchantments that would protect them.

They were safe . . . for a time.

Eleanor pulled back the heavy burlap on the front window just enough to look up at the tops of the trees and the still-dark sky. "I'm dreading the coming of morning."

"Does the transformation hurt?" Reynard's voice echoed with compassion.

She shook her head. "It doesn't, oddly enough. And I don't even feel uncomfortable in the form that I take. I still think as myself. I can still understand people when they speak." She clasped her hands together and pressed them to her chin. "I tried to talk while in pine marten form. I didn't manage it, but I'm not certain if that is because doing so is impossible or if I simply need to continue practicing."

"Do keep trying," he pleaded. "If we could actually speak during the daylight hours, we would have a better chance of sorting out how to end this curse. It is too complex for either of us to remedy alone."

"I will keep trying. I swear to it."

His smile was soft and appreciative. "You are not easily defeated, Your Majesty."

Her eyebrows pulled sharply together as she shook her head. "Please don't call me that."

"But you are the queen. That is how I am meant to address you."

Misery tugged at her features as loneliness began filling her heart. "We were friends once, Reynard."

At the reminder, Reynard's posture grew rigid. "When we were children," he said with firm propriety. "When you were not yet queen. Now that you are, it would be inappropriate for me to think of you in any other terms."

He was attempting to remember his duty.

She was attempting to feel less alone in the world.

Only *he* succeeded.

Pushing from her thoughts the memory of him holding her in his arms and emptying her heart of the hope she'd allowed to grow that he might care for her, Eleanor turned away. She couldn't bear the idea of her heartbreak and misery being so obvious to him.

She took up the wool blanket she'd used when they'd last been in the cottage and wrapped it around herself once more. Dawn would come eventually, and Amesby's queen would again "see through pine marten's eyes." Even in the sorceress's curse, Eleanor had been identified only as "the queen."

That was all she was to anyone. She was the ceremonial robes she wore. The scripted words she spoke. A position but not a person. And everything depended on that continuing to be true.

Reynard's words had hurt, but they were true. And they were a needed reminder of what was required of her. When she had been crowned queen, her personal hopes and dreams and wishes had been set aside, made secondary to what the kingdom needed. She would suffer fewer disappointments if she remembered that.

Eleanor wiped away a tear, feeling foolish and weak.

Reynard watched that tear form, feeling guilty that his words had contributed to her sorrow. He hadn't meant to hurt her.

"For what it's worth," Reynard said into the heavy silence, "I liked being your friend all those years ago. I wish that hadn't needed to change."

She didn't look at him, but kept her eyes on the window. "I'm not allowed to wish for things any longer. Not for myself. I would do best not to forget that."

Several long moments followed, and Eleanor lowered herself onto a pallet in the corner, wrapping her blanket about her. Reynard set himself in a corner, another blanket draped over him. Exhausted, discouraged, and both lost in their separate thoughts, they drifted off into equally fitful sleep, unsure and wary of what the future might hold.

INSTALLMENT V
in which Help is sought and Danger is courted!

Reynard awoke to find soft sunlight peeking around the makeshift burlap curtains hanging in the windows. Morning had come. And looking at the pallet where Eleanor—*Queen* Eleanor—had been sleeping, he saw she had transformed once more. A deep-brown pine marten lay curled in precisely the way it had in the sentry box the day before.

She'd said the transformation didn't hurt. He hoped that continued to be true.

Reynard rose, stretching out the tension that had built in his body after he'd slept in so odd a position. He was not required to stand sentry today. Everyone amongst the palace guards was permitted two days in each month away from their duties. He'd chosen these days weeks ago, having wanted to attend the feats of skill and strength that were held during the week of the Unification Ceremony. That had proven fortuitous.

It is too complex for either of us to remedy alone.

His own words from the night before had returned to him again and again in his dreams. This could not be addressed by only the two of them. They needed others. Others who had magic. Others who might be willing to take a stand against Dezmerina.

And Reynard knew where to find them.

He changed from his sentry uniform, which he'd been wearing for far too long, and into a set of clothing that had once belonged to his father. If ever he needed his parents' wisdom to reach him from beyond, it was then. His mother would have understood the curse without difficulty. His father would have known how to safeguard the queen. Reynard was struggling to manage just one of those tasks.

He set a hat on his head and pulled a knapsack over one shoulder. He intended to awaken the pine marten queen before departing, but she woke on her own. Queen Eleanor had told him she could understand him when he spoke, that she still thought as her human self. So he addressed her as such.

"I know of people who will help us," he said. "People who can be trusted. They were associates of my mother, who built and enchanted this cottage. And while she was here, she was safe. You'll be safe here as well. I am going to see if I can find us help."

She hopped off the pallet and moved swiftly to the wall near the door. Stretching to her full length, she reached up on the wall, her paw nearly touching the amulet hanging from a nail. She looked back at him, then back at the amulet a few times in succession.

He understood. "I'll wear the amulet while I am out. It will protect me, and this cottage will protect you."

She dipped her head in a way that made him think of a nod.

He knotted the amulet's two leather straps and placed it around his neck. "Please be safe," he said. "I will return as soon as I can."

Reynard slipped from the cottage, closing the door firmly behind him. He paused for a moment, concerned for Queen Eleanor, unsure of his ability to complete his task successfully. But being in his mother's cottage had made him feel she was close. She had always believed in him. She would have insisted he forge ahead with confidence.

He moved with swift feet through the forest toward the vast field where the competition of skill and strength was to be held. It had been many years since he'd spoken with his mother's friends, but he remembered them, and he hoped they would remember him.

Spectator benches had been placed in neat rows on the hillside overlooking the field of competition, but the press and pull of so many eager to watch gave the neat layout a decidedly chaotic feel. That suited Reynard's purposes brilliantly. No one would take note of him wandering about, having conversations. He'd be able to learn what he needed and make his pleas for help without adding to the danger of the situation.

I'm not allowed to wish for things any longer. Not for myself.

He'd seen for himself how hard Eleanor tried to be the best queen she could be, doing what the kingdom needed her to do. Was she truly required to lose so much of herself in fulfilling her duties? It seemed terribly unfair.

"Reynard!" Marwen, an older man, one known to him from childhood, called out and waved him over. "How fare ye?" It was the greeting used by those with magic when encountering each other or each other's families.

"I am as I have ever been, though not all know the how or when." That was the reply used when one needed assistance from those with magic. Dezmerina was the reason they were all in hiding; she was the source of nearly all their difficulties.

Marwen walked with Reynard to where a woman sat, awaiting the start of the competition. Her name was Gerhilde, and she had been one of Reynard's mother's dearest friends.

"Reynard," she greeted. "How fare ye?"

"I am as I have ever been, though not all know the how or when."

"Tell us of both."

He sat between them, and all three set their gazes on the field below, giving every impression of chatting casually whilst enjoying the day's offering.

Keeping his voice low, Reynard said, "Our mutual adversary has set a curse."

"Upon what or whom?" Marwen asked.

"To one known as Eleanor."

There was a pause, a silent gasp.

Gerhilde pressed for greater clarity. "Known to us all?"

"Known to us all," Reynard confirmed.

"And what has been done to her?" Marwen's concern filled his soft voice.

"She has been transformed into an animal, but only in the daylight."

"What are the four patterns?" Gerhilde asked.

"The manifestation is while the sun is in the sky. The 'how' is that Eleanor is transformed into a pine marten. The impact is battles and chaos. The ending I cannot truly sort out."

"Tell us the fourth line," Marwen said. "We will help you sort it."

"'Her life will ebb whilst mine remains,'" he quoted. "I have my fears about what that means."

"Your fears are likely well-founded," Gerhilde said. "While the curse is in place, the one it is placed on will slowly die."

"But that is impact, not requirements for ending." Reynard shook his head. "Unless the only way to end the curse is for—" He couldn't bring himself to finish the thought.

"The curse will end when Eleanor's life has been drained," Gerhilde said. "Or—"

"I like the possibility of 'or.'" Reynard liked it very much, in fact.

"Or when the caster of the spell has died," Gerhilde finished.

Whilst mine remains. If Dezmerina's life no longer remained, that would end the curse too.

"But no one has been able to defeat her since she began her reign," Reynard said. "Indeed, many have been lost in the attempt."

"So much so that you will have difficulty finding those willing to join you in your fight," Marwen said.

"And how did you know I intended to attempt a recruitment?"

"Because you know better than most that a single person, or even two, are not enough to stop one as powerful as she."

Gerhilde nodded in agreement.

"But if this curse is not lifted, chaos and battles will tear this kingdom asunder. That must not be permitted to happen," Reynard said.

"She knows how to cause fear," Gerhilde said. "Fear is a powerful thing."

"Then we need to find something more powerful," Reynard said firmly.

But before they could imagine what that something might be, the competition below quite suddenly stopped.

Everything stopped.

An explosion of sparks and a whirlwind of color split the scene, revealing the sudden presence of Dezmerina.

"Where is your queen?" she demanded in a carrying voice, echoing in the silence around her. "She is not at the palace. She is not here."

No one spoke, but eyes were darting about, searching for answers in the faces around them.

Below, Dezmerina cackled. "Your barons are consulting. Tomorrow the Unification Ceremony will be held. But where is your queen? She has failed you. She has flown. War will descend, and chaos will reign in her stead, and I alone will maintain power enough to protect those who choose me."

The already silent air grew heavier with worry and uncertainty.

"You have the night to choose your side. Once the ceremony begins, there will be no changing loyalties." She held her hands to the sky, clouds roiling and spinning above her. "You have the night."

And in a flash of lightning, the sorceress disappeared.

· **INSTALLMENT VI**

in which the Queen discovers things of a most Distressing nature!

Though oblivious to all that had occurred at the feats of skill and strength competition, Eleanor was hardly idle whilst Reynard was away. She felt unequal to the weight of being queen and suspected others also took little comfort in the idea of her on the throne. She wanted them to have confidence in her. She wanted the kingdom to feel safe and well looked after. Discovering their monarch was a three-foot weasel-like creature during daylight hours would only add to their doubts.

The week of the Unification Ceremony was always precarious, with all the kingdom holding its collective breath, praying peace would hold. She could not risk that failing. She would not.

It took doing and a great deal of patience, but she was eventually able to pull out and open a book entitled *On the Creation, Implementation, and Elimination of Spells, Curses, and Enchantments* she found amongst the stacks of jars and pots and other household things.

Eleanor was pleased to discover her assumption on the matter of her literacy was correct. Because she still thought and experienced life as herself, she felt certain she would still be able to read. She'd not felt as energetic today as she had the day before in pine marten form. She was weaker, more worn down. It was the result of worry and the strain of transformations, she didn't doubt. She had energy enough, though, to search the book Reynard's mother had kept in her enchanted cottage. In it, she hoped to find answers and solutions.

Turning the pages proved rather difficult. Her arms were so different in this form than in her natural one. And though she could retract her pine marten claws, she couldn't do so entirely, and she didn't want to damage the book. That slowed her search but did not thwart it entirely.

The book, she discovered, was organized in the same manner Reynard had explained the curse placed on her. Explanations and information regarding manifestations in the first section, how the magic manifested in the second. The third section discussed the impact of the magic. The fourth was dedicated to the wording of endings and what that meant for lifting a curse, ending an enchantment, or countering a spell.

Though she wanted to know how to end the curse placed upon her, Eleanor began with the first section of the book, searching each page until she found a heading that read quite familiarly.

Spells, Curses, and Enchantments Beginning with Variations upon "When the sun lights the sky"

It is a common misunderstanding that the manifestation of magic invoked with these words will be in place during daylight hours regardless of conditions in the sky. While that is generally true, there are notable exceptions.

Exceptions were precisely what she needed. She skimmed over the text devoted to wording that substituted "if" for "when" or included additional specifics such as "when the sun would normally" or "whenever the sun lights the sky, however dimly."

At last her pine marten eyes settled upon the paragraph delineating limitations to curses that used precisely the wording Dezmerina had chosen.

Should magic be implemented with the manifestation declaration of "whenever the sun lights the sky," even should the portion of the sky in which the sun's location be specified, there are rare instances when the magic will not manifest during what would, by all estimations, be deemed daylight hours. A combination of thick clouds and heavy smoke can block out enough of the sun to trick the magic into relinquishing its hold for a time. Locations with particularly high mountains to the east will see the magic delayed until the sun is higher than the mountaintops. Likewise, locations with mountains to the west will see the magic lose its grip once the sun has sunk below those mountaintops, making it last a shorter time than it would in a place without such mountains.

Neither of those things really applied in Eleanor's case. Amesby's mountains were to the north. And she could not imagine, even if clouds rolled in, there would be a fire of such enormous proportions as to block out the sun. It would be far too great a coincidence, and a tragic one at that.

This manifestation of magic can also be temporarily tricked into releasing its grip when a shadow crosses the sun, blocking its light and dimming the world. The sun still lights the sky, but the heart of the sun is covered, and the magic will believe the sun has fled.

A solar eclipse. But it would only lift the curse temporarily.

She needed to know how to end it entirely. That would be found in the fourth section of the book.

Her agility with her clawed paws was improving, but her energy was ebbing. Did pine martens always grow tired so quickly? She didn't think so. They were hunters, after all, needing to capture prey. Feeling as lethargic as she did would make her future efforts virtually impossible.

She searched through various wordings for final lines of curses and enchantments and spells until she found what she was looking for.

Spells, Curses, and Enchantments Ending with Declarations Regarding the Life of Those Involved

The curse had specifically mentioned life: both hers and Dezmerina's.

Several entries below the heading, Eleanor came upon the entry most closely resembling the curse she was living with.

Curses, spells, and enchantments which specify, in their fourth line, the ebbing of a life rather than the ending of one will still be lifted upon the death of the person referred to. The difference is, that person will begin dying as a result of that magic and will, in time, succumb to it. That death will end the curse, spell, or enchantment.

Her death would end the curse. But that death would not occur by accident or as the result of normal aging. The spell, itself, was killing her. It was likely why she was tired today, why she felt as though she was struggling more than usual.

She was dying.

There had to be another way to end the curse and save the kingdom that didn't require her death. And not merely because she didn't particularly want to die. There was no clear successor to the throne. The battles and chaos the curse, itself, would cause, would not end with the curse being lifted. Her death would not save her kingdom.

It was in the midst of this discouraging discovery that Reynard returned. He looked as disheartened as she felt. If only she'd also found a means of speaking while in this frustrating form she was forced to assume.

He spotted her on the floor of the cottage. "My mother's book. I hadn't even thought of it. Brilliant."

She didn't always feel brilliant. That he thought she was, even if only in that moment, was a wonderful thing. That she was dying was not nearly as wonderful.

Eleanor tapped her paw against the page directly atop the bit she'd been reading. Reynard's eyes slid over the page as he read.

He looked more saddened than surprised. "I consulted with two people who are wise in the ways of magic. They said the same thing."

Eleanor leaned against his leg. She was both tired and discouraged and needed the momentary support.

"They did say that the last bit of the fourth line means Dezmerina's death would end the curse as well. But only her death or yours can accomplish it."

People had been trying for years on end to stop Dezmerina. As near as anyone knew, it was impossible. She was too powerful to kill and too feared for others to gather in anything approaching the numbers needed to have any chance of success against her.

Unable to simply tell Reynard what else she had discovered, Eleanor pawed the pages back, stopping when she reached the first entry she'd read. Once more, she pointed with her paw to the bit she needed him to read. And, once more, he did so without hesitation.

"An eclipse. You would temporarily transform back into yourself, long enough to address the barons and the people, to show them that Dezmerina's powers are not infallible, that there are gaps in what she can do, flaws in the spells she can cast. If they feel that defeating her is possible, they'll be more likely to try."

Eleanor nodded, knowing full well the movement looked odd in her current state.

"My mother did not study the sky. There will not be anything in this cottage that will allow us to predict when an eclipse might occur, or if one will happen before—"

He didn't finish the sentence. He didn't have to. They both knew full well that the curse was actively killing her. Each day that passed, each moment, drew her closer to death, speeding her to her untimely demise.

But she hadn't time for dwelling on that. She knew of someone who could, with accuracy, determine the movement of celestial bodies, and who had, while her father was still alive, accurately predicted more than one eclipse. But curse her pine marten's voice, she could not speak to Reynard.

Eleanor turned pleading eyes on Reynard, tapping her leg anxiously, hoping to communicate with him.

Bless him, he understood rather quickly. "Do you know of someone familiar with the skies?"

She gave her best nod.

"Where do we find him?"

That was not a question she could answer with a nod or a shake of her pine marten head, which he realized quickly.

"At the palace?" he asked.

She shook her head.

"The village?"

She nodded.

"Let us go there, then. But I must warn you, fear has already taken hold of the kingdom. Dezmerina disrupted the competition today, issuing a warning to all. She declared that war is on the horizon, the queen has fled, and only those who side with Dezmerina will be protected by her. Once the Unification Ceremony begins tomorrow, she will allow no changing loyalties."

And, because no queen would arrive at the ceremony—at least not a queen in human form as the ceremony occurred during the day—that would be seen as confirmation of Dezmerina's declaration. It would usher in the start of the chaos and battles her curse promised.

The sorceress had, it seemed, thought of every aspect of her sordid spell.

What chance did a pine marten queen and a sentry guard truly have of defeating her?

INSTALLMENT VII
in which the Queen and her Knavish Guard seek the Help they require!

The day was growing late as Reynard Atteberry rushed to the village that abutted the palace. He held the pine marten fast in his arms, both of them encircled by the leather straps of the late Mrs. Atteberry's amulet.

Eleanor used her snout to point Reynard in the direction they needed to go. Her father's one-time astrological advisor made his home above the pub, making him both easy to find and, in that moment, impossible to visit undetected.

All the village had gathered in the public house. There was no mistaking the topic they were discussing. Neither was there any chance of missing the fear they felt.

Gerhilde and Marwen were present and spotted Reynard upon his arrival. They rose and joined him, both asking with their expressions alone what his business in the village might be.

"There is a man here who knows the movements of the sky.

Unfortunately, our friend"—he indicated the pine marten in his arms—"is unable to tell me precisely where or the person's name."

"This is the unfortunate creature we spoke of earlier?" Gerhilde asked.

"Yes, and she is able to understand us."

"I believe," Marwen said to Eleanor, "the man you seek is Orestes."

She nodded.

"Follow us." Marwen led the way up the stairs to the landing above.

A second, narrower, darker stairwell led to a second, darker landing with but one door. At that door, they knocked, and waited.

A man, hair whiter than snow, answered their summons. His was the face of a friendly man who did not suffer fools gladly, a decidedly interesting combination. No one took time to contemplate the contradiction; far too much needed to be accomplished.

"We come with urgent business on behalf of Her Majesty, the Queen," Reynard said.

Orestes found them believable enough to let them in. He closed the door quickly behind them, a sure sign the old man knew that life in the village had that very day grown perilous.

"Her Majesty's inquiry is rather simple," Reynard said. "She wishes to know when the kingdom might expect to experience an eclipse of the sun."

"Soon, actually," Orestes said. "Quite soon."

Eleanor perked up, wishing yet again she could speak.

"One will occur tomorrow. The first time, to my knowledge, that an eclipse will occur during a Unification Ceremony. I do not yet know if that is a good omen or bad."

Eleanor turned about in Reynard's arms, looking up at him.

He met her eyes. "You will be present for the Unification Ceremony. That will undermine Dezmerina's predicted dissolution of the kingdom."

But it was more than that. She could address both the barons and the people. She could tell them what had happened and do so in a way they could not deny it. They would know she had not abandoned them, and that Dezmerina's goal was to destroy their dedication to one another.

This was hope.

"The sun is nearly below the horizon," Gerhilde said, watching at the window.

Reynard set Eleanor on the floor, giving her space to make her transformation.

Orestes watched them with curiosity, his mind sharp enough that he pieced together the situation in the moment before the spinning and twisting caused by the curse transformed Eleanor once more.

She had told Reynard the transformation was not painful. And though that was still true, she was finding that each change was more exhausting than the last.

This time, she couldn't remain on her feet. As she, now in human form, crumpled, Reynard leapt to catch her, saving her from a painful collision with the floor.

"I don't know how many more times I can do this, Reynard," she said, sighing as she leaned against him.

"It seems at least two more," he answered. "Can you endure two more?"

She tried to be brave, tried to be reassuring. But her nod and smile were found lacking by all present. They knew, to a one, she might be nearer to the curse's completion than any of them would like.

"Your Majesty," Orestes said with a bow when Eleanor had regained her feet. "It was my honor serving your father as his Royal Astronomer. I am pleased to have served you as well."

"Thank you, Orestes. Thanks to your help, we might yet save the kingdom."

"Begging your pardon, Your Majesty," Marwen said. "I believe, if we are to have a hope of that, it is your help we need most in this moment."

She wasn't certain what he meant.

He continued. "Below us, so many in this village are quaking with fear over what tomorrow will hold. They are debating what is to be done with someone as powerful as Dezmerina, who has both threatened them and promised to protect them. Their current predicament will soon spread through the entire kingdom, and all because our foe told them their queen had deserted them."

"But I haven't," Eleanor said.

"They need to know that." Reynard stood with a supportive arm still around her. "And now, until the sun rises again, you are able to tell them."

"I have never possessed a knack for grand speeches." The very thought overset her. And yet . . . "If their courage can hold, then mine certainly can. It must."

How brave was their queen! How worthy! If only she truly realized how beloved she was.

"Come." Gerhilde motioned the queen and her errant palace guard to follow her back down the narrow stairs, all the way to the public room below, where the voices were louder than they had been and the atmosphere had grown tense with wariness.

Gerhilde flung her arms out and upward, sending sparks high into the air.

"Dezmerina can sense the use of magic," Eleanor whispered, frantic.

"The magic Gerhilde is casting now will protect this pub," Marwen quietly assured her. "The enchantment will not last long, but it will keep Dezmerina at bay long enough for you to offer those here some reassurance."

Eleanor held tight to Reynard's hand. He knew it was not appropriate, that he ought to pull back and keep the distance required of a palace guard when interacting with the monarch. To allow this closeness was the act of a knave. Yet, he felt certain she needed the touch, needed the connection. He needed it too.

Those gathered at the pub had grown quiet, all watching Gerhilde.

"Let your minds rest, my friends," she said. "I bring you reassurance." She turned toward Eleanor. "Your Majesty."

Eleanor kept hold of Reynard's hand, bringing him with her as she stepped into the center of the room. Whispers bounced through the crowd as people bowed and curtsied to their queen.

"Good people." Her voice wavered, but anyone looking at her would know she was sincere in wanting to be heard. "I know the threats and promises Dezmerina made today, but I also know the lies she told you. She said I had fled, had abandoned you. But, in truth, she cast a spell on me which rendered me unable to be seen during the day. She used that curse to convince you that I am dishonorable, that you have been left alone, that the kingdom is vulnerable to the very chaos that tomorrow's ceremony was created to prevent."

As she took a quick but deep breath, Reynard squeezed her hand. Gerhilde, Marwen, and Orestes offered nods of encouragement.

"She must not be allowed to destroy our peace. She must not be permitted to steal from us our future, our hopes, or our freedom from her tyranny. Those here with me are determined to do all we can to thwart her. But, good people all, we cannot manage it alone. We need you. *I* need you."

"The sorceress will kill us if we defy her," someone in the crowd replied. "She has done so before."

"I know," Eleanor said. "And I will not require anyone to court that danger. But if you are willing to help, please do. Please."

Reynard stepped forward, addressing them himself. "You all know me. My father was born in this village, as was I. My mother had magic, like others in this room." He wouldn't name them, as doing so would put them in additional danger. "Many like my mother were killed by Dezmerina for defying her. I know perfectly well what you would be risking. But it is also why I am taking that very risk. My father dedicated his life to safeguarding this kingdom. My mother gave her life in protecting all of us from the very person who threatens us now."

"For the sake of those who have fought this battle before," Eleanor said, "please consider helping us. Our stand must happen at the Unification Ceremony tomorrow."

"Consider," Reynard said.

Murmurs began amongst those they had addressed. They all had a difficult, seemingly impossible choice to make. Offering them privacy in which to do it seemed the kindest thing.

Reynard and Eleanor held fast to either end of the amulet that had, thus far, protected them from the sorceress who meant to destroy the kingdom and rebuild it as her own. They rushed, unspeaking, away from the village and into the forest, back to the cottage that had sheltered them.

Only once inside, with the door closed and the window coverings drawn, did they at last fully breathe. But though Reynard felt a sense of relief, Eleanor crumpled, her strength nearly spent.

"Eleanor!" He knelt beside her, wrapping his arms around her, studying her face, needing to know he'd not lost her already. "Eleanor?"

She leaned into him, her eyes closed. "I truly think I am dying, Reynard. Ebbing, just as the curse said. A slow siphoning of life."

"Do not lose hope," he pleaded.

"It is not hope I fear I'll lose, but strength." She curled a bit, not entirely unlike the position her pine marten form took when sleeping. "I have to transform at least twice more. I'm not certain I have the fortitude."

Reynard lifted her from the floor and carried her gently in his arms to the pallet, where he laid her down before pulling a blanket up to her shoulders. "Rest, Eleanor. Save your strength. And know you're not alone."

"Reynard?"

"Yes?"

"Will you promise to keep calling me Eleanor?" How she wanted him to!

How well he knew that he oughtn't! "I would be a very presumptuous and insolent sentry if I did."

She forced her eyes open, though it drained nearly all her remaining strength. "I have sentries aplenty," she whispered. "I need you to be more than that."

He wanted to be. He truly did.

INSTALLMENT VIII

in which Choices must be made and Consequences faced!

All the barons were on the palace grounds for the Unification Ceremony, gathered in neat rows according to the ancientness of their various titles. Beyond them, the people of the kingdom stood, sat, and waited with interest for the ceremony to begin. On the dais was a perfectly round table with the three-wicked candle and ceremonial wreath upon it. The bejeweled crown lay atop a velvet pillow, awaiting the arrival of the queen.

But she was already there.

Tucked behind the tapestry table covering, Eleanor, in pine marten form, assured herself of two very crucial things: that Orestes's prediction of a full eclipse would prove accurate and that her pleas at the pub the night before had convinced at least some of the people present to stand up to Dezmerina when she inevitably arrived in fury and nefariousness.

At Reynard's insistence, Eleanor was wearing the protective amulet. She was, after all, alone on the dais and would continue to be even after the eclipse allowed her to transform into her true form once more. She was weaker than she'd ever been and had every expectation of being weaker still after the next transformation. If she had any hope of thwarting Dezmerina, she needed all the help and protection she could call upon.

As often as the gathered people's eyes watched the dais, they also turned them upward to the sky. The eclipse had begun, the encroaching shadow covering more than a third of the orb. The sun's heart had to be covered in order to fool the magic. That would not happen until the eclipse was nearly at its height.

Reynard was amongst the palace guards, recruiting them to the cause, rallying their support, and calling upon their sense of duty and desire to safeguard their kingdom and their queen.

Gerhilde and Marwen had sent whispers out amongst the others with magic, reminding them of those they had lost, encouraging them to stand with those who ought to have support.

Orestes wandered amongst the villagers and other people of the kingdom, speaking of the violence Dezmerina was known for and of the impossibility of one person—even the queen herself—defeating a villain like that if she was required to do so alone.

The time for the ceremony arrived. Word had spread from the pub all the way to the barons of the curse placed on the queen, one that made her unable to be seen in the daylight. Her absence, therefore, was not entirely unexpected, but neither was it reassuring. This ceremony had been the backbone of the kingdom's peace and tranquility for generations. No matter that their monarch was not neglecting it out of indifference or even choice, to not complete the ritual would take them into uncharted waters.

Above their heads, the dark shadow passed farther over the sun, enough so that the sky itself was rendered dim.

From her place hidden behind the tapestry-covered table, Eleanor could feel an odd pulling and twisting. It was similar to what she felt when transforming, but it seemed to be shifting back and forth at the same time. Parts of her attempted to become human, while other parts firmly remained pine marten. In the middle of a transition, her becoming-human-limbs would transform to animal paws again.

It was, without question, the worst transformation she'd experienced. The others, as she'd assured Reynard, had not been painful: exhausting and uncomfortable, yes, but not agonizing.

This one was.

The murmurs from the crowd grew louder. The ceremony was late.

Eleanor silently pleaded with the eclipse to speed its path, to cover the heart of the sun, to grant her both relief from the agony of this broken transformation and the time she needed to address her people as herself. As if fate had chosen to be kind to her, the pine marten fur and clawed paws gave way to her own skin and clothes, to her own hands and fingers.

Drawing on every bit of strength she had left, and there was precious little, she rose and stood, leaning against the tapestried table. A gasp rose from the barons and gathered villagers alike.

"My people," she said quickly, attempting to keep her voice loud enough to be heard, even as she could feel herself fading. "Dezmerina will arrive at any moment, I have no doubt. She has done all she can to stop this moment, to destroy this kingdom. We must not allow her to do so."

Eleanor lit the ceremonial candle and placed the wreath around it with shaking hands. A speech was usually given, pledges both given and received from the monarchy and the barons to live in peace, but it was the lighting of the candle and the placing of the wreath that was the crux of the ceremony. After that, the crown was to be placed atop the monarch's head, a symbol that the royal reign would continue in harmony with the nobility, the merchants, the people, and the kingdom as a whole.

A crash of thunder announced Dezmerina's arrival on the dais before Eleanor's crown was put in place. Some in the gathering ran for their very lives. They could hardly be blamed. Dezmerina did not make idle threats.

"Your time is up," the sorceress declared to them all. "This kingdom will soon be claimed by me, to be ruled as I see fit. Make your loyalties known."

"Queen Eleanor!" The shout went up from amongst the guards. Reynard had convinced them, securing their loyalties.

The guards' declaration seemed to give courage to the barons, who added their voices. The people gathered did so next.

Dezmerina's look of confusion was unlikely to last long. She would be angry soon enough.

"You cannot control them with fear," Eleanor whispered. "They are determined to be free."

Dezmerina flung her arms in a circle, and a pack of unnaturally enormous wolves appeared, lined up along the edges of the dais, keeping the would-be defenders of the throne at bay. Anger having seized her expression, the sorceress looked at Eleanor at last.

"It is daytime. Why are you not as you were cursed to be?"

"Your magic cannot see the heart of the sun." Eleanor's legs shook beneath her, but she stood tall.

"The eclipse," Dezmerina muttered. "No matter. It will pass soon enough, and you will be helpless and hopeless. You cannot survive another transformation. And even if you did, you would never escape my wolves. They are very fond of the taste of pine marten."

The dais was surrounded by those eager to defend their queen and their kingdom. The wolves might have been fond of pine marten, but Eleanor suspected they would not object to a meal made of those they were currently holding at bay.

Her eyes fell on Reynard. She could not bear the thought of him being killed in this fray, of his life, so precious to her, being lost. But what could be done but fight?

> Whene'er the sun lights Amesby skies,
> Her queen will see through pine marten's eyes.

Soon enough, the eclipse would pass, and Eleanor would be transformed. She was the queen, and that was the curse.

Except the recrowning of the monarch was part of the Unification Ceremony.

Eleanor was the queen. But if someone else was crowned as part of the ceremony, by one who had the authority to do so—which Eleanor did—that person would, symbolically, at least, be the monarch. And the curse did not specify that Eleanor was to be transformed, but rather that the *queen* was.

"Will you let them live?" Eleanor asked, rushing her words, hoping to outlast the eclipse enough to prevent her transformation. "If I place this crown on your head rather than mine, will you let them live?"

Dezmerina's eyes narrowed. "I would consider it."

"No, Eleanor!" Reynard called out from amongst the crowd. "Do not believe her."

She looked out at the faces of those who were ready to defend her. "I am certain this will be for the best." How she prayed they believed her!

Her insides were beginning to twist again, a sure sign her time was running short. Eleanor took up the crown but didn't move hastily. She needed Dezmerina to be crowned without enough time to return the favor once she realized what the ceremony would do to her. The pain increased, the tearing apart of her body from within as it struggled to know what form it was meant to take.

Eleanor set the crown on the sorceress's head.

"I am queen," Dezmerina said with satisfaction.

"Whene'er the sun lights Amesby skies," Eleanor repeated, feeling her strength return swiftly, "the queen will see through pine marten's eyes."

The shadow slipped off the sun above.

Dezmerina's body spun and twisted, the crown falling from her head, but the curse had taken hold. Her shrieks of anger turned the heads of her wolves. Their curiosity turned to unmistakable hunger as the sorceress took the shape of the one creature her pack craved the most.

In a dart of fur, the pine marten ran from the dais, the wolves after her. With the canine guards on the chase, some people they'd been holding back ran to the dais, while others rushed around it, following the pack to determine the fate of the one who had hurt them for so long.

INSTALLMENT IX
in which the Queen, at last, is free!

Reynard was at Eleanor's side the instant after she outwitted Dezmerina. He wrapped his arms around her, his words of inquiry rendered inaudible in the chaos. But Eleanor did not need to hear what he said; his love and concern for her was etched in her heart already. She tucked her head against him, knowing by the sound of snarls and growls from the magical pack and the shouts of celebratory relief from the crowd who had followed that Dezmerina was no more.

Directly into her ear, so she could hear him, Reynard said, "You've lost your throne, my dear Eleanor."

"She had to be queen in some way when the sun returned. If that meant I would no longer be, it was well worth it. The kingdom will, at last, be free."

That kingdom celebrated for three days following Dezmerina's demise. The wolf pack was returned to the realm of magic by the efforts of those who'd once been forced to hide their gift.

The people sang the praises of their brave queen, not knowing if she would be their queen again.

The barons undertook two days of consultation, something that had never occurred before. But then, a monarch crowning someone else during the Unification Ceremony had also never happened before.

And thus it was, during this state of uncertainty, that the ball was held which always marked the end of this most important of weeks. All the barons and their families were present. Reynard, having been elevated by the Captain of the Guard to be the second-in-command, was eligible to attend the ball inside the palace.

The rest of the guards and the people of the kingdom gathered on the grounds for a party of their own. The celebration had seldom been so jovial. Yet, underneath the joy, was uncertainty. They had seen for themselves the bravery of their one-time queen. But what was to become of her now?

Into the gathering of glittering gowns and flickering candles, Eleanor stepped, her head held high despite the precariousness of her situation. She had not been lying when she'd told Reynard that her kingdom being free of Dezmerina had been her most important goal. But she was at loose ends and, until the question of her position was settled, she would continue to be so.

She paused at the top of the grand stairs leading into the ballroom. From there, arrivals were to be announced. But how to announce her?

Silence followed, and all eyes watched as the highest-ranking of the barons approached the base of the stairs and climbed them, one by one, to the top.

He turned and looked out at the ballroom. "Barons, gentlemen, ladies, and guests. By decree of the royal barons, I present to you—Queen Eleanor of Amesby."

The cheer that rose shook the crystal chandeliers. The cheer that followed as word reached those outside the palace shook the very trees.

Their queen was theirs once more. As brave and good and loyal a queen as any kingdom had ever known.

And, in the years that would follow, a prince consort—as brave and good and loyal as any queen had ever known—would stand at her side, loving her, loving the people, loving the kingdom.

They were free from the tyranny of one who had ruled with fear and threats. Free from the violence with which that queen would have reigned. Free because they'd chosen to stand together. Because they'd been as brave and good and loyal as any people could hope to be.

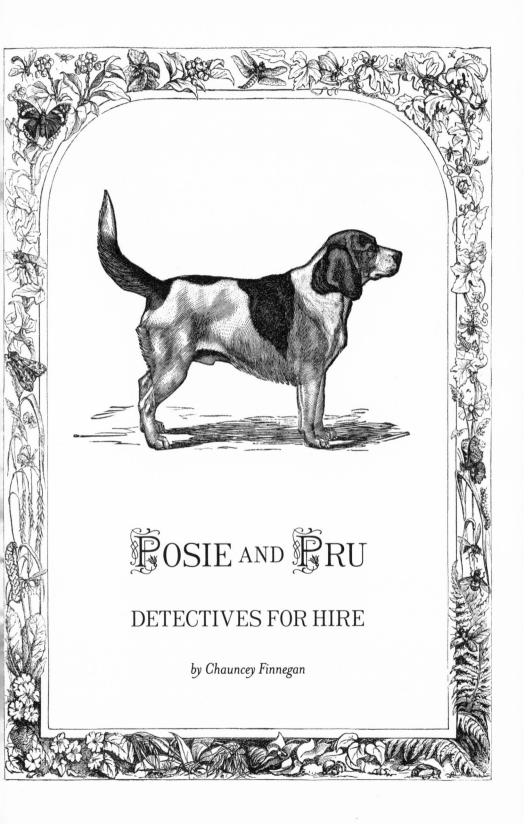

POSIE AND PRU

DETECTIVES FOR HIRE

by Chauncey Finnegan

CHAPTER ONE

Posie Poindexter was bored. Pru Dwerryhouse would have been, too, if she'd realized boredom was an option.

The two had set up house together on the occasion of Pru's seventieth birthday, Posie having already marked that milestone a year earlier, and had continued on in that arrangement for well over a year. They'd known each other from childhood and had the good fortune to have lived near each other all their lives, marrying men whose homes were in the same village. It was, in fact, in the very village of Downsford where they lived still.

The two were well known to all. Posie, with her shockingly white hair and ordinary brown eyes, stood at the height of a child but with the wrinkles of a poorly laundered shirt. And Pru, whose hair would have been as white as Posie's if not for her dedication to dying it an odd shade of dark brown using nuts and oil and other strange things, was built very much like the local church steeple, and she always wore something on her person that was blue.

Though neither of them realized as much, they had become somewhat legendary in their tiny village. It wasn't that either was necessarily more strange than anyone else living in Downsford. Mr. Green had a pet mole he called Walter and walked about on a lead. Mrs. Brennan also had a favored color of clothing, always wearing something that was white, which somehow made her gray hair look more like snow than silver. The local vicar insisted on walking backward for at least one quarter hour every morning. The blacksmith also worked as the farrier yet was terrified of horses.

Downsford was an odd place. It was also, at the moment, a bit tiresome in the eyes of one particularly bored resident.

"I need an occupation," Posie said on a sigh, her eyes on the window and the rain running down it in rivers.

"I believe the army would think you too old. And I do not think the vicar would let you take his living." Pru did not make this observation in jest. Pru never did. Her humor was, without exception, unintentional. "Do you suppose a woman of seventy-two could take up farming?"

"Not an occupation in *that* sense." Posie looked away from the window at long last. "I need . . . a hobby."

"The blacksmith seems to enjoy his hobby," Pru suggested.

Posie shook her head. "Blacksmithing isn't his hobby; it is his occupation."

"I thought you were looking for an occupation." Pru looked up from her knitting, genuine confusion on her face.

Posie rubbed at the spot above her right eye, the bit that had ached on and off with great regularity the last year or more. She'd begun referring to it as *petite pru*, the Frenchified name making the recurring headache more elegant somehow and the one for whom the headache was named less insulted.

"Perhaps we might open a lending library." Posie would enjoy that for a time.

"Who would lend us a library?" Pru asked, her knitting needles clicking quickly and rhythmically.

"It isn't a library that is lent out but a library that lends things *to* people."

"Ooh. What sort of things?"

"It's a *library*."

Pru's look of curiosity remained.

"Books, Pru. Books."

"Where would we get the books from?" Pru's needles clicked

unceasingly. "Seems we would need more than we currently have. Not too many more, though. It's a small village after all."

As was often the case with Pru, she'd stumbled upon a worthwhile insight quite by accident. Posie only owned seven books and hadn't the funds for purchasing more. Even if she came upon a literary windfall, a village of Downsford's size with its rather un-literary mindset would hardly have use for stacks and stacks of books.

"We used to look after dogs," Pru said with her usual smile. "We were good at that."

"When we were six years old. Could you imagine the two of us chasing after dogs *now*? I can hardly climb stairs any longer. You don't always remember where the stairs are."

"Well, each house and building has stairs in different places, don't they?" Pru continued knitting, clearly unconcerned about the possibility of being bored for the remainder of their lives. "Perhaps we could train dogs to find stairs for us."

"I think we can safely eliminate any potential pastimes that involve dogs, Pru."

"Oh, that *is* a shame. We were good at looking after dogs."

Petite pru perked up at that declaration. "There must be other things we are particularly good at," Posie said. "Some other talents we possess."

Pru smiled vaguely, not the least upended by their discussion.

"A shame I did not gain your propensity for knitwork," Posie said. "We might find some occupation involving that."

"I could knit sweaters for dogs!" Pru suggested eagerly.

"Whatever we choose," Posie said firmly, "it will have nothing to do with dogs."

Pru's silver eyebrows pulled low. "Oh, that *is* a shame. We were good at looking after dogs." She knitted another minute, then said, "Do you remember that time when your mother's ear baubles went missing—the ones with pearls—and we found them? That had nothing to do with dogs."

Posie did remember that. They'd gone on a very extensive search, one that included asking a great many questions of a great many people. After a time, they'd realized the jewelry had likely slipped behind a piece of furniture in Posie's mother's dressing room. They'd told her parents of their deduction, the dressing table was moved, and, much to everyone's delight, the baubles were there. It had been an exhilarating experience.

"We did solve that mystery rather expertly, didn't we?" Posie felt proud of herself, thinking back on it. "And I do recall it was not the first nor the last one we solved."

Pru nodded eagerly. "We sorted out why my knitting needles were bent."

They had, at that. They'd been all of twelve or thirteen and had followed the clues until they'd discovered that their brothers, as good of friends as the two of them were, had been using Pru's needles as swords in their reenactment of famous battles, all of which were staged in the back garden. It was, in fact, all the mud they'd found on the needles that had raised their suspicions that the boys had absconded into the garden with the needles.

"We could solve mysteries." Posie sat up straighter at the idea. "People could come to us with their puzzles, and we could discover the answers."

"We would be like the Bow Street Runners used to be: solving mysteries, being very dashing in their red waistcoats." Pru's eyes suddenly pulled wide. "Oh, I could—"

"Please do not offer to knit us red waistcoats."

"They don't have to be *red*."

Solvers of mysteries. Sorters of puzzles. There was nothing boring about any of that. "How do we let people know that we are now detectives?"

"We could tell them," Pru said over the continued needle clicking.

"If we are to be true detectives, then we need something more impressive than starting rumors about our availability."

"What if we made trade cards, like the tradesmen use in London?" Pru offered one of her rare but much appreciated useful suggestions.

Trade cards. Posie liked that idea very much, indeed. The town hadn't a printer, but they could obtain heavy paper and create their own cards by hand. That might prove a very elegant and personal touch.

In the end, it proved intriguing, at least. All around the village, cards began appearing with hand-drawn floral borders and the words *Posie and Pru: Detectives for Hire.*

The bit of advertising paid almost immediate dividends. A mere three days later, the newly minted detectives were visited by someone in great distress.

Mary O'Reilly was employed as a housekeeper in the home of Mr. Flanagan, a local man of not insignificant wealth, who had long been known to be rather dreadful and had for two days now been quite inarguably dead.

Mrs. O'Reilly was given a cup of tea and a shortbread biscuit, both of which Pru had decided were absolutely necessary to the running of their newly opened detective service. The three women chatted about little nothings—from dogs to knitting to the weather—and once they'd reached the amount of inconsequential chatting all conversations in England were, by unspoken agreement, required to include, Posie introduced the true topic at hand.

"What is the mystery we can help you sort?" she asked.

With a deep sigh and a look of worried confusion, Mrs. O'Reilly said, "I cannot be certain, but I think Mr. Flanagan was murdered."

"Murdered?" Posie was careful not to sound excited, though she was. Her excitement was not on account of a murder having been committed but as a result of being in a position to *solve* a murder. "Have you any idea who might have committed this heinous crime?"

Mrs. O'Reilly nodded, her cap nearly sliding off her gray curls. "It might have been . . . *me.*"

CHAPTER TWO

Posie and Pru's very first case, unfortunately, required them to undertake a journey. The late Mr. Flanagan's home was merely down the road, but leaving the house when one required an increasing number of aids and preparations was, no matter the distance, *a journey*.

"I don't know that you need *two* shawls," Mrs. O'Reilly said to Pru. "The weather is not overly chilly."

"One is my *indoor* shawl," Pru was quick to point out. "The other is for out of doors. I must have both."

Mrs. O'Reilly eyed Posie's canes—three of them. "Indoors. Out of doors. And . . . ?"

"No, no, no." Posie held aloft her shorter, hook-topped cane. "For steep paths." She raised the slightly longer, thicker one, with the wide base. "For slick paths." She held up the third one, quite elegantly made and boasting a silver handle. "For indoors."

"Roger the cheeseman would likely let us use his pony cart," Mrs. O'Reilly suggested in tones that grew more doubtful the longer she watched Posie and Pru's preparations.

Young people, Posie said inwardly. Mrs. O'Reilly was barely fifty. What did she know of canes and shawls and such?

"We can walk there," Posie insisted.

And they did. Pru put her out-of-doors shawl on top of her indoor shawl. Posie opted for her slick-paths cane, though she kept her indoors cane hooked over one arm. And they made the almost-half-a-mile walk at quite a clip, arriving at the late Mr. Flanagan's house in forty-five minutes.

"Which door do we use, Posie?" Pru asked. "We're here as tradespeople, being detectives for hire, but we've only ever entered homes through the main door."

It was a valid question, though Posie hadn't thought of it yet. "Being detectives doesn't mean we're not still ladies. I think we'd do best to call at the front door as we would if we weren't now detectives."

"We haven't a butler," Mrs. O'Reilly said. "You'll have to wait until I am inside and can answer your knock."

Which is precisely what they did.

Posie and Pru waited under the front portico until they heard Mrs. O'Reilly call out from the other side of the door that they could knock now.

Which is precisely what they did.

At the opening of the door, Posie produced one of their cards. "Posie and Pru. Detectives for hire," she said with pride.

Mrs. O'Reilly accepted the card and motioned them inside. "May I take your . . . out-of-doors items?"

"Excellent." Posie gave the housekeeper her wide-ended cane and leaned on her silver-handled one instead.

Pru handed over her heavier shawl.

"There are knitting needles in this shawl." Mrs. O'Reilly sounded confused.

"My out-of-doors knitting needles, of course," Pru said.

Mrs. O'Reilly saw to the storing of their items in the small cloak closet before ushering them from the entryway to a small withdrawing room. "This is where Mr. Flanagan was found."

Posie hadn't been in the Flanagans' house before, but she'd heard there was a room inspired by the Hall of Mirrors at the Palace of Versailles. Seeing the half dozen mirrors hanging on the wall proved less impressive than Posie had expected. Most of the mirrors were quite small, and most of the wall was only a wall.

Perhaps Mr. Flanagan had actually died of being entirely underwhelmed by a room that had promised palatial perfection. Posie had read a great many novels in which disappointment had proven fatal.

Or, perhaps he'd caught sight of himself in a few of the mirrors at once and, thinking several people had appeared in the room without warning, was so startled that he died of surprise—another possibility she had learned of through novels.

"Had Mr. Flanagan recently been in receipt of particularly bad tidings?" Posie had also read of people who, upon being told something shocking or mournful, died of unhappy news.

"No," Mrs. O'Reilly said. "In fact, his son had only just arrived at the house for a visit. Mr. Flanagan was beside himself with happiness."

Happiness. Did people ever die of happiness?

"What was he doing in here?" Pru asked. "Other than being dead, I mean."

"One of the maids came in because she'd heard a loud crash and a shattering sound. She felt certain he had been drinking a glass of sherry."

Ah. And had likely been disappointed, surprised, or shocked to death by something.

"Might we talk with the maid?" Posie asked.

"Of course."

"And have a bit of tea and biscuits?" Pru pressed.

Mrs. O'Reilly dipped her head. "Of course."

"And have a seat?" Posie's cane was reliable, but her bones preferred resting.

"Please do," Mrs. O'Reilly said before disappearing out of the room.

"I suppose if a person has to die unexpectedly," Pru said, looking around as she shuffled toward an obliging chair, "this is not an unpleasant place to do it."

"I have three theories already, Pru, each as likely as the next." Posie lowered herself into a wingback chair. She set her cane in front of her and rested both hands atop the handle. Her late husband used to assume that very pose when waxing long about something or other of significance. "We simply must determine if he was disappointed, surprised, or shocked in the moment before his death."

"Are those the only options?" Pru settled into a chair of her own.

"No, but I believe that is where we should begin."

Ten minutes passed before Mrs. O'Reilly, with the maid in tow, returned to the mirror room to find both Pru and Posie sleeping peacefully in their chairs. She was reluctant to wake them, but there was a mystery to be solved, after all, and if she was in fact a murderess, she would very much like to know.

With the two septuagenarians awake once more, the investigation could continue.

"This is Jane," Mrs. O'Reilly said, gesturing to the maid. "She's the one that found him."

"Did he look surprised?" Pru asked. "That is one of our theories."

"He didn't look surprised," Jane said. "I suspect he was, though. No one's expecting to be dead."

Posie nodded knowingly. "What else can you tell us?"

"He was lying on the floor, dead as can be. And the glass he'd been drinking from was shattered on the floor. The sound of it breaking was what brought me in. Saw him lying there. Saw Mrs. O'Reilly in the mirror. Leastwise I thought it was her. Let out a scream, I did, though on account of the sherry stain in the carpet I was going to have to scrub out. I didn't know he was dead. Once I did, I screamed on account of that."

"And did your screaming bring anyone else to the room?" Posie asked.

"Someone who might know if he'd been disappointed or surprised or shocked?" Pru pressed.

"Young Mr. Flanagan—our Mr. Flanagan's son—rushed in. He sorted out quite quickly that his father was dead." Looking as though she'd pieced something together, Jane eagerly added. "*That* Mr. Flanagan looked surprised and shocked. Might that have something to do with it?"

"I suspect he looked upset because his father was dead," Mrs. O'Reilly said.

Posie couldn't argue with that. She addressed the housekeeper. "Jane said you were in the room. What did you see?"

"I didn't know I was in the room until Jane told me later. I don't remember it."

Interesting.

"How did you know it was Mrs. O'Reilly?" Pru asked Jane.

"She was wearing her white dressing gown. It was billowy and flowing in the mirrors. Couldn't help but notice that."

"And you don't remember it?" Posie asked Mrs. O'Reilly.

"Not at all. Which is why I don't know for certain if I killed the poor man. Can't even remember being in the room. I must've been in a trance or something like that."

This was a stranger mystery than Posie had bargained for. If they could solve this, they would be legendary detectives.

"Are there any additional puzzles we might ponder?" Posie asked.

"One other," Mrs. O'Reilly said. "The young Mr. Flanagan is missing a dog."

And at that, Pru sat up straighter than she had in years.

CHAPTER THREE

"Oh!" Pru's eyes lit with excitement. "We are very good at dogs. Posie didn't think we'd be doing any dog-related detective work, but I just knew we would. I just knew it!"

"I think we would do best to focus our efforts on the more critical matter at hand," Posie said. "The issue of the dog can wait until we have determined if Mr. Flanagan was in fact murdered and by whom."

"The young Mr. Flanagan is very fond of that dog," Mrs. O'Reilly said. "And he's heartbroken at having lost his father. It'd be a kindness to relieve him of one source of grief, though we can't relieve him of the other."

The more time Posie spent with Mrs. O'Reilly, the more convinced she was that the woman was not the sort to murder a person. Granted, Posie had not, to her knowledge, been acquainted with any murderers. She had, though, read a great many novels. And the murderers in those novels were very sneaky and very selfish and very . . . murdery.

"We are very good at dogs." Pru was even more animated than usual.

"Nonetheless," Posie said, ignoring the first whispers of *petite pru* sneaking up on her once more. "I think our wisest course of action is to speak with young Mr. Flanagan. He might know things we do not, things that would help us solve the matter of his father's death."

Posie took firm hold of the arms of her chair and slowly rose, doing her utmost to hold back the grunt that usually accompanied the effort. It was such an "elderly" thing to do, and she preferred not to feel or seem old.

"You can converse with him in his library," Mrs. O'Reilly suggested. "He does not like to spend time in this room on account of it being where his father died."

That seemed reasonable enough.

They followed Mrs. O'Reilly down the corridor. Posie had her indoor cane, which was particularly helpful. Pru's indoor shawl was proving well worth bringing also. This was why Posie knew they would be excellent detectives: they thought ahead.

That forward thinking was also why Posie reminded Mrs. O'Reilly that they never had been provided with the requested tea and biscuits. Not only did Posie anticipate being hungry in short order but she knew full well that to begin a proper conversation with Mr. Flanagan, they had to begin with tea and biscuits.

Mrs. O'Reilly provided those basics of any English welcome a mere moment before the grieving son entered the library. He eyed them with obvious confusion but also offered a genteel bow and a kind word of welcome.

"Please sit for a moment," Posie offered. She was well aware that calls required them to follow a certain protocol. They had tea and biscuits. Now they needed to talk about unimportant things none of them truly cared about.

"How have you found the weather of late?" Pru began.

"Pleasant." Mr. Flanagan sat among them, being wonderfully polite, but seeming a bit uncomfortable. "And you?"

"Most pleasant weather," Posie said. "The sky does seem to promise rain before the day is out."

"I shall make certain to be prepared for that possibility."

Pru took a sip of tea before moving to what was usually a very insignificant topic. "Dogs are quite lovely creatures."

Mr. Flanagan's expression grew immediately somber. "I do like dogs. I have a dear little beagle. He's been with me since he was a puppy and hasn't ever run away. But I don't know where he is now. The little thing's disappeared."

"We'll find him," Pru promised. "We're very good at dogs."

"When did your dog go missing?" Posie thought it best to gather information about this less important mystery as quickly as possible so they could return to the more pressing matter.

"I cannot say precisely, but sometime during the day my father died. I realized that night that I'd not seen the little beagle in some time. The horridness of all that had happened had entirely distracted me."

And that brought them nicely back to the mystery Posie most wanted to solve. "Your father's passing is what has brought us here, in fact."

"What about his passing has so interested you?" Mr. Flanagan was being very kind, but Posie recognized the wariness that had entered his expression. He had, thus far, proven himself a more genial person than his father had ever been, which was to his credit, but they would be wise to explain and not try his patience.

"We have our suspicions regarding the manner of his death."

Something oddly like relief filled his face. "I've had similar suspicions but hadn't dared voice them. I think someone might have killed him."

Posie and Pru both nodded in unison. To Posie's relief, Pru didn't say anything about Mrs. O'Reilly's potential involvement. It was best not to give away one's purpose when seeking out those who might attempt to thwart it for their own benefit.

Mrs. O'Reilly stepped inside the library a moment later. She offered a curtsey to her new employer. "Your man of business is here to see you, sir."

"Thank you, Mrs. O'Reilly. Please show him in." He looked at Posie and Pru. "As this is the most fitting room for me to conduct business, I fear I will have to be a little rude and ask if we might end this discussion early?"

"We're needing to collect clues as it is," Posie said. "We'll see to that."

"Collect clues?" Mr. Flanagan repeated with a hint of a smile. "You are dedicating yourselves to the matter, it would seem."

"We are, indeed." Posie shook a bit as she rose but proudly did not make any noises.

"Do share with me anything you might learn." Mr. Flanagan bowed to each of them.

"And we will make certain not to neglect the matter of your dog," Pru promised him.

"That is very good of you."

Mr. Flanagan's man of business was shown in as the two detectives for hire were shuffling out. The slowness of their departure meant Posie overheard a little of the conversation beginning between the men.

"I have looked over the expenses you are anticipating, Mr. Flanagan, and I do believe you can afford to make some changes in the household staff."

Once in the corridor, Mrs. O'Reilly joined them. "Have you learned anything of significance?"

"Quite a few things, in fact," Posie said. "We simply need to sort through them. Jane saw a woman in a flowing white nightdress in the many mirrors in the room where the late Mr. Flanagan died. He'd been drinking and dropped his glass before dropping himself. The young Mr. Flanagan's dog disappeared during this time, and everyone knows dogs are more aware of things unseen than people are."

"I suppose that is true," Mrs. O'Reilly acknowledged.

"I find myself growing ever more convinced that the culprit was, indeed, seen by Jane in the mirrors, but that, contrary to what she thought she saw, the woman in the flowing white nightdress was not actually you."

"Then who was it?" Mrs. O'Reilly asked.

In near perfect unison, Posie and Pru both said, "A ghost!"

CHAPTER FOUR

"A ghost?" Mrs. O'Reilly did not seem to fully grasp how likely that explanation truly was. "What has led you to think the murder was perpetrated by a ghost?"

It was simple, really. For a detective at least.

Posie smiled, eager to explain. "Janey saw a figure in the mirror dressed all in flowing white. Ghosts always dress like that. Always. And it would explain why she thought you were there when you were *not* actually there. The ghost, you see, simply looked like you. And since you have a long white nightdress, she wrongly believed the ghostly gown was your nightdress. It is well-known that people quite regularly die of being startled. What could be more startling than the sudden appearance of a ghost?"

"I suppose that does make a bit of sense." Mrs. O'Reilly began nodding.

"Further," Pru added, "dogs find ghosts particularly worrisome. And the young Mr. Flanagan lost his dog during the time this ghost was being murderous. It all fits brilliantly."

Of course Pru would find clues of a ghostly crime based on the dog's disappearance.

"Little Morris at the stable looks after the dog when young Mr. Flanagan is not around," Mrs. O'Reilly said. "You could ask Morris if the dog seemed particularly worried."

"An excellent idea." Posie pointed ahead with her inside cane before leaning on it once more. "Let us make our way to the back garden."

"I'll need my outdoor shawl," Pru said. "It's blue," she reminded Mrs. O'Reilly.

"Will you be wishing for your outdoor cane?" Mrs. O'Reilly asked Posie.

"That would be preferred, yes."

The two detectives began their slow walk toward the back of the house. Before they reached the doors leading to the back garden, Mrs. O'Reilly caught up to them with Pru's blue outdoor shawl and Posie's wide-bottomed outdoor cane.

"Do you truly think the culprit is a ghost?" Mrs. O'Reilly sounded hopeful if not entirely convinced. "I would feel extremely relieved to know for certain that *I* wasn't the guilty party."

Posie patted her hand. "While I will not discount the reality that someone might commit a crime whilst in a trance and not remember the doing of it, or perhaps suffer a blow to the head and have the memory of that crime erased, I do think it is more logical that this particular crime was the work of a specter."

Mrs. O'Reilly released a tense breath. "What a relief."

They stepped onto the back terrace, aiming for the stables at the far end of the path ahead. It would be a long walk, and it was at a bit of an angle. Posie thought perhaps she ought to have brought her steep-trail cane rather than her slick-ground cane.

Off to the side, Mrs. Brennan could be seen making her way to the stone steps leading down to the rear servants' entrance. She wore a dingy white bonnet and brown coat over a dress of blue-and-white gingham. On anyone else, it would have been a soft choice, pleasant and unobtrusive, but Mrs. Brennan somehow looked all angles and sharpness.

"I didn't realize Mrs. Brennan worked here," Posie said.

"She doesn't," Mrs. O'Reilly said, "though she had applied for positions in the past. The late Mr. Flanagan was not interested in expanding the staff."

"The young Mr. Flanagan is," Posie said. "I overheard him discussing such with his man of business."

"We *are* in need of a couple of extra maids." Mrs. O'Reilly didn't sound pleased at the possibility. "Do you wish me to accompany you to the stables?" She looked very much as if she hoped they would decline her offer.

"We can make our way there on our own," Posie assured her.

They'd only gone half the length of the walk when Morris skipped up to them. His name was simply Morris, as no one knew his surname, not even Morris. He'd arrived in the village a year earlier at only six years old and had worked as the stable boy at Mr. Flanagan's house ever since. Mr. Flanagan was not known for his kindness, but he'd shown a rare bit of compassion in the matter of Morris the stable boy.

"Good day to you, Morris," Posie said.

"We're looking for a lost dog," Pru added. "We're detectives now, and we are very good at dogs."

"The dog *is* missing," Morris said, eyes wide and earnest. "Ran at the house the day Mr. Flanagan died. Frantic and loud and acting like he'd . . . well, like he'd seen—"

"A ghost?" Posie pressed, feeling certain she knew the answer.

"Could be," Morris answered. "But I were going to say like he'd seen a villain, someone terrible."

"Ghosts can be terrible," Pru said.

Morris shrugged. "The little dog gets on with most people. Only them who most people don't like seem to upset him."

"People like whom?" Posie pressed.

"He didn't like old Mr. Flanagan much," Morris said. "Don't like the blacksmith, but most of us don't. He thinks Mrs. Brennan oughtn't be allowed to come anywhere near the house. And young Mr. Flanagan said there's a man in London the dog don't like none."

"The dog doesn't like Mrs. Brennan?" Pru asked.

"Not a bit. But then none of us does, do we?"

There was truth to that.

"Perhaps the dog simply doesn't like the color white." Pru shrugged. "I have tried to tell Mrs. Brennan that if she is to choose a color to wear at all times it ought to be an actual color. White, I think, doesn't really count."

Posie tapped her finger to her lips, musing on the clues they had uncovered so far.

The dog barked at something—or someone—it didn't like.

The murderer, seen in the mirror, was wearing white and bore a resemblance to Mrs. O'Reilly.

Mrs. Brennan had wanted a position, but Mr. Flanagan wouldn't give it to her, yet young Mr. Flanagan seemed more inclined to expand the staff.

"Oh, dear, Pru," Posie said. "I think we might have to *unsolve* this crime."

CHAPTER FIVE

"Morris, rush to Mrs. Brennan's house and see if the poor little dog is there," Posie said. "I suspect it will be."

Morris didn't hesitate. Posie and Pru would do best not to as well.

"To the house, Pru!" Posie pointed the way with her outside cane, and the two of them hobbled at their fastest pace—somewhere between a slow stroll and a moderate walk—back toward the house. Being a detective was exhausting. Who knew there would be so much rushing about!

"Do you truly think Mrs. Brennan stole young Mr. Flanagan's dog? What a horrible thing to do." Pru shook her head. "Which, come to think of it, is rather fitting. She's not a very pleasant person."

"I suspect she didn't steal the dog so much as she took it with her so it wouldn't give her away."

"Give her away for *what*, Posie?"

"For murdering Mr. Flanagan, of course."

Pru emitted a little "Oooh" sound of realization. "Solving the bit about the dog really did help solve the bit about the murder."

"I suppose it did."

They reached the house and found the terrace unlocked. They went through the doors and down the corridor. Unfortunately, no one was there to change their outside shawl and cane for those meant for the indoors. If not for the urgency of their errand, they might have sat down and waited for someone to sort all that out.

By the time they reached the library, where Posie hoped young Mr. Flanagan would still be, they were both a touch out of breath and more than a touch exhausted. Their entrance pulled the attention of the three people in the room: the master of the house, Mrs. O'Reilly, and Mrs. Brennan, whose presence was extremely helpful. They'd not need to go running about the house yet again attempting to find her.

Posie held up a hand to stave off any questions as she hadn't breath enough to answer. Pru had already dropped into an obliging chair. Posie lowered herself slowly; she hadn't her indoor cane, after all.

"Mr. Flan—" No. She still hadn't breath enough yet.

Pru seemed to have regained some of hers. "We think we found your dog."

"Truly?" The poor man looked as though he might grow emotional. "I've been so worried."

"That's not—" Heavens, Posie wasn't fit enough for running about being a detective. "—not the most significant—" Another deep breath. "—most significant thing we've learned."

"Can this wait?" Mrs. Brennan asked. "I was here before you, seeing to business of my own."

"Our business involves you." Posie stood, though her cane was the wrong one for doing so. "Mr. Flanagan, you shouldn't hire Mrs. Brennan to be on your household staff."

"Why on earth not?" Mrs. Brennan demanded.

"Because she stole your dog!" Pru said.

"Again, Pru," Posie said, "this is not the most pressing matter."

"Oh, yes. I forgot." Pru grinned at the room in general. "Because she murdered Mr. Flanagan."

Posie shook her head. "You haven't the first idea how to build a moment."

"I was meant to be more mysterious, wasn't I?"

"It would have been difficult to be *less*."

"Begging your pardons," Mr. Flanagan said calmly but earnestly, "please return to the topic of my father's death and your belief that this woman is connected to it."

"I take exception to—" Mrs. Brennan objected but was shushed by Mrs. O'Reilly and cut off by a wave of Mr. Flanagan's hand.

To Mrs. O'Reilly, knowing she would understand the significance, Posie said, "The person in the mirror was wearing white."

"Oh." Mrs. O'Reilly's mouth remained in a perfect *O* long after the sound dissipated.

"And people have said for years that you and Mrs. Brennan look alike," Pru said.

Mr. Flanagan eyed the two women and nodded his agreement.

"The late Mr. Flanagan wouldn't hire her, which she clearly very much wanted. Having a new master of the house would mean she could try again." Posie warmed to the subject. "And hiding in the room as she did would startle anyone—and being startled has been known to kill people."

"But it was the crash of the goblet that brought Jane into the room," Pru said. "Maybe the crash was what startled him so entirely."

"I think he dropped the goblet *because* he was startled," Posie insisted. "If you saw Mrs. Brennan unexpectedly hanging about the corners of a room, you would drop everything you were holding."

"And then die." Pru nodded emphatically.

"I do not scare people to death," Mrs. Brennan insisted.

"Startle," Posie corrected. "You *startle* them to death. There is a subtle but important difference."

"Oh, yes," Pru said. "If you scared them to death, that would likely mean you were doing something frightening. But you can startle a person simply by being something they aren't expecting, like emerging from a shadow or talking suddenly into the silence or being odd looking."

"I didn't kill him by being ugly," Mrs. Brennan said sharply.

"Then how did you kill him?" Mr. Flanagan asked quickly and casually, though he was watching her very closely.

"Poison in—" She clamped her mouth shut.

Poison in the goblet. Oh. That did make more sense than startling him to death. But Posie took pride in having identified the correct murderer and giving Mrs. O'Reilly the peace of mind that comes from knowing she *wasn't* the murderer.

It was in the very next moment that Morris rushed into the room, holding tight to Mr. Flanagan's missing dog. "He were tied up at Mrs. Brennan's, just like Mrs. Poindexter and Mrs. Dwerryhouse said he'd be."

The dog caught sight of Mrs. Brennan, and he immediately began barking and growling.

"The dog doesn't like her," Pru said. "And he was barking quite a lot at knowing she was inside the house startling people."

"*Murdering* people, Pru."

"Yes." Pru nodded. "That, too."

"Morris, take the poor thing out into the garden," Mr. Flanagan said. "Mrs. O'Reilly, have someone fetch the squire."

Realizing their work was done, and done well, Posie and Pru made to take their leave as well. Mr. Flanagan stopped them, still keeping an eye on the murderer.

"How can I thank you for managing to sort this out, and to do so in such a short time?"

"Simple enough, Mr. Flanagan. Should you hear of anyone else in need of the services of two very fine detectives, send them our way," Posie said.

"I will."

"And tell them we are very good at dogs," Pru added.

EPILOGUE

Posie Poindexter was delighted. Pru Dwerryhouse was *always* delighted.

The two sat in their cottage, perfectly pleased with life. Pru was knitting, an enormous ball of red yarn on the floor beside her, and singing softly to herself a song about dogs. Posie was watching rain run down the window in rivers, a common occurrence in the English countryside.

Their first endeavor as detectives had not merely been successful, it had been very quickly successful. They were, by any estimation, proper detectives.

"What do you suppose our next detective undertaking will be?" Posie mused aloud.

"I hope it's to do with dogs," Pru answered.

Dogs. Of course.

"For my part," Posie said, "I hope we eventually have a case that involves an actual ghost. That would be brilliant."

"A ghost dog," Pru suggested with a slow and emphatic nod.

It was on that unsurprising declaration that Mr. Green, a man from the village, entered the cottage with hat in hand. "Hello, ladies. Are you still acting as detectives?"

"Indeed, we are." Posie sat up tall. "Posie and Pru—detectives for hire."

"Well, then, I have a case for you."

Posie and Pru exchanged grinning glances. "Excellent!"

THE GOVERNESS
AND THE FUGITIVE

by Mr. King

INSTALLMENT I

in which our Heroine begins a new life on a most mysterious Estate!

Miss Josephine Harlow had not always intended to be a governess. She'd not ever been destined for wealth untold, neither was she a lady of such particularly high standing that her future had been heavily bespeckled with grand opportunities. But when her family's fortunes, such as they were, had reversed suddenly and drastically, employment had been her only option.

She reminded herself of the necessity of providing for herself as she made the long and lonely journey to Tullybridge. No one she had spoken with had ever heard of the estate or the resident family. While that had struck her as odd, she'd acknowledged to herself that the offer of employment had noted that the family she would be working for kept very much to themselves. That they were not widely known ought to be seen as confirmation that she had been told the truth, not reason to be suspicious.

And, yet, she was.

The coachman had fetched her from the posting inn where she'd been instructed to report. When she had asked him how long the journey was to her new place of employment, he'd responded with "not far enough." The only person she had yet encountered with any knowledge of Tullybridge, and that had been his response. It certainly had not bolstered her confidence.

A heavy fog hung over the countryside as the carriage crested and dipped over the rolling hills. The sounds of distant, unseen animals offered both the reassurance and concern that she was not alone.

The carriage began to slow. She strained her eyes, attempting to spot anything at all. Fog and more fog. And in the distance . . . a shadow moved.

Josephine pulled back from the window with sharp movements, more startled than she would have guessed. She'd heard animals and knew they must have been out on hills. To see a shadow should not have been alarming or unexpected. Yet, it felt almost threatening.

She took a breath, one made surprisingly difficult by the seemingly heavy air. Fog had never affected her in such a way before. What was different this time? Was she merely nervous, having had so much of her life upended so quickly?

Before she could determine the answer, the carriage came to an abrupt stop, nearly unseating her. She had only just snatched her carpetbag from the carriage floor when the door snapped open. So thick was the fog that she could not even see the footman or stablehand or whoever it was that had opened the door. She couldn't even see the house, though it must have been mere feet in front of her.

She swallowed. Breathed. Set her shoulders.

Earthbound clouds swirled around her, clinging to her feet and dress and face. She could see only the vaguest of shapes in front of her: a person she assumed she was meant to follow, what looked like steps leading up, what might have been the indistinct outline of a large and imposing house.

She climbed steps she could barely see and crossed a threshold into a dimly lit entryway. Behind her, heavy doors snapped closed. Josephine turned in a slow circle but saw no other person. It was customary for a governess to be met upon arrival by the family, or at the very least, the housekeeper.

She was met by no one.

The tall entryway windows flanking the heavy wooden door offered a view of the front drive. The fog that had obscured seemingly all of creation was quickly dissipating. So quickly, in fact, she found the change both fascinating and unnerving.

She moved to the nearest window and watched as the billows of thick, low-lying clouds retreated. So fast did it happen, she could see the movement, almost like a flock of sheep rushing away from the house.

"Best hurry, Miss Harlow," a rasping, high-pitched voice implored. "It don't do to keep the young master waiting. He's a right horror when he's upset."

Josephine turned to find a stooped, angular-featured woman watching her from the base of the stairs. A thick ring of at least a dozen iron keys hung from a chain at her waist, suggesting her position as the housekeeper. Her ruffled cap was stiffly starched but dingy in a way that spoke of age rather than neglect. Indeed, the woman's entire appearance could be described that way.

"I don't wish to keep anyone waiting," Josephine insisted, "but I haven't the first idea where I am meant to go or with whom I am meant to meet."

"To the nursery wing, miss. But hurry. The young master's growing impatient."

Impatient? She'd not been in the house more than a minute or two.

"Come along. Come along." There was something more than impatience in the woman's voice and mannerisms. There seemed to be fear.

Josephine followed, surprised at how quickly the older woman moved. "Is Mr. Northrup a particularly fearsome employer?"

"It ain't the father you need to be appeasing, miss," the woman insisted.

"His son, then?" Josephine had heard of governesses whose charges were difficult, but the anxiety with which the woman spoke of the little boy was unexpected.

"He's no ordinary boy, Miss Harlow." The housekeeper didn't even look back at her as they rushed up yet another flight of stairs. "Others have learned, to their cost, what happens when he grows cross."

"What happens?"

That brought their hasty climb to a sudden halt. The housekeeper turned to face her, a look of warning in her steely eyes. "Strange things happen at Tullybridge, Miss Harlow. Strange and dreadful things. He makes them happen, miss. We all know he does. Makes the wind howl. Makes the fog come. Makes people disappear."

Josephine couldn't help taking a step backward any more than she could prevent the sharp intake of breath that accompanied her involuntary retreat.

"Don't make him angry, miss. Lands' sake, don't make him angry."

With that plea ringing in her ears, Josephine followed the housekeeper to the door of the nursery. She held her breath as the sharply angled woman turned the handle and pushed the door open.

Josephine's heart pounded a rhythm of trepidation as she willed her feet to step inside. *Don't make him angry.* She half expected to find a monster, a horror of some kind. *Strange and dreadful things. He makes them happen.* She swept the room with her gaze and found not a creature of darkest magic but a little boy.

He sat in a tiny rocking chair, a book open on his lap. He looked up at her, his tiny pink lips forming a half smile.

The tension slid from her posture as relief wrapped itself around her as fully and completely as had the fog outside Tullybridge.

"You must be Silas Northrup," she said.

"I must be." His expression did not change. Not at all. "You are Miss Harlow."

"I am," she confirmed. "I am to be your governess."

"And you will stay here," he said. "That is what governesses do."

He had a very direct way of speaking, which she found odd, but she had encountered other children who adopted a formality beyond their young years. His unchanging expression could not help but be noticed, though perhaps he was merely nervous to meet someone new. Perhaps it was his uniqueness of manners that made the housekeeper view him the way she did. Perhaps all the hiccups of heart Josephine had felt arose from unfamiliarity rather than truly sensing something that required caution and worry.

The door to the nursery closed behind her, the housekeeper having stepped out of the room.

Josephine set her carpetbag on the floor. "What ought we to do first, Silas?"

"You are not to call me Silas." He made the observation quite calmly, yet the declaration sent a sliver of ice right through her. "I am Mr. Northrup."

Ah. Some young boys did take pride in more grown-up names. She could oblige him in that. "Mr. Northrup," she corrected with a dip of her head. In time they would come to know each other better and might find more familiar footing. "What ought we to do first?"

"You will put your bag away," he said. His expression hadn't changed, neither had his tone, yet Josephine heard a warning in it.

"I would be happy to do so," she said, "but I do not yet know where my bedchamber is."

He did not move from the rocking chair, but behind him, a door opened, squeaking in protest as if objecting.

"There," he said. "Your bag goes in there."

Strange and dreadful things.

She forced herself to be calm. "You can open doors?"

"Can you not open doors?" His tone betrayed nothing of his thoughts, whether he asked out of actual curiosity or if he did so sarcastically.

"I can," she said, "but I have to use my hands."

"Do you think I do not?" The same sweet expression, the same posture, the same tone.

"That door just opened on its own," she pointed out.

"Wind, perhaps?"

"Perhaps."

Trepidation began quickly replacing the momentary relief she'd felt. Something in him did not match. He was answering her questions, yet he wasn't. He looked content, yet he didn't. He sounded perfectly at ease, yet he didn't.

"The people here would seem to think it was not the wind," Josephine said.

"There are few people here. I don't think you've talked to more than one of them."

That was true. "Did you open the door?"

"I do what I wish," he said. "And I wish for your bag to be in your room."

Still, nothing had changed, but she felt the threat in his words. A boy of no more than five, yet he felt intimidating. And she felt herself on thin ice.

"I have not yet met with your parents," she said. "Do you know when they might speak with me?"

"They will not," he said. "Put your bag away, or I will grow very cross."

Others have learned, to their cost, what happens when he grows cross.

And, for reasons she could not explain or define, she knew in that moment that the housekeeper had not been exaggerating or lying. Strange things happened in this house. Strange and dreadful things.

The hills surrounding Tullybridge were far from silent, though the sound was undetectable by most. Some would sense movement in the shadows. Some would think, for a fleeting moment, that they heard a rustling. Some would even feel a ripple of curiosity mingled with apprehension, the reaction of a heart attuned to the movements of the faerie world when tip-toeing a bit too close to the thinner partitions separating the human world and the magical realm.

And in those shadows and rustlings and heart ripples, a rift was torn in the heretofore impenetrable grasp the world of faeries and creatures and magic claimed on the hills of Tullybridge. A rift. A break. A moment's hope.

INSTALLMENT II

in which a Mysterious Stranger arrives at
Tullybridge, bringing Dangers untold!

Josephine didn't know how long she'd been at Tullybridge. She felt as though she'd spent months there, but also like she'd passed a mere few days. She could remember coming to the estate, yet the life she'd known before her arrival seemed to have existed an age ago. She'd whispered of her confusion to Mrs. Chester, the housekeeper, and had received a knowing nod in return.

"Strange and dreadful things happen at Tullybridge" had been the entirety of that lady's response.

At some point, Josephine had begun to count the people at the estate. It was so large a place, yet so empty. Her first count had been five, excluding herself and Silas, or rather Mr. Northrup, as he insisted on being called: Mrs. Chester and her ever-present ring of keys; Mrs. Green, the cook, whom Josephine had never seen without her apron on; the coachman, a skeletal man who kept to the stables; the gardener, who was as burly as the coachman was haggard; and a footman named Peter, whose thick black hair seemed to perpetually stand on end.

Mr. Northrup's parents were never seen or spoken of. As near as Josephine could tell, they were entirely absent from their child's life, and he was not the least bothered by it. She'd asked Peter once if he knew why the senior Mr. Northrup and Mrs. Northrup were never spoken of.

Peter had paled. "They disappeared."

"What?"

"The child's parents," he'd whispered in reply. "People are always disappearing from Tullybridge, and none of us knows where they go."

"Does no one find that odd?"

"'Course we do. But we don't talk of it. He don't like when we talk about the people who've disappeared. It makes him cross."

Josephine had nodded. "We mustn't make him cross." It was the most oft-repeated rule. The one everyone adhered to.

"We mustn't," Peter had repeated.

Two days later, Peter was gone.

When Josephine had wondered aloud where he might have gone, Mr. Northrup had said in the calm, measured voice and with the unwavering, contented smile he *always* wore, "Peter made me cross."

The gardener was gone now too. The coachman, housekeeper, and cook moved about in terrified tiptoes, desperate to please their tyrannical master, a child of no more than five.

Josephine sat in the nursery of the home that had become her prison, reading yet again the only book Mr. Northrup ever permitted her to read to him. She was careful not to stumble over any words and to read at precisely the pace he preferred. And every time she read, she had the most unnerving sense that the story was different than it had been the previous time she'd read it.

The book had colorful illustrations, yet Mr. Northrup never looked at the pages. He sat in his little rocking chair, wearing his permanent staid expression, listening.

She finished the book and closed it on her lap. "What would you like to do now?"

"The story is done today," he said. "I will have my tea now."

Josephine nodded and rose. She knew this ritual well. When he was ready to eat, she would walk with him to the formal dining room. She did so again now. There, they were met by the housekeeper, who saw him seated. The cook entered the room to deliver the food he had earlier dictated be made. Josephine had one hour before she was required to return and fetch him.

Precisely one hour.

On that day, she chose to spend the hour outdoors. The fog that so often surrounded the house had not wrapped itself over the countryside today. Mr. Northrup was in good spirits, after all.

She did not remain on the grounds. The gardener's disappearance had not yet rendered the gardens or lawns unkempt, but she felt sad walking the paths he had once trod, especially not knowing what, precisely, had happened to him. She also felt uneasy, following footsteps that had led that man to his mysterious fate.

Instead, she slipped through a stile in a stone wall at the back of the eastern lawn and out onto the hillside. The feeling of heaviness that followed her inside Tullybridge didn't dissipate. Not entirely. The estate could not be escaped. She knew instinctively that should she try to run, try to flee away over the hills, Mr. Northrup would still, somehow, be able to stop her, to punish her. She suspected that as long as she remained within reach of the fog that so often gripped the area, he could still make her disappear.

But on the hills, she breathed the tiniest bit easier. For an hour, she could feel as close to safe as she had since her arrival at Tullybridge, whenever that was.

Mere steps from the stile, however, she spotted a shadow ahead. A shadow that moved toward her, staggering and stumbling. Drawing closer. Ever closer!

Josephine took a step backward, watching its approach through widened eyes. Another step and her back pressed against the stone wall. She felt along its face, trying to locate the stile without taking her eyes off the approaching figure.

Before she found the opening, though, the shadow revealed itself. It was a person. A man, likely her age. He lurched, tottering as if in pain, and walked hunched like one who had almost no strength remaining.

She ought to have been afraid, but she wasn't. She felt drawn to him instead. Her feet even moved toward him, bringing her closer.

"Please," he pleaded in a strained whisper. "Please, help me." His legs trembled beneath him, and he began to sink.

Josephine reached out and grabbed hold of him, steadying him as he regained his strength once more. He was worryingly cold to the touch. Clearly, he'd been in the elements too long.

"Please," he repeated. "I mustn't remain out on the hills. Please, it is too dangerous."

"Tullybridge is dangerous too," she warned him.

"I've reached Tullybridge?" That seemed to strike him as significant.

"You know of it?" She'd not met anyone who did, beyond those who lived there.

His legs weakened, and he nearly buckled.

Josephine set an arm firmly around him. "Were I in a position to do so, I would instantly offer you a warm bed and food at Tullybridge. Sadly, I am not." Seeing the fear grow in his careworn face, she quickly said, "But I could hide you. Though you would have to stay hidden. No one could know you were there other than me."

He nodded. "I would not endanger my guardian angel for all the world."

To Mr. Northrup, she was a prisoner, one held under threat of unthinkable punishment. She far preferred being a guardian angel.

"We must hurry," she implored him. "I have not all of my hour's respite remaining. Should we not have you hidden and situated by the end of my hour, we shall be done for."

Over the stile they climbed, he leaning against her as his own strength proved insufficient. Only as they slipped through a ne'er-used back door did Josephine spy in his hand a loop of branches.

"What are you carrying?" she asked in a strained whisper. Though the house was all but empty, she dared not risk drawing the attention of those few who remained.

"A rowan loop. An amulet. Protection against magical harms."

Josephine shook inwardly. *Protection against magical harms.* Had he any idea how needed that was at Tullybridge? "It will protect you if you hold it?" That might help prevent him from being found.

"We can hang it. Above whatever doorway I am placed behind. It will . . . safeguard . . . the room." He was struggling to speak.

"Conserve your strength," she instructed. "We must get you to the nursery wing."

"Why there?" he asked.

"I am nursemaid here. That is where I am most of the day. I cannot look after you nor see to your recovery if you are elsewhere."

He did not object. He likely lacked the strength to do so.

"But it is so very important that you not be found there," she added as they carefully climbed the servants' stairs toward the nursery wing. "Strange and dreadful things happen in this house, sir. Magical harms, as you have called them."

"You must hang the rowan loop," he said. "Above the door of the room I am placed in. Above, but inside—out of sight of anyone glancing into the room from beyond."

She nodded her understanding.

They reached the nursery, empty of its tyrannical overseer. Mr. Northrup's tea would be complete soon enough.

Josephine guided the injured stranger through the nursery and into the room that was her own; she knew not where else to place him!

He rested on the edge of the mattress while she prepared a place for him to sleep on the floor, hidden from view by her own bed.

"This will not be the most comfortable place to recover your strength," she warned. "But it is imperative that you not be seen. Crucial."

"I am grateful for whatever shelter you can offer me." The man handed her the rowan loop, then dropped to his knees on the ground. With a sigh of heart-deep relief, he laid himself on the floor and pulled the blanket she'd provided for him over his shoulders, resting his head on the thin pillow she had provided.

Josephine pulled a chair to the door and climbed atop it. A nail in the molding above the door stuck out just enough for her to hang the loop from it. She wedged the loop as tightly as she could manage into the space. She did not wish it to come loose.

With swift but careful movements, she climbed down and replaced the chair, then rushed to the side of the poor, weak stranger, lying so helplessly on the floor. The man must have been plagued with the worst sort of luck to have found himself seeking refuge in a place such as Tullybridge.

"I will do all I can for you," she promised him.

"Thank you, Miss—?"

"Miss Harlow," she said. "Josephine Harlow."

"You are indeed an angel, Miss Josephine Harlow."

"Might this angel ask what your name is?"

He nodded, his eyelids heavy with the burden of approaching sleep. He took a single breath before he spoke. "I am Silas Northrup."

INSTALLMENT III

in which Terrifying and Dangerous Secrets are uncovered!

I am Silas Northrup.

Though Josephine couldn't confidently recall the given name of Mr. Northrup's absent father, she did not think it was also Silas. Indeed, she recalled that, upon receiving the offer of employment, she thought that the little boy she was charged with tending had a more unique name than his father did. Or was she remembering that incorrectly?

Perhaps *this* Silas Northrup was a cousin of some sort to the one who ruled at Tullybridge. Or an uncle for whom the boy was named.

"Did you know you share a name with—?"

But he was asleep, exhaustion pulling at his features. The poor man looked as though he'd been through a mighty struggle. Bruises and scratches marred his face. His right hand, peeking out from beneath the blanket, was in a similar state.

How very many questions she had for him! Who was he? Where had he come from? Why had he been wandering the hills?

But it was not merely his exhausted state that prevented her from asking them. Her hour of respite was all but gone. Mr. Northrup required her to be in the dining room when he finished his tea. She had mere minutes to be there.

She left the door to her bedchamber open the tiniest bit; that was how she always left it, and she didn't want anything to draw Mr. Northrup's attention. For precisely the same reason, she slowed her steps as she approached the dining room and smoothed her expression. She didn't want to give any indication that she was returning to her post in a state of mind that was at all different from the one she'd left in.

When she stepped inside the room—at precisely one hour after she had left—Mr. Northrup was seated at the table. The tea things had already been cleared. Mrs. Green and Mrs. Chester stood to one side of the room, as still and quiet as stones. That they were desperate for Josephine to leave with the boy was painfully obvious. They would be in less danger momentarily; she, however, would be in far more.

"I will return to the nursery now." Mr. Northrup stood as he made the declaration. When he turned toward Josephine, the hair on the back of her neck stood on end. A child's smile ought not do that to a person, but his did. "I wish to read my book again."

She dipped the small curtsey she always did. "Yes, Mr. Northrup."

Josephine walked beside him. His posture remained precisely perfect.

His little smile and placid expression didn't change. It never did. To her utter relief, his gaze didn't linger overly long on the doorway to her bed-chamber. His eyes betrayed no curiosity or suspiciousness. But, then, they never did.

Mr. Northrup sat in his rocking chair, staring straight ahead.

Josephine collected the book and sat in the chair he'd declared was where she must sit when reading to him. She read carefully despite her mind being continually drawn to the slightly ajar doorway and the stranger hiding inside. Even as she repeated the familiar, yet seemingly changed story, she also watched Mr. Northrup. The repetition and monotony of her time spent with the demanding child had often been unnerving. That afternoon, how-ever, it was reassuring. He hadn't, it seemed, noticed anything unusual.

Josephine finished the story. She closed the book on her lap and waited for instructions.

"Mrs. Green did not have figgy pudding at tea like I wished for." Mr. Northrup didn't sound upset, neither did he look it, yet Josephine could tell he was. The boy's perpetually frozen expression was rather like looking at a painting. But she'd never been afraid of a painting.

"I am sorry you did not have the figgy pudding you wished for," Josephine said.

"Do you think Mrs. Chester knows how to make figgy pudding?" Mr. Northrup asked.

"I don't know. Most housekeepers do not know how to do such things."

Still wearing his vague smile, Mr. Northrup nodded. "Do governesses know how to make figgy pudding?"

She swallowed quickly. "No, Mr. Northrup. Governesses do not know how to do such things."

"Mrs. Green said there would be figgy pudding at supper. And she said she will not neglect it again. I thought she would have to disappear for that. I am still very cross about it. But there will be no one to make figgy pudding if she is disappeared."

"It would be a shame if you were to miss your figgy pudding while she was disappeared." Josephine's heart pounded at the unnerving topic. So many had disappeared. And Mr. Northrup always spoke of them in that way: someone *being disappeared*, as if it were a state of being rather than an occurrence. There was an everlastingness to it that grasped her heart with icy tentacles.

"She also said she will have fewer fruits and vegetables now that there is no gardener." Mr. Northrup's statement struck Josephine as both a question and a source of curiosity. "But the gardener made me very cross. He needed to be disappeared."

Such conversations were how she knew he wasn't a child who merely struggled with expressing and showing his emotions or whose interactions were sometimes labeled odd or uncomfortable. This was much different. This was dangerous.

Over the hours that followed, she did as he bid. She fetched toys as he asked for them, and then he sat in his chair, his expression unchanging, holding the items without playing with them, until she was required to switch them for others. Through it all, he asked about the cook and the pudding and how he was to have pudding if Mrs. Green were disappeared.

By the time she had him dressed for supper and walked with him to the dining room, she was nearly at the end of her endurance. If he would cause the cook to disappear for neglecting his dessert, he would most certainly make Josephine disappear for bringing a stranger into the house, no matter that the man's condition was fragile.

But Mr. Northrup hadn't discovered the man who called himself Silas Northrup, and Josephine had precisely one hour in which to discover precisely who "Silas" was and how he'd come to be at Tullybridge.

She rushed back to the nursery and into her bedchamber.

Silas was awake, still lying on the floor on the far side of her bed.

"The child is having his supper," she explained. "I have only one hour."

"The rowan loop kept his attention away from this room?" he asked, his voice weak but firmer than it had been when he'd first arrived.

Josephine nodded. "He seemed to have no interest in this room."

A look of relief swept over him, and she felt it too.

"I heard you call him 'Mr. Northrup,'" he said.

"That is the name he requires us to use. It is so very important that we never make him cross."

Silas sat up, though doing so took a great deal of effort. "But that is not his name." He didn't state it as a question.

"His name is Silas Northrup." She watched this Silas for signs of surprise, but she saw none.

"Did you ask him if his name was Silas Northrup?" His deep brown eyes settled on her, questioning and earnest.

Josephine sat on the floor near him and thought back on her earliest moments in the house. "I believe what I said to him was 'You must be Silas Northrup.' And he indicated he was."

"Did he, though? Did he truly?"

She thought harder. "He said, 'I must be.'"

Silas nodded. "You were not receiving confirmation, Miss Harlow. You were being told what is being required of him. He was acknowledging, in rather misleading ways, the role he is playing."

"The role?"

He leaned closer. "As I told you in our earliest moments in this room, *I* am Silas Northrup. *I* am the son of this house. *I* am the child he pretends to be."

That made no sense. "You are not a child."

"I was when he took my place. 'Mr. Northrup' is not a child, though he has done his best to appear to be one. He has done well enough to fool most everyone, but his true nature seeps through the cracks."

"*Strange and dreadful things,*" she whispered.

"The hills surrounding Tullybridge are no ordinary hills. They are dotted with faerie rings and cavernous portals, with unseen crossroads and traps for the unwary."

"The shadows I've seen." She was beginning to understand.

"I stepped inside a faerie ring when I was five years old," he said. "Rather than enchant me with a deadly spell, as is so often their punishment, the faeries chose to spirit me to their realm, meaning to keep me there forever. And they left in my place—"

"A changeling." Josephine pressed a palm to her heart. "How has it not been obvious before now?"

"Because Mr. Northrup is powerful, made even more so by his proximity to these hills."

"But surely someone would have noticed that a child had not aged in what must have been twenty years."

"Time in the faerie world is different," Silas said. "Though decades passed there, mere months might have passed here, perhaps only weeks."

"Then Mr. Northrup has only been at Tullybridge a short time?"

Silas nodded. "But those of the faerie realm do not need much time to cause great harm if they choose."

"He makes people disappear. We don't know how nor what happens to them, but if someone crosses him or displeases him, he causes them to vanish, and they are never seen nor heard from again. Magical harm, as you called it."

His dark brows pulled together in thought. "Does time seem odd here?"

"Yes. I cannot say with any certainty how long I have been here. I am nearly certain it has only been a fortnight at most, but sometimes it feels like far longer."

"He is no ordinary changeling, Miss Harlow."

"Josephine, please."

He indicated his acquiescence with a dip of his head. "If Mr. Northrup is not removed, Tullybridge will soon become part of the faerie realm, and all within the estate will be doomed to remain there."

"What can possibly be done, Silas? If he so much as suspected someone was attempting to disobey him, let alone trying to stop him, that person would vanish like all the others."

Silas set his hand atop hers. There was reassurance and comfort in the simple touch. "He must be made to reveal himself. That is the only way to rid the house of him."

"If he saw you, he would have to do so, would he not? You, after all, are the person he is pretending to be."

But Silas shook his head. "He would not merely deny that truth, he would likely disappear us all in an instant. Trickery is our only hope."

"I will do what I can," she vowed.

"You, unfortunately, will have to do most. The rowan hoop protects more than this room from Mr. Northrup's notice. It keeps me safe from the faeries who I know are attempting to find me and drag me back to their home. I mustn't leave this room until it is safe to do so."

"What am I to do, then?"

He held her gaze. "When it is safe to do so, I need to take a look at the book you have been reading him."

"It is significant?"

"I believe it must be. I know every book that was in this nursery when it was mine, but that book is unknown to me."

That was a bit suspicious, but it did not seem outside the realm of possibility that it had been obtained before his disappearance and simply not revealed to him. But, then again, she herself had noticed there was something odd about it.

"I have thought since I first began reading it to him that the book was strange. Though I cannot pinpoint in precisely what way, I am absolutely certain the story changes."

"It is magical, Josephine. And in that magic, we may just find the answers we so desperately need."

INSTALLMENT IV

in which Risks are taken and Danger approaches!

Over the following days, Josephine ran herself nearly ragged. During Mr. Northrup's three meals, she used the hour she had to secretly bring her own meals back to her room to share with Silas. Then she hurried to the grounds to gather as many rowan branches as she could and gave them to her co-conspirator. Together, they created rowan hoops according to the lore Silas had learned from listening to the various tales of woe those in the faerie realms had shared regarding their encounters with the protective amulets. Careful not to be seen doing so, Josephine had begun placing them throughout Tullybridge in places where Mr. Northrup was unlikely to see them.

"I do wish we could place one of these in the nursery," Josephine said, sitting beside Silas as they created yet another rowan hoop. "I would feel so much safer."

"I wish you *were* safer." Silas had grown stronger in the time since he'd emerged from the hills, but that meant he'd also grown more frustrated. He knew the faeries were searching for him, so he dared not leave the protection of this room, lest he draw in more creatures that would threaten the safety of the home he'd fought so long and so hard to return to. "You are taking so many risks. It is too much to ask of you."

"Without risks, there is no hope of escape. If I do nothing, I will be a prisoner here until Mr. Northrup inevitably disappears me as well. I cannot simply resign myself to that."

How brave she was! But she didn't feel overly brave.

Silas paused a moment in his work with the rowan branches. Hesitantly, he asked, "Do you know what became of my parents? They were at Tullybridge when I was taken by the faeries, but you have not mentioned them."

Josephine's heart broke to have to tell him what would, undoubtedly, be a painful revelation. "I do not know any details, only that they are not here and have not been for some time. Mr. Northrup grows cross if they are mentioned, so everyone is quite careful not to do so."

"The faeries had hinted that my parents were gone, and not merely from Tullybridge." He released a shaky breath, disappointment tugging at his features. "I had held out hope that they were wrong."

She set her hand atop his. "I am sorry, Silas. How much you must have missed them these past years."

He adjusted his hand so he was holding hers. "The magic I was surrounded by preserved my memories of them. Without it, I am certain I would have no recollection of them at all, being only five years old when I was stolen away."

"If you would like," she said, "you could tell me about them. Then they will be remembered by both of us."

"I would like that very much indeed. And I would also enjoy hearing about your family."

She smiled at him, a smile nothing like the one affixed to Mr. Northrup's face. Hers was sincere, pleased, happy, inviting.

They resumed the making of rowan hoops, talking as they worked. They shared stories of their childhoods and parents, spoke of their hopes for their futures. They found in each other a kinship that went beyond their currently shared difficulties, a companionship they grew increasingly reluctant to even imagine losing.

That connection between them grew with each meal hour they spent creating protections for Tullybridge. The promise of Silas's company saw Josephine through the difficult times she had to spend in Mr. Northrup's presence. And for Silas, the sound of Josephine's voice just beyond the bedchamber door offered him reassurance that he was not alone.

One evening, upon making her way to the dining room to retrieve Mr. Northrup after his supper, Josephine crossed paths with Mrs. Chester, who was pale and shaking.

"What's happened?" Josephine asked, concerned by the usually stalwart woman's distress.

"Mrs. Green," she whispered. "He disappeared her. I saw it happen. I saw it."

Josephine's heart froze inside her. *He disappeared her.* Even with all the risks she was taking to help create the rowan hoops, she hadn't felt as vulnerable or endangered as she once had. Time with Silas and their work safeguarding the house had allowed her to momentarily forget the reality of her situation.

He disappeared her.

She wanted to take a moment to grieve with Mrs. Chester over the loss of their friend, to acknowledge the horrible circumstances they were all in. "Does Mr. Northrup know you saw it happen?"

Mrs. Chester shook her head. "I don't think so."

"It is likely best if he does not know." She motioned the housekeeper in the direction of the dining room. "You are meant to be in there when I arrive. Quickly. To your post."

Josephine remained where she was as Mrs. Chester rushed to the dining room. *He disappeared her.* She'd not managed to get a rowan hoop into the kitchen, and it wasn't safe to put one in the dining room since Mr. Northrup spent so much time there. All her and Silas's efforts to protect the house—and those who remained inside it—had failed poor Mrs. Green.

Do not let him know you are upset, she silently reminded herself as she followed the housekeeper's path into the dining room.

As soon as she entered, Mr. Northrup stood, wearing his unnerving smile. "I will return to the nursery now. I wish to read my book."

"Of course, Mr. Northrup," Josephine said.

Mrs. Chester stood stoically against the wall where she always positioned herself. For the first time since Josephine's arrival at Tullybridge, the woman stood there alone.

As Josephine walked at Mr. Northrup's side toward the nursery, he said, "You will have to learn to cook. I wish for you to do so."

"Of course, Mr. Northrup." That was the response that always seemed most acceptable to him.

"Mrs. Chester will cook my supper tomorrow. The coachman will prepare my tea. You will cook my breakfast."

She was not versed in cooking, but she knew that would not excuse her. "I will search the library for any books I can find on cooking." And she would hang a rowan hoop in the room at the same time. "That will mean I will not be in the nursery in the morning while you prepare for the day."

"I will allow that," he said.

Mr. Northrup moved directly to his rocking chair upon arriving in the nursery, and Josephine crossed to the shelf where his book was kept. The shelf sat beside a window, and while she ordinarily paid no heed to the land stretching out beyond the glass, something caught her attention just then. Shadows were moving upon the hills. So very many shadows, moving in ways that did not make sense. All were drawing nearer the house, but so slowly. Achingly slowly.

"Why have you stopped?" Mr. Northrup asked.

"I thought I saw something through the window." She took up the book and turned to face him once more, making certain her expression revealed nothing of her concern. "It was merely a trick of the light."

"You are meant to be reading my book, not looking out the window."

"Of course, Mr. Northrup."

She sat in her chair and opened the book. She read the story and knew it was different, but she did not know in what way it had changed. Silas had looked through the book the first day he had been in the house, but they'd been unable to determine what magic it contained. Knowing the story had changed, knowing it was now different, this was likely Josephine's best opportunity to sort out what was different.

Josephine was very careful not to look out the windows. It was not merely a matter of Mr. Northrup's disapproval, though heaven knew that was a strong motivation. She was also willing to admit to herself that the shadows had unnerved her. She suspected she knew what they were—creatures from the faerie realm searching for Silas—and their approach was terrifying.

Somehow she managed to make it through the evening without upsetting the tyrant of Tullybridge. She saw him settled in his bed, his expression unchanging even in sleep. She closed his door, and then moved quickly and quietly through the nursery to the shelf where the book was kept. She took the volume with her into her own bedchamber, closing that door as well.

She and Silas had hung rowan hoops over the window of her room and on the mantel of the tiny fireplace. It was as safe as it could be, and she felt relief every time she closed herself inside her room.

Silas sat beside her on the foot of the bed, and she opened the enchanted book. They flipped through one page at a time, searching for words that were different, for anything unfamiliar.

On a page near the end, she spotted something she knew hadn't been there before. "This illustration is different." She motioned to the corner of the image, which depicted a gathering of people. "This woman was not in it before."

"You're right." Silas leaned closer, just as she did.

Josephine gasped. "Mrs. Green." She pressed her hand to her heart. "Heavens, that is Mrs. Green."

"Mrs. Green was the name of the cook here at Tullybridge when I was taken."

Josephine nodded. "She still is. Or *was*. Mr. Northrup disappeared her just today."

And with that realization, a murkiness seemed to be lifted from their minds. Josephine recognized Peter, the dark-haired footman, and Mr. Jones, the burly gardener. Silas recognized members of the staff he'd known before his abduction.

This was where Mr. Northrup sent them.

"How did we not realize this sooner?" Josephine wondered aloud, though she kept her voice soft, worried Mr. Northrup would hear despite the closed doors and the rowan hoops that surrounded her.

"The book is enchanted. It, no doubt, protects itself from discovery." Silas continued flipping through the pages. "The rowan hoops in this room offer some protection from magic. Bringing the book in here lessened its ability to hide the truth from us."

"But it does not offer protection strong enough for these poor souls to escape the pages?" She looked once more at the sad expressions on the faces of those depicted in the horrid book.

"I don't know if they are able to, regardless of the presence of amulets." His search of the illustrations grew more intent, more focused.

"Are you looking for a clue as to how we might free them?"

He looked up at her, his expression both desperate and forlorn. "I am looking for my parents."

How could she have forgotten? Josephine set her arms around him, her heart breaking for him as he searched a third and fourth time. She rested her head on his shoulder, still embracing him, as he undertook a fifth search.

"Oh, Silas."

He closed the book. "I already suspected they hadn't been spirited away but had departed this life entirely." He put one arm around her in return, offering comfort and connection. "If we are to have any chance of freeing the people trapped in these pages, we must defeat Mr. Northrup and prevent the faeries from reaching this house."

"There are shadows on the hills," she told him from within his embrace. "I saw them. They are coming this way."

"I can feel their approach. We haven't a lot of time."

Though she found solace in his arms, she knew there was not time for such things. Josephine rose and squared her shoulders. "You know more of the laws of the faeries than I do. What do we need to do?"

He fished from his pocket a length of twine with a tiny hoop of rowan twigs hanging on it. "Wear this around your neck. I will wear one as well. And there are two more, one each for the housekeeper and the coachman if we can manage to secretly give it to them. They are not enough to entirely thwart Mr. Northrup's magic, but it will slow his propensity to use it against the person wearing it."

"Will he not sense it? That is the reason we did not place a talisman in the nursery."

"They are small enough that all he will feel is a little disinclination to punish the wearer. And, I hope, large enough to allow me to move through the house without drawing the notice of those pursuing me."

Her heart dropped to her feet. "You mustn't leave this room. You're safe in here. I do not want anything horrid to happen to you."

He took her hand in his and held it tenderly. "None of us are safe. The faeries will reach Tullybridge in the morning. We must trick Mr. Northrup into revealing himself, and I must find the one object in this house that will thwart those wishing to recapture me—a fugitive from the faerie realm."

She didn't know what object Silas was referring to, but she trusted that he did. "While you search for what you need, what ought I to be doing?"

"Now that you have the protection of the rowan hoop on your person, it is time to attempt to force Mr. Northrup's hand."

The prospect frightened her more than she could express, yet the coming of the faeries did as well. This was their one, fleeting opportunity. "I am cooking his breakfast in the morning, on his orders. That gives me a bit more freedom and a bit more time than I am usually granted."

"You are cooking a meal for him?" Silas repeated, the smallest flicker of hope in the question.

"I am."

His eyes lit. "Perfect."

INSTALLMENT V
in which our Hero and Heroine face treacherous Foes!

Before the sun rose the next morning, Silas slipped around his neck a length of twine holding a tiny rowan hoop and sneaked out of the nursery in search of the item they needed to defeat the faeries. He'd lived twenty years in their realm, though likely no more than six months had passed in the world he'd left behind. Those two decades had taught him a lot about their ways.

It also made him keenly aware of their movements, and he could sense them nearby. They had nearly breached the grounds of Tullybridge in their search for him. He would wager the house itself would be invaded in an hour's time. There was something horribly disquieting about a slow inva-sion one had no hope of preventing. The anticipation added another layer of fear.

The rowan hoop Josephine wore would not be enough to protect her if she did not force Mr. Northrup to admit his true identity, and even that would not be sufficient if Silas failed to complete his part of the plan they had hatched the night before.

To that end, Josephine made her way to the kitchens after opening the door to Mr. Northrup's room. She had excused herself, reminding him of her assignment to make his breakfast. He had watched her more closely than usual, which she suspected was due to him sensing the rowan hoop but not fully identifying it, the protection it offered dampening his suspicions.

She'd not crossed paths with Mrs. Chester and, thus, was unable to give the housekeeper a talisman of her own. There was not time to find her. Silas had written out specific instructions for the meal Josephine must cook and present to Mr. Northrup.

Josephine was careful and precise as she prepared a breakfast of barley pottage that she cooked inside an eggshell. She made several, in fact, wanting to make certain that, should she drop one, there would yet be an eggshell meal to place in front of the changeling.

While she toiled in the kitchen, Silas made his way to the room that had belonged to his mother. It was just as he remembered it, unchanged, unweathered. Only the lightest film of dust touched the furnishings, a testament to how short his absence had been, and how recently his mother had been lost.

He opened the jewelry casket atop her dressing table. He needed something small and easily concealed. But it also needed to have personal value to him beyond the monetary. Almost immediately, his eyes fell upon a wooden brooch carved to resemble a rose. He remembered it well. His mother had always worn it to church on Sundays. He would sit on her lap and run his fingers over the wooden petals. The memory was a strong one, which made him reluctant to use the adornment to thwart the faeries. Doing so meant he would lose it; he would never see it again. The very thought pierced his heart.

But that made it perfect for his purpose.

Silas could feel the faeries closing in on the house. They would be inside soon enough. Time was running worryingly short. He made his way toward the dining room.

Josephine had left the kitchen with a tray of eggshell pottages in her hands. She'd chosen a tray with high sides to conceal what she was bringing. Mr. Northrup had to be caught unawares for the strategy to work. Should he sense she was approaching with this particular food, he might manage to avoid its impact.

He sat at the table alone, though Mrs. Chester was meant to have fetched him. Had he disappeared her? If only Josephine had managed to give the poor woman a rowan hoop. If only she'd found her in time.

"I will eat my breakfast now," Mr. Northrup said.

"Of course, Mr. Northrup." Careful to reveal nothing, she set the tray directly in front of him, holding her breath.

"Though I have seen acorns grow into oaks, never have I seen a meal such as this." It was precisely what the meal forced from the mouths of changelings, the admission made in surprise.

For the first time since Josephine had met Mr. Northrup, his expression changed. Shock, anger, fear.

"A child of five has seen no acorns grow into oaks," Josephine declared, "yet you have admitted to such. You have revealed yourself to me, changeling."

He began to transform before her very eyes into the form of an ancient and grizzled faerie.

"You told me your secret, therefore I have charge over you." She repeated what Silas had told her to say. "I command you to take the form of Silas Northrup once more, but as he appears now."

"I know not what shape he takes," the faerie spat.

"Look upon him yourself." Josephine motioned to the doorway where the true Silas stood. "But mind, I further command you to use no more magic in this house against those of this world."

Mr. Northrup glared at the man whose life he had stolen. "This is your doing. You know the world of faeries."

"I know it against my will," Silas said, stepping inside the room. "And you are required by the law of your realm to obey this lady's commands."

With a growl, the faerie took the form of Silas as he appeared now, whilst the true Silas moved to stand beside Josephine.

"Did you find the item?" she asked *her* Silas.

"I did, and not a moment too soon."

Josephine nodded. To Mr. Northrup, she said, "I have five remaining demands of you, and you are required to fulfill them all faithfully."

Though the faerie looked indistinguishable from her Silas, the anger that flashed in his eyes differentiated him. Even when recounting the years of his captivity and the mistreatment he had endured there, Silas's eyes had never held the violent fury Mr. Northrup's did.

"My first demand is that you restore to Tullybridge all the people you disappeared into your book."

Mr. Northrup didn't look away, but she knew he could not refuse.

"The second is that when the faeries breach this house, as they will momentarily, you will convince them that *you* are the fugitive they seek and will do nothing to disabuse them of that belief until after they have carried you back to the faerie realm."

Silas set his wooden rose in her hand.

"The third," she continued, "is that you keep this on your person, concealed from view, and do nothing to make the faeries aware of it until after your identity is revealed upon returning to the faerie realm."

She set the brooch in his hand. The changeling pinned it inside his jacket, then buttoned the jacket closed. All the while, he watched her with anger. She did not let him see the fear that still plagued her.

"Fourth, you will use your magic to disguise the real Silas such that the faeries will not even suspect who he is—a disguise that will remain in place until you have been taken back to the faerie realm."

The furious faerie did not look away from her, yet out of the corner of Josephine's eyes, she could see the true Silas's appearance transform. No longer a man of twenty-five, his dark hair thick and waving, he now appeared to be in at least his eighth decade, with close-cropped hair of snowy white and a face lined with a lifetime of experiences.

"My fifth requirement of you is this: that you will never again, so long as you exist, act as a changeling." Josephine had added that requirement herself to the list she and Silas had compiled the night before. She could not bear the thought of another family and household suffering as this one had.

"It will be done as you demand," the changeling said.

Silas took the tray of eggshell pottage and tossed the contents into the fire. It wouldn't do for the faeries to see it when they arrived, as that would tell them in an instant what had happened.

No sooner had the last remnants of the revelatory breakfast been rendered ash when a harsh wind whipped through the house.

"They are here," Silas whispered, returning to her side.

A moment later, the room was filled with otherworldly creatures, their keen eyes taking in everything. Some among them were skeletal, with sparse strips of torn leathery hide and skulls adorned with horns or beaks. Others were blue-skinned faeries, built not unlike people but smaller, more angular, and moving with a fluidness that did not match what was seen on this mortal clime. Still others were dark, furry rats as tall as a man and standing upright on two feet.

Silas pointed to the Mr. Northrop. "This man has forced his way into the house, claiming to be Silas Northrup, whom we know to be a child."

The faeries turned to look at the changeling, who so perfectly resembled the grown Silas who had escaped their realm. His face no longer betrayed his anger at having been caught out and being under obligation to Josephine. Indeed, if she did not know for a fact that the disguised man beside her was the actual Silas, she would have believed she was looking at him.

"Do not make me go back," the changeling said. "This is my home; I should be permitted to stay."

He sounded so convincing that Josephine, for a moment, thought he was violating his obligation to her. She quickly realized, however, that he was merely speaking the words the *real* Silas would have said.

"There is already a Silas here," someone among the faeries said. "He will remain, and you will return with us."

They, of course, referred to the changeling they had placed in this house.

"You are claiming him?" Silas asked, managing to sound merely curious. It was a crucial question though.

"Him and all" came the answer.

Him and all. That was the phrase they were waiting for.

The faeries took hold of the changeling, being convinced he was the actual human they'd come to claim. They carried him from the house, aloft in their hands. Beyond the garden they went and over the hills, the fog giving way behind them.

Josephine and Silas followed at a distance.

The faeries and their claimed fugitive reached the edge of a faerie circle. They carried the changeling inside—

And vanished.

Josephine looked to Silas, watching with relief as his appearance changed back to his true form and self. She breathed more easily.

"Did it work, do you suppose?"

Silas put his arms around her. "We will know shortly."

She leaned into his embrace, and, their eyes on the very same faerie portal that had stolen away twenty years of Silas's life, the two of them watched and waited.

INSTALLMENT VI
in which the Future of our brave Hero and
Heroine and of Tullybridge is made clear!

From within Silas's embrace, Josephine pressed her tiny rowan hoop to her heart. The two of them watched the faerie circle, knowing the true identity of the changeling would soon be revealed. Inviting the anger of the faerie world was a dangerous thing, indeed. But it was also Tullybridge's only hope.

As if summoned by Josephine touching her talisman, disordered shadows appeared inside the faerie circle. Silas and Josephine kept their distance, careful that not even the tiniest bit of their clothing passed the threshold.

In a flurry of tiny flashes of lightning, a creature not even a quarter the size of a grown person and with skin the shade of a summer sky appeared in the center of the faerie circle. Upon its head rested a crown of flowers, untouched and unharmed by its hair that looked like a flame.

"The queen of this faerie band," Silas whispered to Josephine. This was the moment when all they had done and all they had risked would prove either efficacious or woefully insufficient.

"You have played us a trick, Silas Northrup." Its voice was small yet filled the hills.

"Do not speak to me of ill turns," Silas replied. "You have claimed for your own something of mine, the value of which is found not in its monetary worth but in the treasure of memory and sentiment."

That gave the horrid creature great pause. "What do you accuse us of stealing?"

"Inside the coat of the changeling you took with you is a simple wooden brooch."

"We claimed no brooch," the faerie queen insisted, jutting a pointed chin defiantly.

"You did," Josephine said. "When you took the changeling from the house, you said you were claiming 'him and all.'"

Though her knowledge of the faerie world did not equal Silas's, she knew that claim for what it was. The faeries had taken for their own both the disguised faerie they believed to be the fugitive they sought *and* all attached to him. That included the brooch secreted on his person.

The faerie queen could make no denial, for that was the declaration her band had made.

"You have stolen a heart item from me," Silas said, "and by your laws, you are forever indebted to me."

Though the creature's expression remained defiant, she no longer argued nor faced them with a threatening posture. "We ought not to have allowed you to learn so much, Silas Northrup."

"Having committed this thievery, you are now forbidden from harming or doing mischief to me or anyone or anything connected to me," he declared aloud, knowing that would seal the faeries' indebtedness to him. "And this will be true forever more."

"It is as you say, Silas Northrup." And with that admission, the creature disappeared.

Josephine looked to Silas. "We are free?"

A smile pulled at his lips, and the tension that had permanently resided in his eyes since his escape from the faerie realm eased at last. "We *are*," he said. "At long last."

Hand in hand, they walked over the hills and back toward Tullybridge.

As the house came fully into view, Silas sighed. "It feels like home again. It feels like home."

The house was far from empty when they stepped inside. All the staff had returned, released from their literary imprisonment. Expressions of delight were plentiful. The house was filled with celebration.

"We are free," Josephine told them. "All connected to Tullybridge are forever free of the faeries' mischief and harm."

Shouts of delight accompanied embraces and handshakes. Silas, though older than any of them expected, was not a stranger to anyone. They knew him, recognized him, welcomed him.

As he had said, Tullybridge was once again home.

But it was not home to Josephine. And, with no child in residence, she had no employment in the house.

Only when the celebrations had lulled and the household sought rest was Silas granted a quiet moment in which to ask why her spirits seemed so low.

"I will miss Tullybridge," she said.

"Miss it?" He shook his head. "Why should you miss it?"

"I was brought here to be a governess, but there are no children at Tullybridge."

Silas took her hand in his. "Would you not consider remaining? At least for a time?"

"What would I do?" was the question she spoke, but in her eyes was the question *Might this be home to me as well?* For Tullybridge, which had until that very day been a place of fear and struggle, had become quite suddenly precious to her. *Silas* had become quite precious.

"You could do whatever you pleased," Silas said. "And, if I am very fortunate, I hope you would be willing to spend some time with me, granting me the chance to know you better."

"And I you."

He raised her hand to his lips, gently kissing her fingers. "I would like that very much, Josephine Harlow."

"And I like *you* very much, Silas Northrup."

She did remain, and they did, indeed, come to know one another better. The fondness they felt grew with time. Free of both the fear "Mr. Northrup" had inflicted and the threat of the faeries, Josephine and Silas found in one another . . . a home.

ON A SEA
OF GLASS

by Stone

A MAN OF THE SEA

My father had been a man of the sea. That was all Mother ever told me of him. She didn't seem to dislike that about him, neither did she disapprove when I began a seafaring life as well.

"The sea is in your blood, Rafael," she had said. "I could no easier keep you from it than I could prevent the waves from reaching the shore."

I'd begun as a powder monkey aboard a ship that, once far out to sea, sailed under the Jolly Roger. My next adventure at sea was amongst a merchant crew. Then part of the crew of a passenger ship. By my twentieth year of life, I was a seasoned sailor, a skilled rigger, a tried-and-true man of the sea.

It was on the docks of Portsmouth that I first heard Captain St. John Mortimer speak. He stood atop a crate, a larger-than-life man in all imaginable if not literal ways.

"The sea calls to us, men!" His voice carried over the crowd, reaching my ears and capturing my attention. "It offers adventure, opportunity. Many a man has made his fortune. Many a man has discovered true courage. Many a hero has been forged on the waves. And I need such men to set sail aboard *The Siren Song*."

Anyone who had sailed for any length of time knew of Mortimer and his ship. But no one knew for certain if Mortimer was a pirate or a merchant. The line between the two was often blurred.

"I abide no hooligans or scoundrels," Mortimer continued. "And the slothful don't last long. But all others will find that sailing under my flag can prove a most profitable venture."

The pier was filled with men looking for a position or longing for an adventure; some were desperate to escape various entanglements. Even before he finished his proclamation, Mortimer had more volunteers than he likely had positions.

I took my time approaching him. A person could learn a lot about life on board a particular ship by studying the one who dictated that life. Captain Mortimer was scarred, wind-bitten. He moved decisively but stiffly, a lifetime of injuries evident in the imperfections of his body. And there was a hardness in his eyes that warned any onlooker that he'd not been exaggerating when he'd said that the slothful and incompetent did not last long aboard his ship.

That was evidence enough for me.

Those who'd not yet found their sea legs often thought a grizzled and abrasive captain meant a miserable experience at sea. I knew better. The soft, wavering ones were the nightmares. They didn't respect the sea, and their crews didn't respect them. Both were guaranteed to bring disaster.

"You still looking for men?" I asked as I reached the spot where he stood.

"Might be." He eyed me with a critical gaze. I looked young, which I knew gave him pause. But I was hardly a child. "How many years have you spent at sea, lad?"

"This'll be my fifth."

Mortimer nodded. "And your name?"

"Rafael Funar."

That caught his attention just as I knew it would.

"Albrecht?"

"Was my father."

The wariness in his weatherworn face gave way to a hint of interest. "What is it you do on board, Rafael?"

"I'm a rigger. Best you're like to find."

He must have found that to be a show of confidence rather than arrogance because the next morning, I set sail from Plymouth as the youngest of the riggers aboard *The Siren Song*.

Any doubt we might have harbored about the true nature of this vessel and her aim was quickly put to rest. A quartermaster was elected, and his authority, very nearly equal to the captain's, was immediately established. Such a thing was only ever done onboard pirate ships.

Our chosen quartermaster, a man called Ezekiel, divided the crew, not by roles or skills, but by name. I could read my name and a few nautical terms but little else. And I was *more* literate than most on board. Assigning responsibilities to men by where their names fell in the alphabet was odd to say the least. Still, I took my place in the watch rotation beside Evermond, one of the young powder monkeys, and Jones, a green-around-the-gills seaman. No matter the unusualness of the approach, we were happy enough to be at sea on so worthy a vessel and sailing with so famous a captain.

We had been five days on the waves. I was in the crow's nest, watching the water through my spyglass. A driving wind had kept the sails full. *The Siren Song* leapt over the waves in a graceful dance. In my place high above the deck amongst the rigging, I felt at home. All was well with the world.

Then the wind died. Suddenly. Entirely.

And the ship stopped. Suddenly. Entirely.

So quick was the change that items on the deck were tossed about. *People* on the deck were tossed about. Were I not tremendously nimble and in possession of strong hands, I might have been flung to my death from my mast-top vantage point.

Ships are often becalmed, adrift on the sea, awaiting the return of the wind. But no ship had come to so sudden a halt in open water as *The Siren Song* just had.

And never before in all my time spent watching the sea had I seen water as smooth and as still as glass.

BECALMED

I asked Captain Mortimer on the day after we left Portsmouth why he had christened his ship *The Siren Song*. He said it was because he believed men were called to the sea to meet their fate, be it glory or death. He also told me he didn't think the two were mutually exclusive.

But now, sitting high in the riggings of *The Siren Song,* three days becalmed on an endless sea, I did not find the prospect of death at sea quite so glorious as he'd made it sound.

The wind had not resumed blowing. Not even a slight breeze. The air and the water around us were perfectly still.

"A sea of glass," the ship's boatswain, Cleaver, had called it.

I thought of that description often as I climbed the riggings or watched the horizon from the crow's nest during those first three days. *Sea of glass.*

The ship had stopped rocking the very moment we were becalmed. It didn't lean or roll or ride atop the slight undulation of the ocean. Because there was no undulation.

Becalmed had quickly proven too soft a word. The ocean was not calm; it was utterly unmoving.

From my vantage point high above the deck with my spyglass pressed to my eye, I could see what the others could not. The water far from us moved as the ocean ought. In all directions, I could see hills and valleys of the waves, growing and shrinking, rising and falling. But around us—and *only* around us—the water was as flat and still as a mirror's surface.

Below me, those of the crew on watch paced the deck, eyeing the eerie water. They were at a loss. Cleaver insisted they continue tending to the needs of the ship, as salt water took a toll on a vessel even if that vessel was not moving. But the work had proven insufficient to keep the crew distracted from the unnerving situation we found ourselves in.

Captain Mortimer strode from his quarters toward the starboard railing, the quartermaster at his side. The crew parted for them to pass, an air of worry about them both.

"There must be a reason for this misfortune," the captain growled. "The seas do not punish without cause."

His voice carried on the still air. That I could hear him from my perch so high above the deck was yet another testament to the strangeness of our circumstances. The crew kept quiet, their focus on Mortimer.

Ezekiel, the quartermaster, was as hardened and experienced a seafarer as the captain, and likely older. "I've inquired of all the crew. No one has brought aboard any cursed items or behaved in violation of the superstitions that rule the seas."

The two of them looked out over the unforgiving water.

Captain Mortimer let forth a string of creative and colorful curses, a common thing on any ship but a near constant sound on this one these past days.

Without wind, we might as well have been anchored. Without wind, we could not return to port. We could not obtain supplies. We would run out of food and fresh water. Should illness grip one of us, it would claim all of us.

I raised my spyglass once more and watched the movement of water so far away. There was no clear edge where the water changed from moving naturally to becoming this mirror of ocean we sat upon. It simply became what it was here.

Still.

Still as death.

The captain and quartermaster made their way back to the captain's quarters. The crew began milling about, muttering to each other, grumbling to themselves. In the midst of them, a sailor named Halloran spoke above the din.

"This ship cannot sit becalmed this way forever," he declared. "We must send out a rowboat to search for land or assistance."

Cleaver shook his head. "Rafael has seen no hints of land anywhere on the horizon. Our compass is not working. The measurements taken with the sextant change even as we're taking them. We do not know where we are, Halloran. And there is nowhere to send anyone that could be reached with oars. Those sent on such a mission would die at those oars."

I could not see Halloran's face, but I could imagine the expression he wore. He'd suggested rowing away several times since we'd found ourselves unable to leave this mysterious corner of the ocean. Anytime his suggestion was dismissed, he grew petulant.

Captain Mortimer did not abide petulance, though he'd not lost all patience with the discouraged sailor. Yet his patience was unlikely to last much longer.

"So we will die aboard this ship instead?" Halloran snapped, a rare outburst for him. He grumbled, yes, but he didn't usually bite back.

"It's been three days, you yellow-bellied swab," one of the other sailors drawled. "We ain't anywhere near the longest a ship's been becalmed."

That was true. I'd been on board *The Swallow's Tail* when it had waited ten days for the wind to pick up again. And even that hadn't been the longest some aboard had been in frustratingly calm seas.

But we all knew this was different.

The crew continued laughing at Halloran's fatalistic view of our three windless days, but I knew he wasn't the only one genuinely worried about it. The captain, after all, considered it a punishment of such significance that he and the quartermaster were evaluating everyone on board. But finding something to turn the crews' thoughts to something other than the flat sea was likely a welcome distraction.

I had no such distraction. With my spyglass trained on the horizon, I searched for answers, for explanations, for hope. I slowly angled my search closer and closer to the ship until the water was inanimate once more. The ocean offered no clues.

Then, without warning, a single bubble burst on the mirrored surface mere feet from the ship. Then several more bubbles. And those several turned into what looked to be sea-foam. There was movement below the foam.

"Water moving off the port side!" I shouted down to the sailors. "The water's moving! Port!"

As easily as I could hear them before, they heard me now. All on deck rushed to port, shouting for each other to come see. Captain Mortimer and Ezekiel emerged from the captain's quarters, brought to deck by the commotion.

On the surface of the water, the sea-foam was growing, expanding quickly. It formed a mound—large as a man, then large as two. It expanded upward until the top of the mound towered above the railings at the side of the ship. In width, it surpassed what would be accomplished by ten men standing shoulder to shoulder.

The column of sea-foam bent as it rose, like a wizened old man standing slowly from a chair, his back arched with age. The crew stood like statues, no doubt too shocked and confused to do anything but stare up at the column of inexplicable composition as it towered over them.

All was silent. From my perch above, the scene played out like a moment in a terrible dream, hardly making sense and yet existing somehow.

The sea-foam, for I knew not what else to call it, stilled and froze. Nothing moved beyond the nearly indiscernible rise and fall of tense shoulders as the men attempted to breathe through their uncertainty. For my part, I held my breath.

Then it struck. Like the deadly tail of a scorpion, the column crashed down upon the men standing nearest it. Those not within its path scattered, shouting in panic and confusion. All was chaos and fright.

As quickly as it had formed, the sea-foam column returned to the sea, sinking below the water, which sat as still and unmoving as before. The deck was unmarred where the strike had occurred. No indication of what had happened could be seen.

But the men who'd been standing there were gone. Vanished without any trace.

And just as the sea sat silent and still, so did *The Siren Song* and her crew. Unspoken among us was the realization that windless skies were not the gravest danger we faced.

The sea of glass held a monster.

A TOMB

By the seventh day, half the crew was gone.

Those of us the sea monster hadn't claimed kept below, avoiding exposure on the weather deck. Even Captain Mortimer had installed himself on the gun deck with the rest of us in order to converse with his crew without risking the vulnerability of leaving his cabin to descend into the belly of the ship.

We were prisoners, hostages to a creature we could not name and did not understand.

"We cannot simply sit here and wait for it to take us one by one," Halloran said.

Ezekiel eyed him with the annoyance everyone had come to feel. "Have you heard any of us suggest we simply line ourselves up for the creature to take its pick?"

"No," Halloran admitted.

"Then quit talking like we have." Ezekiel then addressed the rest of us. "We've food and water enough for keeping ourselves alive for weeks yet. But neglecting the upkeep of the ship will mean we can't set sail should the wind return."

Cleaver, the boatswain, spoke next. "The ship won't fall to ruin in the next couple of days. We've time enough for making a plan."

"And how are we to do that?" a sailor named Mercer asked. "We don't know what the creature is. We don't know if it's in the water or if it *is* the water." He didn't sound defeated, but rather frustrated by his desire to move forward but not knowing what path to take.

"And we don't know how it's stopping the wind," Jones, the only other remaining rigger, said. "Or even if it is."

I stepped away from the pillar I'd been leaning against. "What we need is a better understanding of what we're facing. All we know is this creature takes people off the deck and leaves not a trace. We know it either *lives* in this place of unnatural calm or *creates* it. Perhaps both. We don't know its weaknesses. We don't know if anything'll make it retreat."

"Are you volunteering to stand above deck and ask it questions?" Mercer laughed, a nice change from the tension that had permeated every conversation over the past days.

I shook my head. "Nor am I volunteering anyone else to go on such a fool's errand." I looked to Captain Mortimer. "The first captain I sailed under said that knowing *which* weapon to use was even more important than knowing *when* to use it."

"A privateer?" the captain asked, though he seemed to have sorted the answer.

I shrugged. "That's what he told people."

The others chuckled. Pirates often identified themselves as privateers; it gave them a sense of respectability. Halloran didn't seem to see the humor. He continued sulking, a talent of his.

"You're suggesting we discover which, if any, of our weapons might deal it a blow?" Captain Mortimer asked.

"It's too large a thing for a flintlock—even a row of them—to likely do anything." I set my hand on the back of a nearby cannon. "But a gun of this size might make an impression."

Consensus rippled through the group. Most important of all, Captain Mortimer and Ezekiel, whose authority as quartermaster rivaled the captain's, agreed with the idea.

Only Halloran had complaints. "We might only make it angry."

"Might," I acknowledged. "But as someone said a moment ago, 'We cannot simply sit here and wait for it to take us one by one.'"

Halloran either didn't recognize his own words or didn't understand why I'd tossed them back at him.

Jones spoke up. "One benefit is that we can fire a cannon from here. No need to go above deck."

We all discussed the hows of it all: watching for the bubbles to start, needing to decide in the moment which cannon to fire. Soon, we had a strategy. And the feeling of helplessness that had permeated the gun deck eased.

I received a small nod of approval from the captain. On any other voyage, I'd have seen that as reason to believe a promotion lay ahead, which would have pleased me to no end. Given the circumstances, I was too concerned with staying alive to spare a free thought for my nautical ambitions.

We'd lost all but one of our gunners and had only two powder monkeys left. Hours were spent training those who remained in the tasks they'd not anticipated being asked to perform on *The Siren Song*. When the opportunity arose, there'd not be time for scrambling. Everyone needed to know his role and perform it swiftly and well.

Another day passed before sea-foam was spotted in the water again. Jones saw it through an open gunport. In an instant, we were all at our assigned posts, readying the cannon that was positioned above the growing tower of foam.

Just as it had done before, the creature expanded, growing taller and wider. While it did so, we took all the steps necessary to fire the canon directly at it.

Cleaver stood at the gunport next to the one we'd be firing through. Jones stood at the other.

"Taller than this deck now," Cleaver reported.

"Nearly to the upper deck," Jones added after a moment.

The cannon was ready. We all waited, breath bated, for the captain to give the order to fire.

In the very instant we heard Mortimer shout "Fire!" a tentacle of sea-foam shot through the gunport where Cleaver stood, enveloping him precisely as it had so many others before him.

We lit the cannon even as those nearest Cleaver ran toward him with all they had.

The cannon fired, and the tentacle retreated. As had happened on deck, it left behind not a trace of water, a hint of destruction, nor hide nor hair of boatswain Cleaver.

The rest of the crew were running, hiding, cowering. But we had to know what the cannonball had done, if anything.

My heart in my throat, I rushed to the gunport Jones had abandoned.

The cannonball had torn a hole through the creature, the edges of the sea-foam somehow burnt. Could water burn? I'd never heard of such a thing.

As quickly as it had appeared, our foe sunk back beneath the smooth surface of the sea.

I closed the gunport, then turned to face the dark deck and the crew beginning to re-emerge from the shadowy corners they'd retreated to. Only the captain hadn't hidden away. He watched me from his position, stalwart and stern.

"We burned a hole in it," I said. "That's something."

"Little good it did," Halloran said, walking to where Cleaver had stood. "The creature reached right in here and snatched him away. We aren't even safe below deck. This ship might as well be a tomb."

SINISTER SATISFACTION

A day had passed since we'd shot a hole through the sea-foam monster. It hadn't reappeared, but not one of us believed we had defeated it. Tension was growing amongst us all, fear threatening to push us toward panic.

"We hit it at point-blank range," Ezekiel said, "and it still took its time retreating. If a cannonball won't defeat it, what will?"

"But the wound remained," one of the powder monkeys said, showing more grit and logic than many of his adult shipmates. "The blow did damage."

"We've an entire broadside of eighteen-pounders," Captain Mortimer said. "If we hit it with all of that, we'd tear it in two."

"There're only fifteen of us," Ezekiel said, though he didn't look to be dismissing the idea out of hand. "Firing a whole broadside quickly enough to catch the beast would be a difficult feat."

"We would do far better to search out safer waters," Halloran said.

"If I hear you suggest abandoning *The Siren Song* in favor of a rickety rowboat one more time," the captain said, "I'll keelhaul you and let the monster nibble at you at its leisure."

When Halloran had first begun suggesting we row for our lives, I'd dismissed it as cowardice. But to keep suggesting the same thing knowing that the water was far more dangerous now than ever before seemed to me something more.

"If we sort out a means of firing all our guns at the beast," one of the quieter sailors said, "what's to stop the creature from reaching through a gunport and taking us like it did Cleaver?"

That was a sticking point for sure and certain. And yet . . .

"Mercer stood not far from Cleaver," I said. "Though the sea-foam beast has snatched multiple men at a time, it didn't grab him nor any of the rest of us who were nearby."

"Maybe it couldn't see the rest of us?" another of our ragged crew suggested.

"Or couldn't reach," Ezekiel added.

It's reach above deck had been significant. Perhaps fitting itself through so narrow an opening limited it. Perhaps it could grow taller than it could wide. Whatever the answer, we'd found a weakness in our foe; we couldn't ignore it.

While Ezekiel and the remaining gunner talked through the difficulty of firing so many cannons in succession with so few people, I watched Halloran. He appeared on edge but, the closer I studied him, the more clear it became that what he was feeling *wasn't* fear.

The person who, from the start, had continually advocated the coward's escape, and he wasn't actually frightened.

Had he always been such a contradiction? I couldn't say with any certainty. I'd not known him before our current circumstances had made him so vocal. We'd not served in the same watch. What I needed was to discover which watch he'd been assigned to.

I motioned Jones over. He could read and write more than just his name.

"You know your letters," I said. "Where does Halloran fall when putting names in the alphabet order?"

"Near to the front," Jones said. "It'd be after your name."

"How far after mine?" It must've been a fair bit after for the two of them to have been in different watches.

"Two letters over. Closer to your name than mine."

I shook my head, trying to jar my thoughts into a version that made sense. "You and I were in the same watch."

"Oi, we were." Jones clearly hadn't realized the significance of that yet.

I held his gaze. "Why wasn't Halloran?"

Jones waved Ezekiel over. "Did you make any exceptions to the alphabet order watch assignments?"

Ezekiel shook his head. "None but Mortimer, myself, and Cleaver." Obviously the captain, quartermaster, and boatswain wouldn't have been assigned to a watch.

"You're certain of that?" I pressed.

"Full certain."

"Halloran should've been on watch with Jones and me, but he wasn't," I said. "I can't even remember seeing him on board until after we were becalmed."

"Come to think of it, neither can I," Jones said.

Ezekiel's thick eyebrows pulled together in thought. "Neither can I."

"A stowaway?" Jones guessed.

"I make a point of having the ship searched thoroughly the first day at sea. We had no stowaways."

I didn't overly like that answer. "Then when did he come aboard?"

We all turned to look at the man in question and found him watching us from the other side of the ship-long gun deck. Sound carried unnaturally far in this cursed corner of the sea—I'd discovered that whilst perched in the crow's nest—but I hadn't realized until that moment that the phenomenon occurred inside the ship as well.

He didn't look at us with any degree of surprise to have suddenly been the focus of our trio. He'd heard what we'd been discussing.

"When?" I asked him, not bothering to raise my voice, knowing I didn't need to.

A slow smile spread over his face, one not of amusement but a sinister sort of satisfaction.

In that precise moment, our youngest powder monkey shouted, "The foam is forming again!"

There'd not been time enough to prepare the cannons. Panic began filling the space. Yet Halloran stood in his same spot, wearing his same expression of unnerving gratification.

"Get far from the gunports!" I shouted.

The crew rushed away from the starboard side where the monster had been spotted.

Mere moments later, a tentacle of sea-foam reached in through a port, farther and farther into the deck, closer and closer to where we all stood. No one breathed or spoke or moved. I doubted anyone even swallowed.

My heart pounded in my neck, speeding up with each beat. I didn't take my eyes off the tentacle, which had stopped less than a yard from my face. We knew if it touched a person, that person was snatched away.

As quickly as it had reached in, the sea-foam arm retreated.

Still, we didn't move. Long minutes passed without sign of the monster's return. We might have stood there for minutes or hours. Both felt possible.

Finally, Mercer broke from the group and moved tentatively to one of the starboard gunports and peered out at the water below. "Still as glass." He breathed a sigh of relief that was echoed by us all.

"There is a limit to its reach," Captain Mortimer said.

"And the hole was still in it," the little powder monkey added. "That didn't heal."

We now knew two things about our enemy. Two weaknesses.

I turned to look at Halloran, wondering what he thought of our discoveries. But he was gone.

BAIT

We had an enemy below the ship and another somewhere on it, and all of us knew that time was running short. Our next encounter with the monster needed to be our final one.

All was ready for firing the cannons as quickly as possible when the sea-foam next appeared but doing so required us to stand within reach of the tentacles.

"We've not ever seen it reach in more than one direction at a time,"

Captain Mortimer said. "It has either made a single strike on the weather deck or reached with a single tentacle through a gunport. But it can snatch multiple people at once if they are near enough to each other."

"Meaning it might snatch up a whole slew of us in here as we're gathered around the cannons," Mercer said.

"If we leave the gunports closed until the last moment," the older of our powder monkeys said, "it might be searching the deck and not realize what we're doing."

"I suspect it'll sort it quickly," Ezekiel warned.

I'd been giving the matter a lot of thought and spoke those thoughts just then. "We need to bait it, distract it from the gunports."

"How do we do that?" Jones asked.

"Every time we've seen it, it has searched above deck first. I'd wager it'll do so again. We need to make sure it finds something there it wants."

"One of us?"

I couldn't blame the poor soul who asked that question for the disapproval in his voice.

"If we could find Halloran, I'd suggest him," I said. "But since he's proven impossible to locate, I've another idea." I stood from the stool I'd been sitting on. "The first time we saw the creature, I was in the crow's nest. It never grew as tall as I was high."

"You think it can't reach that far?" Captain Mortimer asked.

"I think it's possible."

"You'd sit up there and hope it can't reach you?" Jones shook his head. "A fool's errand, that."

"I've something far more foolish in mind," I said. "The monster needs a distraction not merely a destination. When next we see the foam beginning to form, I'll scramble above deck and up into the rigging." I turned to the captain. "I told you on the pier in Portsmouth that I'm the best rigger you're likely to ever find. That's not on account of my knot-tying skills alone. I can climb better and faster than nearly all the riggers on all the ships on all the seas in the world. I'm not being braggart; I'm telling you I'm capable of doing this."

"You're proposing to let the creature stretch up after you as you climb toward the crow's nest, not knowing at what point its reach will run short."

I gave a single nod. "And, by Neptune, while I'm doing that, the lot of you had better blast that beast out of the water."

For three days we watched for the return of the monster. For three days we listened for the sounds of Halloran sneaking about the ship. But neither appeared.

The other thirteen people on the gun deck ran drills, practicing, but without actually loading or firing the cannons. I spent that same time plotting various paths up the rigging to the crow's nest. Every climb a rigger made on board a ship was dangerous. This one, however, would be unlike any climb I'd ever made.

On the morning of the fourth day, the water began to bubble.

Shocked at how calm I was, I rushed to the weather deck and directly to the mainmast. Up the rat boards I went, not pausing to look for sea-foam or listen for movement. The ropes and boards were completely dry, which was perhaps the only benefit of no rain or wind or sea spray for weeks. The rat boards gave way to ratlines as I climbed ever higher.

I was elevated enough to look portside where the foam had been spotted. It had grown to the height of the railing on the weather deck. I climbed a little higher. I didn't dare go too far. If it didn't see me, I'd not make much of a distraction.

The sea-foam monster bent over the deck as it had done the first day. No one was there. Would it look around? Or would it go next to the gunports, having had success there?

It began shrinking again, down toward the gun deck.

I let forth as loud and shrill a whistle as I could manage. It stopped, then began to grow again. Up I climbed, careful not to slip, with only the quickest of glances to see if I'd baited the monster.

It seemed undecided. It would be moving in my direction on one glance, then retreat again on the next. The indecision was serving its purpose. The monster hadn't caught up to me but also hadn't reached into the gunports.

I pulled myself up a futtock shroud and onto the top above, now higher than I'd seen the monster grow, though I knew that was no guarantee that I was out of reach. I moved along the top to the mast once more and back to ratlines. The crow's nest was higher still.

Something grabbed my foot.

I hooked my arm around the shroud and ratline to anchor myself as I jerked my head around to see what I was caught on. Not a rope. Not a hook. Not even the sea-foam monster.

Halloran.

I tried shaking him loose, but his grip was ironclad. Below and behind him, the sea-foam column continued to grow.

"It'll reach you soon enough," I told Halloran. "You'll be snatched."

He didn't look away from me, didn't let go. "It's hungry."

"Then it can eat you." I kicked my foot as hard as I could, but it didn't break from his grasp.

"It's hungry." Just as there'd been no fear in his expression as we'd discussed the monster before, there was none now.

"That's why you wanted us in rowboats." I twisted and bent trying to break his grip. "You were trying to feed it."

"It's hungry."

And it was far too close for comfort. I either needed to free myself or resign myself to being snatched like all the others before me. I bent my free leg and, with every ounce of strength I could muster, slammed the heel of my boot into Halloran's wrist. At last, he let me go, falling to the platform mere feet below us. My ankle, where he'd gripped me, was covered in sea-foam.

I continued my climb, knowing he'd be pursuing me, knowing he was connected to the monster, knowing the monster itself was still growing taller.

Upward. Upward. As fast as I could climb. Heart pounding. Muscles burning.

The ropes pulled as Halloran climbed after me. The monster grew closer. Halloran grew closer. Even if the foam couldn't reach the crow's nest, the monster in sailor's form most certainly could.

I reached the bottom of the crow's nest just as Halloran snagged hold of my foot again.

"It's hungry."

My hands were losing their grip. My lungs burned with the effort of so fast and dangerous a climb. I couldn't hold on much longer.

I slipped, gripping only with my fingertips. A moment more, and my fingers would give out as well.

I closed my eyes, telling myself at least it'd be over quick.

Then an explosion cut the air. Cannon fire. Then another. And another.

The grip on my ankle loosened. I kicked free, finding barely enough strength to pull myself into the crow's nest.

Another explosion. Another.

I turned to see the sea-foam beast flailing, twisting and bending.

Another explosion. Foam at the level of the gun deck flew in all directions. Then more. And more.

The monster suddenly grew entirely still. After a moment, it fell backward, like a tree being felled in a forest. It dropped into the ocean, shattering like glass against the mirrored surface. On the rigging below me, Halloran evaporated.

I sank to my knees in the crow's nest, my strength entirely gone.

Beneath me, the ship began to roll on the waves.

THE RETURN

Twenty-nine people had left Portsmouth aboard *The Siren Song*. Fourteen returned.

We knew no one would believe us if we explained what had really happened to more than half the crew. We'd be labeled mad. The families of those we'd lost would consider themselves ill-used to not be told the truth of what had happened to their loved ones, convinced we were lying.

"Illness," Captain Mortimer had decided. "We'll say it was illness."

And we did. And we were believed.

And we were lying.

We all said we'd stay away from the sea for a time. We said it didn't call to us any longer.

And we were lying.

Not a fortnight after docking in Portsmouth, *The Siren Song* put out to sea once more. The same fourteen people who'd stood on her deck, battered and wizened as she'd returned to England, stood there again as she left the shore.

Our powder monkeys were made full gunners.

I was made boatswain.

Captain Mortimer stood at the helm, studying the horizon with a look in his eyes that matched the one we all wore. We were a formidable collection of survivors, and we meant to test our mettle once more.

The sea was calling. And we were ready to answer.

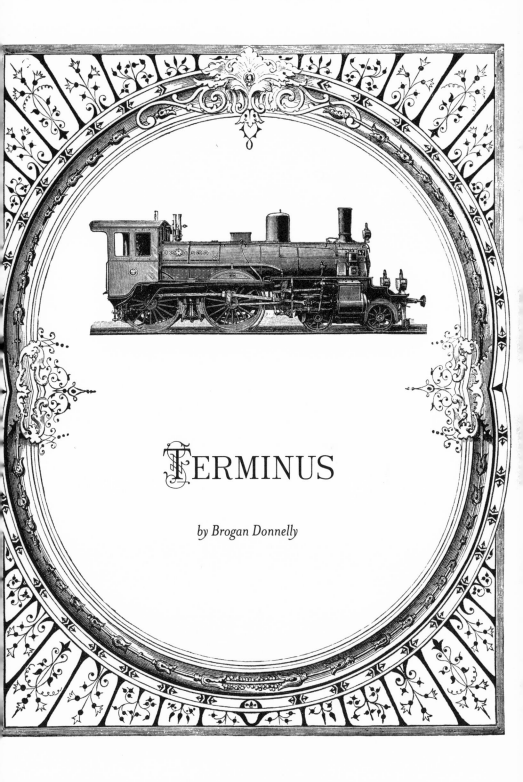

TERMINUS

by Brogan Donnelly

THE JOURNEY BEGINS

Rufus Millard stood, perplexed, in the midst of the bustling Victoria Station, unsure which of the imposing locomotives he was meant to board. He'd never traveled by train before. Rail travel was not entirely new, but it was not yet universal enough to not be intimidating to the inexperienced. And, oh, how inexperienced Rufus was!

Our somewhat intrepid traveler spotted a man wearing a conductor's uniform. Rufus approached, hopeful he would be pointed in the correct direction.

"Begging your pardon," he said to the conductor. "Which train am I meant to board?" He held up his ticket, embarrassed to see it shake under the influence of his nerves.

The conveniently located conductor needed to merely glance at the paper before answering what had seemed to be an unanswerable question. "This one, sir." He motioned Rufus toward a nearby passenger train, not overly large nor overly opulent but nicely appointed.

Rufus counted at least a dozen open doors, all leading to sections in which passengers sat to undertake their journeys. "How do I know which compartment I am meant to enter?"

"This particular train is not divided into travel classes," the conductor said. "You need only pick a door."

That seemed simple enough. Rufus wasn't certain how he'd managed to find a train ticket with so few complications, but he was grateful.

He carried his carpetbag to the first open door and stepped onto the train. The compartment was nearly full, four other passengers having already taken seats inside. Rufus eyed them with misgiving, on account of his being shy of strangers. It had been his understanding that men and women sat in separate compartments on the train unless related to one another.

"Pardon me," he said with a quick dip of his head. He moved to step back out.

"Nonsense," said one of the women. She waved him back inside. "We've room and plenty."

Though there was a significant resemblance between the two women in the compartment, he did not see that same resemblance between them and the two men. Perhaps they were not all related. Perhaps that was not the deterrent he'd been led to believe it was.

"I'd not be in the way?"

All four of his fellow travelers insisted he would not be and encouraged him to join them. And, so, he set his carpetbag on the overhead shelf alongside the other passengers' belongings. He placed himself on the rear-facing bench on the end farthest from the door.

"Have you traveled by train before?" asked the same lady who had addressed him first.

"I haven't," he said. "But my wife convinced me it was well worth the expense on account of how much faster this will be."

A mustached man seated across from him adjusted the umbrella leaning against his leg. "Nothing beats train travel for efficiency. I'm headed for Reigate, myself. My parents live there."

The more vocal of the two women offered their thoughts. "We lost our parents only two years ago. Having no family other than the two of us, we finally decided we ought to do the things we had put off for so long." She had referred to "our parents," which meant the two women were sisters. "Please, tell us, what are your names, and where you are traveling to?"

The mustached man answered first. "I am Melvin."

Next to Rufus sat a man far younger than the others in the compartment, likely only just twenty. He wore a pair of dark trousers and a checkered frock coat and held a folded newspaper in his hands. "My name is Harlow. My family moved from London to Ashford, but I stayed behind to work. Now a job is waiting for me there, and I'm traveling to join them."

The two sisters, sitting beside the mustached man, took their turn. The more talkative of the two made the introductions on behalf of them both. "I am Tillie, and this is Zinnia. Our first stop will be Tonbridge. We have always wanted to visit."

Everyone's eyes turned to Rufus. He would be their traveling companion for some time. It seemed rather ill-advised to not at least be cordial.

"I'm Rufus. And I'm traveling to Dover on a matter of business." That business being an unexpected inheritance. His family was not poor, but they sometimes struggled. He hoped that this unforeseen windfall would allow them to worry less about such things.

Tillie smiled at them all. "I believe we will be a very merry group traveling together."

General expressions of agreement followed. Rufus began breathing more easily. He'd found himself in good company with friendly and welcoming people. The journey promised to be a far better one than he'd anticipated.

The same conductor he'd seen on the platform arrived at the door of their compartment. "Tickets, please."

One by one, the travelers handed him their tickets. He punched them without looking before handing them back. When he reached Rufus, the conductor smiled in a way that set Rufus instantly on edge. There was something unsettling in the conductor's eyes.

"Enjoy your journey."

And though Rufus had fully intended to thank the man as his ticket was returned, his voice suddenly eluded him.

REIGATE STATION

The rocking of the railway car proved a bit unnerving. Rufus repeatedly reminded himself that many others had made this same journey before him and very few had found themselves in true danger.

The ceaseless movement of the train twisted his stomach, while the memory of the conductor's disconcerting smile still sat heavy upon his mind. The combination was not overly pleasant.

"How long have you lived in London?" Tillie asked Melvin.

"Twenty years now," the man answered. "I'm a clerk at a bank and have made a fine life for myself. My wife's passed on, and our children are grown and moved away. But I've friends enough for chasing away the loneliness."

"We certainly miss family when they're not with us." Young Harlow spoke as one who knew all too well. He had, after all, been away from his family.

"We do, indeed, miss them." Tillie pressed a lace-edged handkerchief to her lips.

Zinnia nodded her agreement.

This was a topic Rufus felt equal to discussing. "My family is the reason I'm making this journey by rail: I didn't want to be away from them any longer than I have to be."

"Next time," Tillie said, "you should travel *with* your family. I daresay they would enjoy such a journey."

Rufus hadn't thought of that. If his inheritance in Dover proved sufficient, he would bring Gertrude and the girls on his next train journey, assuming, of course, his stomach did not entirely rebel on *this* one. His family would enjoy the train ride. Perhaps they would all move to Dover and leave London behind entirely.

"Did you grow up in Reigate?" he asked Melvin.

"In Dover, actually."

Rufus perked up. "Did you have a good childhood there?"

"A lovely childhood." Melvin smiled in that way one did when remembering happier times. "Dover is a fine place."

"I am considering moving my family there," Rufus said. "A quieter life might suit us better."

"Dover would be a fine choice," Melvin said. "A simpler life than London, but a large enough city for finding work."

"That sounds ideal."

Taking this train ride was proving a tremendous bit of luck. He would arrive in Dover far quicker than by horse or carriage. He had begun to ponder a change of location for his family that might very well be the best thing to happen to them in ages. And he'd met four people he was coming to like very much.

The train began to slow; they were approaching a station.

"This will be Reigate," Melvin said. "It's been a delight traveling with you all."

"Enjoy your time with your parents," Tillie said.

Melvin smiled at her. "I have every intention of doing so. You two enjoy Tonbridge."

"We have every intention of doing so."

Squeals and screeches accompanied the stopping of the train as brakes were applied and the forward movement was disrupted. The stop was not smooth but jarring, and all the passengers grasped their seats for stability.

Once all was settled again, Melvin stood and fetched a small leather satchel from the overhead shelves. He placed his hat on his head.

The conductor opened the door. Steam from the engine obscured the area around him, giving his arrival an otherworldly appearance. "Your stop, sir."

Melvin gave them all a nod of farewell, then stepped out onto the platform. He disappeared into the clouds of steam.

The conductor remained. "Next stop, Tonbridge."

He closed the door but watched them all through the window. His stern expression transformed slowly, muscle by muscle, into the disconcerting smile that had so unnerved Rufus before. No one else seemed to notice. The sisters were deep in conversation. Harlow was reading his paper.

The conductor met Rufus's eye, tipped his hat the tiniest bit, and slipped out of sight. Mere moments later, the train lurched forward, continuing its journey.

The landscape moved past the window ever faster as they left behind Reigate Station. The sway and rattle of the train became even and familiar once more. Rufus had some hope that, by the time he reached Dover, he would be accustomed to it and the slight twist of his stomach would ease.

"I was fortunate to have met Melvin on this journey," he said aloud. "To have his thoughts on Dover was a boon."

"Melvin?" Tillie asked, eyebrows dipping low.

Perhaps she hadn't overheard their conversation. "He told me before he alighted that he grew up in Dover. I'm thinking of relocating there."

"Did you meet him on a previous leg of your journey?" Tillie asked.

A previous leg? "On this one."

Tillie and Zinnia exchanged clearly confused glances. Harlow looked up from his newspaper.

"Melvin," Rufus repeated. "I do not think I am remembering his name wrong."

"Perhaps not," Harlow said.

Perhaps not? Such an odd response. "Do you remember his name differently?"

"Remember *whose* name differently?" the young man asked.

"Melvin. The man who only just disembarked."

All three of his traveling companions looked increasingly confused.

"The man with the mustache who was visiting his parents in Reigate," Rufus clarified.

"Reigate is where we just stopped," Tillie said.

Rufus nodded. "And Melvin, with the mustache and the leather satchel and the parents he meant to visit, disembarked at that station."

Zinnia spoke for the first time. "No one left us at that station. We are all still aboard."

A weight began to form in Rufus's chest, a feeling of misgiving he could not ignore. "Do none of you remember him?"

"This man with a mustache?" Harlow asked.

Rufus nodded.

"There has been no one but us four in this compartment," Tillie said. "No one alighted at the previous station."

Melvin had.

Hadn't he? Suddenly, Rufus wasn't so certain. He remembered Reigate Station. He remembered the fog from the engine. Heaven knew he remembered the conductor.

What else was there? Who else?

He pictured in his mind the compartment as it had been when he had boarded in London. Harlow had sat in the seat he was in now, the one next to Rufus. The two sisters had sat on the bench opposite.

That was all. There'd been no one else.

Indeed, he couldn't even say why he thought there had been another passenger. Somehow, he'd imagined a fifth person. How very odd.

The vague recollection of a mustached man was slowly replaced by the very clear image of the conductor, framed in the window . . . smiling.

TONBRIDGE STATION

"Tonbridge is not the same place as Tunbridge Wells," Tillie said. Harlow had expressed confusion on the matter, and their very talkative travel companion had quite happily taken up the topic. "*Royal* Tunbridge Wells, if we are being entirely accurate."

Tillie had a knack for talking on and on without rendering herself the least bit tedious. And Zinnia managed to say almost nothing at all and yet not seem any less crucial to a conversation. They had proven rather ideal company, every bit as much as the other two people in the compartment with Rufus. He shook that thought away. The *one* other person in the compartment.

He certainly knew how to count. There were four people in the compartment including himself. Four. That was all.

"Tonbridge boasts a castle, did you know that?" Tillie's eyes pulled wide with excitement. "A thirteenth-century castle, and it is said to be quite interesting. And one can wander the castle grounds to one's heart's content."

"That sounds lovely," Harlow said.

"Ashford is not so terribly far from Tonbridge," Tillie said. "As you are to be living in Ashford with your family now, you could visit Tonbridge."

"I will suggest that to my family," Harlow said.

"How far is Tonbridge from Dover?" Rufus asked.

"Not overly far by train," Tillie said. "You could make the journey with ease."

Perhaps if he and Gertrude and the girls did move to Dover, they could take a holiday to Tonbridge. "What else of interest can one find in Tonbridge?"

"There are a great many swans near the river," Tillie said. "And we mean to look in at the shops on the high street."

Rufus's daughters would like the swans. Gertrude would enjoy the castle.

"And there are horse races held near the castle," Zinnia added, her tone bursting with excitement.

"Zinnia," Tillie whispered through a tightened jaw. "We're not meant to find races appealing."

Harlow's amusement was hidden rather well behind his upheld newspaper. Rufus bit down his own grin. Races weren't always considered an appropriate interest for women, though he didn't find the sisters' excitement truly scandalous.

Knowing races were held in Tonbridge gave him even more reason to visit the town himself. And, should they not actually move to Dover, they could still make the journey from London. By train it was not very far.

How fortunate he was to have finally decided to ride a train. All the world seemed to be opening up to him.

"Where do you mean to go after Tonbridge?" Rufus asked, interested for their sake as well as for the possibility of future travel for himself.

"We mean to visit Maidstone and Canterbury. After that, we'll make our way to Ramsgate and then to the Isle of Sheppey." Tillie held herself quite proudly. "We will be quite well versed in the kingdom by the time we finish our vast travels."

Every place she had mentioned was located in Kent. They were traveling, yes, but hardly far and wide. Still, they were so sweetly pleased with their plans that Rufus hadn't the heart to disabuse them of their exultation.

He listened very closely as Tillie, with the occasional comment from Zinnia, delineated the many things they anticipated seeing in the various towns and villages they were traveling to. Seashores and park lands, rivers and ornate bridges. They meant to spend time looking at fascinating architecture, perhaps even being permitted a tour of a fine house or two. They had great hopes for their travels but also seemed entirely content to accept whatever came their way.

Once more, the train began to slow. They were approaching Tonbridge Station, where the sisters would step off the train.

"This was such a lovely journey," Tillie said. "How pleased we have been to make the acquaintance of you all—" She shook her head, as if catching herself in a moment's confusion. "Of you *both*."

You all. She, too, it seemed, had moments of miscounting. Why would both Tillie and Rufus do that? It seemed too much of a coincidence to simply brush away.

The loud, high-pitched squeal of the train coming to a stop filled the compartment. The sound was not entirely unpleasant, yet it sent Rufus's heart into his shoes. Why was that?

With the train at a standstill at Tonbridge Station, the ladies rose. Harlow and Rufus did as well, helping them to fetch their portmanteaus from the high shelves.

Tillie offered her thanks with a smile. Zinnia patted the young man's cheek in a very maternal way.

The door to their compartment opened. Steam from the engine stack created billowing clouds that made it difficult to see the station beyond. From the obscurity, the conductor appeared just outside the compartment door.

"Your stop, ladies."

It sounded so familiar, as if Rufus had heard that, or very nearly that,

before. Yet, Rufus hadn't ridden a train before. He'd encountered no con-
ductors at previous stops on previous journeys. There'd been only one previous stop on *this* journey, but their door hadn't been opened. No one in
their compartment had needed to disembark.

And, yet . . .

The two sisters stepped from the train. The steam billowed around
them, enormous clouds that enveloped them, rendering them impossible
to see.

Rufus hoped the sisters would have wonderful travels together, that
they would get to see all the things they were dreaming of. They were such
wonderfully sweet people. They deserved such moments of happiness.

"Next stop, Ashford," the conductor said.

He closed the door but remained visible through the window, not stepping away. He'd maintained a staid demeanor as he'd held the door for the
sisters. But, standing in the window, looking in, his smile changed in a most
unnerving way. And Rufus had the most disconcerting feeling of having
done this before.

Harlow was situating himself on the bench across from Rufus, not paying the least heed to the conductor. The man outside the train compartment
tugged the brim of his hat, then stepped away.

Rufus ought to have felt relieved, ought to have been able to shake off
the oddity of his interaction with the man.

But he couldn't.

The train jerked to a start once more. Rufus held the bench to keep his
seat. After a moment, the train was moving forward at a fast clip.

"The conductor is a bit odd, isn't he?" Rufus said.

Harlow shrugged. "I haven't met him."

"Well, I've not *met* him in the strictest sense. But his behavior just now
as the sisters disembarked was unusual."

The young man's mouth tightened, and his eyebrows pulled so tight
they nearly touched. "You have sisters on the train? Why, then, aren't you
sitting with them?"

"They aren't my sisters; they are each other's sisters."

"And you wished they'd ridden with you?" Harlow was clearly confused.

"They did ride with me. With *us*."

"I didn't think you'd made any previous train journeys," Harlow said.

"I haven't."

"Then, on which journey did you ride with these sisters?"

Sisters? Rufus wasn't entirely certain. Had he taken a journey with sisters? Somewhere in his brain, a whisper repeatedly insisted he *had* taken such a journey, that he was currently on such a journey. Yet, that made no sense. He and Harlow had boarded the train at Victoria Station and had ridden this far together.

Just the two of them.

Why, then, did his mind vaguely believe that wasn't true?

ASHFORD STATION

"How long has your family been in Ashford?" Rufus asked. He and Harlow had made this journey together thus far, but he didn't feel he'd talked much to the young man. That seemed a shame.

"Two months," Harlow said. "I've worked for a merchant in London, but my father has arranged for me to work at the dry goods shop on the Ashford high street. So now I get to join them."

"You have missed them terribly these past months." Rufus had been away from his family mere hours, and he already missed them.

"I have." Harlow offered a sad sort of smile. "The position they've secured for me there is something of a step-down, but I'm not opposed to working hard to better my situation."

An admirable trait, that.

"I began as an errand boy for a barrister when I was quite young," Rufus said. "I am now a secretary for another barrister, doing important work."

"Your finances must appreciate the change, as well," Harlow said. "I, too, have been an errand boy. It does not precisely line one's pockets, does it?"

"It certainly does not." Rufus adjusted his position, his hips beginning to ache from the long journey. "Are you the oldest in your family?"

"I am. I've only just turned nineteen. My nearest sibling is my sister, and she's sixteen years old."

"My daughters are eighteen and sixteen," Rufus said. "It's a shame your family isn't in Dover. My girls would likely enjoy meeting you and your sister."

Harlow smiled. "Perhaps you might consider moving to Ashford instead of Dover. There might very well be a barrister or solicitor in the village in need of a secretary."

The prospect was actually a little intriguing. Harlow was proving himself a fine young man. His sister was likely no different. Rufus's girls would have ready-made companions.

"What sort of merchant did you work for in London?" he asked.

"A linen drapers," Harlow said. "We supplied a great many seamstresses and tailors. I found I was quite adept at tracking orders and keeping records of supplies and such. The dry goods shop in Ashford isn't likely to offer as much of a challenge."

"Perhaps, with your abilities, the shop will be able to expand its business," Rufus suggested.

Hope entered the young man's eyes. "That is possible."

"Work hard, and who's to say what might happen."

Harlow smiled broadly. "Thank you, sir. That is precisely the encouragement I needed."

The train slowed.

"This will be Ashford," Harlow said. "I should gather my things."

Rufus had the oddest urge to plead with him to stay. He had been enjoying Harlow's company, but suggesting he stay with a stranger instead of disembarking to be with his family was an unusual inclination to say the least.

The squeals and screeches of the train stopping sounded in his ears. His heart began to pound. Heavens, why was he responding this way? He'd nothing to fear from a simple stop at a train station.

Harlow rose and took down his bag. "This has been a lovely journey. Everyone was—" He shook his head. "You were wonderful company."

"As were you." But "you *all*" nearly fell from his lips. Yet, there'd been only the two of them. Why would he say differently?

"Best of luck to you in Dover," Harlow said.

"And to you here in Ashford," Rufus replied.

The door opened. The train conductor stood on the other side, surrounded by clouds of steam, no doubt coming from the engine at the front of the train.

"Your stop, sir," the conductor said to Harlow.

Rufus had heard that before. At least he thought he had. But he hadn't the first idea where or when.

Harlow dipped his head to Rufus once more before stepping off the train and disappearing into the steam.

"Next stop, Dover," the conductor said.

The door closed.

Through the window, the conductor smiled.

THE FINAL STATION

The train was approaching Dover. The journey had been a quiet one. Rufus didn't know whether to be grateful or disappointed to have found a compartment all to himself for the length of the trip. He might have enjoyed a little conversation. He was not overly talkative, but he did like listening.

Rufus shifted his position, searching for one that offered a little more comfort. He would have put his feet up on the bench, but the newspaper left there was in the way, and as it wasn't his, he didn't feel comfortable crumpling or moving it.

The newspaper wasn't his.

Then, whose was it?

And, for that matter, who did the umbrella placed under the other bench belong to? It wasn't Rufus's.

And there was a lace-edged handkerchief tucked halfway into the cushion of the bench; that was also not his.

Those things, he was certain, had not been in the compartment when he'd stepped inside at Victoria Station. They weren't his. But they hadn't been there before.

In the back of his mind, just out of reach, was a memory of other people inside this very compartment. But he couldn't entirely recall them. He couldn't make them become clear in his memory.

But they had been there. They had been on this train. They had disembarked. And now they were gone.

Not merely gone from the train.

Gone *entirely*.

Squeals and squeaks. The jerking of the train coming to a stop.

Rufus's heartbeat pounded hard in his neck. His stomach lodged firmly in his feet. Every breath he took rattled through him. He could hardly think.

Gone entirely.

Entirely.

All was still. Outside the windows, steam billowed thick and deep. Rufus's mind spun at the familiarity of it but couldn't lay claim to the vague memory.

The door opened.

He swallowed. Tried to breathe.

From the midst of the steam, the conductor appeared. In serious, tense tones, he said, "Your stop, sir."

And then . . . he smiled.

Somewhere along this same line of tracks, a train is traveling from London. Many have boarded it, anticipating a pleasant and efficient journey. But when the train reaches its terminus station, all will be gone.

Entirely.

ABOUT THE AUTHOR

SARAH M. EDEN is a *USA Today* best-selling author of witty and charming historical romances, including 2019's Foreword Reviews INDIE Awards Gold Winner for Romance, *The Lady and the Highwayman*, and 2020 Holt Medallion finalist, *Healing Hearts*. She is a two-time "Best of State" Gold Medal winner for fiction and a three-time Whitney Award winner.

Combining her obsession with history and her affinity for tender love stories, Sarah loves crafting deep characters and heartfelt romances set against rich historical backdrops. She holds a bachelor's degree in research and happily spends hours perusing the reference shelves of her local library.

THE DREAD PENNY SOCIETY

Illustrated by Katherine Eden